Strike Force

ALSO BY DALE BROWN

Edge of Battle

Act of War

Plan of Attack

Air Battle Force

Wings of Fire

Warrior Class

Battle Born

The Tin Man

Fatal Terrain

Shadow of Steel

Storming Heaven

Chains of Command

Night of the Hawk

Sky Masters

Hammerheads

Day of the Cheetah

Silver Tower

Flight of the Old Dog

Strike Force

Dale Brown

HarperCollins books may be purchased for educational, business, or sales promotional use. For information, please write: Special Markets Department, HarperCollins Publishers, 10 East 53rd Street, New York, NY 10022.

FIRST HARPERLUXE EDITION

HarperLuxe™ is a trademark of HarperCollins Publishers.

Library of Congress Cataloging-in-Publication Data is available upon request.

ISBN: 978-0-06-125931-9
ISBN-10: 0-06-125931-4

07 08 09 10 11 ID/RRD 10 9 8 7 6 5 4 3 2 1

This story is dedicated to my son Hunter, who has shown me time and again that he has inherited and embraced the greatest gift I can give any young person: the gift of imagination.

You may be reading this story for the first time, but I can tell you that Hunter and I have told and retold this story to each other dozens of times.

The old man thanks you, big guy.

Acronyms and Terms

2S6M Tunguska—combination missile and cannon mobile Russian air defense system

AGM-170D—supersonic scramjet-powered attack missile

Almaz S-300—Russian surface-to-air missile system, also capable against ballistic missiles

ARB—Air Reserve Base

Armstrong Space Station—first American military space station

BDU—Battle Dress Uniform, the standard utility uniform worn by soldiers in combat

BDU-58 Meteor—releases payloads over a target area after atmospheric re-entry

BERP—Ballistic Electro-Reactive Process, the material worn by "Tin Man" commandos

BOHM—borohydrogen tetroxide rocket fuel oxidizer

CAP—Civil Air Patrol (U.S. Air Force Auxiliary)

CID—Cybernetic Infantry Device manned combat robots

CO—Commanding Officer

COMSEC—communications security

Condor—bomber-launched commando insertion and retrieval aircraft; also large unmanned new technology airship

Crew Exploration Vehicle—next generation orbital and lunar manned space vehicle

DARPA—Defense Advanced Research Projects Agency

Doshan Tappeh Air Base—Tehran headquarters of the Iranian Revolutionary GuardsCorps

EVA—extravehicular activity; a spacewalk

exfil—exfiltration

G-forces—acceleration forces imposed on the human body, expressed in multiples of Earth gravity

hypoplastic thumb—congenital birth defect where the thumb is reduced in size, missing, or fused with another finger

IRGC—Iranian Revolutionary Corps

ISAR—Inverse Synthetic Aperture Radar

JP-7—jet fuel refined with a higher flash point than more common JP-4

KC-77—aerial refueling tanker and cargo aircraft

komiteh—Iranian moral and religious enforcers

LADAR—laser radar

LakeSpotter—private individuals who camp outside secret U.S. military installations to spot classified aircraft test flights

LPDRS—Laser Pulse Detonation Rocket System

magnetohydrodynamic generator—using the movement of liquid metal moving through a magnetic field to generate electricity

Majlis—Iranian parliament

MHD—magnetohydrodynamic

mil power—full aircraft engine thrust without using afterburners

muay thai—kick boxing

NCOICNon Commissioned—Officer In Charge

NSA—National Security Agency

OPSEC—operational security

Orion—next generation manned spacecraft

Pax River—Patuxent River Naval Air Station

Pilatus PC-6—Swiss-made single-engine turboprop trainer

pollicization—surgical creation of a thumb from a finger

PSID—pounds-per-square-inch differential, a measure of cabin pressurization

RFID—radio frequency identification device
RPG—rocket propelled grenade
RTB—return to base
SA-10, SA-12, SA-19, SA-21—Russian surface to air anti-aircraft missiles
SAM—surface to air missile
SDB—small diameter bomb
Shahab-2, Shahab-3, Shahab-5—Iranian ballistic missiles
Skybolt—space-based anti ballistic missile laser
SPAW—supersonic precision attack weapon
SPO—senior project officer
sun-synchronous orbit—orbit that places a satellite over the same spot on Earth at the same time of day
Supreme Defense Council—Iranian military advisory group to the president
TEL—transporter-erector-launcher
Tin Man—commandos who wear advanced protective suits and carry sophisticated weapons
VFR—visual flight rules
XR-A9—Experimental Reconnaissance Article Nine, Black Stallion spaceplane
Zulfiqar—Iranian-made main battle tank

Cast of Characters

AMERICANS

KEVIN MARTINDALE, President of the United States
MAUREEN HERSHEL, Vice President
ARMY GENERAL JONAS HARMAN SPARKS, National Security Adviser
JOSEPH GARDNER, Secretary of Defense
ARMY GENERAL WILLIAM GLENBROOK, Chairman of the Joint Chiefs of Staff
DR. MARY CARSON, Secretary of State
KEN T. PHOENIX, Attorney General
CARL MINDEN, Chief of Staff
U.S. MARINE CORPS MAJOR-GENERAL ANTHONY LEWARS, White House Press Secretary
GERALD VISTA, Director of Central Intelligence

LT. GENERAL PATRICK MCLANAHAN, special adviser to the President

BRIGADIER GENERAL DAVID LUGER, asst. special adviser to the President

BRIGADIER-GENERAL REBECCA FURNESS, commander, First Air Battle Force (air operations), Battle Mountain Air Reserve Base (ARB), Nevada

BRIGADIER-GENERAL DAREN MACE, Air Battle Force operations officer and EB-1C mission commander

U.S. AIR FORCE COLONEL NANCY CHESHIRE, AL-52 Dragon aircraft commander

U.S. AIR FORCE RESERVE MAJOR WYATT CROSS, EB-52 Megafortress aircraft commander

U.S. AIR FORCE RESERVE CAPTAIN MARK HOURS, EB-52 mission commander

AIR FORCE RESERVE CAPTAIN MARGARET "MUGS" LEWIS, EB-1C Vampire aircraft commander

BRIGADIER GENERAL HAL BRIGGS, deputy commander for operations (ground operations), First Air Battle Force, Battle Mountain Air Reserve Base, Nevada

MARINE CORPS SERGEANT MAJOR CHRIS WOHL, NCOIC, First Air Battle Force

U.S. ARMY FIRST LIEUTENANT CHARLIE BRAKEMAN, Tin Man commando

ARMY NATIONAL GUARD CAPTAIN CHARLIE TURLOCK, CID engineer and pilot

U.S. ARMY SPECIALIST MARIA RICARDO, Tin Man commando

COLONEL MARTIN TEHAMA, COMMANDER, High Technology Aerospace Weapons Center (HAWC), Elliott Air Force Base, Nevada

CAPTAIN HUNTER "BOOMER" NOBLE, XR-A9 Black Stallion aircraft commander, Elliott Air Force Base, Groom Lake

FIRST LIEUTENANT DOROTHEA "Nano" Benneton, Ph.D., Black Stallion mission commander

U.S. AIR FORCE CAPTAIN WIL LEFFERTS, XR-A9 mission commander

U.S. NAVY LIEUTENANT COMMANDER JACK OLRAY, XR-A9 pilot

U.S. NAVY LIEUTENANT LISETTE "FRENCHY" MOULAIN, XR-A9 mission commander

STACY ANNE BARBEAU, senior U.S. senator from Louisiana, ranking member of Senate Armed Services Committee; Colleen Morna, her aide

GENERAL CHARLIE ZOLTRANE, commander, Eighth Air Force

GENERAL COLLEEN EDGEWATER, commander, Air Force Matériel Command

ANN PAGE, PH.D., Former U.S. Senator, astronaut, and space weapon engineer

COLONEL KAI RAYDON, Space Shuttle aircraft commander

CIVIL AIR PATROL CADET MASTER SERGEANT DOUG LENZ, Cadet Lieutenant Katelyn VanWie's NCOIC

IRANIANS

MAJOR-GENERAL HESARAK AL-KAN BUZHAZI, former chief of staff of the Iranian military

CIVIL AIR PATROL CADET LIEUTENANT KATELYN VANWIE, aka Shahdokht Azar Assiyeh Qagev, heir presumptive of the Peacock Throne of Iran

IMAM SAYYED MOSTAFA SHĪRĀZEMI, religious leader of Iran

MASOUD AHMADAD, president of Iran

BRIGADIER GENERAL MANSOUR SATTARI, Buzhazi's aide

BRIGADIER-GENERAL KAMAL ZHORAM, commander of the Second Rocket Brigade of the Pasdaran-i-Engelab, or Revolutionary Guards Corps

GENERAL HOSEYN YASSINI, commander-in-chief, Iranian armed forces

FLIGHT CAPTAIN ALI-REZA KAZEMI, transport pilot

LIEUTENANT GENERAL MUHAMMAD BADI, commander of the Pasdaran (Iranian Revolutionary Guards Corps)

COLONEL/GENERAL ALI ZOLQADR, replacement Pasdaran commander; Major Kazem Jahromi, his aide

AYATOLLAH HASSAN MOHTAZ, Director of the Supreme National Security Deputate and military adviser to the Faqih

MAJOR PARVIZ NAJAR, Lieutenant Mara Saidi, Katelyn's bodyguards

COLONEL JAMAL FATTAH, chief political officer, Iranian embassy, Ashkhabad, Turkmenistan

RUSSIANS

LEONID ZEVITIN, president of the Russian Federation

GENERAL KUZMA FURZYENKO, Russian chief of staff

Real-World News Excerpts

PENTAGON PLANNING FOR SPACE BOMBER—by Robert Windrem, MSNBC NEWS, August 14, 2001—An experimental NASA spacecraft could well be the harbinger for a small armada of billion-dollar space bombers—"space operations vehicles" that could be launched from a U.S. base and fire weapons at almost any target on Earth, all within 90 minutes of a presidential order.

. . . The next generation of America's bomber fleet will be a far cry not only from World War II's B-17 but from the stealthy B-2 bomber as well. Speed to target is likely to be just as high a priority as a bomber's payload in the 21st century.

. . . In June, Rumsfeld directed the Pentagon to investigate "suborbital space vehicles" that "would be valuable for conducting rapid global strikes," according to a Pentagon planning document issued under his name. And as recently as last month, Boeing said it was talking to the Air Force about investing millions of dollars more in Boeing's X-37.

Then, in congressional testimony this month, Gen. Michael Ryan, the Air Force chief of staff, acknowledged that a futuristic "space bomber" is being contemplated by the Pentagon's long-range planners . . .

STRATEGIC FORECASTING INC., www.stratfor.com, 9 November 2004—An Iranian official said Nov. 9 that Iran has acquired the capability to produce medium-range ballistic missiles in mass quantity. Defense Minister Rear Adm. Ali Shamkhani told journalists in Tehran that the Islamic republic is able to manufacture in bulk the Shahab-3 missile, whose range was recently upgraded to 1,250 miles.

IRANIANS REFUSE TO TERMINATE NUCLEAR PLANS—by Elaine Sciolino, *New York Times*—26 November 2004—VIENNA—Iran refused Thursday to abandon plans to operate uranium enrichment equipment that could be used either for energy purposes or in a nuclear bomb-making project, European and Iranian officials said.

The refusal threatened to scuttle a nuclear agreement Iran reached 10 days ago with France, Britain and

Germany to freeze all of Iran's uranium enrichment activities, the European officials added. It also gave new ammunition to the Bush administration, which asserts that Iran has a secret nuclear weapons program and cannot be trusted . . .

U.S. FORCE EYES RAPID SATELLITE CAPABILITY—*Jane's Defense Weekly,* 7 January 2005—The U.S. Air Force, along with the Defense Advanced Research Projects Agency (DARPA), plans to conduct a flight experiment midyear to see if it can rapidly place a light satellite payload into orbit aboard a small space launch vehicle. If successful, the demonstration could herald a new technology for space access, said officials involved with the launch.

RUSSIANS HELPING IRAN CREATE EUROPE MISSILE THREAT: British Paper (AFP) Oct. 16, 2005—Former members of the Russian military have been secretly helping Iran obtain the technology needed to make missiles capable of hitting European capitals, a British newspaper claimed on Sunday.

Citing anonymous "Western intelligence officials," The *Sunday Telegraph* said the Russians were go-betweens as part of a multi-million-pound deal they negotiated between Iran and North Korea in 2003.

"It has enabled Tehran to receive regular clandestine shipments of topsecret missile technology, believed to be channeled through Russia," the newspaper reported in a front-page article.

The allegations came after U.S. Secretary of State Condoleezza Rice feuded openly with her Russian counterpart Sergei Lavrov over Iran's nuclear programme while on a brief trip to Moscow on Saturday.

. . . According to the *Telegraph,* Iran would be able to use its new technology to build a missile with a range of 3,500 kilometres (2,200 miles).

"It is designed to carry a 1.2-ton payload, sufficient for a basic nuclear device," the newspaper said.

It quoted a senior U.S. official as saying Iran's programme as "sophisticated and getting larger and more accurate. They have had very much in mind the payload needed to carry a nuclear weapon.

RUSSIA WARNS AGAINST MILITARY FORCE—© Stratfor Inc., August 17, 2005—Military force against Iran would be "counterproductive and dangerous," the Russian Ministry of Foreign Affairs said Aug. 17. The ministry called for a diplomatic solution to the tensions surrounding Tehran's nuclear program, warning of "grave" and unpredictable outcomes if force were employed.

ARMS SALE TO TEHRAN FUELS TENSIONS WITH ISRAEL—Janes *Defence* Weekly, 14 December 2005—© Janes' Information Group—Tel Aviv—Russia confirmed earlier reports on 5 December of the deal with Iran, which includes the upgrading of Iranian Su-24 attack aircraft and MiG-29 multirole fighter aircraft, along with the acquisition of an unspecified number of patrol boats, 32 Antey Tor-M1 (SA-15 "Gauntlet") low- to medium-altitude surface-to-air missile systems (16 tracked, 16 wheeled) and the upgrade of an unspecified number of T-72 main battle tanks. Russian news agency Interfax reported that the missiles would be deployed to protect Iran's soon-to-be-completed nuclear reactor in Bushehr.

The Tor-M1 can simultaneously detect and track up to 48 airborne targets out to a range of 40 km and can engage targets at a maximum range of 12 km and at altitudes from 10 m to 6,000 m. During a test in Russia, the Tor-M1 achieved a high kill probability against cruise missiles, unmanned aerial vehicles, and jet fighters . . .

LOW-COST ACCESS TO ORBIT: MARINES TO THE RESCUE, by Taylor Dinerman, www.thespacereview.com, 6 January 2006 . . . In July 2002, the Marine Corps released a Universal Needs Statement that defined the Small Unit

Space Transport and Insertion (SUSTAIN) concept that, if successful, will give the U.S. a ". . . heretofore unimaginable assault support speed, range, altitude, and strategic surprise" capability. SUSTAIN is an RLV that will carry a squad (13 men) into space and land it anywhere on Earth within two hours with, among other requirements, "flexible launch on demand to any orbital inclination."

A fully operational SUSTAIN-type vehicle would also be the preferred low-cost way to get cargo and personnel to and from LEO [low earth orbit] . . .

TWO-STAGE-TO-ORBIT "BLACKSTAR" SYSTEM SHELVED AT GROOM LAKE?—© *Aviation Week and Space Technology,* 5 March 2006 . . . U.S. intelligence agencies may have quietly mothballed a highly classified two-stage-to-orbit spaceplane system designed in the 1980s for reconnaissance, satellite-insertion and, possibly, weapons delivery . . .

. . . A large "mothership," closely resembling the U.S. Air Force's historic XB-70 supersonic bomber, carries the orbital component conformally under its fuselage, accelerating to supersonic speeds at high altitude before dropping the spaceplane. The orbiter's engines fire and boost the vehicle into space. If mission requirements dictate, the spaceplane can either reach low Earth orbit or remain suborbital.

. . . Exactly what missions the Blackstar system may have been designed for and built to accomplish are as yet unconfirmed, but U.S. Air Force Space Command (AFSPC) officers and contractors have been toying with similar spaceplane concepts for years. Besides reconnaissance, they call for inserting small satellites into orbit, and either retrieving or servicing other spacecraft. Conceivably, such a vehicle could serve as an anti-satellite or space-to-ground weapons-delivery platform . . .

www.Iranian.ws (a U.S.-based Iranian Web site) polls, 13 March 2006—49% of respondents believe the current Iranian regime will "go away because it is in its nature to be deposed by violent means."

As to the question "If (or when) the time comes to choose between Iran or Islam," 92% chose "Iran."

As to the question "Which is the right model of governance for Iran?" 45% chose a republic, 34% chose a monarchy, and only 8% chose a theocracy.

As to the question "Do you support a separation of religion from state in Iran," 81% chose "Yes, of course," and 16% chose "No way."

82% of respondents rate Iran's future under the current regime as "Not good."

The poll Web site page http://www.iranian.ws/poll/ has a warning on it which reads: "According to some, you may turn to solid rock or may burn in hell for eternity by participating in our polls."

PRATT & WHITNEY ROCKETDYNE COMPLETES MACH 5 TESTING OF WORLD'S FIRST CLOSED-LOOP HYDROCARBON-FUELED HYPERSONIC PROPULSION SYSTEM—PR NewsWire-FirstCall, 27 July 2006—CANOGA PARK, Calif.—Pratt & Whitney Rocketdyne (PWR), a business unit of United Technologies Corp., has completed testing of its hypersonic Ground Demonstrator Engine No. 2 (GDE-2) at NASA's Langley Research Center in Virginia . . .

The PWR GDE-2 produced significant hypersonic data results during several test runs conducted at Mach 5 conditions in the eight-foot High Temperature Tunnel at the Langley Research Center. The engine used standard JP-7 fuel in a closed-loop configuration to both cool engine hardware and fuel the engine's combustor . . .

IRAN, RUSSIA: A NUCLEAR MARRIAGE OF CONVENIENCE—Strategic Forecasting Inc., 27 September 2006—Russia and Iran have signed a contract for the delivery of 80 tons of nuclear fuel to Iran's Bushehr nuclear power facility, which is scheduled to be completed in September 2007. Russia appears to be in the process of finishing updating its military doctrine. Closer economic ties with Iran will allow Russia to maintain a foothold in the Middle East while keeping pressure on the United States, which lacks the bandwidth to respond to Russia's provocative moves.

Strike Force

PROLOGUE

ORUMIYEH AIRPORT, ISLAMIC REPUBLIC OF IRAN

March 2008

"Group, atten-*shun!*"

The group of five hundred uniformed young men and women snapped to attention, and the reviewing party marched from their waiting position in a large white tent on the edge of the tarmac. The group leader saluted the reviewing party, who returned his salute. The reviewing party turned about-face as the flags of the Islamic Republic of Iran, the Armed Forces of the Islamic Republic, the Ministry of the Interior, and the Internal Defense Corps were marched out. The presiding officer of the reviewing party saluted, as did the entire assembly, followed by the playing of "Ey Iran," a popular inspirational and patriotic song often preferred by the military over the pro-revolutionary official national anthem "Sorood-e Melli-ye Jomhoori-ye Eslami-ye Iran." After the song concluded, the presiding officer stepped up to a podium, and the crowd of about two thousand guests and base employees were asked to be seated.

"Citizens, friends, families, and fellow warriors, I bid you welcome on this glorious and important morning here in Orumiyeh," Major-General Hesarak al-Kan Buzhazi began. "I am proud to preside over this important occasion for the Islamic Republic of Iran. On behalf of His Holiness Imam Sayyed Mostafa Shīrāzemi, may God bless his name; president Masoud Ahmadad; senior adviser to the Supreme Defense Council His Holiness Hassan Mohtaz, may God preserve him; the chief of staff General Hoseyn Yassini; and the commander of the Revolutionary Guards Corps Lieutenant-General Muhammad Badi, I hereby activate the First Combined Border Defense Battalion."

There was a short ceremony, during which Buzhazi unfurled the battalion flag and tied the combat-ready ribbon atop it, then handed the flag to its new commander and saluted him. Tall and slender, with gray hair worn slightly on the longish side and with a closely cropped gray beard and mustache, Buzhazi looked much younger than his sixty-one years. He wore a dark winter-weight fatigue jacket with no insignia on it except his general's stars on his shoulders (but they were also black and hard to see from a distance), thick black fatigue pants, tanker boots, and a black visor cap with the earflaps folded up. He clasped the commander on the shoulders, kissed him on each cheek, returned his salute, and returned to the podium to finish his speech.

"I hope you all realize the significance of this ceremony today," Buzhazi went on. His voice was deep, sharp, and clipped, and he spoke without notes. "As you know, the Supreme Leader, may God protect him, has ordained that one out of every ten citizens of Iran over the age of majority serve in the active or reserve military forces, so in case the forces of evil attack us, we can be ready. As we are a peaceful nation, maintaining a force this large is difficult and expensive, so persons not serving in the active-duty military forces are assigned to local militias, the *Basij-i-mostazefin,* what used to be called the 'Army of the Oppressed.' I don't know about you, my friends, but I would not have liked being assigned to an army with the term 'oppressed' in its title.

"When I resigned my post as chief of staff of the Armed Forces of the Islamic Republic and accepted the post of commander of the Basij, I found a force of willing and energetic men and women of all ages who desired nothing more than to serve their country, both as hard-working citizens and as defenders. What they lacked was proper training, motivation, and purpose. My goal was to transform the best of the Basij into a true fighting force, capable of not just assisting the active-duty forces, but complementing them. Ladies and gentlemen, and especially my fellow warriors, may I present to you, the First Combined Border Defense Battalion, The Lions, of the newly designated Islamic Republic of Iran Internal Defense Force!"

Amidst a round of enthusiastic applause, a procession of vehicles moved onto the tarmac from the north hangar area, surrounded by security guards in armored vehicles. The first vehicle was a ground support vehicle towing a single engine, two-man aircraft; the second was a road-mobile surface-to-air missile vehicle; and the third was a mobile anti-aircraft artillery vehicle.

"My friends, let me introduce you to the three main weapon systems now being deployed with the First," Buzhazi went on. "The aircraft is a Swiss-made Pilatus PC-6 turboprop aircraft. Normally these aircraft are just trainers—Switzerland does not build any of its aircraft to be used for combat—but we have modified them to act as close air support, photo-intelligence, and counter-insurgency attack aircraft. They even carry heat-seeking missiles to combat enemy aircraft.

"The second is an Almaz S-300 mobile surface-to-air missile launcher. It is designed to engage and destroy aircraft at very low altitude, even stealth aircraft, helicopters, and cruise missiles—it can even detect and destroy helicopters hovering close to the ground or behind trees; it also has an excellent high-altitude engagement capability, and is effective out to fifty kilometers. It is designed to deploy to isolated field locations so as to make it more difficult for enemy aircraft to target it. It is an older air defense system, but our best military engineers have upgraded and refurbished it so it is far better than new.

"The third vehicle is a 2S6M Tunguska anti-aircraft artillery system, with two 30-millimeter radar- or infrared-guided cannons, capable of a combined firing rate of five thousand rounds per minute, plus eight 9M311M anti-aircraft missiles, capable of destroying low- to medium-altitude targets out to a range of ten kilometers."

Buzhazi applauded along with the audience as the three weapon systems were towed right behind the unit members. It truly made a very impressive sight. Behind them, security and maintenance vehicles cruised slowly along the taxiway. "These weapons represent the first time a reserve force has been given such advanced weapon systems," Buzhazi went on. "I am proud to award this unit the combat-ready ribbon, which represents this unit's high marks in field exercises, testing, and inspections. I am pleased to present to you the officers and senior non-commissioned officers of each regiment. They are the most important element of this new, vital defense force that will ensure the security of our great nation. They have undergone a rigorous and intensive training program, trained not just to use these weapon systems but in how to best deploy them in case of national emergency, to counter whatever threat exists to our great land and defeat them. They are some of the best I have ever had the pleasure of commanding, and I am proud of each and every one of them."

As Buzhazi read the names and watched as the men came forward, he sensed a slight disturbance somewhere distant from the audience. He turned to look over his left shoulder but saw nothing out of the ordinary—plenty of security on hand to keep any curious onlookers from straying too close to the hardware.

He read off a few more names, but still that feeling persisted, and so this time he turned fully around and studied the area. A security vehicle with blue flashing lights on the roof was escorting what appeared to be a technical maintenance vehicle, basically a medium-sized eight-ton truck with a small crane on the front to load and unload missiles and ammunition. Both were common sights—why was he feeling so uneasy? Everything looked completely . . .

. . . and at that instant, the two vehicles quickly accelerated and headed straight for the ceremony area—and now Buzhazi could see a line of security cars and armored vehicles racing out of the hangar area toward them, lights and sirens on, pursuing the two vehicles!

"Get out!" Buzhazi shouted into the microphone. "Get out of here, now!" The crowd stood still, heads excitedly turning back and forth, but no one was moving. "I said, run! *Everyone run!"* He turned to a couple of guards who were standing about thirty meters away, AK-47 rifles slung on their shoulders. "You! Guards! Stop those vehicles!"

But it was too late. Buzhazi had enough time to run away from the podium toward the base operations building, wildly motioning for the crowd to follow him, when the truck plowed into the S-300 surface-to-air missile launcher. There was a small explosion, perhaps from a bit of gasoline ignited by a spark . . . and then seconds later the thousand kilos of high explosives packed into the rear of the truck detonated. Buzhazi felt himself picked off his feet by a red-hot wave of energy, along with pieces of concrete, burning fuel and metal, and body parts, and flung through the air.

ELLIOTT AIR FORCE BASE, NEVADA

That Same Time

"You're *where?*"

U.S. Air Force Lieutenant-General Patrick McLanahan smiled at the Vice President's astounded and somewhat angry tone. "I'm still at the 'Lake,' Maureen," he said. Even on a secure radio connection, he or anyone he knew never mentioned the name "Groom Lake" or even "Elliott Air Force Base" to anyone. The top-secret weapons and aerospace development and testing facility in the Nevada desert north of Las Vegas, named after its first controversial firebrand commander Lieutenant General Brad Elliott, was always called "the Lake."

"Did you forget, Patrick? We have a meeting in Washington in three hours!"

"I didn't forget," Patrick said. "I'll be there."

The other man in the back of the Air Force blue Suburban with him, U.S. Air Force aerospace engineer and test pilot Captain Hunter "Boomer" Noble, smiled. Everyone at the High Technology Aerospace Weapons Center, or HAWC, nicknamed

"Dreamland," was wired with subcutaneous satellite transceivers that allowed worldwide two-way communications—and the ability for the government to track and listen in on that person worldwide, for life—and so he was accustomed to listening to persons talking into thin air. "Say hi to the Vice President for me, General," Noble said. Patrick nodded, and Boomer went on checking maintenance logs and reports on his tablet PC.

"Who was that, Patrick?" Vice President Maureen Hershel asked from her office at the Old Executive Office Building in Washington, D.C.

"Boomer said hi," Patrick said. "He's going to fly me to the meeting."

" 'Fly you to the meeting?' Why is he . . . ?" And then Maureen stopped. She had been briefed on this mission, several days ago—she just didn't know that Patrick would be the one flying it. "You do know what you're doing, don't you?" she asked.

"Don't worry. I'm looking forward to it."

"Patrick . . ."

"I'll be there," he asserted. "Gotta fly."

"That's an understatement," Maureen said. "Call if you'll be late. See you . . . whenever." And the connection was broken, leaving his reply, "I love you," unheard except by "Boomer" Noble.

Patrick stepped out of the Suburban with his flight helmet bag and took a deep breath, barely able to contain his excitement. The early-morning air was crisp and cold, with barely a hint of a breeze. The sky was completely cloudless, as it was for much of the year in south-central Nevada. He and Boomer reviewed aircraft documents on the hood of the Suburban, signing off the various pages and transmitting the forms to HAWC's maintenance and records computers.

"The bird's code one and ready to go, General," Boomer announced. "Let's get you to that meeting." He looked at the three-star general standing beside him. Patrick was staring at something intently. "Something wrong, sir?"

"No . . . no, not a thing, Captain," Patrick responded. A huge grin spread across his face, and he looked at Noble with an unabashedly childlike expression. "Not . . . a . . . damned thing."

Boomer looked at the object of Patrick's amazement, nodded knowingly, and took a deep breath himself. "Yes, sir, I know what you mean," he said. "I know exactly what you mean."

Years ago it was known as "Aurora," the unclassified code name for America's first hypersonic reconnaissance plane, able to fly over five times the speed of sound; at the High Technology Aerospace Weapons

Center that now owned all five of the prototypes, it was simply the XR-A9 (Experimental Reconnaissance Article Nine). About the size of the SR-71 Blackbird recon plane it was meant to replace, it greatly resembled the Blackbird with its thin wings and fuselage and jet-black skin. Its official unclassified nickname was the Black Stallion, but everyone around Dreamland simply called it the "Stud."

As they walked toward the huge craft, more and more changes were evident. There were a number of odd-shaped nozzles around the nose and fuselage. This plane had no conventional aerodynamic flight controls like flaps, elevators, and ailerons—instead, the XR-A9 used mission-adaptive technology that used microhydraulic actuators to change almost the entire surface of the wings and fuselage, making every part of the airplane a lift or drag device. Unlike the SR-71, this aircraft had four engines mounted underneath the fuselage with a movable vane in the center of each elongated rectangular engine inlet and wide exhaust nozzles.

After their walkaround, McLanahan and Noble climbed up the boarding ladder along the side of the plane. "Last chance, sir," Boomer said at the top of the boarding ladder, and held out a small round plastic container. The flight surgeon and other fliers had recommended that all flight crewmembers take anti-motion sickness medication—promethazine hydrochloride was the most common—before each flight, whether or not you had a history of motion sickness, but Patrick had steadfastly refused. "You'll thank me."

"No thanks, Boomer," Patrick said. "I've been airsick before, and it's not fun, but I don't like taking any kind of medication."

"Where we're going, it's different, sir," Boomer said. "If you don't need it you won't feel any differently, but you don't want to be hurting through your whole trip. It'll ruin it for everyone, believe me." Patrick finally relented and took the pills. "Thanks, sir." He held out a gloved fist, and Patrick punched it. "Have a good flight, sir. Have fun. I'll see you on the ground afterward."

The XR-A9's interior was arranged in a tandem arrangement in two separately pressurized compartments, with the aircraft commander, or AC, in front, and the mission commander, or MC, in back, like the SR-71 Blackbird spy plane or the F-15E Strike Eagle. The cockpit was cramped for such a large plane, and some contortions and quasi-gymnastics were necessary to get into the cockpit seats. Patrick silently cursed the extra five pounds he had put on recently and vowed once again to get rid of his now-noticeable "executive spread" ASAP.

There was a bit of hesitation and confused expressions when Patrick got ready to step into the forward aircraft commander's seat. "Uh . . . sir . . . ?"

"I'm flying this baby today, Boomer," Patrick said as he began to "build his nest"—arrange his personal and life-support equipment in the cockpit just so.

"I realize you're technically qualified, sir," Noble gently argued, "and you obviously know what you're doing, but I always . . ."

"Not today, Captain," Patrick said, emphasizing the word "captain." "I've played back-seater long enough. I'm going to fly the hot jet."

"But sir, the flight plan says . . ."

"Boomer, I'm flying the damned plane," Patrick insisted, almost an order. "You can fly along and back me up, or I'll find someone else to fly in the back." Patrick had to smile at the young officer's worried expression. "That was exactly like my dad's expression when he handed over the keys of his car."

"Why? Did you bend the car too, sir?" Patrick gave him a half-amused, half-irritated expression, which terminated the conversation.

Once seated, both officers found the seats quite comfortable, hugging the body like a luxury sports car. There were no ejection seats on the XR-A9—instead, it used the capsule ejection system found in the original B-1A bomber, in which the entire cockpit section separated from the rest of the aircraft and floated to Earth on six huge parachutes. Like the B-1 Lancer supersonic bomber and many fighter aircraft, Patrick found that a crewmember wore the XR-A9, rather than sat in it . . .

. . . which was a piece of cake for a young guy like Hunter "Boomer" Noble, just twenty-three years old, but problematical for a guy pushing fifty like Patrick McLanahan. But he was experienced, determined, and still in pretty damned good shape, thank you very much, and it took him only a few moments longer to get situated and strapped in than it did Boomer.

The ground technicians had already performed the "Preflight," "Before Power On," "Power On," and "Before Engine Start" checklists, but both crewmembers checked them again before allowing the computers to proceed with engine start. Like all of Dreamland's aircraft, checklists and most everything else were accomplished by computers and checked and monitored by humans—they merely prepared themselves to take over in case of a major malfunction, which was rare. Much of what the engineers did at Dreamland these days was design unmanned aircraft and convert formerly manned aircraft to unmanned ones—in fact, unmanned aircraft far outnumbered manned ones at Dreamland.

Ten minutes after strapping in, the canopies motored shut and the aircraft was ready to taxi. There was no control tower at Elliott Air Force Base—ground control and tower functions were handled by cameras and sensors that detected the position of any object larger than a rabbit for miles in any direction. Like most everything else, taxiing for takeoff was done by computers—the sensors and satellite-based navigations systems on board the aircraft were much more precise than a human's senses, and the bomber never left the yellow taxi lines as it lined up for takeoff.

It was another opportunity for Patrick to think about all the oddities of not just this mission, but the entire XR-A9 program. Although Lieutenant-General Patrick McLanahan was fully qualified to fly any aircraft based at Elliott Air Force Base, including the XR-A9, he always flew with a fully qualified pilot—but he was unaccustomed to flying with someone less than half his age. Hunter "Boomer" Noble was one of the new breed of men entering the twenty-first-century aerospace industry: highly intelligent, highly motivated by technical challenges if not geopolitics and military affairs—and completely unresponsive to the notion that there was just one way to do anything, or that anyone over the age of thirty knew anything about anything worthwhile.

But in the cockpit, this young playboy test pilot was all business. “Ready to go, General?” Boomer asked.

“Yep,” Patrick replied, and he put his hands on the side-stick controller and throttle. “I’ve got the airplane.”

“Uh . . . sir, I thought the rules said no manual takeoffs on operational test flights,” Noble pointed out.

“We’ve been working together for about a year, isn’t that right, Boomer?”

“Yes, sir.”

“Then you should know by now that if a three-star general wants to fly the plane, even manually, you say ‘yes, sir’ in a smart military manner, and then doing everything in your power to make sure he doesn’t crash the plane.”

Boomer smiled and put on his oxygen visor. “Yes, sir. It’s your ass, I guess.”

“That’s more like it. I’ve got the airplane.”

“You got it, General.” Boomer switched all of the navigation and flight control screens over to Patrick’s supercockpit display and placed the engine and system monitor screens on his panel. “Aircraft configured for manual takeoff, mission-adaptive systems set to auto, navigation display set, everything’s in the green. You’re ready for takeoff.”

“Roger. Brakes on,” Patrick said. He applied the brakes, then slowly advanced the throttles. When he was at full military power he let the brakes go, then eased the throttles into full afterburner. It did not take long for the Black Stallion to reveal its legacy as the fastest air-breathing aircraft in the world as the speed built up quickly. It leapt off the runway in less than three thousand feet and climbed at a dazzling ten thousand feet per minute to forty thousand feet.

They proceeded to the air refueling track, which led westbound out over central California to the Pacific Ocean, then descended to twenty-four thousand feet, rendezvoused with a Dreamland KC-77 tanker, a modified Boeing 777 airliner a few minutes later, made contact with the tanker's refueling boom, and started to take on fuel. The tanker made two contacts: the first to fill up the Black Stallion's jet fuel tanks in the wings and aft fuselage, and the second to transfer another substance into a separate, larger storage tank in the center fuselage section of the aircraft. The second transfer took much longer because the substance was much thicker than jet fuel, but after almost an hour the refueling was complete. The aircraft was now over three times heavier than it was at takeoff: the aircraft carried twice its own weight in fuel. If it had this same fuel load on the ground, it would never have been able to take off.

After the tanker departed the area, Hunter reconfigured the bomber's computers for the next phase of flight, then began checking all of the engine and flight systems carefully. Patrick steered the Black Stallion north, then began a slow climb and gradually began applying full throttle. At full afterburner power at forty thousand feet about a minute later, they were at Mach 1.8, or about fourteen hundred miles an hour. "Airflow has stabilized and is in the green, lasers ready—we're ready to spike the leopards, General," Boomer reported.

"Let's see what this thing has under the hood," Patrick said. He hit a small control stud on the side-stick control and spoke, "Spike engines."

"Engines spiking, stop spike," the female computer-synthesized voice responded, adding the command to stop as a reminder. The airspeed slowed to Mach one point six, enough to tug at their shoulder harnesses. On the front of each engine, heat-tolerant vanes extended across the engine inlets, diverting airflow around the fan blades and compressor section of the engines. As the air was turned it was also mixed with tiny amounts of jet fuel and compressed. As the air-fuel mixture was squeezed, several diode laser emitters in each engine ignited it, and the jet exhaust was forced out of the back. The airspeed almost immediately jumped back up to Mach one point eight and quickly rose, exceeding Mach two, three, four, and even began approaching Mach five. The vertical

velocity readout was equally as impressive—as the airspeed increased, the pitch angle became steeper and the Black Stallion climbed faster.

The LPDRS, or Laser Pulse Detonation Rocket System, nicknamed "leopards," was Boomer's engine design that would change the face of high-speed travel. The LPDRS engines were a new generation of advanced rocket engines that used instantaneous, pulsed detonation of jet fuel using blasts of laser energy, producing fifty percent more thrust than the conventional chemical rocket engines. Patrick was squished back into his seat as the "leopards" engines began their high-frequency hammer-like pulsing and the spaceplane rapidly picked up speed.

Finally, the engines began to throttle back and the pitch angle decreased, until they were straight and level again. The curvature of the Earth began to become apparent, although a few thunderheads on the horizon seemed to reach their altitude. "All engines stabilized and running perfectly at Mach four point five-one," Boomer reported a few minutes later. "We're level at flight level eight-zero-zero—eighty thousand feet. Incredible," Patrick breathed. "Simply incredible. Almost five times the speed of sound." He glanced at the engine readouts. "And I don't even detect any fuel burn at this speed."

"The lasers are hot enough to ignite the compressed air, but we use a few hundred pounds of fuel an hour to help the process along," Boomer said. He checked some position readouts, then said, "We can turn eastward now and I can have you in Washington in about forty minutes, sir."

"You could . . . but that's not why I came on this ride, Boomer," Patrick said. "Besides, we have a job to do too—this isn't just a taxi ride. Let's do it."

"Yes, sir," Noble said excitedly. He checked some more readouts; then: "Ready for suborbital burn, sir."

"Roger that," Patrick said. He took one last sip of water from a canteen, then flipped his oxygen visor back in place, tightened up all of his straps, and situated himself in his seat. "Here we go," he said. "Computer, commence suborbital insertion burn."

"Commence suborbital insertion burn, cancel suborbital insertion burn," the computer responded. When the countermanding order was not received, the computer said, *"LPDRS engines activated . . . ignition in three, two, one, zero."*

At that moment they heard four distinctive and rather unnerving "BAARRK!" sounds reverberating through the fuselage, and the XR-A9 suddenly accelerated so fast that a puff of air was forced out of Patrick's lips. Patrick's vision blurred and tunnel-visioned as his eyeballs were squished against his skull, but the last thing he saw clearly was the airspeed jumping past Mach five, less than a minute after main engine start. As the airspeed increased, the flight control computer nosed the XR-A9 higher and higher, until their climb rate now exceeded one hundred thousand feet per minute. At that point the readouts switched to thousands of feet per second—two, five, then ten thousand feet per second. The Mach numbers, or times above the speed of sound, were approaching double digits.

Once above three hundred thousand feet at the edge of space, the spikes in the inlets of the four LDPRS engines closed even more. Instead of using the atmosphere to burn jet fuel, the "leopards" engines used borohydrogen tetroxide, or BOHM—nicknamed "boom"—as the oxidizer. The thick soupy substance was a hundred times more efficient as liquid oxygen, and increased the specific thrust of each engine by several thousand percent.

As the numbers climbed, so did the G-forces—the number of times the forces of gravity was being exceeded on the human body. Patrick had pulled as much as twelve Gs before, but only for a few seconds at a time. The G-forces now were not excessive, only about 2.75 Gs (times the force of gravity), but it had been going on for a relatively long time, something that Patrick was definitely not accustomed to. Patrick practiced moving his arms to activate switches on the instrument panel in case voice commands didn't work, which was a real possibility since his chest felt like someone was sitting on it, and it took effort and control to breathe, let alone speak.

Patrick began to feel as if he had been tackled by the entire Penn State linebacker squad. His vision blurred, then tunneled, and the air was forced out of his lungs—fortunately the life support system immediately sensed this and started shooting pure oxygen into his lungs under pressure to keep him from asphyxiating. Although he was quite uncomfortable, the pressure was not painful, just disconcerting. Could a crewmember stand this kind of pressure flight after flight? he wondered. How long could someone serve with the Black Stallion before something bad happened?

After what seemed like an eternity—but he knew from flying the simulator that it was less than eight minutes—the engines shut down. Suddenly the cockpit was deathly quiet and the G-forces, which had built up to about four times the normal force of gravity, stopped suddenly as well. The sudden quiet and relief from the pressure on his chest made Patrick pause in fear. What caused that sudden stoppage? Was everything OK? Was this the end . . . ?

"General?" Patrick found he had his eyes closed and his breathing had all but stopped. "General sir?" Still no response. Then, louder: *"Yo, Muck!"*

Patrick took a deep breath, like a free-diver coming up from three minutes underwater, then blurted out, "What?"

"Welcome to space, General," Boomer said.

Patrick opened his eyes—and he saw the Earth from space for the first time. The view was simply unbelievable. He had to look on his supercockpit display to see what he was looking at: it was northern California and Nevada, all the way from Lake Tahoe to the Pacific Ocean—at least five hundred miles in all directions. The edge of the Earth was rimmed in bluish-white; the sky was absolutely stark black. He still had a sense of altitude and velocity: he could discern differences in altitude of peaks of the Sierra Nevada Mountain range, and he could see enough ground details to get a feeling of how fast they were traveling over the ground. As he watched in absolute awe, the Bitterroot Mountains hove into view, and on the horizon he could start to see the snow-capped Rocky Mountains. The speed was amazing.

"We made it," Patrick breathed, quickly regaining his composure. "Station check."

"In the green up here, General," Boomer said. "You okay up there, sir?"

"I'm in the green." He moved his arms and shoulders experimentally, then took a couple deep breaths. "Everything seems OK. How did the Stud do?"

"Another typical suborbital insertion," Boomer said casually. "Altitude seventy-four point two-one miles, velocity Mach twelve point one-two-eight. Fuel flows looked a little high on number four—I'll give that a check when we get back. Good job, General. You just earned your astronaut wings—any flight above sixty miles is considered a space shot."

"Thanks, Boomer." He tore his eyes away from the beauty and grandeur around him and checked all of his instruments, flipping quickly through all of the different display pages on the supercockpit screen. "On course, on speed," he reported. "Fuel levels in the green."

"Always the navigator, eh, General?" Boomer chided him. "Sit back and enjoy the ride, sir—you're in space. Only a handful of humans have ever done this."

The air inside the cockpit was filled with tiny bits of floating dust and dirt and the occasional tiny washer, which Patrick collected and put into a plastic bag. He then took a pencil from a storage compartment near his right elbow and let it go in front of his face to watch it hover in mid-air. He had done that a few times in terrestrial aircraft, putting it in a gentle dive so the object fell at the same speed as the aircraft, making it seem "weightless." But that had lasted only seconds, and the windscreen had been filled with clouds or the ground coming up to meet him. This would last for a lot longer period of time, and his windscreen was still filled with clouds and Earth, but at this rate he wouldn't hit it for quite some time.

"Feeling OK up there, General?" Boomer asked.

"No problems so far," Patrick said. That wasn't quite true, but he wasn't going to admit anything else.

He had been fortunate in his Air Force career and had only been airsick a couple times, during really violent maneuvers or disorienting, smoky, tense situations as in combat, but he never suffered from plain motion sickness. Right now there were no violent maneuvers going on; there was stress, certainly—they were over seventy miles in space, cruising at almost seven thousand miles an hour—but in microgravity, with no real sense of up or down, he could feel that creeping queasiness building in the pit of his stomach. The shoulder and lap belts helped to maintain his sense of weight and orientation, and he had to turn his attention to his assigned tasks instead of stare out the windscreen and think about how high up he was—or even try to determine which way was up. Despite Boomer's rakish tone and the immense beauty outside, it was not hard for

Patrick to turn his mind to the task at hand. This was not simply a joyride: they had work to do.

Patrick made several radio calls and entered commands into his computer terminal. "We're ready for payload release," he announced a few minutes later. "Range reports clear. Bomb doors coming open . . . Meteor away. Doors closed."

The BDU-58 Meteor was a simple orbital delivery system designed specifically for the XR-A9. It was nothing more than a large heat-shielded container fitted with a liquid-fuel rocket booster, guidance system, datalink communications system, and payload release mechanisms. Once the BDU-58 was released, the first stage rocket motor pushed the weapon down and away from the Black Stallion, then up on a tongue of fire into its own Earth orbit. Once in orbit, the Meteor's rocket engine could push the spacecraft out of orbit, change course, or propel it to a higher or differently shaped orbit, depending on the payload. After releasing its payload, the Meteor could be deorbited and allowed to burn up in the atmosphere, or it could be retrieved by another spacecraft, brought back to Earth, and reused.

On this mission, the Meteor carried three inert test articles, each weighing about twelve hundred pounds. The Meteor would be deorbited at a particular point in its orbit, penetrating all the way through the atmosphere in order to protect the test articles inside; then each test article would be released at different altitudes above the target area. Each test article had a triple-mode guidance system that would locate targets using millimeter-wave radar, infrared, and satellite steering signals, but then each test article would "tell" the other which target it was tracking and the quality of its target identification and lock, so the other test articles could locate and attack other targets. The test articles had tiny winglets that allowed it to home in precisely to its target or glide long distances if necessary to locate targets. When released from extremely high altitudes, the test articles could glide for as far as two hundred miles, or loiter over an area for several minutes searching for targets.

"Payload released successfully, bay doors closed," Patrick reported. "It'll make two orbits, then attack its targets inside the White Sands Missile Test Range."

"I'd hate to be under those bad boys when they come in," Boomer remarked. "Okay, sir, we'll alter course slightly southeast, then in exactly eleven minutes and nine seconds we'll start our descent for Washington. Let me brief you on the descent procedures . . ."

"I've got a better idea, Boomer," Patrick interrupted. "How about we take her up?"

"Up? You want to go to a higher altitude?"

"No. Let's take it up . . . into orbit."

"Are you sure, sir? That wasn't on the flight plan."

"I'm sure."

"But during takeoff . . ."

"I'm okay, Boomer—really. Maybe I blacked out a bit, but I feel fine now."

"I'm thinking about re-entry, that's all," Boomer said. "The g-forces are heavier and more sustained."

"I'll be fine . . . Captain," Patrick said, adding the formal title "Captain" again to signify his desire to terminate the discussion.

"Yes, sir." There was only a slight hesitation as Boomer considered whether or not to use his prerogative and not do this, but he decided that the required phase of this flight had been accomplished—if the general became incapacitated, it wouldn't affect mission completion. Besides, what aviator wouldn't want to fly into orbit if he had the chance? "Ready when you are, General," Noble responded. "Let me make a few changes to the flight plan and get them entered into the computer . . ." It took only a few minutes, with Patrick carefully monitoring Boomer's inputs and the computer's responses. "Done. Isn't there anyone you need to call first? Don't we need to get permission from someone?"

"Nope. Let's do it."

"You got it, sir. I've got computer control and engine monitoring."

"I've got the aircraft."

"You got the leopards. Ready anytime you are."

"Here we go." Patrick pressed the voice-command button: "Computer, orbital burn."

"Ready for orbital burn, stop orbital burn," the computer responded. "LPDRS engines reporting ready . . . engines firing in three, two, one, now."

Patrick had steeled himself for the push, but he never expected the punch he received as the high-tech rocket engines fired off. Because there was less atmosphere to let airspeed build up more gradually as before, the shove was ten times worse than takeoff. Patrick used every ounce of strength he possessed to keep his legs and stomach taut, forcing every milliliter of blood to stay in the upper part of his body. Soon he found doing the H-maneuver wasn't that necessary, because soon he had to pressure-breathe against the regulators forcing oxygen into his helmet—in a reversal of the normal breathing mechanism, he had to carefully sip the high-pressure oxygen into his lungs, then forcibly push carbon dioxide out. If he tried to breathe normally, the high-pressure oxygen would pop his lungs like over-filled balloons.

"General McLanahan."

"I'm . . . okay . . . Boomer," Patrick grunted. He strained to look out the side of the canopy toward Earth, but he couldn't see anything, and the G-forces pressed painfully on his neck and vertebrae.

"Keep your head and back still, sir. The boost isn't a good time for sight-seeing."

"I figured that out real quick, Boomer."

"Ninety seconds left. How are you doing?"

"O . . . kay." Even saying one letter was difficult, like talking while facing into a hurricane. "No sw . . ." And then Patrick felt his chest shudder, and his vision tunneled and spun. He grunted out the bad air even harder, then had to fight to keep the pain down as he slowly, carefully let the high-pressure oxygen refill his lungs.

"General! Can you hear me?"

"R . . . og . . . er . . ."

"I'm going to cutoff . . ."

"No . . . no . . . keep . . . go . . . ing." Patrick wasn't sure if he meant it, but he did hear the words come out of his gritted teeth . . . and the pressure and the pain remained, so Noble must've heard him.

It seemed to take an hour, but in fact it was over in less than sixty seconds. Patrick barked out a breath, forgot to reverse-breathe, and was surprised when he took a deep breath and the pain didn't come back. "Sta . . . station check," he snapped.

"MC's in the green, sir," Boomer replied.

"AC's in the green," Patrick said before checking his oxygen, cockpit pressurization, and mission displays.

"That was a hairy one, sir," Boomer said. "I hope it was worth it. Take a look."

He looked . . . and he gasped in surprise despite himself. The horizon was no longer flat in any direction—it was all curvature now. Out the right side he could see all of the New England states and beyond almost to Nova Scotia, and out the left he thought he could see all of the Great Lakes to the very western tip of Lake Superior. The ground was sliding under them at an amazing speed. "Are we . . . ?"

"Seventeen thousand one hundred miles an hour . . . Mach twenty-six point zero-two-one, altitude crept up a little to eighty-seven point eight-nine miles," Boomer said. "Welcome to low Earth orbit. You've really earned your astronaut's wings now."

"How did I do?"

"A little worse than last time, although you kept on pressure-breathing—instead of screaming, you were grunting like Atlas lifting the weight of the world onto his shoulders," Boomer said. Patrick silently thanked the aerospace medical and life support technicians for repeatedly drilling the pressure-breathing routine into him while preparing for this mission—he doubted he was lucid enough to consciously do the drill. "The G-forces hit hardest going from Mach fifteen to Mach twenty-six. Sit back and relax for a few minutes, sir, and then I'll brief the re-entry procedures."

The coast of Canada slid underneath them, and minutes later Greenland came into view. The scenery changed with amazing speed. It seemed every time Patrick did a computer check or read a procedure, then looked up again, he was in a completely new corner of the globe. He could see the southern coast of Ireland, with the British islands and the coast of Europe already in view on the horizon. He could see London, Brussels, Paris, and all the way to Hamburg to the north. Soon they were over Eastern Europe, with Moscow on the very horizon to the east and the Black Sea stretching out before them. "I'll bet the Russkies don't appreciate us flying over their territory like this," Boomer said.

"Ask me if I care," Patrick said. He motioned toward the horizon. "Ever get shot at, Boomer?"

"Shot at?" he asked. As if on cue, a warning tone blared and the computer reported, *"SEARCH RADAR ACTIVE."* The computer did not identify the radar signal or even attempt to classify it except as a "search radar."

"The Russians have a pretty good anti-ballistic missile base on the Kola Peninsula that has the capability of reaching us," Patrick said. "The SA-21 'Boa' missile is Russia's version of our Ground-Based Interceptor—the 'Star Wars' missile defense anti-missile system. It's supposed to be in initial deployment testing right . . . there." He pointed at a spot on the ground. "It has a max altitude range of one hundred and twenty miles."

"You're kidding me!"

"You guys in Dreamland need to get more intelligence briefings before you take these things for a ride," Patrick said. He pointed at the threat display on their computer screens. "Your software needs to be updated too—because I'll bet that's their ABM tracking radar we're picking up. They're tracking us and probably the Meteor as well."

"I've flown this track at least three times and no one's ever said anything to me!"

"That's because no one officially knows what you're doing," Patrick said. "NORAD can see and track you of course, and they may even suspect you're a Dreamland bird, but they'll never start an inquiry except at the very highest levels, and it'll stop right away once they confirm who you are. It's up to you to get the intel you need."

"Yes, sir," Boomer said. "You get to feel pretty safe up here."

"You can't afford to—not in this day and age," Patrick said. "I'll start sending you a daily file on global threats, and I'll get the techs at Air Intelligence Agency to get you the software to update your threat receiver. You may have to replan your missions accordingly, depending on the geopolitical situation."

"We don't need to get permission to fly in space over Russia—do we?"

"Legally space is open to all nations," Patrick said. "Russia usually doesn't squawk when a new spacecraft flies overhead—they would certainly like nothing more than to bring down an XR-A9, or at least study it—but since we can go in and out of orbit so easily, they may complain. If they complain loud enough, we'll stop. Maybe." Both crewmembers were on high alert for any sign of danger until they were well past the area.

Things were quiet for several minutes; soon, Patrick heard through his subcutaneous transceiver: "Luger to McLanahan."

"Go ahead, Dave."

"You received a 'go.' "

"Roger that." On intercom, McLanahan said, "Give me payload command, Boomer."

Noble hit a key: "Transferring payload command, now. I've got flight command."

"Thank you." McLanahan's multifunction displays now showed the status of the BDU-58 Meteor device. He hit a few keys, then casually announced, "I'm having a problem with the Meteor. It's not responding to commands. Everything looks normal—relay network, datalink, orbital control computers—but it's not responding."

"Want me to look at it, General?" Boomer asked.

"I'll give my command override one more try, then turn it over to you." But a few moments later: "Still no good. I'll take flight control, Boomer, and you take payload control. I've got the spacecraft."

"You've got the spacecraft." Noble checked the payload control displays. Sure enough, the Meteor was just completing its deorbit push burn and was quickly losing altitude. He tried to command the device to stop its burn, translate around, and boost itself back to its correct orbit, but nothing happened. "No response," he said dejectedly. "It almost looks like your command override is locking out any other attempts to change trajectory."

"I know, but I never entered my override code," Patrick said. "It already locked me out, and my code can't override it."

"I can try to recycle the payload control computers . . ."

"Go for it," Patrick said. Noble switched off both payload control computers, then turned them back on again and let them boot up. As soon as they were back and running, Noble tried again. "The computers look like they're fine, but your override command is still not letting any other commands to be entered. Should I try to have Elliott send an override command?"

"I already tried that, but let's try it again now that we've recycled the computers," Patrick said. But nothing happened. The master command code radioed from mission command at Elliott Air Force Base did no good.

"Looks like the master override command was received, but the payload command system is still locked up," Noble said. He tried several more times but was still unsuccessful. "That's a bummer, sir," he said. "It's coming down and there's nothing we can do about it. Sorry about that." He checked some more displays. "Looks like it's going to hit in central Iran. That's pretty uninhabited territory—I don't think it'll hurt anyone. The Iranians will probably find it, though."

"If they do, all they'll find are hunks of metal," Patrick said woodenly. "You take flight control again and get us ready for deorbit and landing. I'll report this incident to the Pentagon."

"You got it, General," Noble said, and he got to work on entering and checking the computer routine for deorbiting the spacecraft.

SOUTH-CENTRAL IRAN, NEAR ZARAND, KERMĀN PROVINCE

That Same Time

"Ninety seconds to launch, sir," the launch control officer announced. "Launch pads are clear. All weapons reporting fully functional."

"Very well," Brigadier-General Kamal Zhoram, commander of the Second Rocket Brigade of the *Pasdaran-i-Engelab*, or Iranian Revolutionary Guards Corps, responded. He smiled and nodded resolutely as he monitored the pre-launch procedures from the command vehicle. Ever since taking command of this operational test unit, he had been driven to succeed, and his vision was finally taking shape. The Shahab series of ballistic missiles represented the cutting edge of Iranian military technology, even more than its fighter aircraft, air defense systems, and submarines. After years of pleading, arguing, and cajoling his superiors for additional funding, the fruits of his labor were ready to be demonstrated this morning.

This missile was the most advanced of the Shahab series now in operation: the Shahab-5, code-named "*Takht*," or "throne." The model being tested today was a three-stage rocket, with two liquid-fueled boosters stacked upon one another plus a small solid-motor third stage. Although Iran never officially discussed details about its military arsenal, when launch tests were scheduled the Shahab-5 was described as a space launch vehicle, and it certainly had the capability of placing a satellite into orbit. But more importantly it was also capable of carrying one thousand kilograms to any target in Israel, the Persian Gulf, half of Africa, most of Europe, and even western China. It was extremely accurate and reliable, thanks to improvements made over the original North Korean Taepodong-2 missile technology.

Although this was an above-ground pad launch, the other three mission-ready Shahab-5 missiles operated by the Iranian Revolutionary Guards arsenal were housed in below-ground hardened silos, which gave them added security and protection from attack . . .

. . . which was necessary, because the three ballistic missiles carried nuclear warheads. Iran had purchased Chinese 350-kiloton nuclear warheads from North Korea years ago, along with a variety of test rockets and anti-ship missiles, in exchange for generous oil and natural gas shipments, and had worked for over five years to fit the warheads on the North Korean–derived missiles. With today's successful test—this missile carried two independently targeted dummy re-entry vehicles—Iran's intermediate-range nuclear ballistic missile could be declared fully operational, making it the first Islamic country with a nuclear strike capability.

Zhoram glanced up at the last security zone report: it was ten minutes old. A good commando squad could move two kilometers in ten minutes—it was unacceptable. "I want all security zone officers to update their security status immediately."

"Right away, sir."

"Update guidance system alignment at zero minus sixty seconds."

The clock ticked by—it seemed to get slower and slower every second. Finally: "Inertial measuring units updated, alignment is well within Class One tolerances."

Zhoram went over to the guidance control officer's console and hit the button that told the difference between the inertial navigation system's position, heading, and velocity values versus those of the last fix—they were indeed well within tolerances. He checked the master target coordinates and verified them against the flight plan—good, all was in order.

His targets were sets of geographical coordinates in the northern Indian Ocean, about two thousand kilometers downrange. The target area was surrounded by Iranian patrol vessels and warships that would document the test package's accuracy as well as to keep out any spy ships. But the general secretly hoped that an Israeli or American submarine or spy satellite would be on hand to witness the results of this important test flight, because he knew it was going to be a successful one—and then the world would know that Iran had a powerful, fast-response weapon that could threaten any enemy.

"Very well," Zhoram said. "Prepare to release batteries on my order."

There was a brief flurry of activity on another console as the master launch crew ran their checklists, then waited for ready indications from the individual controllers. Normally a Shahab-5 launched via commands issued from the master control vehicle, transmitted by radio with a hardwire fiber-optic cable backup, but each launcher was able to launch independently as well, and they had to be prepared to do so in an instant if communications were cut or jammed. Zhoram watched carefully, making sure all proper procedures were being followed. "Standing by, sir."

"Send to all units, stand by for launch." Zhoram picked up the phone datalinked directly via satellite to Pasdaran headquarters at Doshan Tappeh Air Base in Tehran. He listened for the encrypted satellite link to connect, then spoke: "Faraz, Faraz, this is Heydar, Sorush, I say again, Sorush."

"Reza," the reply came. "Reza. Acknowledge."

"Heydar copies Reza," Zhoram responded. "Out." He turned to his command-post controller. "Send to all units . . ."

At that instant there was a loud "BANG!" like a car accident, but ten times as loud, reverberating the walls of the command vehicle. "Sir, lost connectivity with unit . . . !" There was another loud crunch of metal, followed by a tremendous explosion that shook the command vehicle on its tires.

"Stay at your posts!" Zhoram shouted. "Secure all systems and prepare to move immediately!" The general dashed out of the command vehicle, knowing that it was a violation of procedures to open the pressurized cab, but he had to see for himself what was going on. He stepped into the airlock, sealed the door behind him, donned a chemical weapon protective mask and gloves, undogged the outer door, and stepped out . . .

. . . into the midst of a raging inferno. The Shahab-5 missile launch pad to the northwest was ablaze, with thousands of liters of burning rocket fuel spreading quickly across the ground in all directions. He picked up the phone inside the airlock: "Move the command vehicle one kilometer to the northeast, and do it now, or you will all roast to death within sixty seconds. Go!" He sealed the outer door to the command cab and jumped clear of the vehicle just as the hydraulic legs began to retract.

How in hell could this happen? Zhoram shouted to himself. They were at least twenty kilometers from the nearest bit of civilization, and they had three hundred security personnel deployed all around this area. It was impossible for any commando to . . .

. . . and out of a corner of an eye, he saw it—a flash of dawn sunlight in the sky, directly overhead. He stood, transfixed, as his eyes scanned, then saw another glint of light, even closer this time . . . headed right for him.

The command vehicle had moved no more than fifty meters away when the object from the sky slammed into it, directly in the center. The metal top of the vehicle splintered and collapsed like balsa wood, then blasted straight up into the sky as the power transformers, backup batteries, and high-pressure air conditioning units inside ruptured and exploded. In seconds, huge belching streams of fire were gushing from the top and bottom of his command vehicle. As he watched, he saw several more objects hit the vehicles again, but of course by that time they were consumed by the immense fireballs that were once his rocket and command post.

They were under attack! Zhoram screamed at himself as he watched his launcher and command vehicles ablaze. Someone had launched some sort of precision-guided weapon at them from above that destroyed them almost instantly.

Realizing immediately that there was nothing he could do to rescue any of his comrades from the twin infernos, his thoughts turned to the investigation that he knew would commence within hours. No one was going to believe him when he reported that it was an attack—his superiors would argue that it was some sort of malfunction or error in pre-launch procedures. He knew better—but he had to do his best to convince his commanders of it. If he survived the inquisition and punishment phase that he knew was going to begin very soon, he vowed he would find out who carried out this attack from the sky, and do everything he could humanly do to avenge himself on him. God willing, he was going to make them pay . . .

CHAPTER 1

"If you're looking for a sure way to make enemies, change something."
—President Woodrow Wilson

THE WHITE HOUSE, WASHINGTON, D.C.

A Short Time Later

"Is this how you usually get into the White House, sir?" Captain Hunter Noble asked as they turned into a guarded underground parking structure a couple blocks from 1600 Pennsylvania Avenue.

"Only when I'm in a flight suit," Lieutenant-General Patrick McLanahan responded. Both he and Noble still wore the plain black Dreamland-style flight suits they were wearing on their suborbital flight in the XR-A9 spaceplane less than two hours ago. "The boss thought we might attract too much attention going in the main entrance."

"Doesn't want to be seen with the line grunts, eh?"

"Doesn't want to have to explain you, me, and the Stud to the world . . . yet," Patrick corrected him. "Believe me, the President is on our side. Once the Stud goes public, I'm sure he'll want to be the first sitting president to fly in space."

In the very back part of the parking garage they came upon a nondescript locked steel door with a sign on it that read "DANGER HIGH VOLTAGE." Patrick opened a hidden panel a few steps away, punched in a code into a keypad, returned to the steel door, and waited. Moments later Boomer heard a buzzing noise, and Patrick pulled the door open. They stepped inside a very small, dark room, and Patrick secured the steel door behind them. A few moments later they heard another buzzing sound, and Patrick pulled another door open. They entered a long, dark, concrete-floored hallway illuminated with bare lightbulbs wired up with surface conduit. Steel and PVC pipes snaked overhead, some leaking. The air was dank and it felt most definitely claustrophobic.

"Ooo. Secret hallway," Noble murmured. "Very cloak-and-dagger. I suppose there are lots of these hidden hallways around the capital."

"I suppose. I only know about two of them, and the one between the Pentagon and the White House isn't that secret."

"I didn't know about that one."

It was a very long walk, during which they passed several cameras in the ceiling. At the end of the seemingly endless hallway there was yet another steel security door. Patrick picked up a telephone on the wall and spoke briefly to someone inside, the door buzzed, and Patrick pulled it open. They entered another small room with a uniformed Secret Service guard sitting behind a thick bulletproof glass. Patrick and Boomer exchanged ID cards for ID necklaces, signed in, and were buzzed inside.

The hallway they entered was just barely nicer than the long tunnel they just crossed—it was carpeted and better lit, but it still had that musty, wet smell and feel to it. "Your usual entrance, sir?" Boomer asked.

"That was one of the Secret Service alternate entryways and emergency exits," Patrick explained. "They let me use it when I need to. It's closer to my office."

They weaved around boxes of files stacked up in the hallway and old copy machines scattered here and there, then went down another flight of stairs to an even dirtier, mustier level. There were even fewer signs of life down here. Boomer had a peek into an open lavatory door, which looked like a fifties-era Army barracks latrine with a concrete floor complete with large drain in the middle, trough urinal, open showers, polished metal mirrors, metal shelves for towels and cleaning supplies, and very dated toilets and sinks, although it was clean enough.

The door they entered was a few down from the latrine, and unlike most of the other ones on this floor it was thick, new-looking, and well-maintained. Inside the feel was actually pretty comfortable—thick light-colored carpeting, plastered sheetrock walls with a few photographs and award plaques on them, a coffee pot and small refrigerator, computers, copy machines, a couple upholstered chairs, a convertible sofa, nice bookshelves, and a small but nice desk. “Nice office, General,” Boomer commented. “After seeing your latrine, I was expecting the modern version of the dungeons in the Tower of London.”

“That’s exactly what it was before I started working on it,” Patrick said. “I’m not much of a handyman, but I think I did okay. They don’t encourage self-help projects in the White House, but I think they took pity on me down here. Make yourself comfortable.” He picked up the phone and punched a button. “Hi, Miss Parks, General McLanahan here . . . Yes, just got in . . . Yes, he’s here too . . . Utilities OK, do you think? That’s all the captain has . . . OK, we’re on our way.” Boomer had just made his way over to the coffee machine and was just getting out supplies. “Sorry, no time,” he said as he replaced the receiver on its cradle. “We’ll get some coffee upstairs.”

"Upstairs? You mean . . . ?"

"Yep. Let's go."

"Then I gotta use your facilities first, sir," Boomer said, and he stepped quickly to use the latrine. His ears were fairly buzzing with excitement, and he found his own plumbing wouldn't work as advertised, so he gave up, washed up, took a nervous gulp of water (ignoring the old, corroded fixtures), and headed out.

They retraced their steps upstairs, then walked up one more flight of stairs beyond where they entered. The sights, sounds, and smells were noticeably better now. They passed by a dining hall, where Boomer recognized several politicians and senior White House staff members from TV. They ascended one more flight of stairs, had their IDs checked yet again by a plainclothes Secret Service agent, and made their way into a circular outer office with a secretary, pictures of presidents on the walls, a fireplace with a small sitting area with a couch and several chairs before it, and several more chairs arrayed against the walls, most of them occupied. There seemed to be an almost constant parade of persons coming and going down the hallway leading to the Oval Office. "Who are all these people?" Boomer asked.

"Congressmen, senators, aides, staffers, assistants, constituents, reporters . . . you name it, they flow through this place constantly," Patrick responded quietly.

"Is it always this . . . chaotic?"

"Yep. Twenty-four seven. Not only does this place never sleep . . . it never even rests."

At that moment Vice President Maureen Hershel emerged from the doorway leading to the Cabinet Room, walking alongside Secretary of Defense Joseph Gardner. Gardner, the former two-term senator from Florida and Secretary of the Navy, was an immensely popular and well-liked politician, widely considered a front-runner in the upcoming presidential elections. Tall, impossibly handsome, and instantly likable, he was one of the most influential and important members of Kevin Martindale's administration. He whispered something into Maureen Hershel's ear as they headed out of the Cabinet Room, and it made Patrick feel good to see her smile and laugh. As if sensing Patrick's presence, she turned, saw him, and gave him a relieved, pleased smile. She nodded at Gardner and let him pass, then gave Attorney General Ken Phoenix a few parting words, clasped him on the shoulder, then motioned to Patrick with two fingers.

Phoenix, a younger-looking clone of President Kevin Martindale with longish dark hair, thin glasses, and piercing dark eyes, shook his head woefully at Patrick as they passed in the hallway. "You should have brought your flying helmet, General," he whispered to him as he flipped open his cell phone. "You're going to need it."

"Thanks for the heads-up, sir," Patrick said. Patrick motioned for Boomer to follow him.

Maureen Hershel intercepted Patrick in the hall just outside the door to the Cabinet Room. She had always been trim and shapely, but the office had taken a toll on her and made her thin. She kept her brown hair long but tied up in a French braid behind her head, off the collar of her brown business suit, which only served to make her face seem even thinner. Her blue eyes still shined behind her simple rimless glasses, but the worry and edginess of her position had deepened the lines around those beautiful eyes.

"I knew you wouldn't make it," she said.

"Sorry." He reached out with his right hand and touched her left in their little expression of love in that very public of places, but her hand was as cold as stone, as cold as her voice. "Traffic was murder."

"I don't think anyone's in the mood for jokes, Patrick," she said. She gave Boomer a nod and shook his hand. "You two okay?"

"We're fine, Miss Vice President," Noble said.

"Good." She was all business again. "It'll be you two meeting with the President, myself, SECDEF, NCA, and CJCS. The press somehow got wind of the spaceplane proposal, and they might have info on the flight you just took."

"We knew they would, ma'am."

"Why is that? The project is supposed to be classified."

"We began daylight ops two weeks ago, Miss Vice President," Patrick said. She noticed Maureen's eyes narrow a bit when Patrick addressed her formally—she knew it was only proper, but she felt isolated and detached from him whenever he did it. "I warned everyone it was going to be just a matter of time before it was all over the press. We saw the first 'LakeSpotter' reports four days later on the Internet . . ."

"We were notified that the report was coming out in tomorrow's paper just this morning," Maureen said. "No requests, no opportunity to squash it—just notification. Everyone's pissed."

"It's no secret who wants what, Miss Vice President," Patrick said. "Congress has made that quite clear. Everyone has got their own ideas, and none of them include the Stud."

"You're still going with your original recommendations, Patrick?"

"Yes, ma'am."

Maureen's lips went hard and straight with concern, but she nodded. Miss Parks, the Oval Office assistant, approached and informed her that the meeting had been moved to the Oval Office and the President was waiting. "Okay. Ready?"

"Ready." He tried to reach out again to her, but she had already spun on her heel and headed toward the door to the Oval Office. He swallowed his feeling of dejection, then turned to Hunter. "Ready to do it, Boomer?" Patrick whispered.

"Do I have time to change my shorts first, sir?" Noble asked.

"Negative. Follow me."

Maureen peeked through the peephole in the door, saw nothing out of the ordinary, knocked lightly, then thrust open the door, and before Boomer knew it they were inside. Like much of the rest of the place he had seen, the Oval Office was not the largest or most ornate office he had ever been in—in fact, it was pretty plain. Boomer expected that, but what he was waiting for was the experience of feeling the aura of power that was supposed to emanate from this historic room. This was the place, he knew, where hundreds of decisions a day were made affecting the lives of billions of people all over the world, where the word of a single man could commit the resources of the most powerful nation ever to inhabit the planet to a goal.

But he didn't sense that either. This was a workaday office—he felt nothing more. No sooner had they walked into the room than the outer office assistant came in and handed papers to the Secretary of Defense, Joseph Gardner, and hustled out, only to be followed by someone else a few moments later. There was no sense of anticipation, no excitement, no . . . nothing, really, except for a sense of business, perhaps with a slight undercurrent of uncertainty and urgency.

The one thing he did notice was the large rug in the middle of the room with the presidential seal on it. Boomer knew that before World War Two the eagle's head had been turned toward the thirteen arrows it was clutching in its talons; after World War Two, President Harry Truman redesigned the seal so that the eagle's head was turned toward the olive branches, signifying a desire and emphasis for peace. But after the attacks on the United States, President Martindale ordered the eagle's head on the seal turned back toward the arrows, signifying America's de facto perpetual readiness for war.

Boomer wasn't sure if he agreed with that sentiment or not, but clearly the President did, and it hung heavy like a fog in the famous historic room.

The Chairman of the Joint Chiefs of Staff, Army General William Glenbrook, looked as if he was going to get to his feet when Maureen Hershel stepped into the room, but he kept his seat. Apparently there was some informal but clearly understood rule that no one rose for the Vice President entering any executive office unless she was the senior official present or unless the President did, and he was too distracted by his chief of staff, former U.S. House of Representatives Majority Leader Carl Minden, to notice. Minden himself noticed, but he only scowled and turned back to whatever he was showing the President. Finally the President impatiently looked up from his desk, wondering when his next meeting was going to start and finding the participants waiting on him.

Kevin Martindale was a long-time fixture on Capitol Hill and the White House. A former Congressman and former two-term vice president, he served one term as president before being defeated by the ultra-isolationist Jeffersonian Party candidate Thomas Thorn. He had been gearing up for another run at the presidency when the Russian Air Force attacked the United States. Amidst Thorn's decision not to seek a second term and with only twenty percent voter turnout, Martindale and Hershel—the only candidates to run for the White House that year—were elected. "Well well, the rocket boys," he said jovially. "Welcome home."

"Thank you, Mr. President," Patrick responded. "Nice to be home." Per protocol, he waited in place quietly until told where to go.

The President finished what he was doing then got up, stepped toward them, and shook hands with Patrick. Martindale was thin and rakishly handsome, a little more than average height, with dark secretive eyebrows, small dark eyes, and longish salt-and-pepper hair parted in the middle. He was famous for the "photographer's dream"—two curls of silver hair that appeared on his forehead without any manual manipulation whenever he was peeved or animated. While out of office Martindale had grown a beard which had made him look rather sinister; he had shaved the beard after the American Holocaust, but kept the long hair, so now he just looked roguish. "I hope you know," he said quietly into Patrick's ear, not yet releasing his handshake and keeping Patrick close to him, "we created quite a ruckus out there, Patrick."

"I was hoping so, sir," Patrick responded.

"Me too," the President said. "Did you get it?"

"You bet we did, sir," Patrick replied. "Direct hit."

"Good job," the President said. "No radiation detected?"

"They'd be crazy to put real nuclear warheads on that test shot, sir."

"But you checked anyway . . . ?"

"Of course, sir. No radiation detected."

"Great." He shook his head with a smile. "Did the bastards really think we were going to allow them to base a nuclear-capable medium-range missile within striking distance of Diego Garcia, one of our most vital air bases in Asia?"

"Apparently so, sir," Patrick said. "But we only took out one of those Shahab-5s—they've got possibly a half-dozen more ready to fly. And we know they still have as many as three or four nuclear warheads, plus any number of chemical, biological, or high-explosive warheads deliverable by the Shahab-5s."

"This one was a warning," the President said with a smile. "We'll keep an eye on the others and take them out if we need to."

"Faster than you can imagine, sir."

"Outstanding." His voice turned serious, and the "photographer's dream" devil's locks slowly appeared as he went on: "I should have guessed you were going to fly the thing, but I sure as hell didn't know you were going to go into orbit. That was unwise and unauthorized. What made you think you could do that without permission, Patrick? You work for me. I make the calls."

"Sir, you know me," Patrick said. "As long as I've been in uniform I have flown the first operational test flight of every manned aerospace vehicle coming out of the 'Lake' for the past twelve years. This one was no different just because we went into space."

"Next time, mister, you tell me when you plan on flying anything, and I don't care how high or how fast it goes," the President hissed angrily into Patrick's ear. "This is no longer about you and how you do things. You are special adviser to the president of the United States, in uniform or out, on the ground or in orbit. I don't like surprises. Am I making myself fucking clear to you, General?"

Patrick was a little taken aback by the President's admonition—he looked carefully for even the faintest glint of humor or forgiveness and, finding none, was ashamed for even looking. "Yes, sir."

"Good." He stepped back, smiled, shook Patrick's hand warmly and firmly, and, so everyone could hear, said, "Job well done, General. Job well done."

"Thank you, sir." When the President looked at Boomer, Patrick continued, "Sir, may I present my mission commander and designer of the rocket engines on the Black Stallion spaceplane, Captain Hunter Noble, U.S. Air Force, call-sign 'Boomer.' "

"Captain Noble, a pleasure to meet a real rocket scientist," the President said. Boomer was about half a head taller than the President, but he didn't notice that because suddenly he found it very difficult to speak or even think: he was shaking hands with the President of the United States! Now the full force of where he was hit him, and it came much more suddenly than he ever believed possible. He felt Patrick steering him to his right and someone said something about getting his picture taken by the official White House photographer, but he felt as sluggish, as if he was standing in quicksand. "'Boomer,' huh?" the President asked as the photographer worked. "Where did that call-sign come from—making sonic booms all the time?"

Patrick waited a few breaths to see if Hunter would answer; when he found he was still too starstruck to do so, he chimed in, "It does now, sir. But when Captain Noble started at Dreamland, most of his designs went 'boom' on the test stands with frightening regularity. Fortunately for us, he perfected his designs, and now he's created the fastest, most efficient, and most reliable manned spacecraft in existence."

"Excellent. That's what we're here to talk about. Take seats." Patrick steered Boomer to the proffered chairs. The President was pointing to the others in the Oval Office as Patrick led him to his seat. "Boomer, I know you've met the Vice President; let me introduce Dr. Carson, secretary of state; Mr. Gardner, secretary of defense; General Glenbrook, chairman of the Joint Chiefs of Staff; and General Sparks, my national security adviser." Both remained standing as they were introduced to the others in the room and shook hands, then took seats after the President took his seat at the head of the meeting area. "First off, General McLanahan, I want to know about the flight."

"I'll let my mission commander describe it for you, sir, if I could."

" 'Mission commander?' " General Sparks commented. "Isn't that the new Air Force term for 'copilot?' "

"Yes, sir," Patrick said. "I flew the spacecraft this morning."

"You?"

"I may not wear pilot's wings, sir, but I fly every aircraft that goes through the 'Lake,' " Patrick said.

"Is that so?"

"Yes, it is," Patrick said, meeting Sparks's questioning glare with a confident one of his own, then turned to Boomer. "Captain? Tell us about the flight." They could all see Boomer's face turn several shades of red and his mouth open. Patrick decided he was going to give him just one more chance: "Boomer, fill us in."

"Uh . . . it was . . . well, it was pretty routine, actually . . ."

" 'Routine?' " Vice President Hershel remarked, trying to help the young Air Force officer out of his funk. "Boomer, less than three hours ago you were standing on a dry lake bed in southern Nevada—now, you're sitting in the Oval Office. In between you orbited the Earth! What's routine about that?"

"Wait a minute, wait a minute—you say you went into orbit?" Sparks interjected, his eyes wide in surprise. "I didn't know about this! Why wasn't I briefed?"

"I knew the XR-A9 had the capability, sir," Patrick said. "I decided to try it out."

"You flew that experimental and still-classified spaceplane into orbit without permission, General?" Sparks thundered. "You 'decided' on your own to do it? You're not even a pilot! Do you think that it is your own personal property, your own private conveyance? If so, you are sadly mistaken."

"It's okay, Jonas—this time," the President said. "I didn't authorize General McLanahan to go into orbit either, but I didn't prohibit it either. What I asked for was a demonstration of the spaceplane's capabilities, and I believe I got one."

"I see," Sparks said. "Thank you for the clarification, sir." He turned to Patrick and added, "I've heard this about you for many years, General—now I see why."

"What would that be, sir?" Patrick asked.

"Your proclivity to authorize yourself to take action; your willingness to take unnecessary and in many cases dangerous risks; your horse-blinder view of the world. Do you need me to go further, General?"

"I didn't know you took such an interest in my career, sir," Patrick said wryly. "I'm flattered." Sparks gave him a look like a snake that was busy digesting a mouse, but said nothing.

"It's still pretty incredible," General Glenbrook commented, suppressing a grin at the quiet interchange taking place before them. "Climb into a jet, take off, and shoot yourself into orbit minutes later? Impressive."

"I'll say," Maureen added. "And can it be done again?"

"Yes, ma'am," Boomer said, finally relaxing a bit. "We're parked over at Patuxent River now—we can gas up, do a flight plan, and be in space in about an hour."

"No launch pad, no space suits, no massive boosters—none of that stuff?" the national security adviser asked, his voice skeptical.

That was just the right level of technical questioning and curious disbelief Boomer needed to ignite his brain. "That stuff is unnecessary and outdated technology," he said. "We had to change our way of thinking about space flight first, and then we built the equipment to do the job."

"What do you mean, Captain?"

"Government and military space was always predicated on lifting large payloads—big multi-function satellites mostly—into high orbits," Boomer said. "Those payloads are very versatile and can stay in service for years, even decades, but are expensive, difficult, and take time to put into orbit. With the invention of small single-purpose satellites designed to be used for short periods of time—weeks or a month or two at the most—we don't need a big expensive launch system to get them up. Black Stallion is designed to place small payloads into low Earth orbit quickly and efficiently."

"Can't we already do that, Captain?" Sparks asked, emphasizing the word "captain" to give Noble one more chance to remember who he was talking to.

"Yes, we can," Boomer replied. "But Black Stallion can do it faster, better, and cheaper, and it's more versatile."

"How so?"

"The Stud—er, the Black Stallion—can not only insert payloads into orbit, but can also fly passengers anywhere on the planet in just a few hours," Boomer said. "None of the other quick-launch systems, like Pegasus or Taurus, can fly passengers. Our other advantage is sustainability and quick-reaction capability:

we can launch payloads into orbit once per day in normal use or twice per day in dedicated surge mode, where other so-called 'quick launch vehicles' could take weeks or months to prepare."

"But how do you get that kind of power and thrust?" General Glenbrook asked. "The Space Shuttle orbiter needs two immense solid rocket boosters and a huge fuel tank to reach orbit, and then it has to glide back for a landing."

"Because the empty weight of the orbiter is about three times heavier than the Black Stallion, sir," Boomer replied. "It carries ten times the payload and four times as many crewmembers. The Stud is designed to get into orbit quickly from almost any military base in the world and carry small payloads. The Stud can't replace expendable launch vehicles and the Shuttle, but it can do things that the others can't."

"The other difference is the 'leopards' engines Captain Noble developed, sir," Patrick added. "The engines are very high-tech and at the same time remarkably simple, using upgraded designs first drawn up almost fifty years ago. The engines are hybrid jet-rocket engines that burn jet fuel and a hydrogen peroxide compound oxidizer . . ."

"Hydrogen peroxide? You mean, the stuff you use to clean wounds with?"

"The same, only highly purified and combined with compounds such as boron to increase the specific impulse," Boomer explained. "But we can do it with regular hydrogen peroxide also. Outside of the atmosphere, the fuel and oxidizer are burned in a combustion chamber that uses laser pulses for ignition and to superheat the gases, which also increases thrust. In the atmosphere, the engines switch back to regular turbofan engines and it flies like a conventional jet fighter."

"What's wrong with what we have now, Captain?" Sparks asked. "We have the most reliable launch systems and satellites in the world. Our satellites are designed to stay in space three times longer than the Russians', and they often stay up three times longer than planned."

"All that's okay—for the older generation," Boomer said. Sparks ruffled again but tried not to let it show. "Today and for the near future, that system is slow, inefficient, costly, and not flexible enough for current-day missions." Patrick tried not to grimace as he listened to the test pilot not only interrupt a superior officer and throw a challenging remark at the national security adviser, but forget to call him "sir" when addressing him. "We should scrap it and build a brand-new system."

"Your system, I assume, eh, Captain?" Sparks asked. "We replace satellites that stay in orbit for ten years for satellites that stay in orbit for ten weeks, max? Scrap a shuttle program that can carry sixty thousand pounds into orbit and back again for a system that can carry six thousand?"

"We build a system that can do the jobs the military needs done today, not forty years ago." Still no "sir," Patrick noticed, and Sparks was getting pissed.

"You've been in the Air Force for how long, Captain? Six years?"

"Five."

"Five years. And you think you have all the answers, Captain?" Boomer finally, finally realized who he was talking to, and he wisely just shook his head. "Well, Captain?"

"N-no. Sir," Boomer stammered.

"I don't think so either, Captain Noble," Sparks said, "but thank you for your input anyway. I'm sure we'll give it all due regard."

"You made your point, General Sparks," Joint Chiefs of Staff chairman William Glenbrook said, not raising his eyes to directly challenge Sparks, but not backing down either. To Boomer, he asked, "What's your max payload, Captain?"

"Depends on the orbit, sir," Boomer replied. "I believe we can shoot five hundred pounds to the moon." That got a lot of folks' attention in the Oval Office.

"We can put a four-thousand-pound bunker-buster bomb down on a bad guy's head anywhere on the planet in about ninety minutes."

"A more typical attack payload, sir," Patrick interjected, "would be a spread of three precision-guided supersonic attack missiles, or sixteen two-hundred-and-fifty-pound small-diameter precision-guided bombs. Launched from over the U.S., the bombs could hit sixteen individual targets anywhere on the planet within hours. But Captain Noble is correct: with a small payload and a booster section similar to the Air Force's Payload Assist Module, we can push a small satellite out beyond Earth orbit into space. A moon shot is certainly not out of the question."

"The stealth bomber can attack over sixty targets with the SDB, General," Sparks pointed out.

"Yes, sir, but the stealth bomber needs time and tanker support to fly to the target area," Patrick said. "If both planes were loaded and sitting alert and were ordered to launch and attack a target three thousand miles away—say, Diego Garcia to Tehran, Iran—a stealth bomber would take six hours and a minimum of two refuelings to do the job; a B-1 bomber could do it in five hours. The Black Stallion can do it in less than two hours, and do it with approximately the same cost. By the time the bombers arrive over the target area, the Black Stallion can land, reload, refuel, and fire another salvo."

"That's still a lot fewer targets attacked in the same amount of time."

"Yes, sir, but the Black Stallion did the job without putting any personnel or hardware over enemy territory, and without the need for any overseas bases," Patrick pointed out. "Plus the Black Stallion has the advantage of speed and reaction time: if satellite imagery, human intelligence, or unmanned reconnaissance picks up an enemy presence, we can respond quickly."

"And the bad guys won't see us coming," Boomer added.

"The whole *world* saw you coming today, Captain," Secretary of State Mary Carson said perturbedly. Carson was in her early fifties, tall, slender, and very serious-looking, with a clipped pattern of speech that made it sound as if she was snapping at anyone she spoke to. "The Russians inquired about our unannounced launch activities minutes after you fired the rockets to boost yourself into space, suggesting that some believed it was an intercontinental missile attack; and they inquired about the payload shortly after you released it. Several of our European allies also queried us about the flight. It was no secret to anyone."

"Then another part of our mission was a success," Patrick said.

"What part is that, General—spooking half the world?" Carson asked. "Demonstrating our intent to conduct our own 'bolt-from-the-blue' aerial bombardment attacks, like Russia did? Is that the message you're trying to send here?"

"Madame Secretary, we have no conventional strategic long-range strike forces except for a handful of bombers," Patrick explained. "Our ability to project power abroad is limited to the ten existing carrier battle groups and deployed tactical air power. Even if every group is put to sea and every Air Force and Marine fighter wing is deployed to forward operating bases, it still leaves most of the planet unreachable by American military air power simply because smaller aircraft have less range and need more support to operate far from home or friendly bases. If we show the world that we can successfully launch a viable quick-reaction single-stage-to-orbit aircraft, the world will be caught off-guard, and our enemies will be scrambling to catch up. That gives us much-needed breathing space to decide which direction we want to proceed."

"I don't like playing those kinds of games, General," Carson said. "This gives the State Department nothing to work with. It's brinksmanship." She turned to the

Secretary of Defense, Joseph Gardner. "Do we even need long-range bombers any more, Joe? Everyone keeps on saying that the bombers are outdated—why spend billions on outdated technology?"

"General McLanahan has stated the situation accurately, Mary," Gardner replied. "We need a long-range quick-reaction non-nuclear strike force to fill the gap between tactical ship- and land-based air forces and nuclear missiles, able to respond to a severe crisis anywhere in the world in a very short period of time with sustained and devastating firepower. With the Russians still a threat and China growing stronger every year, that mission hasn't changed." He turned to Patrick and added, "But frankly we're very disappointed in General McLanahan's recommendations. With the kind of money we're talking about, we can triple the size of the previous B-2 stealth bomber fleet, procure all of the latest state-of-the-art precision-guided weapons we'd need for the next ten years, and still have money left over for other needs."

"The 'Barbeau Formula,'" Vice President Hershel interjected.

"It's a good plan, Miss Vice President," Gardner said. "Two wings with twenty B-2 stealth bombers each, fitted with the latest technology and armed with the latest standoff precision-guided munitions.

They are still unmatched for performance and striking capability over any heavily defended target complex on Earth. The Navy takes care of maritime, littoral, medium-range strike missions, nuclear strike, and space; the Air Force takes care of tankers, transports, long-range conventional strike, and air superiority." Again, he turned sullenly to Patrick and added, "With General McLanahan's background, the Pentagon assumed he'd agree with this strategy. I'm somewhat perplexed by his current stance."

"Sir, I don't have a 'stance' here," Patrick said. "My directive was to evaluate several different proposals to replace the strategic conventional strike forces destroyed by the Russians. That's what I'm doing."

"But you came to this meeting riding in one of those 'proposals,' General," Joint Chiefs of Staff chairman Glenbrook pointed out with a wry smile. "You didn't come here on a B-2 stealth bomber. That sounds like an endorsement to me."

"It was an opportunity I couldn't pass up, sir, that's all," Patrick said. "Besides, I've already got plenty of hours in the B-2."

Glenbrook's conciliatory nod was almost a bow—he was very familiar with Patrick McLanahan's record, including his combat record. McLanahan had not just helped design and test aerospace weapon systems, but he was often chosen—or volunteered—to take his ultra high-tech war machines into battle. Many conflicts around the world over the past eighteen years had been prevented from escalating into a major war because of McLanahan's skill, bravery, and outright audacity. He had a very long list of awards and decorations, most of which he was not allowed to wear on his uniform or ever have revealed to anyone until after his death: some would never be revealed for a generation.

"I think it was a dangerous and foolish stunt, General," National Security Adviser Sparks said hotly. "You exposed yourself to unnecessary danger just for a thrill ride."

"Sir, men and women from the 'Lake' expose themselves to the same dangers every day," Patrick said. "I wouldn't characterize it as 'unnecessary.' "

"It is if a middle-aged White House staffer does it," Sparks said.

"May I suggest we get back to the subject at hand, gents?" Maureen Hershel interjected. She had to stifle a smile at Patrick's expense at the "middle-aged White House staffer" comment. "Congress is bugging the White House for a recommendation the President will support for the new long-range strike force. If we don't recommend something soon, we'll risk losing part of the appropriation."

"I take it," the President said, "that we have no consensus here on which direction we should proceed?" His comment was met by uncomfortable silence, so he rose, poured himself another cup of coffee, and sat down. "All right, let's talk about the Black Stallion track once again." After he had settled into his chair at the head of the informal meeting area, he asked, "So, Patrick, tell me what it was like to go into space."

"In a word, sir—incredible," Patrick replied with a smile. "I still can't believe what we did this morning: one orbit around the Earth and landing at an air base all the way across the country in about two hours."

"And we can fuel up the Stud and do it again, right now," Boomer added excitedly. "Patuxent River or Andrews Air Force Base both has everything we need to blast off again."

"Could I fly in it?" the President asked. Boomer chuckled. "What's so funny, Captain? Don't think I can handle it?"

"No . . . no, sir, it's not that," Boomer said, the smile disappearing from his face as he realized he might have unwittingly offended the President of the United States of America. "General McLanahan said you'd want to fly in it."

"He's right—he knows me too well," the President said. "The general and I go way back—I knew him when he was a young, cocky, know-it-all captain like yourself. So what sort of training would I need to fly your spaceplane, Captain?"

"Training? No training, sir," Boomer responded. "You look like you're in good shape—I think you'd do fine. Let's go. We'll gas up the Stud, hop in, and in three hours we'll be on the beach in Australia."

"Fly right now? No one can get ready to fly into space that fast!" Sparks said perturbedly. "NASA astronauts train for years to get to fly into space!"

"That's NASA's way of doing things, sir," Boomer said. "In the Stud, passengers are just passengers. We're not interested in turning anyone into Buzz Aldrin or Captain James T. Kirk of the Starship *Enterprise*—we just want to make sure you don't flip the wrong switch at the wrong time. Let's go."

"The crewmembers spend considerably more time training, sir," Patrick quickly pointed out, "but Captain Noble is perfectly correct: we don't require anything from passengers except to be in good health—if you suffered some sort of injury or difficulty you'd have to hang on without any possibility of assistance for an hour or two, possibly longer, since the front-seat crewmember can't get to you." It was obvious that President Martindale's head was churning—he wore a mischievous grin, as if running through his datebook and trying to figure out if he could spare the time. Patrick was sure he was going to agree. "Sir?" he asked. "Would you like to go for it?"

"Don't be ridiculous, General," Sparks said. "The President is certainly not going to . . ."

"Carl, call Bethesda," the President said to his chief of staff. "Ask the doc to come see me."

"Mr. President!" Vice President Hershel exclaimed. "Are you really going to do it?"

"Why the hell not?" Martindale asked. "I was given a clean bill of health from the doc just a couple months ago, and that was the straight story, not just a blurb for the media. I've piloted a B-1 Lancer and a B-2 stealth bomber, landed a Hornet onto an aircraft carrier, drove a tank, and been in a submarine down to twelve hundred feet—all while I've been president or vice president. And no offense, McLanahan, but if you can do it, I can do it."

"No doubt, sir. No offense taken."

"We have meetings all day, Mr. President, and then we have the reception for the Turkish prime minister tonight, and that is a function we can't postpone," the President's chief of staff Carl Minden said. "If you're really thinking about doing this, let me discuss it confidentially with the White House counsel, the Cabinet, and the Leadership. They all have a stake in what happens if you didn't come back."

"He'll come back—faster than you can imagine," Boomer interjected.

"Riding in the spaceplane would be seen as an endorsement of the program," Sparks said, "and I don't think that's what you want just yet."

"All right, all right, I get the message," the President said. "Carl, I still want to meet with the doc as soon as the schedule permits. And go ahead and put out the feelers to the usual players about this. And I want serious comments, not horrified reactions."

"Yes, Mr. President." Minden shook his head, already dreading the calls he had to make. "You realize, sir, that the press and the opposition will have a field day with this—they'll call it an election-year stunt, an abuse of privilege . . ."

"An old Navy destroyer captain once told me that every month he went down to the turrets and fired the big guns, took a patrol shift in his helicopters, took the helm of his ship, and even spent a couple hours in the ship's laundry and galleys," the President said. "Being the commander-in-chief means more to me than flying in Air Force One—it means getting out in the field and experiencing the life your soldiers live every day in uniform. I will do it, and I don't care what the opposition says."

"If they had the office and the guts, they'd do it too," Boomer chimed in.

Both Sparks and Minden gave Boomer warning glares, silently ordering him not to speak unless spoken to, but the President nodded. "Well said, Captain," he said. "Someone's got to be the first sitting president to fly in space or orbit the earth—I'm determined that I'm going to be the one. But Mr. Minden is right: business before pleasure, I guess." He turned to Patrick. "Let's hear it, Patrick. I nominated you four years ago to draw the new long-range strike blueprint to replace the aircraft and missiles destroyed by Gryzlov. What do you recommend I do about the bomber force?"

"Sir, I feel the decision isn't just about the long-range bomber force but the entire future of the air force—even the future of the U.S. military," Patrick said. "I strongly believe we're on the threshold of changing the entire force in preparation for the future, and we shouldn't shy away from it."

"And what future might that be, General?" Sparks asked skeptically.

"Space," Patrick replied simply. "The technologies demonstrated in weapon systems like the XR-9A Black Stallion spaceplane are clear indicators that the future of the U.S. Air Force and possibly the entire U.S. military rests in space. The Black Stallion today demonstrated the ability to carry out and improve upon two core centers of gravity of the Air Force and indeed of the entire U.S. military: rapid airlift and rapid long-range strike."

"You were late to the meeting today, Patrick," Maureen pointed out with a smile.

"It took longer for our helicopter to fly the sixty miles from Patuxent River to Andrews than it did to fly the Black Stallion from Nevada to Maryland, Miss Vice President," Patrick replied with a smile of his own. "Instead of boosting up to three hundred thousand feet to launch the Meteor payload, we could have flown a straight-line trajectory and shaved sixty minutes off the flight time."

"Or instead of a Meteor orbital payload," Noble interjected, "we've developed a pressurized cabin module with seats and luggage space. We can fly eight passengers from Washington to Tokyo in less than an hour and a half, and they don't need to wear space suits."

"Damn," the President muttered. "Now I know I want to ride in that thing."

"Mr. President, I believe orbital and suborbital travel will soon become as commonplace as transcontinental commercial airline travel is now," Patrick said. "In less than five years I believe we can stand up a wing of twenty spaceplanes and dedicated refueling tankers, plus the necessary hardware to allow us to deliver a wide variety of ordnance, satellites, and even people anywhere around the globe within hours. The array of payloads we can lift right now is small, but within those five years I believe the range of payloads will jump exponentially as manufacturers start building more microsatellites compatible with the Black Stallion."

"Based at Battle Mountain or Elliott air bases, I assume," Secretary of Defense Gardner interjected.

"The beauty of the Black Stallion launch system is that we can launch from almost any runway, sir—if it can handle a big fighter jet like the F-15 Eagle or F/A-22 Raptor, it can launch a Stud," Boomer said. "Vandenberg and Cape Canaveral are good for large rocket launches not only because it's more efficient to launch polar and equatorial flights from those bases, but the various stages fall safely into open ocean. We don't drop anything. If the folks down below don't mind a distant sonic boom, a Stud can go into orbit from anywhere."

"That nickname is starting to get on my nerves," Sparks commented under his breath.

"General Glenbrook, would the spaceplanes fill the requirements we've established for long-range strike?" Vice President Hershel asked.

The Joint Chiefs chairman nodded noncommittally. "It certainly is an impressive system," he said. "As the

Pentagon sees it, the Black Stallion is in the same class as a fighter or light bomber but with almost twenty times the speed and range of present aircraft. Its performance envelope gives it capabilities that very few bombers have—namely, the ability to put small payloads—or itself—into Earth orbit in a very short period of time. It has the huge advantage of hypersonic speed, suborbital flight, and payload delivery throughout its flight envelope."

"What are the negatives?"

"Well, we can always use more payload—six thousand pounds max is very small for today's weapons," Glenbrook said, "although with advances in weapon and satellite technology, soon we should be able to do the same mission with smaller payloads. The biggest negatives are that we have no idea what sort of tactics and procedures we'd need to match the system with the mission. Normally we never change the mission to adapt to the weapon system; we don't field a weapon, then change procedures and tactical doctrine to match the weapon. It looks like we're being forced to do exactly that. With the stealth bombers and sea-based systems, we have well-developed doctrine in place suitable for a large array of contingencies."

"Doesn't sound like a ringing endorsement, General."

"It's not, sir," Glenbrook admitted, "but only because I don't know that much about it. Quite frankly, I think it's too advanced. But after reading the reports from General McLanahan, Captain Noble, and their team for the past year during advanced development, I think the system is worth serious consideration. But I'm not yet ready to endorse it, or fly in it . . . and I don't think you should either, sir. We test aircraft and weapon systems every day—the President of the United States has no business riding in any of them before they're made fully operational."

"Hear, hear," Sparks said under his breath.

"I get the message, General," the President said a bit perturbedly. The outer office secretary entered and handed the President a note. His face adopted a half-excited, half-amused expression. "Well, well, it seems this meeting has been leaked to Congress already," he said. "Senator Barbeau is here and wishes to speak with me"—he turned to Patrick and added—"and General McLanahan."

Maureen Hershel couldn't help noticing General Glenbrook, Chief of Staff Minden, and Secretary Gardner straightening up in their seats and adjusting ties, and even the President wore a rather goofy schoolboy-in-love expression. But National Security Adviser Sparks was anything but anticipatory: "Damn the information leaks in this town," he muttered. "If I ever catch who it is, I'll roast his balls on my radiator."

"Mr. President, do you want to do a meeting like this?" Minden asked. "She doesn't have an appointment, and it's improper etiquette for a member of Congress to just show up at the White House unannounced—the Senate would squawk if you just showed up on Capitol Hill like this, without notifying the leadership. Besides, if you allow one to do it, they'll all want the privilege."

"I'm not one to stand on formality, Carl," the President said. "Miss Parks, ask the senator to come in." The outer office secretary had barely left the room before a red-haired whirlwind whizzed past her, and the men in the room were scrambling like startled chickens to get to their feet.

Boomer had seen Stacy Anne Barbeau on TV, of course, but she looked even more striking in person. He noted she was not the tallest woman he had ever met, nor the thinnest or most curvaceous. But whatever it was, Stacy Anne Barbeau had it. He couldn't tell if it was the round green eyes, the flowing curly red hair, the lush red lips, the killer body, or the attitude of supreme confidence and control she exuded—perhaps all of the above—but she made an entrance all right, like a famous actress exiting her limo and walking down the red carpet in front of thousands of adoring fans. She created a presence, a force that drove almost everyone before her—mostly the men, even the very powerful ones in this very powerful office—to their hormonal knees.

"Mr. President, how good of you to see me," Barbeau said in a rather loud but at the same time sweet Southern voice—sweet like indulgent champagne, not sugar, was the thought that entered Boomer's head. She strode quickly over to him. "You are looking mighty fine, Mr. President, the best I've ever seen you. You wear the mantle well, I must say."

"Senator Barbeau, this is an unexpected surprise," the President said. He was a head taller than she and eight years older, and Boomer had to admit they made a fine-looking couple—or maybe he had already heard that in any number of celebrity gossip magazines that continuously postulated on the bachelor President's love life. Boomer noticed the sudden presence of the President's famous "photographer's dream," the two locks of thick curly silver hair that automatically tumbled over his forehead, one above each eye, whenever the President became agitated—obviously they also appeared when he was aroused too. "Welcome back to the White House. Let me introduce you to some folks you probably haven't met."

She interlocked her left arm with the President's right, snuggling the side of her left breast seductively to him, then turned toward the others in the office and flashed her most brilliant smile, nodding collectively to the others as she greeted them. She gave Boomer a quick appraisal from head to toe, then a hungry look, a mischievous smile, and an appreciative nod after apparently liking very much what she saw. The President stepped over to Patrick. "Senator, allow me to introduce . . ."

"Lieutenant-General Patrick Shane McLanahan needs no introduction, Mr. President, none what-so-ev-er," Barbeau interrupted. She unwrapped herself from the President's right arm, went over to Patrick, and extended her hand. "An honor to meet you, General," she cooed, locking her green eyes on his. She reached out with her left hand, placed it on the back of his neck, drew him closer, and kissed him lightly on both cheeks. "A true American hero. It is a pleasure to meet you, sir. A real pleasure."

It felt as if all the air had been sucked out of the room as the other men looked on, wishing they were getting some of that preferential treatment from the Southern belle—and what little air was left was being ignited by Maureen Hershel's fiery stare at Barbeau. She quashed it right away and impatiently checked her watch.

"Nice to meet you, Senator," Patrick said finally.

"Thank you, General," she said, her voice still low and . . . husky, Boomer thought. Barbeau ran her left hand down Patrick's shoulder, and her eyes widened a bit as she gently ran her fingers over his shoulders and arms. "You're pretty tense, General." She paused, then looked at him with that mischievous smile and added, "Or is that all you?"

"I'm afraid it's all me, ma'am."

"Well, you must get out of the weight room more often and visit me on Capitol Hill, General," she cooed. She glanced over at Hershel, noticed her impatient expression, hid a smile, and added, "And maybe take a bath before you do, if I may be so bold, Patrick—may I call you Patrick?" She didn't wait for a response. She turned and shook hands with Boomer. "Captain Noble, a pleasure." She slid closer to him, placed her cheek against his, then gave him a kiss on the cheek as well. "Mmm, nice," she whispered to him.

"That goes double from where I'm standing, Senator," Boomer whispered back.

Barbeau stepped back, affixing Noble with a mind-blowing smile and a wink, then turned to the others in the Oval Office. "Good Lord, Mr. President, these men smell as if you have sentenced them to hard labor," she said gaily, waving a hand under her nose and batting her eyes in her best Scarlett O'Hara imitation. "Do you normally allow airmen to come into the White House in flight suits, smelling like they just walked in from a thirty-six-hour mission?"

"Now you leave those boys alone and stop making fun of them, Senator—recruiting is bad enough these days without a senior senator chasing the good ones away," the President said. Was it her imagination, Maureen asked herself, or was the President adopting a Southern accent all of a sudden? "Sit down, and tell me what I can do for you."

"With your permission, sir, we'll return to duty," Patrick said.

Chief of Staff Carl Minden nodded and started to herd the two toward the door, but Barbeau said anxiously, "No, General, Captain, please stay. Mr. President?"

"You're the one who said they stink, Stacy," the President quipped.

"Looks like a serious political discussion gearing up here," Boomer said. "Way above my pay grade, I'm sure."

Barbeau flashed her bright green eyes at Boomer and gave him a smile that could have been either amused or devilishly angry. "You are a deliciously plain-spoken young man, Boomer. Mr. President, I'm madly in love with both of them. You must order them to stay."

"We've got a full schedule this morning, Senator," the President warned, then nodded for Patrick and Boomer to remain. The chief of staff's mouth hardened in exasperation, but said nothing.

"I am so sorry to impose myself on you, Mr. President," Barbeau said as she took a seat at the end of the sofa opposite Maureen—that way she could keep an eye on everyone in the room while she spoke to the President, and she could also see whoever came into the Oval Office and even see anyone in the corridor outside when the door was opened. "But as you know, my committee will begin hearings on the new defense appropriation bill in a couple weeks, and I wanted to personally ask if there was anything at all I could do for you or Secretary Gardner to assist you in preparing your proposals for my committee?"

"Secretary Gardner sent the committee a letter stating our timetable for making our recommendations, Senator," Chief of Staff Carl Minden said. "We won't be late, I assure you." Boomer noticed that the chief of staff stayed on his feet during this meeting, standing opposite the President instead of on his left side as he had always seen him in photographs, almost outside the informal meeting area. It appeared as if Minden had situated himself so Barbeau would have to turn her head all the way to her right to speak to him. Do they sit around all day thinking of ways to gain every bit of advantage over a political adversary, even in the Oval Office? Boomer wondered.

"Your entire staff is the hardest-working and most dedicated in recent memory, Mr. Minden—ruthlessly so," Barbeau said in a slightly flatter tone, only briefly glancing at him before returning her eyes to the President. "We did indeed receive the letter from the Pentagon, and thank you for the courtesy of keeping the committee informed. Mine is an informal and completely off-the-record courtesy call of my own, Mr. President—I'm not here at the request of the chairman or the committee."

"I appreciate that, Senator," the President said, "and I appreciate your time and attention, but we have everything well under control, and we'll be ready for both the closed- and open-door hearings, as scheduled."

"I had absolutely no doubt of that, Mr. President," Barbeau said. She looked at Patrick and Boomer, who were sitting farthest away from her. "The committee will be very anxious to hear from General McLanahan as well, and I in particular will look forward to his testimony with much anticipation."

"The general's not scheduled to testify, Senator," Defense Secretary Gardner said.

"He's not?" Barbeau made a show of looking completely surprised, although as ranking member she had certainly seen the list of government witnesses scheduled to appear before the committee and would have had to approve each one. "May I ask why, Mr. President? Patrick McLanahan is the nation's acknowledged expert on long-range aerial attack. He's been in charge of your fact-finding mission to replace the assets lost after the American Holocaust . . ."

"Senator, as I'm sure you well know, General McLanahan is an active-duty Air Force officer who has been temporarily assigned to the White House as a military adviser," the President said. "He receives no compensation from the White House and has no budget. He serves at my pleasure but his service here is dependent on the needs of the Air Force. While here he reports directly to me, and to the best of my knowledge his activities haven't been announced publicly."

"This is all very mysterious, Mr. President," Barbeau said, her smile returning. "I'm sure I don't recall where I heard of what Patrick's responsibilities might be, but my sources are mostly well-placed and accurate. I didn't mean to presume." The President nodded but said nothing. "Patrick's thoughts and opinions would be of enormous value to the committee, I'm sure. Could you please add him on the witness list,

Mr. President? One day would be more than enough time, with minimal written follow-ups."

"I respect the needs and wishes of the committee, Senator, and I appreciate your consideration, but in my opinion it's not General McLanahan's decision—it's the National Command Authority's," the President said. "As you rightly pointed out, General McLanahan's the expert, but he's not the decision-maker. It's his job to answer my Cabinet's questions."

"We have hundreds of experts, agencies, analysts, and consultants advising the White House and Pentagon on this very important matter, Senator," Minden said. "We can recommend a number of them to appear before your committee . . ."

"Thank you, Mr. Minden, but as the President acknowledged, General McLanahan is the expert in the field as well as a national hero," Barbeau said rather testily. "His testimony would add unlimited authority and weight to any argument you'd care to make to the committee, watched and listened to by millions around the world. If he didn't appear, everyone would want to know why. Do you intend on putting him on the Sunday morning talk show circuit instead?"

"Senator, our witness list is complete," Carl Minden said firmly. "It's always possible that we could add witnesses later, but at this stage we don't anticipate doing so. We know the debate will go on for quite some time—we don't need to waste ours or the committee's time with a parade of witnesses all saying the same thing."

"If there is such a thing as a 'parade of witnesses,' Mr. Minden, I would think General McLanahan would be leading that parade—in fact, he should be in the grand master's limo, being bombarded by confetti and ticker tape," Barbeau said. "Speaking of which, Mr. President, as you recall, I presented a proclamation on the Senate floor after the general returned from Russia, congratulating his courage and dedication and recommending he be given a hero's parade in his home town. The proclamation was unanimously approved. Yet the White House kept him hidden away. If anyone deserved to be honored, it was General McLanahan."

"As you recall, Senator, the nation wasn't celebrating anything in those days—especially anything having to do with the Russian attacks or the extreme losses the nation suffered," Vice President Hershel reminded her. "We were going to over a dozen funerals or memorial services a day for weeks; half the government was spread out in secret reconstitution facilities; the citizens were too busy building bomb shelters to be out throwing confetti . . ."

"I am well aware of that horrible time, Miss Vice President," Barbeau said in a clipped voice, only glancing at Maureen as she spoke. "But America is strong and we have proven once again that we can take a licking and still prevail with honor and pride. The incident may have been years ago, but Patrick still deserves the honor."

"We'll consider it, Senator," the President offered.

"Then may I suggest, Mr. President, that one way to honor Patrick's service and patriotism is to allow the American people to hear what he has to say regarding the future of America's ability to strike back at our enemies," Barbeau said, a bit more insistently this time. "You could pick no better point person for this very important campaign, Mr. President, I assure you."

"Thank you for your advice, Senator," the President said. "I'll consider it very carefully as well."

The outer office secretary came in, escorting someone else, who dropped a note into Barbeau's hand and scurried away. "I feel it would be an insult to General McLanahan to subpoena him to appear before the committee," she said, casually glancing at the note, "but I suppose that is always an option—unless you intend on exercising executive privilege."

"That is always an option," the President said. "But I'm sure we can come to some understanding to avoid any appearance of confrontation."

"That is always our desire, Mr. President," Barbeau said, giving the President another heart-melting smile. She then immediately turned to Patrick and said, "General, I know you've been out to Eighth Air Force headquarters many times, but just three or four times in the past six months. Are you getting all the information you need? I asked General Zoltrane to give you anything you require, any time, day or night." Eighth Air Force, based at Barksdale Air Force Base near Boissier City, Louisiana, was the command responsible for all of the surviving long-range B-52, B-1B, and B-2A bombers—and the northern Louisiana districts were her base of power too.

Patrick glanced quickly at the President, whose smile began to dim but nonetheless nodded his assent to respond. "I receive outstanding support from General Zoltrane and all of the units, Senator," Patrick replied.

"I had absolutely no doubt. But if there is anything at all you need, Patrick, please do not hesitate to call on me. At any time."

Patrick noticed everyone in the Oval Office sigh and squirm with pleasure at Barbeau's invitation, sad that it wasn't directed at them. "Thank you, Senator. I will."

"I was quite surprised to see you here this morning, General," Barbeau remarked. "If I recall correctly, my staff had tried to make an appointment to speak with you just yesterday afternoon, and was told you'd be available later this afternoon. Yet here you are in Washington. My, you do get around, I must say." Patrick said nothing but merely smiled and nodded. Barbeau's eyes flared a bit as she added, "Almost as if they shot you out here from Nevada on a rocket ship."

Patrick again glanced at the President and Vice President, who had both adopted stony expressions. Carl Minden stepped over to Patrick. "I hate to interrupt, Senator, but if we're going to get that report in to your committee on time, we'd better get back to work."

"Can I speak plainly, Mr. President?" Barbeau asked. "We are aware of the three major proposals being bandied about by the pundits for a long-range attack force: rebuilding the manned stealth bomber fleet, building a fleet of unmanned attack planes, and converting cargo planes to cruise missile launchers. But we have heard inklings of another proposal, using untested and very radical spacecraft technology." She stepped a bit closer to Martindale. "I want to work very closely with you on this, Mr. President, very closely."

To everyone's surprise, the President responded, "You're right, Stacy. We're developing a fourth option, one much more advanced than the others."

"The spaceplane, I do believe?"

"It's called Black Stallion," the President said. "It's a single-stage-to-orbit spacecraft that can take off and land from any conventional runway in the world but boost itself into low Earth orbit, fly coast-to-coast in minutes, or around the world in less than two hours."

"It sounds incredible, Mr. President!" Barbeau exclaimed. She looked at McLanahan and Noble and immediately understood how and why they were in Washington now. "I can't wait to hear more. When can my subcommittee get a briefing on this amazing aircraft?"

"We're still making the decision about whether or not to present it as an alternative to the others for the next long-range strike force," the President said.

"And I do believe you have the most qualified man working on it—Patrick McLanahan," Barbeau said. "Wonderful. Well, I hope it doesn't hold up the bill for too much longer, but I completely understand the need for careful deliberation—we're talking about a lot of money. The subcommittee staff would be happy to assist the general in writing his reports and gathering data, Mr. President."

"The Pentagon and the White House national security staff are on it, Senator."

"Yes, of course. But couldn't we convince you to let General McLanahan make a closed-door presentation to the subcommittee and give us a sweet little taste of this mysterious new technology."

"I promise you, Senator, that your committee will receive all of our proposals and supporting data as soon as it's available, at the appropriate time," the President said. "We are certainly not going to waste your time or keep you in the dark." He glanced quickly at Minden, an obvious signal to get McLanahan and Noble out now.

Minden didn't miss his cue—he stood behind them and tapped them on their shoulders. "General, we'll be looking forward to your report. Thank you for . . ."

"Mr. President, may I take General McLanahan and Captain Noble to lunch?" Senator Barbeau asked sweetly. "It would give us an opportunity to get acquainted."

"I'm afraid I have to excuse myself, Senator," Patrick said. As he rose to his feet, he was surprised to feel the room seem to move and spin a little, and he had to concentrate to stabilize himself. "I really do have a lot of work to do."

"Then we'll have lunch right here in the White House dining room—with your permission, of course, Mr. President?"

"I'm going to have to defer to the general's busy schedule, Senator. Have your staff give Carl a call and

I'm sure he'll have it set up right away for the earliest possible time."

"I want the spaceplane impounded and a full investigation started, including complete details on the mission it just flew, who authorized it, and who's paying for it," Senator Barbeau said to her aide, Colleen Morna, as they exited the West Wing of the White House. "And I want a full background check on Captain Hunter Noble."

"Noble? Who's he?"

"He could be the back-door source I need to break Dreamland and HAWC wide open," the senator said. "I thought I could get to McLanahan, but the guy is a clueless Boy Scout, and I can't waste the time on him. Find out everything about Noble—where he comes from, his family, his girlfriends or boyfriends, his schooling, what he drinks and smokes, who he fucks, how often, and how."

"What he smokes?"

"You can learn a lot about a man just by smelling him—and how he reacts when you do," Barbeau said. "McLanahan likes the occasional cigar, but Captain Noble likes cigarettes—and he's not afraid of making a pass at a woman, even a U.S. Senator standing in the Oval Office in front of the President and Vice President of the United States. That means he's a partier, a ladies' man, a player. If he's got a weakness, or ambition, I want to know about it."

"He made a pass at you?"

"His eyes had me undressed faster than I've had in months," Barbeau said with a pleasured smile. "He's no shrinking violet, that's for sure. McLanahan might be the goody-two-shoes, but Hunter Noble is more like the captain of the swim team—and I like jocks, a lot."

OFFICE OF THE CHIEF OF STAFF, ARMED FORCES OF THE ISLAMIC REPUBLIC, TEHRAN, ISLAMIC REPUBLIC OF IRAN

A Short Time Later

"This is more than a major blunder, Buzhazi—this is an embarrassment to the entire Iranian military and leadership," the commander in chief of the Iranian Armed Forces, General Hoseyn Yassini, thundered. Younger by eight years and shorter by several centimeters than the man standing at attention before him—and, the man noticed, much softer around the neck and middle since leaving the field for headquarters in Tehran—Yassini was obviously not accustomed to dressing anyone down, and it appeared that he had to put some effort into doing so now. He glared at the man standing at attention before him. "And I thought I ordered you to change your uniform before you came here."

The man standing at a brace in the center of the office was General Hesarak al-Kan Buzhazi, still wearing his field utility uniform stained with blood and dirt and smelling strongly of smoke, gunpowder, and a large dose of fear. "I thought since you did not see fit to go to Orumiyeh yourself," Buzhazi said, "that I should come directly to you and give you a little taste of what's happened out there."

"I don't need a lecture or a demonstration from anyone, Hesarak, even you," Yassini said. "If you look like a jihadi reject here in headquarters, you'll be treated like one." He picked up the casualty report, glanced at it, and shook it in Buzhazi's face. "Two hundred thirty-seven dead, five hundred and eight wounded, most critically, including the brigade commanding officer and three Majlis members." The Majlis was Iran's Parliament. "What do you have to say for yourself?"

"I say give me a single Shock Battalion and I will round up and present you with all of the terrorists—or their heads—within two weeks," Buzhazi said.

"The Shock Battalions no longer exist, Hesarak, and you know it," Yassini said. "They have been disbanded for years."

"I know that all regular army and marine special forces troops have been merged with the Pasdaran," Buzhazi said. "You have them spread out all over the damned planet, in every lousy backwater mud pit, assisting psychopathic nut-cases who don't know which end of a rifle is which."

"Watch your mouth, Buzhazi," Yassini said. "You may have been the former commander-in-chief, but I am commander of the armed forces now." He paused, then added, "The Pasdaran was created to protect, defend, and support the Islamic revolution throughout the world . . ."

"Don't give me that madrasa indoctrination crap, Hoseyn," Buzhazi said. "The Pasdaran was initially created as the faqih's private army to hunt down and assassinate any of the monarchy's and republic's sympathizers still left in the country after the revolution. When it was discovered that most of those sympathizers were in the military, the Pasdaran was transformed into a branch of the armed services so they could more effectively spy on fellow soldiers. When it was determined that the Shock Battalions were the greatest threat to the cleric's regime, they were absorbed into the Pasdaran. I was there, Hoseyn—I saw it with my own eyes."

Yassini could not argue with Buzhazi's assessment, although he was careful not to say or do anything that could even be construed as agreement—the walls had ears, and probably eyes as well. "The reason you were sent away to command the Basij, General, is because you have this habit of speaking before thinking," he said. "I strongly advise you to stop."

"You know as well as I why I was allowed to command the Basij instead of being executed, Hoseyn—the Supreme Defense Council was hoping some enterprising young radical Islamist would assassinate me so the mullahs could disavow any responsibility for disposing of me," Buzhazi said. "There were ten thousand such crazies willing to do it."

"You made sure any dissenters were eliminated."

"You're wrong, Hoseyn—I didn't have anything to do with the so-called 'purges' in the Basij," Buzhazi said. "What I did was simple: I showed the youth of Iran what real leadership was. I gave the really dedicated kids direction, and I isolated the rest. I turned that organization from nothing more than prowling gangs of murderers and extortionists into a real fighting force." He shrugged and added, "When the true soldiers realized how badly the radicals and Islamists were hurting their organization, they took action. No one had to order them to clean house. It's nothing more than natural selection and survival of the fittest."

"It was a purge, Hesarak—that's what everyone believes," Yassini said. "You may or may not have ordered it, but you certainly were the inspiration for the purges, and you did not punish the offenders as harshly as the Supreme Defense Council wished." It was Yassini's turn to shrug. "But, because of your record of service and your considerable political connections, you survived anyway . . ."

"I survived, Hoseyn, because even the deaf, dumb, and blind idiots on the Council saw that my forces did exceptionally good work," Buzhazi said. "While the Pasdaran and Air Force were busy scratching their crotches and fingering worry-beads, my national guard forces were capturing infiltrators and shooting down American spy drones."

"They were in the right place at the right time, nothing more," Yassini said—but he knew that, again, Buzhazi was right: the Basij, what Buzhazi wanted to call the Internal Defense Force, had done some remarkable work in the past few years. Their biggest achievement was setting up an ambush for an American Predator-A spy drone near a nuclear research facility. Buzhazi set the trap, computed when and how the little unmanned aircraft would approach the target area, and set his forces in place at precisely the right moment. It was only a Predator-A, the lowest-tech version of the unmanned remotely piloted spy plane, but the catch yielded lots of valuable data on the plane's capabilities and systems. Buzhazi's forces had shot down another Predator-A and uncovered dozens of remote data collection and relay devices in the deserts as well, shutting down a good portion of America's covert spy network in Iran.

Yassini's aide came in, bowed politely to Buzhazi, and handed Yassini a memo. Here it comes, Buzhazi said to himself—this whole conversation had been nothing more than a way for Yassini to stall until a decision had been made . . . "General, the Supreme Defense Council has ordered you to be placed under arrest until the conclusion of its investigation into the attack on Orumiyeh," Yassini said tonelessly.

"If you have me put in prison, Hoseyn, the investigation will get bogged down and nothing will ever happen except the obligatory rounding-up of the 'usual suspects,'" Buzhazi said. "Let me, or the members of my staff, lead a special forces team into Iraq and Turkey. It was Kurdish commandos, I know it. It won't take long to . . ."

"The investigation is already underway, General."

"Who is in charge?"

"I am."

"No, Hoseyn—I mean, really in charge." The commander-in-chief's face turned stony with anger. "Listen, General, you have some discretion here. Put me under house arrest—that way I can continue to receive reports and coordinate activities with . . ."

"That's not possible right now, Hesarak," Yassini said. He hit a button on his desk telephone, and his aide entered the office, followed by two security guards with AK-74 rifles at port-arms. "Someone has to pay for what's happened. There was a major breach of security protocols, and the Supreme Defense Council believes it was a lack of leadership and attention to detail."

"Sounds like they've already made up their minds," Buzhazi said. Yassini said nothing in reply. Buzhazi knew he had only one chance left. "Listen to me, Hoseyn," he said, stepping close to the commander-in-chief so he could lower his voice. "Don't play along with this. Imprisoning me is just a knee-jerk reaction to a much broader problem. Iran is concentrating too much on foreign affairs and neglecting internal and frontier security—you know this as well as I. They're masking their inept military policies by blaming it all on me."

"No. There will be an investigation. I will . . ."

"You know how these so-called 'investigations' turn out, Hoseyn—you've conducted just as many as I," Buzhazi said. "The report is dismissed and destroyed as soon as it reaches the Council. The Supreme Defense Council—check that, the mullahs on the Council—have already decided who's to blame. I'm the scape-goat, nothing more."

"I will conduct a thorough investigation," Yassini insisted, "and if it's shown that you did all you could to prevent the attack, you'll be exonerated and restored to duty with all privileges."

"Have you ever known an officer to be returned to full active duty status after landing in prison, Hoseyn?"

"Yes—you."

"I wasn't sent to prison, Hoseyn—I was stripped of my rank and privileges and sent to the hinterlands to be killed by young radical Islamists," Buzhazi corrected him. "Some of the mullahs thought I defended the republic adequately—all the others wanted to see me dead."

"I think you are becoming a bit paranoid, Hesarak," Yassini said. "I'll protect you the best I can, my friend, but sometimes I think you are your own worst enemy. Serve your detention in silence, accept responsibility, appoint one of the Council member's deputies to take your place, beg for forgiveness, and I believe you will be given a short time in a work camp and then a common discharge. You have served this nation well—they won't punish you severely unless they find true negligence or criminal misconduct."

"The deputies serving for the Council are nothing but brainless spoiled rotten sycophants . . ."

"Maybe you deserve to spend a little time in prison, General—a little hard labor might improve your attitude." He shook his head and wrote orders on the message he received from the Supreme Defense Council. "You are to be sent to a Bureau detention facility. I'll see to it that . . ."

"A Bureau facility?" Buzhazi retorted. This bit of news really scared him. The Edarehe Hefazat va Ettelaate Sepah, or Intelligence Bureau, was the Pasdaran military and internal intelligence agency, run by a Pasdaran two-star general. If the Pasdaran itself was fearsome, the Intelligence Bureau was a hundred times worse, because it was from their intensive espionage and monitoring activities that the Pasdaran derived its power. Even though the Pasdaran itself had been officially merged into the unified military command, the Intelligence Bureau still operated quite separately from the military. "I thought you said you were handling the investigation? Why don't you assign me to your staff investigation directorate? Why aren't they handling the investigation if you have been assigned the task?"

"The Pasdaran handles investigations involving possible security breaches inside military units . . ."

"No, the Pasdaran handles the 'wet work' for the mullahs," Buzhazi interjected. "You might as well just put a bullet in my brain now, Hoseyn. They'll come up with whatever verdict the mullahs want."

"Be sure not to say any of that at your deposition, General," Yassini said, nodding to the guards to take him away.

The Pasdaran headquarters, including their diretoates of operations and intelligence, was located at Doshan Tappeh Air Base on the eastern outskirts of Tehran; the heavily fortified installation was also the headquarters of Iran's air force, air logistics command, and several aircraft maintenance, repair, and modification centers. Buzhazi was taken inside the Pasdaran headquarters compound, a thirty-acre walled fortress on the northwestern side of the air base, and turned over to a very large, burly, bearded jailer who looked as if he lived in the subfloor jails. He was ushered into the central building, down two flights of stairs, and down a long corridor to the detention facility. He was taken past several dozen locked solid steel jail cells to an in-processing room, which had a fingerprint station, desk, computer, stainless-steel examination table, file cabinets—and, Buzhazi noted, sound-deadening tiles on the walls and ceiling.

"Strip, prisoner," the big jailer ordered after his handcuffs had been removed.

"As you were, Corporal," Buzhazi said. "You're speaking to a general officer."

"I said strip, prisoner," the jailer growled again.

"My name is General Hesarak al-Kan Buzhazi, commander in chief of the Iranian Internal Defense

Forces. You will address me as 'sir' or 'general.' " The jailer reached out to grab Buzhazi, but the general deflected the jailer's hands away. "You dare use physical force against a superior officer?" He was careful not to scream or curse at the jailer—he wanted to sound authoritative, not crazy or threatening. "Before I was chief of the general staff, I was commander of all Iranian Shock Troops." The jailer was surprised to hear that his prisoner was the former chief of staff. Buzhazi hoped that the corporal would equate the disbanded "Shock Troops" with "Pasdaran" and back off a bit—the Pasdaran had no respect whatsoever for the regular army. "We were taught how to immobilize the biggest man without weapons. I won't hurt you, but I will not allow you to abuse me like a common criminal."

"You will stop resisting and comply, prisoner." He reached for him again, eyes blazing in fury. Buzhazi let the jailer grasp him by his tunic, then easily broke the jailer's grip and shoved him away, digging the tip of his thumb into the man's sternum. Even though the jailer easily had thirty kilos on the general, Buzhazi knew exactly where the vulnerable pressure points on a man were.

Now the jailer was completely confused. Buzhazi saw him glance at the red alarm button on the wall, and he knew if he reached that button, Buzhazi would be restrained . . . or, more likely, shot for resisting. "Corporal," Buzhazi said quickly, in a bit more conciliatory voice, "I am not going to tell you again: I am a general in the Iranian military, and I have not been charged with a crime. You will address me as 'general' or 'sir,' and you will not attempt to touch me, is that clear? If you extend to me this ordinary sign of respect, I will comply with your instructions."

The jailer was obviously now concerned that he couldn't handle this thin, older man by himself; afraid that he would be dismissed from this post, perhaps even punished, for not doing his job. "You must obey my orders . . ."

"And so must you, Corporal," Buzhazi said. "What are your orders?" The jailer blinked and said nothing. "You were not given any orders, so you assumed I was to be treated like any other prisoner and processed in the usual manner, correct?" The jailer was obviously still mentally wrestling with this very nonstandard encounter. "What is your name, Corporal?"

"Tahmasbi . . ." Buzhazi let his eyes dig into the jailer's until he added, "Sir."

"Corporal Tahmasbi, as your superior officer," Buzhazi said in an even, trusting, measured voice, "I instruct you to secure me in a conference room, with access to a telephone and computer if available. Bring in some fresh juice for me from the mess. If there are any other flag grade officers in this facility that have not been charged with a crime, bring them in here as well." The jailer just stood there, dumbfounded. "Corporal? Do you understand these instructions?"

"Yes, sir, but . . ."

"But what? Do any of my orders violate your general orders or any other orders you have been issued since you have assumed this post?"

The jailer thought for a moment, and his eyes brightened. "No, sir, they do not."

"Then get your ass in gear, now," Buzhazi said. "If your sergeant major has any questions, have him come see me. Now take me to a conference room."

"Yes, sir." The jailer averted his eyes and opened the door to the processing room.

"Corporal Tahmasbi." The jailer stopped as if stuck in concrete. "You can't just let me walk out of here, can you? I'm supposed to be in your custody." The jailer meekly nodded and carefully, almost gingerly, took Buzhazi by the arm. "And, Corporal?"

"Sir?"

"Just because you work in the jails and generally only see the scum of our proud military does not mean you can go around with an unkempt beard, dirty uniform, and unpolished boots," Buzhazi said, looking the man directly in the eyes, not raising his voice at all but speaking firmly and authoritatively. "If you want to act like a soldier, look like a soldier. And get yourself into a gym and replace that fat with some muscle. I can teach you how to control a man with the lightest touch, but I need something to work with first. Get yourself into shape and I'll make a shock trooper out of you in no time."

Things went much easier from that moment on. Buzhazi allowed himself to be led by the upper left arm—it would look better to others if the jailer physically held him—through the hallway to a large briefing room where each shift was briefed before beginning their tour of duty. That was where they found a Pasdaran master sergeant at a desk, doing paperwork. As soon as Buzhazi saw the noncommissioned officer in the room, he loosened himself from the jailer's grasp and strode ahead of him. The master sergeant saw the general enter the room, shot to his feet, and stood at attention. "Room, atten-shun!" he said.

"As you were, master sergeant," Buzhazi said. "I am General Buzhazi, commander of the Iranian Internal Defense Forces. I have need of this room." He turned to the jailer. "Thank you, Corporal. Carry on." The jailer snapped to attention, then got out of there as fast as he could. Buzhazi turned back to the NCO. "Your name, Master Sergeant?"

"Fattah, sir."

"Do you recognize me, Master Sergeant?"

"Yes, sir. You . . . are the former chief of staff. I believe you are currently commander of the Basij . . ."

"I prefer they be referred to as the Internal Security Forces," Buzhazi corrected him. The master sergeant nodded, his mind obviously still in a bit of confusion as to what was going on. "You were notified of my arrival here?"

"The message informed me that you are to be held here until further notice. You will be sent to a separate wing until . . ."

"Until my office is ready, this room will suffice."

The NCO hesitated. "Office, sir?"

"I'm here to organize the detail that will be sent out to hunt down the terrorists that perpetrated the attack on my units in Orumiyeh."

"But I thought . . . er, I thought . . ."

"We don't think around here, Master Sergeant—we have orders which must be obeyed until officially countermanded by legitimate orders from a verified higher authority. What are your orders regarding me, Master Sergeant?"

"I . . . I was told in the message to hold you and await instructions."

"I am issuing additional instructions to you now," Buzhazi said, "that do not violate any other orders and as such you will obey immediately. You will clear two phone lines for me and give me the passcodes to access the secure high-speed computer network lines. Where are my staff officers?"

" 'Staff officers,' sir?"

"I was assured that other officers that are to be under my command were sent here, with orders that they are to be detained until further notice. They were to report to me as soon as possible. Where are they?"

"I'm sorry, General, but I'm not familiar with any officers sent here to be detailed to you," Fattah said. He paused for a moment, then added, "We have several in detention awaiting interrogation or disciplinary action, but I don't think they would be suitable for any activities such as you are describing."

"That's for me to decide, Master Sergeant," Buzhazi said. "Have them report to me immediately."

"I can bring them here to you, sir," Fattah said, "but I may not release them to you without written orders from headquarters."

"Understood. The passcodes?" Fattah handed Buzhazi a card. The passcodes on the card, which were changed regularly, were combined with each soldier's own personal code to allow access to the secure worldwide network. "Very well. Carry on." Fattah snapped to attention and departed.

As soon as he departed, Buzhazi hurriedly composed several messages on the computer to his staff officers and unit commanders around the country—using coded phrases and "virtual" e-mail addresses so the Pasdaran or their Intelligence Bureau investigators would hopefully find it more difficult to trace and decipher the messages or their intended recipients—advising them on what happened in Orumiyeh and the Supreme Defense Council's reaction. He knew it was very possible for the Pasdaran to keep him here permanently without anyone else knowing he was here, or for him to just disappear without anyone being able to investigate or question any action. All communications in and out of all headquarters complexes were screened in real time by the Intelligence Bureau, but hopefully at least one message would make it out.

If none did, he would end up worse than dead—it would be as if he never existed.

He had barely hit the "SEND" button on the last message when Fattah returned with three men, all secured at the wrists with waist chain restraints. Two of the men wore gray and white striped prison overalls; the third, to Buzhazi's surprise, wore a battle dress uniform with subdued brigadier-general's stars on it! Like Buzhazi himself, it appeared he had come in directly from the field, without the opportunity to change uniforms or clean up. "Here are the men you requested to see, sir," Master Sergeant Fattah said.

Buzhazi got to his feet and looked the men over. The first officer in prison garb stood at attention but returned the general's glare. "Your name?"

"Kazemi, Ali-Reza, flight captain, One-Thirteenth Tactical Airlift Squadron, Birjand, sir."

"Why were you brought here, Captain?"

"I am not aware of any legitimate charges brought against me, sir."

Buzhazi glanced at Fattah, who said, "Accused of stealing a transport jet to smuggle goods from Afghanistan and Turkmenistan, and for running a black market operation on government property, sir."

"What sort of goods?"

"Food, medicine, weapons, fuel, clothing."

"Is this true, Captain?"

"I am innocent of all those charges, sir."

"Of course you are," Buzhazi said sarcastically. He turned to the general officer. "I know you, don't I, General?"

"I believe we have met, sir. Brigadier-General Kamal Zhoram, Commander, Second Rocket Brigade."

"Pasdaran."

"Yes, sir."

The sooner he got rid of this guy, Buzhazi thought, the better. "Why are you here, General?"

"I am to be questioned about an incident this morning at a field test in Kermān province, sir."

"What sort of incident?"

"An attack, sir."

"Someone attacked you—in Kermān province?" Kermān province was completely surrounded by other provinces, shared no boundaries with any foreign countries, and had no cross-border or ethnic problems—it was considered as safe and secure as any Persian province could be. Orumiyeh was much more dangerous and had a long history of clashes with Kurds, Turks, and Turkmen, but this story of another attack really got Buzhazi's attention. "What sort of attack, General?"

"An air attack, sir."

"An air attack?" Buzhazi was shocked. He had a thrill of spine-numbing fear as he recalled the American B-2 stealth bomber attacks that devastated Iran's air defenses and naval forces not that many years ago. Were the Americans gearing up for another attack? Unfortunately, he didn't have time to question Zhoram about it. "I find that highly unlikely, General, but we'll discuss it later." He moved to the third prisoner, then immediately stepped back, out of smell range. The man had deeply sunken cheeks and eyes, thin hair, wasted neck muscles, and he trembled slightly. "What the hell is your story, soldier?"

"Heroin addict, sir," Fattah said.

"What is he doing here? Why are you wasting valuable resources on him?"

"He's an officer that we suspect is running a drug smuggling operation in Khorāsān province," Fattah said. "We're drying him out so we can question him on the others in his network."

"How long have you been 'drying him out,' Master Sergeant?"

"Three days, sir."

"What do you think the others in his network are doing while he's in Doshan Tappeh getting 'dried out,' Master Sergeant?" Buzhazi asked angrily. "Do you expect them to be sitting around waiting to get caught? They are long gone by now."

"We must conduct an investigation nonetheless, sir," Fattah said, "so we will continue using a rapid-detox protocol which includes high doses of sedatives and naltrexone to alleviate the withdrawal symp . . ."

"I'll show you the proper treatment protocol for a heroin addict, Master Sergeant," Buzhazi said . . . and drove his right hand into the man's throat, splitting his trachea and cracking his vertebrae. The man's eyes bugged out until they looked as if they'd pop out of his head, then rolled up inside his skull, and he hit the floor like a bag of rotten pomegranates.

"General, no!" Master Sergeant Fattah shouted. He pushed Buzhazi away and bent down to examine the nearly decapitated body.

As he was being pushed away, Buzhazi grabbed Zhoram and pulled him close. "Do you expect to get your command back once the Pasdaran completes its investigation of the attack, General?" he whispered urgently.

Zhoram hesitated, shocked at the sudden flurry of action around him, but the shock lasted only moments. "I'll be dead or in prison, General," he said simply. "If I'm lucky, I'll be simply discharged and returned to my family penniless and disgraced."

"As will I," Buzhazi said. "So. Will you fight or will you submit?" Zhoram hesitated again, looking away, but Buzhazi's grasp and urgent growl locked his eyes back on Buzhazi's. "Answer me, Zhoram—fight or submit?"

"Fight," Zhoram said. "The Pasdaran doesn't want answers—they want someone to blame, and the sooner the better. I want the ones that attacked my rocket forces."

"I'll come for you," Buzhazi said. "Join me and you will get your fight. Cross me, and I'll cut your guts out with a spoon."

"Free me, and I'll fight with you, General," Zhoram said. "I swear on the eyes of Allah."

Buzhazi grabbed Zhoram's crotch. "You'll be swearing to me by these, General—because if you cross me, I'll make you eat them."

"I swear, General. Free me and I'm your man."

"Good." He turned to Kazemi, who was watching the two generals and not paying any attention to the dead officer. "What about you, Kazemi? Are you Pasdaran?"

"Air Corps, yes, sir."

"Are you a smuggler?"

"Only when my squadron's supplies are siphoned off by the regional headquarters at Shīrāz, sir," Kazemi said. "I was tired of losing my men to cold and hunger and flew some helicopters to the border to trade with nomads and black marketeers. I find it faster and easier to trade with Afghan nomads than confront corrupt Pasdaran supply officers. If you're getting out of here, sir, take me with you."

"I don't trust thieves, no matter how noble their reasoning."

"I stole only for my men and their families, sir, not for myself," Kazemi said. "I'd do it again if necessary." Buzhazi hesitated. "If you won't take me, sir, then do me a favor and shoot me on your way out," Kazemi added, "because I'd rather die at your hands than be turned into a drooling blubbering vegetable by these Pasdaran goons—and they'll do it, because I'm not implicating my men or the Afghans that helped me. I'll bite off my own tongue before I talk."

"Brave words, Captain . . ."

"You . . . sir, you have killed him!" Master Sergeant Fattah exclaimed. "He's dead!"

"Exactly what he needed to cure his heroin addiction," Buzhazi said proudly. He looked at Kazemi but said nothing. "Get that piece of human garbage out of my sight, Master Sergeant, and let me get back to . . ."

"To what, General Buzhazi?" a voice asked. Buzhazi looked up and saw a Pasdaran three-star general standing in the doorway, hands casually behind his back. "Do you think you're going somewhere?"

"General Badi," Buzhazi said, choking down a shiver of panic, "how good to see you." Lieutenant-General Muhammad Badi, commander of the Pasdaran-i-Engelab, or Islamic Revolutionary Guards, was about Buzhazi's height but several kilos heavier, with slick-backed dark hair, a thin moustache, and a thick jowly neck. He wore a black Pasdaran battle dress uniform, high-topped black riding boots, and a web belt with a large Belgian or Austrian-made pistol in its holster. Badi wore an amused smile as he surveyed the scene in the conference room, but Buzhazi knew it was a crocodile's smile—Badi was as dangerous and unpredictable as they came in the Iranian military forces. "I was expecting you."

"And you prepared a gift for me—a prisoner with a broken neck? How touching, Hesarak." Badi felt comfortable calling Buzhazi by his first name because to him Buzhazi was nothing but a disgraced, incompetent officer that should have been eliminated years ago.

Back when Buzhazi was chief of staff and nominal commander of the Pasdaran, Badi was the senior Pasdaran officer in charge of deploying Iran's limited stockpile of reverse-engineered Russian nuclear weapons. Thanks to Buzhazi's influence with the Supreme Defense Council, Badi convinced them to agree to deploy the weapons aboard a refitted Russian and Chinese nuclear-powered aircraft carrier called the *Ayatollah Ruhollah Khomeini.* Badi was dead-set against such a move—the American naval superiority in the Middle East and Indian Ocean region was unquestioned—but Buzhazi's plan was put in motion despite his strident objections.

The ultimate insult: as the senior officer in charge of all of Iran's nuclear weapons, Badi was assigned as the second in command and chief tactical officer aboard the *Khomeini,* under Major Admiral Akbar Tufayli. The admiral was the fifth highest ranking Pasdaran officer and the highest ranking Pasdaran naval officer, and he never missed an opportunity to let everyone around him know it. He was an incompetent boob that had no idea what power he commanded. Tufayli was killed by the Americans as he tried to flee the carrier; in the meantime, the American air force decimated Iran's air defenses.

The blow to Iran's military and the mullahs' plans to dominate the entire Persian Gulf and Arabian Sea region was severe, especially for the defeated and disgraced chief of staff Buzhazi, but for Muhammad Badi the episode was his ticket to the top. The Supreme Defense Council realized that everything Badi had been saying was true: it would take Tehran years, perhaps decades, to match American military power in the Middle East, so why waste the resources to try to do so? Instead, build small tactical nuclear weapons, place them in the hands of Pasdaran special operations forces around the world, and challenge the Americans in the one area they were not prepared to handle—guerrilla warfare.

That's exactly what the Supreme Defense Council decided to do, and they placed the program in Muhammad Badi's hands, along with a fast promotion and almost unlimited money and authority. While

Buzhazi was sweating away in the Iranian hinterlands trying to teach young Iranian men and women to fight like Persian soldiers instead of common street thugs, Badi was the master of the Pasdaran . . . and the nuclear arsenal that was secretly being assembled.

"I just thought I'd relieve you of some human garbage, Muhammad," Buzhazi said. "You're not angry, are you?"

"If you feel the need to show off your big bad commando skills in front of my men and these other prisoners, Hesarak, be my guest," Badi said. "Are you quite through now?" He turned to the master sergeant. "Sergeant, what in hell are these prisoners doing out of their cells?"

"I . . . er, the general, he ordered them brought here, sir."

"The general, eh? General Buzhazi is a prisoner here, Sergeant—perhaps one small step up from that dead officer lying there, but only just."

"But I . . . Sir, I received no orders regarding the general except that he be held here. I received no list of charges, no sentencing order, no . . ."

"Are you this stupid every day, Sergeant, or is today something special?" Badi asked. "Buzhazi is an enemy of the republic and is considered a traitor and possibly a spy, assisting terrorists to enter the country and attack military bases. He deserves to be hung naked by his thumbs for the rest of the year, but that decision will be left to the Supreme Defense Council. Until then, he will be placed in isolation and monitored twenty-four-seven. Understood?"

"Yes, sir."

"Any more words that the general utters in your's or your men's presence is to be recorded and transmitted to me immediately, to be collected and used against him at his court-martial—if he's still alive when it commences. Clear?"

"Yes, sir."

"Now get that piece of diseased meat out of here, put those other prisoners back in their cages, then place yourself on report. I will escort the general to his cell—after we have a little chat. Get moving." The master sergeant barked orders, restraints were placed on General Buzhazi, and Badi took him by the arm and led him out of the briefing room. As they walked down the corridor, Badi remarked, "I see the old Buzhazi charm is still working. Don't tell me—it was your superior powers of persuasion that prompted one of the most senior soldiers at Doshan Tappeh to not only let you out of your cell but to let three others out as well."

"It's called 'leadership'—treating a soldier like a fellow warrior instead of an idiot," Buzhazi said. "You should try it some time."

"Actually, I'm sure it was our fearless leader Yassini's fault for not leaving specific instructions regarding your arrest and detention," Badi conjectured.

"Another example of poor leadership: blaming others for your own failures," Buzhazi said. "Fattah and Tahmasbi were just following orders."

"Who?"

"Yet another example of poor leadership—you don't even know the names of your key personnel, not even the master sergeant on duty. And it's 'master sergeant,' Muhammad, not 'sergeant.' Calling Fattah a 'sergeant' is an insult to his years of service."

"I guess I'm getting quite a lesson in leadership from you this morning, aren't I, Hesarak?" Badi said. They approached the office of the security detachment commander, where another very large guard resembling Tahmasbi, except perhaps bigger and meaner-looking, was standing at attention. Badi told the security commander he needed his office, and he motioned for Buzhazi to step inside after he had departed.

Buzhazi stepped to the center of the room. "So what brings the chief of the Pasdaran to the dog pens, Muhammad? I would think you'd want to distance yourself from me as much as possible."

"I've had little trouble doing that since I worked on your headquarters staff, Hesarak," Badi said as he moved to sit behind the security commander's desk, leaving Buzhazi standing before him. He started drawing geometric shapes on the polished sandalwood desk before him. "My investigators collected sixteen bodies from the disaster at Orumiyeh, Hesarak. Most died in the truck bomb explosion and the gunbattle that followed; several others had burns and other serious injuries but had a single shot to the head, execution-style."

"A dead Kurd is a good Kurd."

"I didn't say all were dead, Hesarak," Badi said. "A few were still alive and even conscious."

"Good. Make them talk. We'll find out where their base or home cities are and launch a punitive attack immediately." He looked at Badi suspiciously. "You know, Muhammad, I'm very suspicious about the details of that attack."

"Oh?"

"It was almost perfect . . . too perfect," Buzhazi said. "My Internal Defense Force personnel at Orumiyeh were the best of the best—the showpieces of my new force."

"Looks like they weren't as good as you thought, eh, Hesarak?"

"The Border Defense Battalion was specially trained to detect and repel foreign invaders, especially Kurdish terrorists, because of their location so close to Kurdish-controlled territories . . ."

"Guess they screwed up—the outcome of your vaunted leadership skills, no doubt."

"Security was airtight," Buzhazi went on. "I've encountered some experienced and excellent Kurdish soldiers, but this attack was uncharacteristically precise, fast, and lethal, even for the most highly trained Kurds I've ever known."

"What are you getting at, Hesarak?"

Buzhazi looked carefully at Badi, then shrugged. "I don't know, Muhammad. I have nothing. I might still be in shock—I can't concentrate on any details. All I can see when I think about it is body parts scattered around me like ripe fruit fallen from trees in an orchard."

"Well, concentrate on this for a moment, Hesarak," Badi said. "The men we are questioning have already given us a great deal of information, almost all of it corroborated with each other and with intelligence information we've already received—such as the number in their attack squad."

"That could be useful—or it could be a lie," Buzhazi said. "If it's a lie, we can use it against them in later interrogations. However, I'd be cautious of exactly-matching responses, Muhammad—they could have been coached as a group to give false or misleading information."

"I don't think so," Badi said. "They told us other interesting pieces of information—such as some of them were captured by your men."

"My men? I came to Orumiyeh to preside over a stand-up ceremony for a border defense unit—I didn't bring any men. I didn't even bring . . ."

He didn't hear him coming until it was too late. While Buzhazi was distracted, Badi's bodyguard had closed the office door, withdrawn a metal baton, and swung it full force, striking him in the right kidney area. Buzhazi's vision exploded into a cloud of stars, and all he could hear was the terrifying sound of a freight train out of control rushing at full volume in his ears. He gasped at first until the full shrieking tsunami of pain rolled over him, and he cried aloud and dropped to the carpet, writhing in agony.

"If I didn't know you better, Hesarak," Badi said, "I'd say you captured those prisoners and are secretly interrogating them." Buzhazi didn't hear him until Badi repeated himself a few moments later after the roaring in his ears had subsided. "What do you have to say to that, General?"

"I . . . I'd say you know me pretty well, Muhammad, my old friend," Buzhazi said through the choking clouds of pain.

"Where are they? I want them."

"Of course you do, you piece of shit—because they're Pasdaran, aren't they?"

Badi's eyes widened in surprise and his mouth dropped open in confusion, but only for a moment, and then the crocodile's smile came back. "Very clever, Hesarak. Did you know, or did you just guess?"

"I suspected it, but when you showed up here, I knew," Buzhazi groaned. "It's the only logical reason why you would come down here and interrogate me personally. You sent Pasdaran Special Forces disguised as Kurds to attack fellow Iranian soldiers? Why, for God's sake?" Badi didn't answer—but his eyes told the whole story. "You're shitting me, Badi—you did it because you thought the Internal Defense Forces would replace the Pasdaran as guardians of the revolution?"

"Your units were good . . . almost too good," Badi said. "You stood up that base at Orumiyeh for a tenth of what it would cost the Pasdaran, and in less time than anyone would have guessed. Yassini and the Supreme Defense Council were starting to take notice. A few on the Council argued that paramilitary forces couldn't take the place of the Pasdaran, that they would flee at the first sign of the enemy—I just took his suggestion and staged a little raid. Your men didn't run, I'll give them that, but they were completely unprepared. It was easier than I ever could have hoped . . ."

"Except for some of your men being captured, you mean?"

"Before long you will be terminated, and soon after so too your Internal Defense Force project," Badi went on, "and the Pasdaran's budget and border security responsibilities will be fully restored—perhaps even increased, as they should be."

"You're nothing but a sick, egomaniacal bastard, Badi," Buzhazi said. "You can't stand to be subordinate to anyone, so you stayed quiet about Tufayli's incompetence as captain of the aircraft carrier *Khomeini,* and then after he was dead you blamed the whole defeat on me. I never would have thought you'd stoop so low as to kill your own people to advance your career."

"Why not, Hesarak? Your career certainly isn't going anywhere. You could have raised the Prophet up from the dead, and you'd still be known as the one who lost Iran's regional military domination to a numerically inferior Western force. And since Yassini is such a proponent of this idiotic Internal Defense Force idea, he'll go down too . . ."

"And you'll be promoted as chief of staff and remain head of the Pasdaran."

"Why stop there? If I can plant enough false memos and directives, I might implicate the president in the whole Internal Defense Force scheme and take him down too—and I can slip into that position as well."

"All I have to do is trot out your Pasdaran agents captured in the raid wearing Kurdish terrorist outfits, and your game is up."

"Not if I can get to them first, Hesarak," Badi said menacingly. "That's why you're going to tell me where they are."

"Screw you."

"General, I'm going to take great delight in watching you be tortured by my man here," Badi said, nodding to the very large man standing over Buzhazi. "He's going to do it the old-fashioned way—not with unpredictable drugs, but with good old-fashioned physical torture. You're too old to resist it. My man is an expert on knowing exactly how far he can take old geezers like you through the corridors of pain, to the very thresholds of coma and death, without crossing over. All of your Shock Trooper training from thirty years ago won't help you one bit."

"Fuck you, Badi."

"It's going to take us a few minutes to get set up, Hesarak. We'll let you think about what is about to happen to you. If you talk, and if what you say is true and my men are recovered, I'll kill you quick and painlessly. Otherwise, you will experience levels of pain that you can't imagine. And it won't be continuous or cause unconsciousness—it'll be slow, lingering, sharp, and unexpected. Before long you'll be screaming information at me and begging for mercy. You can end any such unpleasantness by telling me what I want to know. I know my man here will be disappointed by not performing his tricks on you, but he'll get over it, I'm sure."

Badi rose from the desk, grabbed Buzhazi by the hair, and said in his face, "You'll be taken to an interrogation room, Hesarak, and prepped. You'll be 'wired for sound,' as they say—your tongue, your testicles, your heart, and your entire nervous system will be plugged into a nice big electrical transformer that we can precisely control. But there is no 'volume control' on this device, Hesarak—just an 'on' and 'off' switch. It's full voltage every time. It'll be interesting to see how you do. I strongly recommend you tell me what I want to know, now, before the fun really begins."

"I said, go screw yourself, Badi," Buzhazi said. "By the time you get anything out of me, my men will have changed locations a half-dozen times. If I'm dead, my men will trot out those captured Pasdaran commandos and release their videotaped confessions. The warrant for your arrest will be issued shortly after that. You might as well start getting out of the country now. May I suggest South America?"

"At the very least, we can find out what else you might know," Badi said. "As I said, as we go on, you'll be most anxious to tell us all sorts of things. This I guarantee. Good-bye, Hesarak. This will probably be the last time I see you with all of your faculties still intact." Badi patted Buzhazi's face, then motioned to the bodyguard. "Have the general taken to an interrogation room and prepared for his 'debriefing.' Have them notify me immediately when he breaks." The bodyguard nodded and opened the door for the general . . .

. . . and Badi saw a man in light gray fatigues, desert combat boots, and the blue beret of the Iranian Air forces standing in the doorway. Behind him stood three soldiers, similarly dressed, carrying automatic rifles. "What is this?" he shouted.

"Greetings, General Badi," the first soldier said—and in the blink of an eye he raised a sound-suppressed Russian Makarov automatic pistol, fired three shots just past Badi's left ear and directly into the torturer's face, then pushed Badi inside and closed the door, leaving his three soldiers to guard the outside. The soldier dumped Badi to the carpet with a kick to the side of his left knee. The Pasdaran general screamed aloud at the pain and shock of the sudden attack. "Who in hell are you?" he cried.

"You don't recognize me, General?" the soldier asked. "You took great delight in ruining my career about eleven years ago." He tossed a set of handcuff keys to the Pasdaran commander, then pressed his pistol against his forehead. "While you're thinking, release General Buzhazi, now."

Badi crawled over to Buzhazi and unlocked the handcuffs; Buzhazi grabbed the keys and released the waist chain. "Now I remember . . . Sattari. Mansour Sattari, Buzhazi's chief of staff."

"Very good, General," the young officer said. After the handcuffs were removed, Sattari had Badi place them on himself, then helped Buzhazi to his feet and waited until the injured general was able to stay on his feet by himself. "If the general is injured, Badi, you die right here and now."

"Killing me won't help you get out of here," Badi said. "There are over a thousand armed Pasdaran guards here."

"Your security force here at Doshan Tappeh is exactly three hundred and fifteen soldiers per shift, Badi," Sattari said. "I brought a team of just a hundred lightly armed Internal Defense Force soldiers and killed or captured every one of the guards on duty already. Your day shift got too cocky and overconfident, Badi—they obviously thought no one ever wants to break into a Pasdaran compound, especially at daytime."

"You won't get out of here alive, Sattari."

"We've got units monitoring the eight other Pasdaran bases in the city, and if they move on us they'll be neutralized as well. We'll be out of here before any other security forces arrive—and you'll be long dead." He raised the pistol.

"Wait," Buzhazi said. He took the pistol from Sattari's hands. "I think it'd be better to put him on trial for the murders of all those men and women in Orumiyeh. We have positive proof that the men we captured alive were Pasdaran?"

"No question, sir," Sattari said.

"All your evidence could've been faked with ease," Badi said. "Besides, the Supreme Defense Council won't accept any evidence you give them. They'll blame it all on internecine rivalry and warfare and send us both on our ways—except the Pasdaran will be after you and all the traitors who joined you as soon as the Council adjourns. You might as well use this temporary advantage to flee the country, Buzhazi, before you are publicly executed for treason—by me." Sattari and Buzhazi looked at each other—obviously the very same thought had crossed their minds. Iran was no place for them now, and it was too late to turn back. "The Basij have no hope of eliminating the Pasdaran, Hesarak. It was created solely as a means of providing the Pasdaran with cannon fodder so the Iraqis would waste their bullets on them and allow the Pasdaran to attack during the War of Glorification. Your Basij forces will always be nothing but cannon fodder."

"We took your headquarters with little trouble," Sattori said.

Badi ignored him. "With you in temporary control of this base, you can hijack an aircraft that will easily take you to Africa, Europe, or Asia. Better get out now, while you can." He smiled as he watched Sattari silently pleading for Buzhazi to agree, and he saw Buzhazi's eyes start to dart back and forth as his mind examined his options over and over again . . .

. . . milliseconds before Buzhazi said, "No, Mansour. We continue as planned," then fired three bullets into Badi's brain.

Sattari spit on the nearly headless corpse and nodded. "Good riddance. That should've been done years ago."

"We're committed now, my friend," Buzhazi said, checking the pistol, accepting a full magazine from Sattari, and reloading it. "Let's avenge the deaths of our brothers in the Internal Defense Forces, and then let's get this revolution started."

CHAPTER 2

OVER THE HIGH TECHNOLOGY AEROSPACE WEAPONS CENTER, ELLIOTT AIR FORCE BASE, GROOM LAKE, NEVADA

Weeks Later

Boomer always thought that it felt like hitting the water on the Splash Mountain ride at Disneyland, bumpy and noisy amidst the sudden shock of deceleration—except the feeling lasted eight minutes, not two seconds.

With a one-hundred-eighty-degree x-axis turn and a ninety-second burn from the Laser Pulse Detonation Rocket System, the XR-A9 Black Stallion spaceplane slowed down to about five thousand miles per hour and immediately began its descent through the atmosphere. Once slowed down, Hunter Noble used the spaceplane's maneuvering rockets to turn forward again, then lift the nose slightly to the proper altitude to expose the heat-proof carbon-carbon underside of the Black Stallion to the worst of the friction. He followed an electronic cueing system displayed on his primary multi-function display, similar to a terrestrial Instrument Landing System—as long as he kept the crosshairs perfectly centered in the middle of the display, he was on course and on glidepath for atmospheric reinsertion.

"Boomer, check your flight control computers, they're not engaged," the crew mission commander, First Lieutenant Dorothea Benneton, call-sign "Nano," said from the forward compartment. Benneton was a high-energy, type-A personality, barely contained by an engineering degree and an Air Force commission—she liked to party and she liked being in control of every situation. She had to take a deep breath and force her words from her mouth through the high G loading during re-entry. "Did they pop off-line?"

"No, I just didn't engage—I thought I'd hand-fly this re-entry," Boomer replied, his voice shaky and hoarse as well.

"Don't you screw with my test parameters, Boomer, or I'll kick your butt," Benneton warned only half-jokingly. "Stay on glidepath."

During re-entry the air around the spacecraft got so hot that it ionized and disrupted normal radio communications, so the team normally used a laser radio system that bounced laser beams between satellites to communicate with the spaceplane. But the message they received was actually over the normal encrypted UHF radio channel: "Stud Two, this is Control, how do you hear?" radioed Air Force Colonel Martin Tehama, the commander of the High Technology Aerospace Weapons Center, from his headquarters at Elliott Air Force Base.

"Three by, Control," Boomer replied. He turned to Nano and gave her a wink. "Looks like your gadget is working, Dottie." Enough heat was being sucked away from the skin to keep the air from ionizing, permitting regular radio communications.

"Why aren't you on auto control, Two?" Tehama asked. "I show the flight control system in 'STANDBY.' Is there a problem?"

"Now I'm getting the nagging in stereo," Boomer said. Reluctantly he switched on the autopilot, keeping his hands on the controls until he was sure the system was responding properly. "Everyone happy now?"

"Why do we bother writing up a test flight plan if you're not going to follow it, Boomer?" the commander asked. To Benneton he said, "Nice job on the protection system upgrades, Lieutenant. Looks like it's working pretty well."

"Thank you, sir," Nano responded, grunting through the G-forces. "I've still got some higher than expected temperatures in the cargo bay, but it looks like the temperature's holding—Boomer hasn't fried anything yet."

As they continued their descent the aerodynamic flight controls took greater and greater effect, and soon they were executing some lazy-eights and steep-banked S-turns across the sky, which helped to slow and cool the spacecraft even more. With the outside thermal protection layer temperatures now below 3,000 degrees Fahrenheit—the safe structural temperature limit for the spacecraft's titanium-vanadium skeleton—Boomer was clear to maneuver as he pleased, and he headed straight for Elliott Air Force Base's 23,000-foot long runway on Groom Lake in south-central Nevada.

It was not Hunter's best landing. He turned toward the runway late and landed about three hundred feet short, on the overrun—fortunately the overrun, while not stressed as highly as the main runway, supported the Black Stallion's weight adequately. He noticed fire and rescue trucks racing toward him as he zoomed down the runway, then slamming on the brakes and reversing direction as he zipped past the preplanned stopping point. He used almost every foot of the three-mile-long runway to stop, but he safely turned off before reaching the end and headed for the hangars.

"The cargo compartment monitors shut down—probably due to high heat," Nano said as she monitored the computerized shutdown process. "If my experiment is trashed, Boomer, I'm going to give you a smack in the head." Noble didn't respond. As soon as the onboard data was collected, the spacecraft completely shut down, and the inspection stand rolled into place, she hopped out and climbed up onto the platform to look at the cargo bay passenger module.

Hunter had a bad feeling about the outcome when he saw daggers flying out of Nano's eyes, aimed directly at him. "What?" he asked.

"Black streaks coming out of the seam in the bay doors," Benneton said frostily.

"The whole spacecraft is black, Nano. How can you . . . ?"

"It's built-up heat and oxidation, Boomer," she said. "I'm going to slit your throat, I swear." A few minutes later, with firefighters and paramedics standing by, they opened up the cargo doors—and an undulating, shimmering gray cloud of smoke and heat rolled out. Nano was shaking her fist in the spaceplane pilot's direction as she stared into the cargo hold. "Boomer, wait till I get my hands on you . . . !"

It took several long, agonizing moments to move a crane into position to lift the passenger module out of the cargo bay and onto a cradle in the hangar. Luckily the cradle was covered with heat-resistant materials, because the module was definitely hot, like a fat steak fresh off the barbecue. As expected, the electrical door opening mechanisms didn't work, so the ground crews started to work on the mechanical locks. By the time the locks had been twisted free, a small crowd had gathered at the hatch, morbidly curious as to what the insides looked like. Nano herself grabbed a pair of insulated gloves and grasped the latch . . . but before Benneton could open the hatch, the levers moved and the door swung open from the inside.

"About time, Doc," the electronically synthesized voice of Air Force Brigadier General Hal Briggs said. A wave of heat rolled out through the open hatch. "We thought you guys forgot about us."

"For God's sake, General . . . are you all right?" Benneton asked breathlessly.

"I'm okay—a little bored, that's all," Briggs said. He was inside a "Tin Man"–powered exoskeleton, a protective suit of electronic armor made up of composite materials thousands of times stronger than steel but just a fraction of the weight. The suit was composed of a material called BERP, or Ballistic Electronically Responsive Process, that kept the material flexible but instantly hardened into an almost impenetrable shell if struck. The BERP material was surrounded by thin microhydraulic actuators in a lightweight composite framework that gave the wearer superhuman strength, agility, and speed. The suit had a variety of sensors, communications equipment, and weapon control functions built into it, as well as its own environmental controls to keep the user comfortable in extreme conditions.

Benneton started to reach in and undo the straps securing Briggs in the aft-facing seat. "Let's get you out of there, sir . . ."

Briggs held up a large armored hand. "Better not, Doc. My readouts say it's over one-seventy Fahrenheit in here." He looked over at his comrade while he undid his harness. "You okay over there, Sergeant Major?"

"Affirmative, sir," the second passenger, U.S. Marine Corps Sergeant Major Chris Wohl replied, also wearing Tin Man armor, his usual emotionless monotone clearly identifiable through the electronic voice synthesizing system. The big Marine was seated in a forward-facing seat. He turned to Benneton while he unbuckled his harness. "I assume it's not supposed to get this hot in here, Doc?" he deadpanned.

"The sergeant major has just expended his allotment of quips for the year," Briggs interjected.

"Take it up with the aircraft commander," she responded perturbedly. "If he had let the computers fly the re-entry and it stayed precisely on the programmed glide path everything would have been fine." The bug-eyed helmeted figure looked at Benneton, then Noble, but said nothing in reply.

After downloading and checking all of the recorded data from the Tin Man suits, Briggs and Wohl disconnected and stepped out of the exoskeleton, removed their helmets, and shuffled off to the back of a Security Forces flatbed truck, helping themselves to cigars and bottles of water as they rested. "It was a good ride until the re-entry, Doc," Briggs said. "I think normal folks would have trouble with that re-entry, though—other than the heat, the g-forces are pretty severe. Can't you make it so you pull fewer g's?"

"We did a two-point-five-g re-entry, which is about half of normal," Hunter Noble said. "The Tin Man suits may have made it feel heavier than normal. How do you feel, Sergeant Major?"

"I feel fine, sir," Wohl said. "Perhaps all of the seats should be forward-facing—the aft-facing seats get a pounding during both takeoff and re-entry."

"Roger that," Briggs agreed. "I know what 'Spam in a can' feels like now."

"I'd also suggest maybe a few windows in there too," Wohl added. "The commando delivery vehicle the Air Battle Force uses has windows."

"I'll bet it doesn't go suborbital, Sergeant Major," Hunter said. "Were you getting a little airsick up there? We noticed your vitals getting up there." A warning glare from the big Marine told Boomer to terminate that line of questioning immediately. "Maybe we can put a computer monitor up front that can transmit mission data as well as outside horizon views. Good suggestion, Sergeant Major." Wohl nodded, which instantly made Boomer feel that his life had just been spared.

"I'm sorry you had a rough ride, General," Nano said, concern still evident in her voice.

"Hey, I had a great time, Lieutenant," the Air Force Security Forces one-star general said. Hal Briggs was always an animated, energetic guy, but his face was fairly beaming as he remembered the flight he just took. "Man, I was in space. Me! I joined the Army to see the world, but I never thought I'd see it from space!" Hal Briggs had originally joined the U.S. Army but transferred to the Air Force when being a Ranger got too unexciting for him. "I'll fly with you anytime, boys and girls, with or without the suit. Just call."

After a brief physical exam, the first stop was maintenance debrief, which usually lasted a couple of hours. Mission data automatically datalinked to Earth stations during the flight was compared to digital mission logs collected on the ground, and then the smallest departure from flight-planned or nominal readings was examined and discussed. The flight crew sat together at a desk surrounded by six computer monitors, each linked to a different main office of the maintenance complex—propulsion, environmental/life support, electrical/hydraulic/pneumatic, payload, communications/computers, and airframe—and answered questions transmitted to them by technicians in the control center, aircraft hangar, and records room.

It was past noon and well over one hundred degrees Fahrenheit outside in the Nevada sunshine when Noble, Benneton, Briggs, and Wohl finally stepped out of the maintenance debrief building, where they found Colonel Martin Tehama waiting for them. He saluted Briggs. "I hope you are okay, General, Sergeant Major," he said. "I'm glad to hear the medics gave you a clean bill of health."

"Actually, I feel pretty good, Colonel—like I had a really vigorous workout," Briggs said. "I guess whatever doesn't kill you makes you stronger, eh?"

"Yes, sir. And you, Sergeant Major?"

"Fine, sir," Wohl said in his typical low, almost growling voice.

Briggs lit up a cigar, watching with interest as Tehama's eyes widened in concern. "Uh . . . sir?" the

HAWC commander said apologetically. "We don't allow smoking here at the complex."

Briggs nodded and looked directly at the Air Force full colonel. "Is that so, Colonel?" he asked simply, taking another deep drag of his cigar. "I've been assigned here for . . . what, Chris? Damn near twenty years?"

"A very long time, sir," Wohl rumbled.

Briggs continued to stare at Tehama. "I don't believe I've ever heard of a ban on smoking outdoors except on the flight line, weapon storage area, and hangars," he went on.

"Well, there is, sir."

Briggs nodded, took another deep drag of his cigar, took it out of his mouth, and blew a cloud of smoke into Tehama's face. "Duly noted. Is there anything else for me, Colonel?" he asked.

"Sir, I think it's a bad example for the men to have a general officer flouting my regulations," Tehama tried one more time.

"Do you think your men will be flouting your regulations because of me, Colonel?"

"I don't believe they will, sir, no."

"Then I don't believe we have a problem here, Colonel."

"But if the men see you violating one of my regulations . . ."

"Will that prompt them to go ahead and disobey your regulations?"

"I don't think so, sir. But it . . . it shows a lack of regard for my regulations."

"A lack of regard for some of your regulations, Colonel . . . like having a cigar after my first space flight, away from the flight line, outdoors, in a parking lot." Tehama said nothing. "You are free to report my flagrant violation of your regulations to General Edgewater at Air Force Materiel Command, or to Major-General Furness at Air Battle Force. Want their numbers?"

Tehama briefly appeared as if he was going to argue with him, but he decided against it, scowling. "No, sir," he said, saluting. Briggs raised his cigar to return his salute, and Tehama turned to depart.

"Oh, Colonel—what did you come out here for anyway?" Briggs asked.

Tehama stopped and half-turned, kicking himself for forgetting. "I need to speak with Captain Noble." He could smell another waft of fine cigar smoke traveling his way and wished he had one himself right now.

"Very well. Carry on."

Tehama strode quickly yet stiffly over to where Boomer and Nano were loading gear into a staff car. They both saluted their superior officer, but Tehama didn't return their salutes. His conversation with Boomer and Nano was very short: Tehama stopped in front of them and, with his eyes averted and his face a mask of anger and frustration, said simply, "Benneton, I want the report on the module on my desk by sixteen hundred hours."

"Yes, sir," Nano responded, wondering if she had enough time and then immediately deciding, based on Tehama's pained and angry expression, that she had better make the time.

"Noble, you're off the flying schedule," Tehama said. "You will report to the flight surgeon for a complete medical and psych eval."

"A psych eval . . . ?"

"I find you moody, irritable, refusing to follow orders, argumentative, and distracted, possibly depressed or in some way unbalanced," Tehama said. "Further, and much more seriously, you willingly violated a major operational security directive by landing during an enemy satellite overfly window period—I shouldn't need to remind you that we are still technically in a state of war. You're grounded until I get the report from the flight surgeon. Get on it, both of you." He walked away without another word, not returning their salutes, or even looking up.

Boomer wore a stunned expression as they watched Tehama walk away. "Can you believe this shit?" he exploded. Nano averted her eyes. "Grounding me is one thing . . . but a psychological evaluation? If that shows up on my records, I'll be out of this program in the blink of an eye! I won't be able to get a job spraying fertilizer over a bean field, let alone fly in space ever again. He can't do this to me! Maybe he's the one who's come unhinged, eh, Nano? Wonder what he and General Briggs were talking about? Wonder if they'd get mad if I asked them?" When Nano didn't respond, he looked at her, and saw her still looking at the pavement. "What's up, Nano?"

"I gotta go write that report," was all she said.

But she didn't need to say anything else—her blank expression told him everything. "You agree with Tehama?" he asked her. "You think I need a psych eval?"

"You were acting real weird today, Boomer," she responded woodenly. "You were fighting everything and everyone, wanting to do it your own way. What's up with that?"

"We do that on *every* mission, Nano—you know that," Boomer said. "This isn't Edwards, Eglin, or Pax River—we don't always follow a set program because our job is to get the weapon systems in the flight test units' hands as soon as possible. Before Tehama showed up, no one was complaining when I'd hand-fly a re-entry or land a little hot. Why am I getting shit now?"

"You're getting a psych eval because you argued with the boss, Boomer."

"Tehama's worried about his promotion and his pension—he doesn't want anybody messing up his perfect little world. We need to get someone in charge here who cares more about putting hardware on the line rather than his career."

"When are you going to learn that you're not going to find a field grade officer bucking for general's stars who's not afraid of ruining his career?" Benneton asked. "A guy's been in the service twenty-plus years and he wants everything to go nice and smooth so he can nail down his retirement; he wants no black marks on his record so he can show off a clean, successful résumé to defense contractors or consulting clients after he punches out. Guys like Tehama are looking at the end of their Air Force careers, not the beginning, and they need that job after retirement to supplement their pitiful government pensions. You and me, we get employment offers every week, and for a hell of a lot more money than guys like Tehama will ever see."

"Hey, I'm not an idiot—I know all that," Boomer said, the frustration evident in his voice. "But we can do amazing stuff out here if we're allowed to do it. Technical and scientific hurdles I can handle—it's the bureaucratic and personality junk that get me angry. Why can't they just let us do our thing?"

"You sound like a complete adolescent nerd, Boomer," Nano said. "Go see the shrink, and try not to aggravate him or he'll put you in a straitjacket and then I'll have twice as much work to do around here." She started walking toward her office inside the guarded flight test compound, then turned and shouted over her shoulder, "And I'm still pissed at you for ruining my test flight. Like I said: payback's a bitch."

QOM, ISLAMIC REPUBLIC OF IRAN

That Same Time

"Is everyone in position?"

"Yes, sir," Sattari said. "Looks like just a skeleton crew on duty."

"As we expected," Buzhazi said. "Let's do it."

Buzhazi didn't usually go for symbology, "winning hearts and minds," or going for shock effect—it was risky to commit precious men and equipment to anything that didn't have concrete tactical purpose—but in this particular case, the mission could have tremendous psychological and morale impact if properly executed . . .

. . . and if improperly accomplished, he would simply just revert to the original plan: go in and kill everyone who dared stand in their way.

The Faqih Sayyed Ruhollah Khomeini Library of Jurisconsult, located just outside the Jamkaran Mosque and next to the Hazrat-e-Ma'sumeh shrine in the city of Qom, was the largest and most modern of the many libraries of Shi'ia Islamic thought and scholarship around the world. Completed two years after the death of the Imam Khomeini by tens of thousands of volunteers from all over the world, and intended at first to be Khomeini's final burial place, the library was considered the home of the concept developed by Khomeini of *velayat-e faqih,* or "guardianship of the Islamic jurists," in which all law, jurisprudence, and governance should be controlled and carefully supervised by clerics, not the people, scholars, lawyers, royalty, the wealthy, or any elected representatives.

Without question, *velayat-e faqih* was the root of all evil in Iran. All law in Iran under the mullahs was based on their interpretation of the Koran, a centuries-old book that was as much fable and mysticism as it was a guide on how to conduct one's life as set forth by God. Getting around the law was simple: just get a more favorable interpretation. Whatever Iran's parliament, the Majlis voted for could be overturned or changed in a heartbeat by the whim of the faqih, the Imam Mostafa Shīrāzemi, through the authority of the Council of Guardians, and there was no recourse. Shīrāzemi—his real name was Kazemi, but as was the custom after being chosen as an ayatollah, he adopted the name of the city of his birth—was a former commander of the Pasdaran and a close political adviser to the previous faqih before assuming the role of the Supreme Leader of Iran, and he knew how to manipulate the system. He appointed six of the twelve members of the Council of Guardians and had approval authority over the other six members chosen by the members of the High Judicial Council, who themselves had been appointed to their positions by the faqih.

In other words: the system was infested with vermin; the vermin had to be eradicated, and the nest incinerated—and this place was most definitely the nest.

Dressed in uniforms as the Pasdarans, Buzhazi's forces situated themselves near three of the library's entrances. They were careful not to deploy any forces on the west side of the library—that side faced the holy shrine of Hazrat-e-Ma'sumeh, Shi'ite Islam's second holiest shrine, about a hundred meters away. What they were about to do would certainly inflame a lot of religious passions already—there was no use in angering the faithful even more by desecrating one of their holy places, even if it was by accident.

Buzhazi had a plan ready to break down the large concrete and steel doors to the library, but that wasn't necessary—a guard waved him over when he noticed them assembling outside. Buzhazi ordered his men to drive their vehicles right up to the gates as if they were deploying to protect the entrances—and when they did so, the guards inside, young Pasdaran troopers fresh out of school, admitted them immediately. "Status of your security detail, Specialist?" Buzhazi asked as he stepped inside the heavy door, casually looking around.

"My God, sir, where have you been?" the young enlisted trooper asked. "We have not been relieved since our security regiments departed."

"Is that any reason to abandon safety protocols, Specialist?" Buzhazi asked. "Get your finger off that trigger. Never place your finger inside that trigger guard unless you're prepared to kill someone." He grasped the young trooper's rifle and flicked the safety switch on. "Same for the safety."

"Sorry, sir. Sorry."

"Pay attention from now on, soldier. Where is your platoon leader?"

"Gone, sir."

"To whom do you make your post reports?"

"Uh . . . we inform the imams when they ask, sir," the trooper said. "We weren't told who else to report to."

Buzhazi shook his head. "That's fine, Specialist. You and your comrades will report to my company commander from now on. I relieve you. Report over there right now and do as you're told." The trooper started to hurry off toward the vehicles arrayed outside the gate, then stopped, returned to his spot, rendered a salute, and managed to wait until it was returned before hurrying off again. Within moments the entire security detail on this gate, just a dozen men, had left their post and were in custody; within minutes, the other two entrances were secure as well. The prisoners would be given a choice: swear allegiance to Buzhazi and join his insurgency, or die. Not one moment of hesitation would be tolerated.

Buzhazi, Sattari, and a group of six security men entered the library. The place was as beautiful inside as it was stark outside: tall soaring ceilings capped with a beautiful mosaic tile dome, polished marble columns, shining marble floors inlaid with gold and silver, and long rows of oak bookshelves surrounded by tables, chairs, rugs, and computer workstations. A magnificent thick topaz carpet outside of an ornately decorated archway signified the entrance to the Khomeini mosque.

There was no one in the library at this hour. Just as Buzhazi started to worry about how to find the mullah in charge of the place, his wish was granted the moment he set foot on the topaz carpet without removing his boots: a man in a white turban and long flowing white and gray robes came running out of nowhere, waving his hands, followed by several assistants. "You! You! I have told you a hundred times, you may not enter the shrine of the faqih without permission from the imam! Now go!"

Buzhazi stood his ground. "I wish to speak with the imam immediately, priest," he said.

"Have you gone mad? Morning prayers are not for another two hours—the imam receives no one until after prayers unless it's an emergency, and normally not until after breakfast and morning rituals." The mullah looked at Buzhazi. "I do not recognize you, soldier. Remove your helmet in this holy place and identify yourself."

"I have information that you have important visitors here from Tehran with you, priest," Buzhazi said, keeping the helmet in place. "I want to speak with the imam, immediately."

"You will remove yourself from this place immediately!" the mullah shouted. "I shall see to it that you are relieved of duty and flogged for this act of gross disrespect!"

Buzhazi turned to one of the young men that had followed the mullah. "Does this man know where the imam is?"

"We all serve the imam of this library. But he will do nothing except . . ." He didn't finish his sentence . . . because Buzhazi had withdrawn his pistol from its holster and shot one round through the mullah's forehead. In a flash Sattari had his pistol out as well, covering the other acolytes.

Buzhazi kept the smoking pistol in his hand but did not point it at anyone. He turned to the young man he had just referred to: "Okay, son, now I'll ask you the same question: do you have some special guests from Tehran here, and will you take me to them?"

The young man hesitated, then nearly fainted from fear as he saw Buzhazi roll his eyes impatiently and begin to raise his pistol. "Yes! Yes! We have guests staying here! Important men from Tehran, members of the Leadership Council, the Assembly of Experts, the Council of Guardians, and the Majlis."

"And?"

"And . . ." He looked at the dead body of the mullah lying on the once-immaculate marble floor, his face ashen, and nodded. "Y-yes, I will take you."

"Good boy." Buzhazi motioned to Sattari, who radioed for more units to follow them inside and secure the library. "Describe where we're going first, then take us."

THE WHITE HOUSE, WASHINGTON, D.C.

A Short Time Later

"So what about your spaceplanes, Patrick?" President Kevin Martindale asked. "Where do we stand?"

"The second Black Stallion spaceplane is ready for operational flight testing, and the third will be ready in six months, sir," Patrick replied. "The contractors are already tooled up for spare parts production and spiral upgrade development. They can be ready to restart full-scale production within two months of initial funding: we could have two more spacecraft ready within twelve months; the tankers can be ready in six months. Fuel and oxidizer are commercially produced worldwide, readily available, easily shipped and stored, and require no special training to handle—no need to expose the program by procuring or storing large amounts of cryogenic materials. The aircraft and tankers are easily concealed and deployed, need no special security or storage, and blend in with the tactical military inventories of any air base in the world."

"So you can build another Air Battle Force made up of spaceplanes and park them out in Dreamland—with you in command?" National Security Adviser Sparks asked. "Got this all figured out, eh, McLanahan?" To the President he added, "The committees will see right through that, sir. Barbeau will get what she wants; then, at the first inkling of trouble from Dreamland—and I can guarantee there will be trouble—she'll spearhead the charge to cut off funding and pillory you as the grand architect of the failed spaceplane scheme." He glanced at McLanahan and said plainly, "With all due respect, sir, McLanahan is damaged goods."

"He might be right, Patrick," the President said. His attention was redirected at his chief of staff's surprised expression. "Carl? What's going on?"

"A call from Secretary of State Carson, sir," Minden replied, releasing the dead-man's silencer button on the handset, his eyes darting over in McLanahan's direction. "There's an Iranian general by the name of Buzhazi . . . that asked to talk with McLanahan. He says it's urgent."

"Buzhazi? Hesarak Buzhazi?" McLanahan exclaimed. "The ex-chief of staff of the Iranian armed forces?"

"What in hell's going on, Carl?" the President asked.

"The State Department verifies that the call is coming from a secure official government telecommunications facility from Qom, Iran, relayed via satellite phone through the Swiss embassy in Washington," Minden said. "But we have no way of verifying if it's really Buzhazi."

"I thought Buzhazi was dead," Vice President Hershel said. "Wasn't he executed by the Ayatollah or the Iranian Revolutionary Guards after the attacks in the Straits of Hormuz? Can you bring us up to speed, Patrick?"

"Yes, ma'am. Hesarak al-Kan Buzhazi was the chief of staff of the Iranian military and head of their Revolutionary Guards Corps, the Pasdaran, several years ago. He tried to close off the Strait of Hormuz between the Persian Gulf and Gulf of Oman by ringing the shipping lanes with anti-ship missiles, with bombers carrying supersonic anti-ship missiles, and even using an ex-Russian aircraft carrier. We slapped him down pretty hard, and he was removed from his post—permanently, I thought. We had no hard evidence that Buzhazi had been executed; we thought he was driven deep underground or escaped Iran to a neighboring Arab country. We were surprised when he turned up as the commander of the Basij, their volunteer federal paramilitary force. Command of the Pasdaran was turned over to a deputy."

"Why is he calling you, McLanahan?" National Security Adviser Sparks asked.

"I have no idea, sir." Sparks scowled, not sure if he should believe him and deciding to check that out for himself.

"I remembered talking to the cocky bastard," the President said acidly. "He can lie and deceive with the best of them. If he thinks he speaks for the Iranian government, he's up to something. I want to find out what." He turned to Patrick. "Talk to him, Patrick, but don't give him anything until we get a chance to check out whatever he says."

Jonas Sparks didn't like junior staffers like McLanahan taking over his responsibility, and he decided to move quickly before this got completely out of control. "Mr. Minden, route the call to my office and I can take it in there."

"No, take it here," the President said. Minden shook his head in surprise: the President never allowed any business other than his own done in the Oval Office—the place always seemed a madhouse, but the chaos always centered on him. "Patrick, talk to him. I'd like to hear what that bastard has to say."

The chief of staff looked warily at Sparks, worried that the President's most senior advisers were being displaced by McLanahan, but right now powerless to do anything. He hit a second line button: "Signal, this is the chief of staff, verify that the voice translators are functioning and sending the real-time transcripts to the Oval Office . . . very well." He went over to a hidden credenza beside the President's desk, withdrew a tablet computer, logged in, inspected a script streaming on it, then hit the speakerphone button and motioned to McLanahan with a reluctant nod.

"This is General McLanahan in Washington," Patrick said. "To whom am I speaking?"

In a thick Middle East accent but in very well-spoken English a young man replied, "Good evening, sir. My name is Kamran Ardakani, and I am a student of theology and government at the Faqih Sayyed Ruhollah Khomeini Library of Jurisconsult in Qom, in the Islamic Republic of Iran. I am translating on behalf of General Hesarak al-Kan Buzhazi, the officer in charge of the military force here."

"How do I know you are translating for Buzhazi?"

There was a rather long pause; then: "The general tells me to tell you that he knows that your black friend Briggs sent the assassin to kill him and that she begged for mercy like a diseased whore before he executed her . . . may Allah have mercy on her soul."

"It's fucking him all right, the bastard," Patrick said. Over ten years earlier, Patrick and a task force from the Air Force, Marine Corps, and Iranian anti-government groups attacked Iranian military targets throughout the country before the Iranian military, led by Buzhazi, could completely disrupt shipping through the Persian Gulf. The last target was Buzhazi himself, led by a female commando from the Gulf Cooperative Council's special operations military force by the name of Riza Behrouzi. Hal Briggs had worked very closely with Behrouzi and formed a personal bond during the operation—but she was killed during the assassination attempt, and Buzhazi escaped. "So what does he want?"

Another pause; then: "The general has ordered me to inform you of what has just occurred here, in my own words," the translator said. "A force of approximately two hundred armed men has taken over the Khomeini Library here in Qom. The soldiers guarding this facility have been captured and the imam in charge has been killed, by the general's own hand. Before the general's raid, the library was being used by many members of the government, both clerics and laypersons, who sought shelter here following insurgent raids in Tehran."

" 'Insurgent raids in Tehran?' I hadn't heard anything about this!" Sparks exclaimed beneath his breath. Chief of Staff Minden immediately went to another phone to get confirmation.

"I do not know the status of the imams and government officials who were staying here—the general is not allowing the staff to attend to them," the student named Ardakani went on. "He and his men have barricaded themselves inside the library and appear to be preparing for a very large battle."

Patrick was silent for a few moments; then, to everyone's surprise, said, "Ask General Buzhazi if he is requesting assistance from the United States of America."

National Security Adviser Sparks's eyes grew wide in disbelief and he emphatically drew a finger across his throat. "Stand by please, General," Patrick said, then hit the "MUTE" button on the speakerphone.

"Are you insane, McLanahan?" Jonas Sparks thundered. "You're asking Buzhazi, the nutcase who tried to start an all-out naval war in the Persian Gulf—with nuclear weapons, I might add—for our help?"

"Buzhazi is up to something," Patrick quickly explained. "I remember reading about him when I was at the Air Intelligence Agency. He was sold out by the clerical leadership and the Pasdaran at the end of the Gulf of Oman conflict. The leadership was afraid simply executing him would have incited the regular army to declare him a martyr and avenge him, so they demoted him and put him in charge of the Basij, the volunteer paramilitary force in Iran—sort of a militarized AmeriCorps. Speculation was that the clerics were hoping someone in the Basij would do the dirty deed.

"Instead, Buzhazi went about purging the Basij of all the fundamentalist Islamists and just plain-old wackos, and in a few years' time had transformed it into a real fighting force he renamed the Internal Defense Force. Rumor was that his IDF might actually take some duties away from the Pasdaran, like border security and rural police. But the Basij went down in numbers from almost a million to less than fifty thousand, still mostly very young or very old volunteers, so it was mostly disregarded as a military force." He fell silent for a moment. "Qom is the religious center of Iran and the second most important Shi'ite Islam city in the world. The library he mentioned was built for the Ayatollah Khomeini's burial site. When Khomeini's body was moved to Tehran, the place was turned into a center of Islamic legal thought, training, and indoctrination—but its design makes it look more like a fortress."

"What does that have to do with offering Buzhazi assistance, McLanahan?"

"The translator mentioned 'insurgent raids,' " Patrick explained. "What if the leadership in Tehran evacuated the city and moved to the Khomeini library in Qom? No Iranian in his right mind, religious or not, would dare invade a holy city like Qom—except a nutcase like Buzhazi. What if Buzhazi is the insurgency? He guesses or discovers that the clerical leadership evacuated the capital and hid out in Qom, and he went down there to . . ."

"To what, McLanahan?"

"To snuff them all out," Patrick concluded, his eyes wide. "He's getting his revenge on the clerics who stripped him of his rank and title." He turned to the President and said, "He's staging a military coup in Iran—and he's asking for our help."

The President's eyes widened in disbelief. "My God, that's incredible," he breathed. "What an opportunity . . ."

"You can't trust Buzhazi, even if he had a snowball's chance in Hell of pulling it off," Sparks said. "He's just as likely to turn on his friends and allies as he is the clerics in his own country!"

"But it's worth a try," Vice President Hershel said. "At least with an active and capable opposition group in Iran the place could be greatly destabilized for years—even if Buzhazi fails, any other home-grown anti-government groups might have a chance."

The President turned to his chief of staff and said, "Carl, call in the National Security Council and as many members of the Cabinet as you can convene in an hour. Have them bring every scrap of data they have on the current military, anti-government, insurgent, and political status in Iran. I want analysis of this situation and suggestions on an American response." Minden was on the phone in an instant. To Sparks he asked, "Jonas, what seaborne strike assets do we have available in the Persian Gulf area right now?"

"Not a whole lot, sir," the national security adviser said, rattling off the information off the top of his head as presented to him in his daily status briefings. After the devastating Russian attacks that destroyed almost all of America's long-range land-based strike capability, the most common question from the President's lips whenever a crisis was brewing was "Where are the carriers?" "There is one aircraft carrier battle group in the Persian Gulf now, but it's scheduled to rotate out with another group in two days."

"That'll have to be delayed for now."

"Yes, sir. The second carrier from Seventh Fleet is in the Indian Ocean, within two days' steaming time to Iran, and another carrier group is a few more days behind in the South China Sea—with just ten carrier battle groups in the fleet now, we're stretched thin. Fifth Fleet is reporting fully operational, but they are heavily committed to operations in Iraq already." Fifth Fleet, based in Bahrain, was the U.S. Navy's permanent presence in the Persian Gulf, but it normally had no aircraft carriers assigned to it except in wartime.

"So the chances of sending a Marine Expeditionary Unit to Iran to help Buzhazi defend himself and rally the people to support his coup . . . ?"

"Dropping two thousand Marines into central Iran, with their entire military alerted? Slim to no chance, sir," Sparks said. "General Glenbrook would have to give us the exact figures, but I would guess it would take several days of planning and a week minimum to mobilize those kinds of forces. An assault from the Persian Gulf or Gulf of Oman would be out of the question—that's the first place they'd be watching for such a move—so we'd try a feint from that direction and bring the main force in overland from Turkey, Turkmenistan, or Afghanistan. That would take even longer to set up."

"But all of this is assuming we want to support a military coup in Iran," Minden said. "As I recall, Buzhazi was one of the most aggressive military leaders ever in Iran. As far as we know, he was the architect of Iran's nuclear program—he certainly made it clear he would use the few nuclear weapons we know were in his control. We need a lot more information before we'd ever contemplate supporting him—it would be akin to deciding whether or not to support a Saddam Hussein or Pervez Musharraf all over again."

"This is an opportunity we shouldn't pass up, sir," McLanahan said to the President. "Buzhazi has taken a small force of volunteers and captured one of Shi'ite Islam's most holy sites, apparently along with several high-ranking members of Iran's clerical government. There's only one reason he's taken a chance to track me down and call me in the middle of this operation, and that's because he knows he's teetering on the brink of success or failure. If he fails, the clerical government will purge the entire country of any other opposition and completely crush them. Iran will be driven even deeper into fundamentalist isolation for another generation . . ."

"And if he wins, we could be looking at another military dictator in the heart of the Middle East, astride one of the world's most important shipping routes, with trillions in petrodollars—and nuclear weapons—at his disposal," Minden said.

"We don't know that, Carl," the Vice President said, "but I agree with the former: if the clerical government survives, they'll squash any group that even hints at opposing the government. We support a dozen Iranian opposition movements: the National Council of Resistance, the Mujahedin-e Khalq, the National

Liberation Army, a number of student anti-theocracy groups, and even surviving family members of the deposed monarchy. The Pasdaran will fan out all around the globe to track down any groups that might gain inspiration for another coup from Buzhazi."

The Oval Office fell silent. The President was stone-faced, masking his own doubt and indecision; after a few moments he motioned back to the speakerphone. Patrick hit the button: "General Buzhazi, are you still there?" Patrick asked.

They could hear a man's voice speaking in the background; then the young English-speaking theology student said, "The general wants to know who else is listening to this conversation."

"Tell the general it's none of his damned business," Patrick snapped. "Ask the general what he wants of me."

After a slight pause: "He says you have said it yourself, sir."

"I want the general to say it, in his own words," Patrick said. "You don't have to translate, Mr. Ardakani—we'll do it ourselves."

There was a rustle on the line as the receiver was apparently passed from hand to hand. The President took the tablet PC in his hands to read the computer-generated translation himself. As the older voice spoke in the background, the streaming text read: "That cursed bastard McLanahan . . ." then: "Very well. The Internal Defense Forces under my command are committed to destroy the Pasdaran and the murderous religious regime that spawned them, or die trying. This so-called library is the birthplace of disaster, betrayal, and ruin for the Iranian people. It will become either the killing grounds of the new defenders of the people, or it will be known as the place where the people of Iran began to take back their homes and government from the religious tyrants. You can choose to help us, or sit in your comfortable chairs and do nothing."

"I still haven't heard a request from you, General Buzhazi," McLanahan said. "Make a request, sir, or this conversation is at an end."

The computerized translation noted several unintelligible words, interspersed with profanity; then: "Help me, General McLanahan. Send your stealth warplanes, your shadows of steel, and help me destroy the Pasdaran. I am outnumbered over fifty to one. I have killed or wounded a number of Pasdaran infantry when they tried to ambush me at Arān, but I discovered the plot against me and prepared a response. The rest of the Pasdaran are undoubtedly on their way to Qom to finish the job."

"How many?"

"I estimate the Pasdaran have mobilized three infantry battalions, possibly one armored battalion, and one helicopter assault battalion against us," Buzhazi responded.

"Five battalions?" Sparks exclaimed. "Almost an entire Pasdaran division up against a few insurgents? There's no way Buzhazi's going to survive, no matter how good or lucky he is."

"What about the regular army, General?" Patrick asked.

"The regular army has not been mobilized and remains in their garrisons," Buzhazi responded. "We have intercepted communications between Tehran and the military districts commanding them to begin mobilizing for battle."

"Will they join the Pasdaran?"

"If my forces are crushed, everything stays as before—they will stay quietly under the heel of the Pasdaran or face being purged," Buzhazi said. "But if my forces appear as if they might prevail, they may join the revolution. I have attempted contact with several friends in the regular armed forces, but none have responded, so I do not know if I shall receive any help at all from anyone."

"Why should the United States join you if the regular army, the forces you once commanded, won't?" Jonas Sparks asked.

"Who is this? Identify yourself."

"This is National Security Adviser General Jonas Sparks, General Buzhazi," Sparks said. "What does the United States get in return for helping you?"

"You would want to see the clerical regime crushed too, I think, General Sparks."

"Only to be replaced by someone like you, General?" Sparks thundered. "You're the one who tried to close off the Persian Gulf to every warship except yours. You were ready to destroy an American aircraft carrier with nuclear weapons . . . !"

"All that was eleven years ago, Sparks," the translated text read. "The only thing that has not changed is the bloodthirsty nature of the clerical regime. You know they have nuclear weapons, Sparks—they have many more than when I was chief of staff, and the Pasdaran is more ready than ever to use them."

"What makes you better than the clerics or the Pasdaran? Frankly, I don't see much difference between you."

"Do not let your bigotry against all Iranians blind you, Sparks," Buzhazi said. "The difference between us is I want Iran to succeed, flourish, and prosper—the current administration and the clerics only want themselves and their twisted brand of Islam to flourish, at the expense of all else. I want Iran to stop all foreign intrigue, stop sponsoring terrorism and revolution in other countries in the name of Islam, and stop threatening its neighbors. Iran can be the desert flower of southwest Asia and take its place among the great powers of the world if the theocracy can be defeated."

"How do we know this isn't some trick?" Sparks asked. "You'd like nothing better than to shoot down a stealth bomber, spy plane, or special ops transport over Qom, wouldn't you, Buzhazi? You'd become the defender of the holy city, the hero of Islam, the sword of Allah avenging the ass-whupping you got eleven years ago. You'd get your stars and your command back and look real good in the eyes of the ayatollah if you sucker-punched the United States, isn't that right, Buzhazi?" They waited for a response, but nothing came. "The bastard hung up. Confront him with the truth, and he runs scared. It's a bluff, Mr. President. He's got something up his sleeve."

"It sounded to me like he was desperate, General," Patrick said.

"If half of what he said is true, I'll bet he's desperate," the President said. He put away the tablet PC translator, rubbed his eyes wearily, then said, "A lack of judgment or poor planning on Buzhazi's part doesn't constitute an emergency on my part, no matter how interesting or important the opportunities may be. General Sparks."

"Sir?"

"Meet with the National Security Council staff right away and come up with some recommendations," the President ordered. "If you don't have the intelligence data you need to make a decision, get it as quickly as you can. I'd like to hear your thoughts as soon as possible."

Patrick knew right away that the President was done thinking about this topic—he was intentionally vague about when he wanted anything, and he wasn't talking about a "plan of action" as he normally did—he was asking for "thoughts" and "recommendations," which were something entirely different. This development was definitely going on the back burner unless he did something. He quickly interjected, "Sir, in the meantime, may I recommend . . ."

"Patrick, talk it over with General Sparks at his earliest opportunity," the President said distractedly. "He'll assemble all the recommendations from the Joint Chiefs together with State and other sources and present all possible options to me, including yours. I've gotta move on to other issues. Thanks, everyone." That was the unmistakable signal that the meeting was at an end.

As they filed out of the Oval Office, National Security Adviser Sparks pushed past McLanahan. "Excuse me, sir," Patrick said, "but I'd like a minute to brief you on . . ."

"Have it on my computer in an hour, McLanahan," Sparks interjected impatiently, "and I don't mean the spaceplanes—I want a plan of action from you using the Air Battle Force unmanned and manned bombers and ground forces at Battle Mountain. If it's not on there in an hour, it won't factor in."

"It'll be there, sir," Patrick said. "About the nomination to HAWC . . ."

"Jesus, McLanahan, don't I have enough to chew on right now?" Sparks thundered. Over his shoulder, he spat, "Send me a full written proposal, a command itinerary report, an outline of all the projects ongoing at HAWC, a staffing and budget proposal, and your full medical report and summary from the attending physicians on my computer regarding their opinions for your suitability for a command nomination. When things calm down I'll look at it . . . but I don't anticipate that happening any time soon."

RUHOLLAH KHOMEINI LIBRARY, QOM, IRAN

Early the Next Morning Iran Time

Brigadier General Mansour Sattari joined Major General Buzhazi in the minaret tower attached to the mosque of the Khomeini Library. It was just an hour or so before dawn, and the first glow of sunrise was already starting to illuminate the sky. "Are you ever going to let proper lookouts back up here, sir?" he asked him. "We're not that far away that a good sniper couldn't get a shot off at you in daylight."

"I've never been in one of these crier's towers before," Buzhazi said. He was busy scanning the terrain all around them with a pair of binoculars. Two soldiers accompanied him, one with a sniper rifle. "Have you?"

"No. I've been told I have the voice of a muezzin, but I was never that religious."

"Your voice was made for barking orders, not calling the faithful to prayer."

"I agree, sir." Sattari motioned out to the outer walls of the Khomeini Library compound. "There's no doubt that the Khomeini Library was designed as a fortress," he observed. "Three-meter tall, meter-thick walls; narrow roads with clear fields of fire and no hiding places; entryways too narrow for most armored vehicles to pass; gates made of thick rolled steel obviously designed for functionality and not just for decoration; and another one-hundred-meter-wide clear zone inside the wall to the main building."

"It's not going to be enough, Mansour," General Buzhazi said. "I reviewed the plans for this place as a young Pasdaran officer. It was designed to withstand riots of faithful mourners, not an armed invasion. You probably don't remember the riots in this country after Khomeini's death, do you?"

"I certainly do, sir," Sattari said, his face turning hard and pallid. "I was already lying low—I had been in the United States in pilot training, but when I returned I denied ever having gone there because foreign-trained officers were being executed by the Pasdaran. I pretended to be an enlisted man for a year! I was in charge of a security detail guarding embassies in the capital, but spent all my time trying to convince the Islamists that I was one of them." He adopted a faraway expression, then added, "I killed a man to prove to the mob that I was on their side. I think he was Dutch, or Belgian, a reporter—I don't know, the Europeans all look the same, and the mob thought all white-skinned blue-eyed men were Americans. I was so ashamed of what I did that I almost turned the gun on myself."

Buzhazi was silent for a long moment, then said woodenly, "I gave orders to my Pasdaran units that probably resulted in thousands of such street executions, Mansour. The more so-called 'insurgents' and 'infidels' we killed, the more the clerics congratulated us." He shook his head. "So went the 'religion of peace.' I'm sorry for giving those orders. I thought that's what I was expected to do to support my government."

"You were following orders."

"The authorities are supposed to protect the weak. I was a soldier, a commander. I knew what my responsibility was—to protect the people, protect the weak, and defend the constitution, not give in to the bloody mobs." He paused, then lowered the binoculars, thinking back to that time twenty-five years ago. "That was a crazy time, Mansour. One million rioters in the streets of Tehran. One million. A thousand people a day, mostly children, died just from being suffocated by the crowds. The rioters were like wild animals—completely out of control. The Pasdaran tapped into that fervor and convinced millions of them to sacrifice their lives on the battlefield against the Iraqis."

"You changed all that by transforming the Basij into a real fighting force."

"But that's never going to erase the blood from my hands, Mansour—never." Buzhazi motioned to the east. "There's a lot of open territory around those farms along the Qareh River."

"Yes, sir, but our scouts say there is a lot of irrigation equipment—pipes, pump houses, farm implements, that sort of thing—through those fields that might provide a few barriers to smaller armored vehicles until they are cleared away. That will slow them down."

"For a short time," Buzhazi said. He walked around the catwalk and peered north. "The Saveh Mountains are damned close, Mansour—we'll only have a few seconds of warning when the attack planes crest those ridgelines."

"I still don't think they'd bomb the compound, sir," Sattari insisted. "An infantry assault—definitely. A helicopter assault—yes, to cover the ground troops, perhaps to breach the walls, but not to shoot up the library grounds. That will give us an advantage—they'll be reluctant to lay down a lot of heavy cover fire."

"The Pasdaran likes helicopters," Buzhazi mused in a quiet voice. "The common person can't relate to a jet screaming overhead at a thousand kilometers an hour no matter how sophisticated it is—but even a small helicopter is a weapon of terror and confusion to everyone." Just then, Buzhazi's radio crackled to life, and he listened. "Our scouts in Qom report several armored vehicles destroyed by our booby-traps on the Ali Khani and Masumah bridges in central Qom. The Ali Khani Bridge is heavily damaged and passable by units on foot only; the Masumah Bridge is intact and passable."

"I'm surprised they decided to use the bridges in the first place—they could have just rolled right across the Musa Sadr," Sattari said. The city of Qom was bisected by a river that was so dry that large parts of it had been paved over and turned into open space for bazaars, playgrounds, parking lots, and campgrounds for pilgrims visiting the holy sites. "That'll slow them down a bit while they look for more booby traps, but they won't be so sloppy around the other bridges."

"Every little wound, no matter how small, weakens the most fearsome enemy," Buzhazi said. "Get the lookouts up here and have them feed us constant updates—we have less than an hour before they'll be in attack range. Let's get to the map room, build a picture of the Pasdaran's deployments, and . . ."

"Warning! Helicopters inbound from the north!" Buzhazi's radio blared.

"Hopefully just scouts, using low-light TV or infrared to take a look as the main force moves in," Buzhazi said. He and Sattari quickly scanned the skies. "Two Mi-35 attack helicopters," he announced. "Staying pretty high. Get out the Strelas and let's see if we can . . ." At that moment he saw two bright flashes of light from one of the helicopters. "Get out! Get out!" he screamed, then jumped through the doorway leading to the spiral staircase that threaded down the inside of the minaret. He never let his boots touch the steps, but half-slid, half-tumbled down the stairs as fast as he could. He was being pushed along by someone cascading down the steps even faster than he . . .

. . . and seconds later, the darkness was split open by a thunderous explosion, a wave of searing heat, and the force of a thousand pieces of stone being propelled in all directions. Whoever was above Buzhazi was now on top of him, and they cartwheeled down the stairs together until they reached a landing about seven meters from the top.

The minaret was wobbling and shuddering, threatening to shatter apart at any moment, so as soon as he could, Buzhazi grabbed whoever had fallen on top of him and began hauling him down the steps. The tower somehow held as they emerged into the sanctuary adjacent to the mosque.

"Allah akbar! Allah akbar!" Mansour Sattari cried as Buzhazi half-carried, half-dragged him outside and away from the teetering minaret. "They fired a damned missile on us!"

"I'm a damned fool—I believed the Pasdaran still only used handheld weapons on their helicopters," Buzhazi said. "They've obviously upgraded to guided air-to-surface missiles."

"And I thought they wouldn't dare attack the mosque," Sattari said, trying to clear the unbelievably loud ringing in his ears. "I guess we were both wrong."

Buzhazi raised his walkie-talkie, fighting to get his breathing under control before keying the "TALK" button: "Strela teams one through twenty, prepare to engage, north quadrants, but stay out of sight until they're within range," Buzhazi ordered. "Repeat, no one fires until we're sure the Mi-35s are within range. Report when secure and ready. All other Strela teams, hold your positions."

Just then a strange voice came through the walkie-talkie: " 'Teams one through twenty?' How interesting, General."

Shit, he thought, their frequency was not just being monitored—they were talking on it now as well! "All teams go to Yellow," Buzhazi ordered.

But he knew that wasn't going to work—after all, they were fighting fellow Iranians, not foreigners. A few moments after he switched to the secondary frequency, he heard: "Sorry, General, but we know that channel, and we know the third one you have available as well, so you might as well stay on Yellow so you don't confuse your fellow traitors. So, did you like the fireworks show up in the minaret? You move pretty fast for an old man."

"I have plenty of surprises in store for you."

"I'm sure you do, General," the caller responded. "May I suggest you stop with the claims you have twenty or more Strela launchers—we inventoried all of the missiles you or the other deserters, traitors, and criminals could have possibly stolen, and subtracting those you have already fired, we think you have perhaps a half-dozen remaining. A good diversionary tactic, though. My congratulations on your quick thinking."

"This sounds like Ali Zolqadr," Buzhazi radioed back, trying any way he could think of to regain any sort of advantage in the eyes of those who were listening in. "I thought you were running the Pasdaran interrogation centers, torturing and killing honest soldiers just to prove your loyalty to the mullahs."

"Another good piece of disinformation on an open channel, General," the man said. This time, however, it wasn't a complete lie: Ali Zolqadr had been Muhammad Badi's "wet worker," supervising the capture—or assassination—of anyone wanted by the state, no matter what nationality or where in the world they might be. He was obviously so good at his job that he had been promoted to deputy commander of the Pasdaran and was now, with Badi's death, in charge of destroying the insurgency. "Let's get down to business, General. As you saw, I have full authority from the Supreme Defense Council to take any and all steps necessary to crush this pitiful insurgency."

"Like firing a missile at a mosque? Aren't you afraid of burning for eternity in the fires of Hell?"

"This from the man who invaded one of Qom's holiest sites and are holding a number of clerics hostage,"

Zolqadr said. "Your fate is sealed, General, and anything I might do pales in comparison to your crimes. Any destruction of the holy sites or deaths of anyone inside the Khomeini Library will of course be blamed on you.

"I simply want you to realize that I have the capability, authority, and temerity to simply level that building if I so desired. I want to avoid any more bloodshed and desecration. The deaths of your followers would be entirely on your head, and I don't think you want to spoil their memories by sentencing them to eternal condemnation in the eyes of their fellow citizens. Your leadership skills are legendary, but I don't think you wished to use your extraordinary skills to lead these men to public and humiliating executions.

"Therefore, my demand is simple: surrender immediately and only you and General Sattari will be held criminally responsible for this uprising. The others will be tried in military courts under jurisdiction of the Ministry of Defense, not the Pasdaran. Only those who have been identified as actually raising a weapon against a fellow Iranian will face capital punishment—all others will face confinement only. All will be dealt with as Iranian soldiers, not as common criminals, with all rights and privileges."

"Zolqadr, all of my men have been told in no uncertain terms they have the option at any time to turn over their weapon and leave," Buzhazi radioed back. "The men that marched into this house of lies and corruption did so willingly, knowing that the Pasdaran, the Ministry of Defense, the Supreme Defense Council, and the Council of Guardians would consider them not just criminals but unclean infidels unworthy of Islamic justice under the Koran. They had every opportunity to leave, remove their uniforms, and disappear into the population. Some did just that. The rest stayed, and we will fight."

"Brave words, General," Zolqadr said. "Their deaths will be on your head. You have one more chance, General, and then anyone in that place not wearing a Pasdaran uniform will die. I will give you and your men thirty minutes to throw open those gates and come out with your hands on your head, or my men will roll in, slaughter everyone inside, and burn your bodies in a hole in the desert like garbage. To all of General Buzhazi's men listening to this message, I promise you if you surrender now you will not be harmed. Ignore Buzhazi's megalomania and come out peacefully. This war is at an end."

Buzhazi mashed the mike button: "All units, this is General Buzhazi. Any man who wants to surrender, report to the main astan-e in the Khomeini mosque without your weapons. I order that any man who wishes to surrender to the Pasdaran not be harmed. May Allah preserve you—because I guarantee the Pasdaran won't. You have fifteen minutes to report to the sanctuary. All others, prepare to repel invaders."

Buzhazi looped the walkie-talkie over his shoulder, and he and Sattari trotted from the mosque across the courtyard to the library. Buzhazi was thankful he didn't see any men heading the other way toward the mosque. Inside the library, he made his way to the roof, the best place to observe the Pasdaran's deployment. His staff officers were down behind the front wall of the roof, drawing diagrams of the approaching armored vehicles. He noticed none of his senior staff had departed, although the roof had fewer guards on them than before—and he noticed none of the officers or senior enlisted men had weapons in hand. The thought had crossed his mind that they might save their own skins by killing or arresting him—he was glad that option had apparently not been exercised. "I hope I'm worthy of the loyalty you show me this morning, gentlemen," he said. "Status report."

"We count three battalions approaching our position," the operations officer responded, "one from the northwest, one from the west, and one from the southwest. We can't see them yet, but we expect a fourth battalion to position itself east to cut off any escape, and the helicopter attack units to come in from the north with a clear field of fire to the south."

Buzhazi crawled over to the edge of the wall and peeped over the top, with just his binoculars and the top of his helmet protruding above. "Platoons appear to be motor-rifle units in BTR-60s led by one Zulfiqar main battle tank," he observed. "One or two mortar platoons breaking off from the echelon to set up. I see the battalion headquarters vehicles—looks like they have BMPs, riding right up front, the cocky bastards. They are still marching in echelon at reduced speed, range approximately four kilometers."

"I think the mines on the bridges got their attention," Sattari said, laughing. The laughter was a welcome break to the decidedly funereal mood that had descended on the roof.

"Nine BTRs and one Zulfiqar tank per company, still in echelon formation, command vehicles still in the fore. What are they waiting for?"

"Same formation to the southwest, sir," Sattari reported. "Command vehicles out front, no flank guards, and just a few scouts. They'll have us surrounded and within a kilometer of the wall in less than thirty minutes."

"A hundred BTRs, nine tanks, a mortar platoon, and a thousand troops—we have to assume the fourth battalion is waiting to the east," Buzhazi said.

"It's only a six to one advantage," Sattari said. "Normally the Pasdaran doesn't engage in any battle unless they're ahead ten to one." He looked at his commanding general. "I was expecting more. I'm disappointed." He returned to his scanning, adding under his breath, "We're still going to get slaughtered, but they could have expended a little more effort to do it."

"This is a massive operation for the Pasdaran—they're accustomed to sabotage, kidnapping, sneak-and-peek, and kicking down doors of frightened civilians in the dead of night," Buzhazi observed.

"The radio chatter between those battalion headquarters vehicles must be fierce," Sattari said. "They're spread out too far to see each other or use light signals. If we could only destroy those command vehicles, we might have a chance to stall this offensive."

Buzhazi thought for a moment—it was obvious he had been thinking the same thing. "There might be a way," he said.

Sattari looked at his commanding officer's face and read it immediately. "I thought you said the spirit of the old Basij was dead, sir," he said.

"Maybe not quite yet, my friend." He outlined his plan to Sattari, who issued orders right away.

Colonel Ali Zolqadr stepped out of his BMP command vehicle, hands on his hips, and observed the battalion spread out behind him with immense glee. He took a deep breath of already-warm, dry desert air. "A nice morning for a bloodbath, eh, Major?" he asked.

"Yes, sir," Zolqadr's aide, Major Kazem Jahromi, responded. He nervously looked outside the armored personnel carrier.

"Uh . . . sir, we're only at three kilometers range to the wall, sir. Perhaps you'd better get back in the vehicle."

"I'll be up there in the commander's cupola before too long, Major, but I wanted to step out onto the field of battle before we start to roll in," Zolqadr said. "This is my first armored field assault—in fact, I believe I'm leading the first Pasdaran armored assault since the American attacks against us over eleven years ago." He took another deep breath. "This is where every commander belongs, Major—at the head of his forces, leading the charge. This is definitely where I belong." He looked at his watch. "How long before their deadline to surrender is up?"

"Just a few minutes now, sir." A few moments later, from well inside the armored vehicle: "Sir, scouts report trucks coming out of the compound with white flags."

"How many?"

"Six, sir. Covered five-ton delivery trucks. Two approaching each battalion formation."

"Six! With . . . what, twenty men per vehicle? Maybe thirty? Looks like a good percentage of Buzhazi's rebel forces are deserting him! Excellent news!"

Soon they could see two trucks moving slowly toward them, a white bedsheet tied to the radio antenna serving as their flag of surrender. For the first time he felt a thrill of panic for being at the head of this column of vehicles as the trucks moved closer. "Don't let the bastards near the battalions!" Zolqadr shouted to his headquarters unit commander. "Stop them well short of the battalions and have them get out of the vehicles one by one. Make sure the men don't rough them up. Let the others still inside see how well they'll be treated, and maybe we'll draw a few more out. Make them all feel welcome—before we execute their traitorous asses."

"Don't shoot, Zolqadr," he heard over his radio. "We're waving surrender flags. May Allah condemn you and your descendants to eternal damnation if you violate a flag of surrender."

"It's Buzhazi!" Zolqadr shouted in glee. He raised his binoculars and, sure enough, saw the general himself driving one of the trucks! "Tell the rest of First Battalion I want Buzhazi alive!" he shouted to his aide. "If he tries anything, disable the truck, but don't kill

Buzhazi!" He picked up his portable radio. "Are you surrendering too, General? How surprisingly wise of you."

"I'm only doing this to be sure my men who wish to surrender will be treated fairly, as you promised, like Iranian soldiers and not criminals," Buzhazi radioed. "I intend to return to the library after I drop off these brave men and continue my fight for freedom, and if you try to capture me, the whole world will know what a coward you are."

"Fine, fine. I'll let you live—plenty of chances to kill you or see you hanged in Shahr Park, along with the other criminals," Zolqadr said. The trucks were too close for binoculars now. "Stop right there and let the men out. I promise they will not be harmed."

"I want to be close enough to look at you face to face, Colonel," Buzhazi said. "I want to look you in the eye before I kill you, just like I did to Badi."

"I said, stop right there, General," Zolqadr radioed back, "or my men will open fire!" He whirled around and screamed, "Get two BTRs and their dismounts up here and cover those trucks, now!" His aide relayed the order.

Buzhazi's truck slowed, and at that moment there was a tremendous explosion to the north, followed by a second explosion seconds later. "What was that?"

Zolqadr cried. Two massive mushroom clouds of black smoke rose into the sky. "What's happening?"

"Suicide bombers!" someone screamed. "The trucks are packed with explosives! They've destroyed one command vehicle and a tank!"

Zolqadr nearly tripped over his own feet in confusion as he whirled around and returned to his own armored vehicle. "Don't let them any closer!" he yelled to his aide. "Open fire! Open fire!"

"Look out!" someone cried. "Take cover!"

Zolqadr turned. The two trucks heading toward him had not stopped but had accelerated—they were less than a hundred meters away now! "All units, open fire!" he screamed. "Stop them!" A machine gun immediately opened fire right above his head so close that he thought he had been hit, and he ducked and dodged left around the BMP.

The second truck weaved and dodged as it barreled toward them, and it appeared as if it was going to keep on coming, but soon its engine compartment hood blew open when its engine block was shredded by the twenty-three-millimeter cannon shells. It weaved a few more times, then its front tires were blown out and it half-collapsed, half spun to the ground. "Good shooting!" Zolqadr said. "Do the same to Buzhazi's truck—try to take him ali . . ."

And at that instant the second truck detonated, the force of two thousand pounds of high explosives—part of an immense weapons cache found on the grounds of the Khomeini Library, brought in by the Pasdaran when the clerics and politicians from Tehran arrived—bowling over the Pasdaran infantrymen like clay jars hit by a whirlwind. But Buzhazi's truck was not far away, and the force of the blast knocked the truck completely off its wheels and over onto its right side.

"Cease fire! Cease fire!" Zolqadr shouted—not just to relay the order but because he couldn't hear his own voice very well from the ringing in his ears caused by the detonation of the second truck. He drew his side-arm. "I want Buzhazi alive!" He turned to his aide. "Grab a rifle and follow me, Major!" The aide blanched at first by the order and then by the smug, amused expressions of the Pasdaran infantrymen around him; he almost dropped the AK-47 rifle offered him, and he grasped it like it was a snake waiting to bite him.

Zolqadr flinched at the sound of yet another explosion to the south, and the chatter on his portable transceiver told him another BMP command vehicle had been hit. His was the only command vehicle to survive this cowardly attack! Buzhazi was going to pay dearly for this! He aimed his nine-millimeter Zoaf pistol at the driver's door as he approached. "Buzhazi!" he shouted. "Come out of there! You are my prisoner!"

"Sir, be quiet!" his aide shouted, ignorant of the fact that half the battalion could hear him just as loudly. "He might hear you!"

"I don't care!" Zolqadr shouted. "I want the great Hesarak Buzhazi to know that I think he is a craven coward to order a suicide bomb attack against the Pasdaran! I hope to personally pull the lever to drop you in the gallows, you worthless piece of shit! Can you hear me, Buzhazi? Your attack has failed, and now I'm going to execute each and every survivor in that library, and I'm going to have you watch each execution. I'm coming for you!"

Zolqadr jumped up onto the truck and pulled open the driver's door. He saw Buzhazi crumpled up against the passenger side door, his head bleeding from a half-dozen wounds, his body covered with soot and broken glass, his hands . . .

. . . were repeatedly pressing a switch—and he realized with shock that it was a detonator switch! Had it not malfunctioned, Zolqadr and anyone within fifty meters would've been blown into a million pieces! He immediately but carefully climbed off the truck, stepped away from the vehicle as if moving to join his aide, then radioed for men to get Buzhazi out of the stricken truck.

"Your attacks failed, General," Zolqadr shouted triumphantly as the semi-conscious former chief of staff of the Iranian military was dragged before him. He made sure Buzhazi was awake, then pointed back the fifty meters toward his BMP and the three armored personnel carriers that had moved up to guard it. "See? My battalion is intact, and we have more than enough firepower to . . ."

At that instant there was a blinding flash of light, several globes of smoke in the sky directly above his command vehicle . . . and then a massive series of explosions as his BMP and all three BTRs blew apart like firecrackers. The shock waves and the surprise of the sudden attack again knocked them all off their feet. When Zolqadr looked up, he saw several more armored vehicles in his battalion on fire . . . and the rest turning and racing madly in the opposite direction! Echoes of still more explosions rolled across the ground from the other battalions' directions. The Pasdaran infantrymen around him didn't know what to do, until finally they simply ran off toward Qom. Soon only Zolqadr, his aide—frightened into complete immobility—and Buzhazi remained.

"What . . . in . . . hell . . . happened? Zolqadr muttered. He turned to Buzhazi, his face a contorted mask of fear, confusion, and blinding rage. "What did you do, Buzhazi?" But the general was in absolutely no condition to respond. Zolqadr drew his pistol and aimed it at Buzhazi's left temple. "Answer me, you traitorous piece of filth! What happened here? Whose work is this? Who are you working with?"

"The . . . devil," moaned Buzhazi. "Or maybe the angel of death. Let's go visit her together, Zolqadr."

"I've changed my mind, Buzhazi," Zolqadr cried. "I'm not going to turn you over for a public trial and execution—I'm going to kill you right here, right now, for what you've done!" Zolqadr grasped Buzhazi's jacket, pulled him up off the ground, pressed the muzzle of his pistol against his head . . .

. . . and suddenly there was a dark blur of motion. The Zoaf pistol was snatched out of his hand, and Zolqadr was sent flying backward by an iron-like blunt object as if he had been hit by a speeding car. Dazed and with his breath knocked out of his lungs, he struggled to a sitting position and looked up . . .

. . . and saw two figures standing over Buzhazi, clad in dark gray outfits. Their arms, legs, and torsos were covered in some kind of structural framework; they wore thick belts around their waists, large fairings on their shoulders and calves, very largecaliber long weapons resembling oversized sniper's rifles, and large bullet-shaped helmets that completely covered their heads, necks, and shoulders. One figure stood guard, aiming his rifle toward the battalion, while the other attended to Buzhazi.

"Who are you?" Zolqadr shouted. "Who are you?"

The figure with Buzhazi turned to look at the Pasdaran colonel. "Be quiet," the figure said in some sort of electronic voice in Farsi. "This battle is over."

Zolqadr heard a creak and rattle of heavy metal, looked to the west, and smiled. "Not quite, my friend," he said. The figure looked around. One of the Zulfiqar main battle tanks was racing across the desert toward them. Zolqadr started to half-crawl, half-stumble backward as the tank's coaxial machine gun opened fire, and the ground erupted into hundreds of bursts of smoke as the shells hit home. "Looks like your battle is over, bastards!"

But when the shooting paused, Zolqadr was shocked to see . . . the two figures still standing! They had been directly hit by twenty-three-millimeter cannon fire and were still in one piece! Then, the second figure calmly raised his big rifle and fired. There was no recoil and no sound, just a laser-straight line of orange-red fire. The round looked as if it had missed the tank because Zolqadr could see the orange-red line go right past the tank as if the tank was nothing but a desert mirage . . . but the tank suddenly shuddered to a halt as if its driver jammed on the brakes. Seconds later smoke began billowing from the tank, and moments later fire was billowing from several blow-out ports and through melting steel.

"Who are you?" Zolqadr screamed. But the two figures ignored him. The first picked up Buzhazi as easily as if he was a doll and headed toward the Khomeini Library, while the second covered their retreat with the big tank-killing weapon, swiveling it in all directions as if it was weightless as well.

The big figure with the large, unidentified rifle said, "Salam aleikom. Have a nice day, sir," in Farsi to the dazed and confused Pasdaran commander as he walked by.

The cheering inside the Khomeini Library could be heard from half a kilometer away as the two strange figures approached. Men came running out to join their leader. The first gray-clad figure put him down on the ground just inside the walls. "Are you alive, Buzhazi?" he said in Farsi through his electronic speakers.

"Yes, thanks to you," Buzhazi said weakly, still dazed but able to rise up on one knee, then motioning for his men to pull him to his feet. He noticed two more similarly clad and equipped figures entering the compound. "I think I recognize you."

The first figure ignored Buzhazi and turned to the others. "Report," he ordered in English.

"The northwest battalion scattered," another figure responded. "No further contact with them. We downed two Mi-35 Hind attack helicopters attacking from the north; three more turned away toward Qom. Systems reporting sixty-three percent and thirty-five percent ammo."

"The southwest battalion departed as well," another reported. "They have reassembled near the city center about seven klicks away and they are reporting the situation to their headquarters. I count a force of six APCs and one T-72-sized main battle tank. We're at fifty percent power and thirty percent ammo."

"Very well. The west battalion has left the area but appears to be rendezvousing with the southwest survivors," the first figure said. "They had five APCs and a number of men on foot. I still have contact with the mortar team that set up—they're still in place but I haven't detected any rounds headed our way, yet. We can expect some sort of counterattack or probe shortly. Me and the sergeant major are at fifty-seven percent power and seventy percent ammo left. All of you, stop wasting your ammunition. Those aren't machine guns you're firing."

"You are Americans, the so-called Air Battle Force ground units, the ones who helped the Sanusi liberate Libya," Buzhazi said.

The first figure handed his rifle over to his comrade, then quickly removed his helmet, revealing the angry face of a rather young black man. He stepped over to Buzhazi and grasped him by his jacket, pulling him toward him until they were face to face. Buzhazi's men moved as if they were going to help him, but backed away when the other armored figures shifted their weapons to a more threatening port-arms position. "I'll tell you who I am, Buzhazi," the black man spat. "I'm the guy who swore if I ever found you alive I'd twist your head right off your shoulders with my bare hands, orders or no orders to the contrary."

"Briggs," Buzhazi gasped. "Harold Briggs, the American commando and leader of the Tin Men. I thought so." Hal's face was a mask of pure rage. "You still mourn your woman, even though she died as a spy serving her people, trying to assassinate me."

"Go ahead, Buzhazi. Say one more word to me. Give me a reason to rip you limb from limb."

"Sir, let's get the hell out of here," the second figure said.

Briggs tossed Buzhazi out of his hands and into the arms of his men surrounding him. "The message is, General," Briggs said, "that you asked for our help, and you got it. If it was up to me, I'd shove you headfirst into the sand up to your ankles and call it self-defense.

But General McLanahan seems to think you have the ability to turn this country around. Personally I think he's insane, but he thinks differently."

"Tell him thank-you from my men and myself."

"He can hear everything you say and has been monitoring this battle, and he will continue to monitor what you're doing from now on," Briggs said. Buzhazi's eyes drifted up to the sky as if he was searching for the eyes watching them. "He convinced a lot of very powerful people that you were going to bring down the theocratic regime and help stabilize the region. If he's found wrong, he will be extremely embarrassed, and I will take great pleasure in removing the source of that embarrassment—you."

"He shall have no fear—the theocracy will die, or I shall," Buzhazi said. "Iran is done sponsoring death and destruction in the name of the religion of peace. If I am successful, I shall pursue peace with the rest of the world—Arab, Westerner, Zionist, Asian, and European, as well as Persian, I swear it. Again, I thank you for your help."

"We're done helping you, General—we're outta here," Briggs said. "Your promises don't mean shit to me—only your actions matter. Make sure no one tries to follow us east of this place, or we'll come back and finish the Pasdaran's job."

"No one will follow you, I swear."

"Better pray that's so, General. If you have any friends in the regular armed forces who aren't friends with the clerics, I suggest you give them a call and get them out here to give you a hand against any other Pasdaran forces who might try a counterattack. And I've got one more promise for you, General: The next time I come back here, it'll be to finish the job—on you." With that, the four figures ran off, and in the blink of an eye were gone—last seen jumping over the walls of the compound and bounding across the farmlands to the east.

"Those were the American armored commandos you called, sir?" Mansour Sattari asked breathlessly. "But that is impossible! You called them just last night! How could they have gotten out here so quickly?"

Buzhazi stood dumbstruck for a few moments, then shook himself out of his shock and smiled. "I would imagine that's the secret east of here they don't wish to share," he said. "No matter. The Americans did the impossible, and they have delivered to us a miracle and turned the tides in our favor. Now it is time to push forward and take the clerical regime down once and for all!"

It took the team thirty-seven minutes to run twenty miles east of the Khomeini Library—they attracted a lot of incredulous stares from farmers and townspeople, and Hal Briggs was sure there were going to be some frantic phone calls to local gendarmerie, but they continued on without any interference. For safety, they changed their main battery packs for fresh ones before moving into the target area—their batteries were almost depleted, and it would not be prudent to have to defend their destination area with spent batteries installed. Eight miles west of the Kavir Buzurg dry salt marsh and three miles north of a smaller dry lake bed, on the very western edge of the Dasht-e Kavir wastelands, they came across a stretch of paved construction highway in the center of a narrow valley. There were dozens of natural gas wells along the road, and Hal remembered passing a large industrial complex several miles back that had to be the natural gas processing plant for these wells.

In the center of the highway, just east of a bend, sat their objective: an XR-A9 Black Stallion spaceplane, the "magic carpet" that took them from Dreamland to north-central Iran in less than two hours.

"I was starting to get worried, sir," Captain Hunter "Boomer" Noble said as the four Tin Men approached.

"We radioed you we were on our way," Hal said.

"Not about you, sir—I was worried we'd miss lunch back at the Lake," Boomer deadpanned. "Sounds like it went well."

"We got lucky, Boomer," Hal said.

"That Iranian commander sure has balls of steel, eh, General? Not one, not two, but six truck bombs—and he decides he's going to drive one of them? Gutsy."

"The man's a coward, Captain," Hal said acidly. "He probably said he'd drive one because he'd rather die in a blaze of glory than be tortured or killed by the same bastards he trained to torture and kill."

"Still, you gotta admit his timing couldn't have been better. He initiates his attack just before the Pasdaran forms up to attack, and right when you . . ."

"You want to go back there and give him a big wet sloppy one, Captain, go right ahead," Briggs snapped. "Otherwise, let's mount up and get the hell out here. Briggs to McLanahan."

"I've been listening, Hal," Patrick responded via their subcutaneous global transceiver system. "Good job. We see a possible sign of pursuit—several small vehicles heading your way, about fifteen minutes out. No general defense alert yet, just a lot of confused radio traffic from your area, but I expect they'll issue a nationwide mobilization order soon. The regular military's got to get involved sooner or later."

"We'll be out of here in ten, if only your boy Noble would just shut his face for a second," Hal said.

After taking one more security scan of the area to be sure there was no pursuit, the four commandos climbed inside the passenger module in the Black Stallion's cargo bay. Boomer and his copilot started the engines, and in less than ten minutes they were racing down the highway-turned-airstrip and airborne.

"Just airborne, and we're already close to emergency fuel," said the Black Stallion's copilot. The spacecraft flew east, but only long enough to just clear the Alborz Mountain range on the coast of the Caspian Sea, then they headed north, not more than sixty miles east of Tehran.

"No such thing as 'emergency fuel' on this flight, Dr. Page—there's no friendly place to abort to within range," Boomer said. "We either reach the tanker or we jettison the passenger module, then punch out."

"Hey, I signed for this aircraft—no one is 'punching' or 'jettisoning' anything," the copilot, Ann Page, said.

"I second the senator's remark," Hal Briggs said.

"I told you boys to call me 'Ann,'" Page said. "Remember it's costing you a shot of top-shelf tequila at the Bellagio every time you call me something other than 'Ann.'"

"Crossing the coastline now," Boomer said. "The computer will start the pre-contact checklist automatically when we're within fifty miles of the tanker's Mode Four transponder. You can follow along on the MFD if you'd like; the checklist routine will prompt you when you come to a check and response step."

"Computers running checklists . . . what is the world coming to?" Ann mused. "I can't believe I'm saying this, but I feel naked without a library full of paper checklists in a cubby around me."

"You'll get over it, ma'am," Boomer said.

"You owe me another shot of tequila when we get home, Boomer—that's the fifth time you've called me 'ma'am' on this flight," Ann said. "By the time we're back on the ground, I won't have to buy myself another drink long past I retire."

"Double or nothing if I plug the tanker on the first try," Boomer said.

"You're on—and no using any computers," Ann said, laughing. She found it incredibly easy to relax with this crew. Although she sounded like a rookie, Ann Page actually had more miles in space than anyone on board the Black Stallion—in fact, she had three times as many miles in space as all of the men and women who wore astronaut's wings in the U.S. armed services combined.

A native of Springfield, Missouri but a Navy brat who had traveled the world with her father, a nuclear guided missile cruiser skipper who had lost his life in a battle with the Russians in the Persian Gulf over a decade ago, Ann Page had never served in the military but had always been considered just as much a part of the armed forces as anyone who wore a uniform. Thin and athletic, with large green eyes and auburn hair she was unabashedly letting turn gray, Ann could have easily been confused with any female senior general officer—and in fact she was regularly treated as such by military and civilian leaders who knew her.

After receiving several degrees in physics, aeronautical and electrical engineering, and astronautics, Ann became the chief engineer and project manager of the most ambitious and top-secret defense program ever devised: Skybolt, a space-based laser weapon system, installed on Armstrong Space Station, America's first military space station. Originally designed for the Space-Based Radar system for the U.S. Air Force, Armstrong Space Station—nicknamed the "Silver Tower" because of its special silvery coating to protect itself from enemy laser attacks—with its two large electronically scanned radar arrays three times as big as a football field had been expanded and transformed from an unmanned radar array to a manned military space station.

Armstrong and Skybolt's involvement in a Russian invasion of Iran over a decade earlier was crucial, and Ann Page and the station's firebrand commander, Air Force Brigadier-General Jason Saint-Michael, became instant heroes. But the political controversy that arose over the offensive use of Skybolt—it proved to be just as effective as an anti-aircraft and anti-ship weapon as it was a defensive anti-ballistic missile weapon—became too much of a foreign affairs liability for the American administration. Skybolt was canceled, and Armstrong Space Station was converted once again to an unmanned orbiting platform, with only occasional maintenance visits made.

But the end of Skybolt didn't mean the end of Ann Page. She continued to work on a variety of military, government, and even private space projects, becoming universally acknowledged as the Burt Rutan of space travel—any innovation, any new spacecraft, any risky or dangerous mission, and Ann Page was flying it. At the age of forty-eight she was elected to the U.S. Senate from California on a pro-military, pro-space exploration, and strong science education platform, even flying several times in space as a sitting U.S. senator, making speeches to Congress and doing TV talk shows and educational broadcasts to schools from space.

When the United States was hit in a sneak attack by the Russian Air Force and over a dozen air and missile bases had been destroyed, Ann Page decided not to run for re-election, and she disappeared from the world stage. What she actually did was join the U.S. Air Force as a civilian space systems designer and engineer, helping to build the next generation of space-based offensive and defensive weapons to help the United States defend itself better from another sneak attack. She was director of a secret program out of Los Angeles Air Force Base that sought to rebuild and redeploy the Skybolt space-based laser system when Patrick McLanahan asked her to join the Black Stallion program at Dreamland.

As compartmentalized as the Black Stallion project was, she had never heard of it before—but when she did, she instantly agreed to join. She had been involved with the America hypersonic space transportation system years ago, a combination scramjet-rocket-powered craft three times larger than the Black Stallion but with almost the same limited cargo capacity. Rapid and flexible access to space was the biggest challenge with working and defending space, Ann knew, and now they seemed to have the answer: the XR-A9 Black Stallion spaceplane. Not only were two of this beautiful little aircraft actually flying, but she had been asked to be in charge of building and standing up the first air wing of these amazing spaceplanes.

Needless to say, she jumped at the chance to work with McLanahan and the XR-A9—not knowing that her first mission was just days later, where she would have to fly into harm's way. But she was in heaven—back in space, where she belonged, leading a brave bunch of airmen in a race to defend the United States of America, just like before aboard Silver Tower.

Ann heard a soft beep in her helmet and scanned the large supercockpit multi-function display for whatever the ship's computer was trying to tell her. "Is that the tanker?"

"Yep. Acknowledge the alert . . . that's it, hit the F-ten button . . . you got it, and that's the computer running the pre-contact checklist," Boomer said. "Step twenty-one is the first crew-response item. F-ten again to go back to the main . . ." But another beep stopped him short. "Okay, looks like the computer is telling us that our fuel status is outside the safe contact parameters."

"Which means . . . ?"

"We're within five minutes of flame-out by the time we reach the pre-planned contact point, which means we're in deep shit unless we do something," Boomer said. "Okay. I don't think there's time to send a text message to the tanker, so let's go ahead and break radio silence, use the encrypted UHF radio, and get the tanker over here now. Hit F-three for the comm panel . . ." But Ann had already switched over to the proper display. "Aha, good, a fast study. You've got the number one radio."

"Sunshine to Mailman," Ann radioed.

"Check switches," came the reply on the channel, a warning that she was broadcasting in the clear on an open frequency.

"You need to give them the code-word for . . ."

"Screw that, Boomer," Ann said. On the radio again she said, "Mailman, just put the pedal to the metal and get the hell down here now 'cuz we're skosh on gas. You copy?"

There was a slight pause; then: "We copy, Sunshine. Pushing it up." Within five minutes, the fuel warning went away as the tanker accelerated and the rendezvous point moved farther south. Once the two aircraft were twenty-five miles apart, the KC-77 tanker started a left turn heading north along the center of the Caspian Sea, rolling out precisely in front and a thousand feet above the Black Stallion in a picture-perfect point-parallel rendezvous.

"Genesis to Sunshine," Boomer heard on his encrypted satellite transceiver.

"It's God on GUARD," he quipped. "Go ahead, Genesis."

"Just a reminder: don't zoom past the tanker on this one," Patrick McLanahan said. "You'll have one chance to plug him."

"Do I have to have someone back home looking over my shoulder from now on?" he asked.

"That's affirmative, Boomer," Patrick responded. "Get used to it."

"Roger that."

The faster rejoin and precision maneuver was sorely needed, because as the refueling nozzle made contact with the XR-A9's receptacle, the "FUEL CRITICAL" indication sounded again—they had less than ten minutes' worth of fuel remaining. "Mailman has contact," Boomer and Ann heard through the boom intercom.

"Sunshine has contact and shows fuel flow," Ann acknowledged. "You're a very welcome sight, boys. Drinks are on me back home."

"We're a Cabernet crew, ma'am," the tanker pilot said.

"The copilot doesn't like being called 'ma'am,'" Boomer said. "Now you owe her a shot."

"The tanker crew's money's no good in any bar I'm sitting in," Ann said. "Just keep the gas coming."

Hunter Noble rejoined with the tanker once more to top off, turned east over the Caspian Sea, and blasted the Black Stallion over Kazakhstan.

"Boomer, I'm altering your flight plan for your return," Patrick radioed. "Instead of heading southeast and doing two orbits to line up for landing back at Dreamland, I'm going to have you go north direct for home. I want the Black Stallion turned and ready for another mission ASAP."

"Fine with me, sir," the aircraft commander replied. He called up the flight plan being datalinked to his flight control computers and made sure it was being properly received and processed.

"You sure you want to do this, General?" Ann Page asked. "This takes us directly over Russia. We're only at forty thousand feet now. According to the flight plan we'll still be below one hundred K and Mach five when we cross the border."

"I know—that's well within the lethal envelope of Russian SAMs," Patrick said. "There's only one known SA-12B brigade in our flight path, near Omsk. You'll be at one hundred sixty K altitude and Mach five point one and accelerating when you get close to the known missile batteries. Missile flight time is at least ninety seconds. With that much time you should be out of the missile's envelope by the time it reaches you."

Boomer looked at the rear-view monitor in the cockpit and saw Ann Page looking at him through the camera, the doubt evident in both their eyes. "Cutting it awfully close, aren't you, General?" she asked.

"The problem is initiating the return over Kazakhstan and the lack of secure recovery bases in the north," Patrick responded. Many of the military air bases in Alaska, Washington State, Montana, Wyoming, and North Dakota were destroyed by the Russian Air Force four years earlier—it would be many years, possibly even decades, before they were inhabitable again. "Flying south over safer territory means an extra orbit, which reduces your reserves, which means bringing you down early at a civilian airfield near Seattle, Vancouver, or Calgary. I'll do it if necessary, but I'd like to have you land at a military base if possible.

"My calculations show you'll be out of the SA-12 envelope by the time the missile reaches you—it'll be close, but you'll be out," Patrick went on. "If they fire the less-capable A-model missile or don't react very quickly you'll be even safer, but you'll be OK even going against the B-model SA-12 fired within seconds of coming in range. As always, the final decision is up to you guys. I've already put you through a lot on this mission."

"I'll say," Boomer muttered on intercom.

"Unfortunately, you only have a few more seconds to decide," Patrick said.

"Figures." He clicked on the radio: "Stand by, General." He looked at the rear cockpit monitor again into his mission commander's eyes. "What do you say, Ann?" he asked on intercom.

"I know McLanahan by reputation only—he hired me to help with the program just a few days ago, and I've only met with him twice," she said. "I know he has a reputation of doing what he thinks best, which is not necessarily what his superior officers want."

"Checks."

"But he also has a reputation of getting the job done and looking out for the men and women under him. I know everybody blames him for inciting the Russians to attack us and kill thousands of people, but I believe it was because Gryzlov was a nut-case, not because of what McLanahan did, which was protecting his forces from another attack."

"I don't know much about what McLanahan did to piss off Gryzlov," Boomer admitted, "but I do know that McLanahan kicked the Russians' butt pretty good afterward. He knows what he's doing. And he's definitely not a glory-hound. I've seen the man's office in the White House—the janitor has a nicer work environment."

"So you trust him."

"I trust him."

"Same here."

"Maybe they'll write that on our headstones, huh?" Ann did not respond. "General Briggs? What do you say, sir?"

"We're just passengers back here, Captain," Hal Briggs replied. "Whatever you do is fine with us."

"Not on my ship it's not," Boomer said. "Everyone gets a say."

"I'm all for getting home earlier," Briggs said. "I've put my life in General McLanahan's hands for most of my military career, and he's never let me down yet. I don't think he will this time either."

"The rest of you guys agree?"

"Affirmative, sir," Master Sergeant Chris Wohl replied immediately. The other Tin Men responded likewise.

"We who are about to fry salute you, General McLanahan," Boomer deadpanned. He clicked open the radio channel: "We're ready to activate the new flight plan, sir."

"Very good. See you back at the barn. Good luck."

"I wish he hadn't said that last thing," Boomer muttered. He recalled the flight plan and pressed the "ACTIVATE" soft button on his multi-function display. The flight control computer immediately entered the countdown for igniting the Laser Pulse Detonation Rocket System, and he and Ann had to scramble to complete the pre-programmed countdown holds on time before their flight path window closed on them. Within seconds the engines rumbled to life, and they accelerated quickly and blasted skyward at a very steep climb angle. At Mach three and sixty thousand feet, the computer altered course, and they headed almost directly north toward the Russian border.

"Unidentified aircraft, unidentified aircraft, one hundred and fifty kilometers south of Omsk, this is Russian air defense sector headquarters," they heard moments later. "Warning, you are entering the Russian air defense identification zone. Respond immediately on any emergency frequency."

"Not too late to turn around," Ann said.

"In four seconds it will be," Boomer said. "Suborbital burn commencing in three . . . two . . . one . . ." Seconds later the airspeed indicator clicked past Mach four, and the three remaining LPDRS engines kicked on.

"Warning, warning, warning, unidentified aircraft approaching Omsk, you are in violation of Russian sovereign airspace," the warning messages on all of the emergency channels declared. "Turn right and reverse course immediately or you will be fired upon without further warning. Acknowledge on any emergency frequency. Over." The messages continued in Russian and Chinese, then repeated.

Moments later the threat warning receiver announced, "Warning, warning, air defense search radar locked on, three o'clock, one hundred miles, SA-12 . . . warning, warning, missile tracking detected, SA-12, four o'clock, eighty miles . . . warning, warning, missile launch, SA-12, five o'clock, seventy-five miles . . ."

"Pedal to the metal, Boomer," Ann Page said.

"Eat my exhaust, Russkies," Boomer said confidently—but he did keep a close watch on both the airspeed readouts and the threat display.

"We're right on the edge of its envelope," Ann Page said. "We should be able to fly away from it here in a second."

Sure enough, a few moments later: "Warning, warning, missile tracking, SA-12, six o'clock, eighty miles . . . warning, missile tracking, SA-12, one hundred miles . . ." Finally, as the Black Stallion continued its climb and gradual acceleration, the warning indications went away.

"Never outran a Russian SAM before!" Boomer exclaimed. "Incredible!"

"The hotline is already heating up," Patrick McLanahan radioed a few minutes later. "Russia is already complaining about your overflight."

"Do we care today, sir?" Boomer asked.

"Not particularly."

Boomer took the spaceplane right up to three hundred and sixty thousand feet, above most of the atmosphere, then throttled back and stabilized the airspeed at Mach nine. "We'll start the descent in eighty-three minutes, everyone," he said. "Check your oxygen, check your buddy, and report in when the station check's done."

"Everyone's good back here," Hal Briggs said from inside the passenger module. "We had to wake 'the Kid' up to do his safety check—the guy can sleep in the middle of a typhoon." "The Kid," U.S. Army First Lieutenant Russ Marz, was the Battle Force ground ops team's newest and youngest member, and Hal had taken "The Kid" under his wing—probably, Patrick had surmised, because he was very much like Hal himself when he was twenty years younger.

The time went quickly. In less than an hour they had crossed the entire width of Russia and the Arctic Ocean, and the coast of North America was in sight a few minutes later. "The computer has started the pre-descent checklist, everyone," Boomer announced. "We're going to do a one point five G descent profile this time instead of three so NORAD won't think we're another Russian cruise missile sneak attack, and I'd like to keep the belly cool in case we have to do a quick-turn and launch again. Keep ahead of the plane and G-forces and sing out in case you're having any problems. I'd like you all to . . ."

Suddenly the threat warning receiver blared, "Warning, warning, target tracking radar, two o'clock, one thousand three hundred fifty miles."

"What did it say?" Boomer remarked. "I've never heard of any radar tracking at that kind of . . ."

"Warning, warning, warning, laser spike, laser spike . . . warning, warning, warning, emergency cooling circuit activated . . . warning, spot hull temperature increasing, station three hundred . . . warning, spot hull temperature increasing, station three-eighty . . . warning, warning, warning, hull temperature reaching critical, station four-twenty . . ."

"What in heck is going on?" Ann Page asked.

"I don't know, but we're going to melt here in a second," Boomer said. He immediately disconnected the autopilot and rolled the Black Stallion hard left using the control thrusters.

"What are you doing, Boomer?"

"We're getting a sudden uneven heating of a small section of the fuselage," he replied. "I don't know what's happening, but I need to expose a different part of the fuselage to whatever that heat source is and give the emergency cooling system a chance to bring the temps down, or it'll fail. General, are you reading this?"

"Just keep turning, Boomer," Patrick McLanahan radioed. "Don't stop maneuvering. We're analyzing the information now." And then they heard him say under his breath, "My God, I don't believe it. They couldn't possibly have done it . . ."

"Warning, warning, laser spike, laser spike . . . warning, warning, spot hull temperature rising, station . . .

warning, warning, hull temperature reaching critical, station one-forty . . ."

"Boomer! Keep rolling!" Patrick radioed frantically. "As hard as you can! Don't worry about depleting thruster fuel now! Move!" Boomer rolled the spaceplane hard to the right, nearly going inverted . . .

. . . and then he saw it—a bright orange-blue dot on the horizon with the familiar shimmering three-dimensional texture of collimated laser light. "We're being hit by a laser—a big mother laser hot enough to almost burn through our heat shields!" he shouted. At that instant, it winked out. "Did you see that, Ann?"

"No—I was too busy praying we wouldn't turn into a shooting star."

"We saw it down here, Boomer," Patrick said. "It's something I prayed we'd never see again . . . but it's back, and it's operational."

CHAPTER 3

QOM, IRAN

Later That Day

A flight of three Mi-35 attack helicopters swooped in from the west in perfect formation. As two helicopters hovered and took up a protective position, the third landed just a hundred meters from the outer wall of the Ruhollah Khomeini Library and shut down its engines. A general officer and three bodyguards stepped out moments later. They carefully surveyed the outer walls of the library compound; then, one of the bodyguards made a radio call, and the two hovering attack helicopters moved away and out of sight.

As the general waited, a captured armored personnel carrier emerged from the library compound and drove out to him. The general's bodyguards had assault rifles and grenade launchers at the ready, but the general did not try to take cover, standing defiantly, almost impatiently, fists on his hips.

Hesarak al-Kan Buzhazi emerged from the APC with Mansour Sattari and three bodyguards of his own surrounding him. He saluted the newcomer, and the general returned the salute. Both men were silent for a few long moments; then General Hoseyn Yassini, chief of staff of the Iranian armed forces, said, "Well well, Hesarak, it seems you have been quite busy lately." Buzhazi said nothing. The officer looked at the men assembled behind Buzhazi, nodding to Sattari. "Hello, Mansour. Quite the daring raid you pulled at Doshan Tappeh. That'll teach the Pasdaran not to be so cocksure next time, eh? Think you taught them a little lesson?"

"I hope so, sir," Sattari said, nodding respectfully.

"Unfortunately you didn't use the opportunity to get out of the country with your hides intact," Yassini said. "Instead, you decided to throw in with the general's plan to . . ." He turned to Buzhazi: "What, Hesarak? What's the plan? Where do you go from here?"

Buzhazi took a thick packet of files from Sattari and handed them to Yassini. "Copies of the evidence we've gathered from Orumiyeh," he said, "proving that Badi ordered the conspiracy to attack the base and kill Iranian soldiers with Pasdaran forces disguised as Kurdish rebels in order to discredit the Internal Defense Force and further his own political ambitions."

Yassini took the files but didn't look at them. Keeping his eyes on Buzhazi, he dropped the files to the ground beside him. "You are too funny, Hesarak," he said, shaking his head with a wry smile. "Don't bullshit a bullshitter. Are you seriously trying to tell me all this is just you wanting to get back at that worthless piece of walking crap Muhammad Badi for concocting that ridiculous plan to discredit your precious Basij? It was obvious to everyone with half a brain in Tehran what happened in Orumiyeh. Do you expect what's in that folder to make one bit of difference for what you've done in the past few days?"

He shook his head. "Hesarak, you magnificent idiot, if you had just stopped with killing Badi and escaping from Doshan Tappeh, you'd have become a legend in the Iranian military," he said. "Hundreds of very powerful and influential men would have silently cheered for you, including some who could have pardoned you after a short stay in Anzali Prison. Badi got too powerful and pried into too many personal affairs—you just saved some other poor bastard from having to do the job. You could have even escaped to Syria or Yemen—hell, man, I probably would've helped you get out of the country! You'd be living like a prince in charge of some sheikh's personal security detail." He looked at the walls of the Khomeini Library compound. "But then you did . . . this. Strategically clever, I must say. If you were going for maximum shock value to the clerics in Tehran, you couldn't have picked a better spot. Foolhardy, but clever."

" 'Shock value' had nothing to do with it, Hoseyn," Buzhazi said. "Are you blind, or just preferring to act the obedient, brainless soldier? Don't you see what the clerical regime has done to our country? The Pasdaran is out of control. There are Pasdaran troops stationed in dozens of countries from Morocco to Malaysia, and they are running al-Quds death squads in every corner of the globe. The Pasdaran has nuclear weapons, long-range ballistic missiles, submarines, and long-range bombers. For what? Some dead cleric's idea of a global Persian empire? The return of the caliphate? This is the twenty-first century, for God's sake."

"Listen to you, Hesarak—fretting about empire and caliphates and political intrigue." Yassini laughed. "Twelve years ago you were the clerics' toughest supporter. You were ready to take on the United States of America in the Persian Gulf in support of the government—the very same government we have today!"

"I was blind and stupid back then," Buzhazi said.

"Perhaps—but when they took the opportunity to get support from China, they abandoned your grand plan. That's what you're angry about, isn't it? So which is it, Hesarak—do you truly feel the government is headed in the wrong direction, or do you just want revenge on them?" He waited for an answer; when one wasn't forthcoming, he went on: "Do you think you've changed anything, Hesarak? There's an interim government already in place, and I guarantee they'll be tougher and more bloodthirsty than the current ones. I've already spoken to the acting president and defense ministers, and they want action."

"We'll see what kind of stomach they have for fighting."

"You're insane, Hesarak, insane," Yassini chuckled. "Look, my friend, I think you've made your point here. The best thing you can do now is to get out and survive. I don't know if what you've begun will lead to the downfall of the clerics, but alive and in exile in some other country will be better for your supporters and your cause than being dead and forgotten. Take your impressive victories and get out, while you can."

"What is it you want, Hoseyn?"

"Simple: I want the hostages," Yassini said.

"Because then you'll be the hero, their savior, right?"

"What the hell do you care, Hesarak?" Yassini asked perturbedly. He shrugged, then said, "Their precious Pasdaran couldn't save them—maybe if I lead them out of there and back to Tehran, they'll think more of the regular armed forces and less of their ideological goon squads, and restore the military to its proper role."

"So you do believe the Pasdaran is misguided and out of control."

"I believe in me, Hesarak, and the forces under my command," Yassini snapped. "Exacting your revenge on the Pasdaran is your battle, not mine. I'm here to protect my country and my government from all enemies, and right now that includes you. If the Pasdaran can't stop you, it's my duty to make sure the job gets done."

Buzhazi nodded, falling silent. The two men looked at each other carefully, sizing up each other's words and mannerisms. Then Buzhazi said, "Let's get down to it, Hoseyn."

"Whatever you say, Hesarak," Yassini said. "This deal is between you and me. Tehran thinks I'm coming down here tomorrow morning to take personal command of the forces that will pry you out of Qom, dead or alive. I'm here early and without the interim Supreme Defense Council's notice or authority as a colleague, a fellow soldier of Iran, and someone who has learned and studied under you and now has the opportunity to repay you for your dedicated years of service to our country.

"Let us speak like men and warriors, Hesarak," Yassini went on, pointing to his right eye, a symbol that he was pledging to tell the truth. "The Pasdaran number approximately one hundred and fifty thousand. You have taken perhaps three percent of that number out of action—an impressive feat, but not nearly enough for your mission to succeed. You and I both know this to be true.

"You may get some regular army soldiers and perhaps even some Pasdaran to join you, but how many? Five thousand? Ten thousand at the very most? Even if you get fifteen thousand to join you, you are still outnumbered almost ten to one. You cannot hope to win, my friend. It is a simple numbers game. The Pasdaran may not be the best infantry fighters in the world, but they don't have to be—the numbers are against you. You could be the greatest battlefield commander on Iranian soil since Alexander the Great, but even he had a massive army and access to all the supplies his forces needed. You have neither.

"Here is what I propose, Hesarak, and if you were smart and truly cared for the soldiers in that compound, you would accept immediately," Yassini went on. "You must release the clerics and politicians you hold hostage. That is nonnegotiable. I trust you have not harmed them—they are politicians and may be your ideological adversaries, but they are not combatants. You are too honorable of a soldier to harm unarmed noncombatants."

"And the second step?"

"There is no second step today, Hesarak," Yassini said. "Release the hostages to me. As you can see, I have no army behind me—yet. In twelve hours I'll have one special ops brigade ready to go, with another on the way. By dawn I will present my assault plan to the interim Supreme Defense Council for approval, and shortly after that I will begin to retake the Khomeini Library by force. If you or anyone else still in that compound tries to resist when I come in, I'll slaughter every last one of you."

"What about the Pasdaran in Qom?"

"My plan only involves the regular army and air force, not the Pasdaran," Yassini said. "I think after their earlier debacle they'll be happy to turn over this operation to the army. They'll stay away from this part of the province—I can guarantee it."

"So you don't like the Pasdaran either," Buzhazi observed. "You think they're corrupt and ineffectual, as I do."

"The Pasdaran will fall because of their own mistakes and blind ideological allegiances, not because I'm fighting them," Yassini said. "As incompetent as I think they are, I'm not stupid enough to take them on directly, like you."

"So you'll simply let us escape?"

"I have no idea what you are doing or where you go, Hesarak, because officially I'm not here," Yassini said. "All I know is that any of your forces still in that compound by tomorrow afternoon will be either dead or my prisoner."

Buzhazi was silent for a few moments, then nodded his head. "I understand, Hoseyn," he said. "I thank you for your fairness and honesty."

"Don't thank me, General—just get the hell out of here. Go to France; go to South America; go to Indonesia, I don't care, but just go. Don't ever come back. You're an old man—let the younger men fight. Become their inspirational leader from the comfort of a secure hideout someplace where the Pasdaran or their death squads can't reach you, or at least you can see them coming. Just don't set foot in Iran ever again, because if I'm still in charge of the armed forces—which I fully intend to be—I'll bury your bullet-ridden body so deeply in the desert that it'll take scientists a millennia to find your bones."

"I understand your warning, Hoseyn."

"You'd better do more than that, Hesarak."

"And I have a word of warning for you, my friend: keep the gates of your bases locked and guarded, and don't let anyone in—especially Pasdaran," Buzhazi said. "Don't go back to Tehran or the Ministry of Defense—I suggest the alternate command center at Mashhad or someplace where Pasdaran forces aren't heavily concentrated. Whether I'm dead or alive, whoever is in charge of the regular army will be blamed for everything I've done. Protect yourselves at all times. Trust no one."

"You don't have to worry about me, General—worry about yourself. Get out while you still can. This is my final warning."

Buzhazi nodded again, then saluted. Yassini shook his head, puzzled and amused by the older officer's weird schizophrenic personality swings between seemingly sociopathic mania and by-the-book military bearing, but he returned the salute. As Buzhazi turned and started walking to his armored car, he added, "And Hesarak? Remember, don't harm one hair on those old men's heads, or all bets are off." His voice got louder and more strident as Buzhazi continued to walk away. "Understand me, Hesarak? Not one hair mussed up, or they'll be after both our skins." But Buzhazi and

Sattari returned to their vehicle with their bodyguards and were gone without saying another word.

"Sorry son of a bitch," Yassini mused. "It'll be too bad to see that proud old neck stretched at the end of a rope, but that's what he's destined for." He waved for his bodyguards to return to the helicopter. He chased the pilot out of his seat and strapped himself in, preferring not to think of the meeting with Buzhazi but to concentrate on something else for a while—time enough to think about how he was going to get those clerics and politicians out of the Khomeini Library alive once he got back to Mehrabad. Flying was always a good way to help him clear his mind before making tough decisions.

"Do you think he believed you, sir?" Yassini's aide asked through the helicopter's intercom.

"I don't know, but I think so," the chief of staff said as he prepared to start engines. "It doesn't matter. If he goes or stays and fights, the status of those hostages is the important factor. If he's harmed them, the replacement clerics and the Pasdaran survivors will engineer the bloodiest purge in the history of the entire country. That's why tonight's raid is important—we need the element of surprise if we have any hopes of saving those men. For our sake as well as the country's, we need to win this one."

"Has Buzhazi given any indication he's harmed them, sir?"

"He's too honorable to kill unarmed civilians," Yassini said. "He might use them as bait or bargaining chips for his men, but he won't kill them. What's the status of the deployment?"

"Ahead of schedule as of the last report, about a half-hour ago," the aide responded. "Airborne infantry regiment Avenger is staging at Mehrabad as briefed. They'll drop three waves of three companies each of paratroopers inside and outside the compound via high-altitude low-opening parachute insertion. The Fifty-first special operations battalion will drop in by helicopter minutes later from Hamadan, followed by the rest of Fifteenth Brigade by armored vehicle and truck. They should be on the move from Esfahan now and will be in position in three hours outside Qom."

"I want to speak with each brigade commander personally and get assurances that they won't come anywhere near the compound unless he is dead on force timing," Yassini said. "Timing is essential. I want five hundred troops to suddenly appear inside that compound in the same room where those hostages are as if they appeared out of thin air. The Fifteenth especially will blow this entire operation if they're spotted by Buzhazi's scouts before the rest of the strike force is in position."

"Understood, sir. I'll notify the brigade commanders to stand by for a conference."

Yassini started engines, completed the pre-liftoff checklist, and had just lifted off and pedal-turned the helicopter to the south to pick up a little forward speed when he heard a voice on the Iranian air force's emergency frequency, which all aircraft constantly monitored: "General Yassini."

"Is that Buzhazi?" Yassini asked angrily. "What in hell does he want?" He switched over to the emergency channel. "Is that you, Buzhazi? I'm done talking with you. You have my final words. Comply with my instructions or face the consequences."

"You sounded so impassioned and so reasonable, General—I just wanted to tell you again how impressed I was by your words," Buzhazi said. "No one else would have ever guessed that you were lying through your teeth the whole time."

Beads of sweat popped out on Yassini's forehead, his mouth turned instantly dry, and his finger trembled a bit as he pressed the microphone switch on his control stick: "What are you talking about, Buzhazi?" he radioed back.

"The Avenger regiment, the airborne infantry regiment you secretly deployed to Mehrabad? They won't be joining you in Qom tonight. Neither will the Fifty-first."

Yassini set the big Mi-35 helicopter back down on the ground so hard that the crewmembers were bounced several inches off their seats. "Say again, Hesarak?" he asked over the radio.

"We've only gained about three thousand men—like you said, Hoseyn, we're still heavily outnumbered by the Pasdaran," Buzhazi went on, "but the new recruits are bringing a few Antonov transports, about twelve helicopters, a bunch of armored vehicles, and some supplies with them. A journey of a thousand miles starts with one step, as some Chinese philosopher once said."

Yassini hurriedly switched to intercom. "Call Tehran and find out what in hell's going on in Mehrabad!" he ordered. He forced calm into his voice. "I'm warning you, Hesarak," he said, "that if you attempt to use those traitors to help you escape from the Khomeini Library, a lot of Iranian soldiers are going to die."

"Don't worry, Hoseyn—I'm already out of the library," Buzhazi said. "I left while you were trying to fly your big bad helicopter around out there—you used to be a good stick, but I see your skills have faded. I recommend you don't try to follow me—we still had a few shoulder-fired anti-aircraft missiles around."

"You're . . . out?" Yassini gasped. His mind spun furiously; then he turned to his aide and shouted, "Get every man you can find—local police, construction workers, farmers . . . I don't care, anyone except the Pasdaran, and get them over to that library compound!" he ordered. "Then call on the discrete command channel and get every available air or infantry unit out here immediately. Do it quickly, but do it quietly. Those Pasdaran units must not know what is happening." He realized that it was very possible for Buzhazi's radio broadcasts to be intercepted by the Pasdaran as well, but he hoped the remnants of Zolqadr's brigade hadn't had time or thought about organizing an intelligence-gathering detail yet. He turned back to the radio: "Hesarak, what have you done with the hostages? Where are they? Over."

"Hoseyn, they were nothing but scum, the twisted filthy corrupted dredges of Muslim extremism," Buzhazi radioed. "Don't bother trying to put together a rescue mission for them—they're not worth the effort. I would recommend that you radio your remaining forces and advise them to lock themselves in their garrisons in full protective defensive posture, because the Pasdaran and their al-Quds thugs will be out looking to avenge the clerics on anyone they deem a threat to their continued existence. They'll hunt down and murder the regular army before you have the chance to stop them, and they'll claim they're bringing the guilty to justice."

"Hesarak . . . my God, what have you done?"

"Better yet, Hoseyn, come join us," Buzhazi said. "Don't wait for the Pasdaran to come hunting for you—join my freedom fighters and help me eliminate those corrupt bloodthirsty warmongers from the face of the planet. It's the only way to guarantee not only your survival, but the survival of our country and our race. Otherwise, you know as well as I the Pasdaran will not stop until they've secured ultimate power for themselves once again."

Yassini looked back outside the helicopter and saw several vehicles racing in his direction—they did not appear to be Pasdaran, thank God. "Listen to me, Hesarak," he radioed, "whatever you do, don't go on a rampage and start a killing spree in this country. The only way to keep this under control is to take command . . . you and I. Let's do it together. We'll take what's left of the government, weed out the radicals, and start fresh. Let's meet, Hesarak. Over."

There was a long pause. Yassini waved at the newcomers, gesturing frantically toward the compound. "Get in there!" he shouted. "Find whoever's being held captive in there and get them out! Hurry!"

"Hoseyn?"

"Hesarak, meet me"—he thought furiously—"in the Esplanade," Yassini said. "We need to march off a few. Acknowledge if you understand. Over."

There was another pause; then: "Here's my acknowledgement, Hoseyn. Out."

"Shit!" Yassini cursed. He gestured even more emphatically to the helpers to get inside quicker . . .

. . . but he ducked and covered instinctively as four massive, brilliant balls of light erupted from the Khomeini Library, followed moments later by four tremendous explosions that knocked Yassini clear off his feet and set the helicopter rocking on its wheels so violently he thought it might flip upside down. The blasts were followed by strings of smaller explosions. When he looked up, he saw several large mushroom clouds of smoke and fire billowing from the library, with massive columns of flames rolling skyward. It took several minutes for the clouds of smoke and fire to travel vertically instead of in all directions—and when they did, he saw that the entire compound had been leveled, with only blackened and crumpled skeletal outlines of the mosque and library buildings remaining.

ELLIOTT AIR FORCE BASE, GROOM LAKE, NEVADA

That Same Time

"Dave, I need a full analysis of the Kavaznya region—military deployment, infrastructure, construction projects, the works," Patrick ordered. At that moment, Colonel Martin Tehama, the commander of the High Technology Aerospace Weapons Center, entered the battle staff area and stood stiffly before Patrick's console, almost at parade rest. He was wearing his service dress blue uniform, not a utility or short-sleeved service uniform as was customary at Dreamland. "The damned Kavaznya laser just fired on the Black Stallion."

"I'm already on it, Muck," Dave Luger, seated beside Patrick, said breathlessly. "My God . . . how could they have rebuilt that facility without us knowing about it?"

"We thought the Russians were knocked on their asses following our bomber attacks," Patrick said. "We got too overconfident. Plus we were too concerned about rebuilding our own strategic military forces to watch over them. We never thought of looking at the Russian Far East—we thought they'd be concentrating on shoring up their military forces in the West."

"You forgot one thing, sir—you were just too damned cocky to pay attention to anything else but your own pet projects," Tehama interjected acidly.

Dave Luger's eyes bulged first in surprise, then in sheer anger. "As you were, Colonel!" he snapped.

Patrick showed little reaction to Tehama's comments. "I heard you got an assignment, Colonel," he commented.

"I finished outprocessing just now," Tehama said. "Since you showed up I haven't had much to do, so I thought I'd put in a few phone calls and redeem a few favors. I report to my new assignment next week."

"I'm sure you'll do fine . . . wherever it is you're going," Patrick said. He briefly looked up from his console, saw the expression on Tehama's face, and shook his head. "But you are just dying to tell me something first, aren't you?"

Tehama glanced quickly at McLanahan, then caged his eyes away again. "I'll save it for my report to General Edgewater at Materiel Command. But I did want to advise you that I will make it clear that you diverted that Black Stallion flight against all established HAWC directives about overflying hostile territory, and that you did so against my advice and without my authorization."

"Noted."

Tehama glanced at McLanahan in disbelief. "General, what's with you?" he asked finally. "You risked those men's lives for no reason. I don't get it."

"The reason you don't 'get it,' Colonel, is the reason you're leaving here today."

"I don't understand it . . . I don't understand you . . . any of you," Tehama sputtered. "Do the lives of these men mean so little to you?"

"I don't think this is the time to discuss this . . ."

"No, go ahead, General—I've got time," Tehama said. "Explain it to me. It might help me make some sense of the twisted mind-boggling bullshit atmosphere you've created in this place and in these people." He motioned around the room. "What is all this? You have a battle staff area at Dreamland. What's up with that? We're a research base, for God's sake—except the planes are never around long enough to do any research on them because you or someone under you keeps on requisitioning them. Our budget is blown all to hell with your secret operations. Now one of our most classified, highest priority, most expensive aircraft has been hit by a Russian laser, and with good reason—you authorized them to fly over hostile airspace! Do you want to get those men killed?"

"Colonel, if you don't get it after being here for three years, you never will," Patrick said. "You're dismissed." It was obvious that Tehama really, really wanted to tell Patrick off, but he snapped to attention, then turned on a heel and exited the room.

"Can you believe the balls on that guy, mouthing off like that?" Dave Luger asked.

"There's only one reason he'd have the guts to do that—his new boss has more than three stars," Patrick said.

"Hal can find out who that is in no time."

"It'll be easier to just assume he's been reporting on our activities to our biggest opponents . . ."

"SECDEF and Senator Barbeau, among many others."

"Might not be enough to get him in legal trouble," Patrick said, "but enough to fill in the details to any bureaucrat or politician who doesn't have the entire picture on what we do at Dreamland." He thought for a moment, then nodded to Dave. "Have Hal find out anyway."

"My pleasure, sir," Dave said with a smile.

THE WHITE HOUSE PRESS ROOM, WASHINGTON, D.C.

A Short Time Later

"Good morning," White House Press Secretary Anthony Lewars said curtly as he stood before the members of the White House Press Corps in the newly refurbished press briefing room. Unlike many of the recent White House press secretaries who came from the media or public relations, Lewars, a tall, bald, broad-shouldered, mean-looking veteran combat officer, was a former Marine Aircraft Wing commander, and he ran the White House press offices as tightly as he did his combat air units. Although he wore a suit and not a uniform, he still looked every bit the hard-as-nails combat veteran he was. “The President is scheduled to meet with the delegation from the Association of South East Asian Nations in the Oval Office to discuss oil and trade policy, and will then travel to Wilmington, Delaware to address the American Bar Association convention luncheon. He’ll return to the White House sometime this afternoon and meet with several state political delegations to discuss campaign travel schedules. He’ll meet with the national security staff later on this afternoon for a detailed briefing on events in the Middle East. He remains in close contact with his national security staff at all times and receives constant updates.

“The President has been fully briefed on the incident in Qom, Iran, but most of the information the White House has received has been through unverified Middle East news sources,” Lewars went on brusquely. “The President reiterates that his main desire is peace, stability, and democracy in the entire region, and indeed the entire world, and the United States stands ready to assist any group that stands for the very same things.” He made a few brief remarks on several other matters, then closed his briefing folder and offered, “Questions.”

The questions came rapid-fire, but Lewars was accustomed to dealing with lots of panicked, babbling individuals, and he waded through the Q&A with a distracted, almost detached indifference—most times he did not even look at the questioner, but shuffled his notes without expression or gestures. It was a lot like watching grass grow. "Is there a coup taking place in Iran, General?" one reporter blurted out. "Are we going to war?"

"No one's going to war. We don't know the details yet. It could be Kurdish rebels, anti-clerical insurgents, or a Sunni Muslim retaliation against the Shi'ite dominated theocratic regime."

"Does the President want to see the Ahmadad government or the clerical regime fall?"

"I refer you to my earlier remarks," Lewars said, almost spitting the words. Then, deciding he'd better tell them rather than leaving it up to their powers of recall: "The President wants peace, stability, and democracy. The President doesn't agree with or endorse the Iranian way of picking candidates for office—basically the Ayatollah Shīrāzemi picks the candidate he wants, and the Council of Guardians rubber-stamps their approval and pulls any other candidates off the ballot. The people have no say. That said, the fact remains that Ahmadad was put in power peacefully and constitutionally, as flawed as their electoral process is.

"As far as a military uprising, rebellion, or whatever might transpire in Iran: again, any such action usually doesn't contribute to peace, stability, and democracy, and so President Martindale views such violent actions as undesirable for the people of Iran, their neighbors, customers, and other interested persons and powers in the Middle East. The President believes that military coups take power away from the people by force of arms."

"But if the clerical regime is deposed, even if by force of arms, and is replaced by a regime friendlier to the West . . . ?"

"That's speculation. We don't have the facts." He left that reporter a dark scowl and glanced at another, then resumed taking notes, head down, not making eye contact with anyone. "You. Question."

"There are reports that the United States sent a special operations team inside Iran to assist the rebellion. Comment, General?"

"That report did not originate within this administration, so I can't comment on it."

"So you're denying it?"

"I said I can't comment on it."

"General, 'no comment' is not an answer," the reporter persisted. "I understand if you don't want to confirm or deny it, but you must have some comment.

Either you don't know or you refuse to say, but you can't just . . ."

"Excuse me . . . Mr. Richland of the *Sun,* correct?" Lewars said, looking up from his notes and impaling the reporter with a deadly asphalt-melting stare. "Let me make myself crystal clear to you: I don't have the time or the inclination to comment on rumors, innuendo, guesses, or anything but the Administration's official statements. If you want to fantasize, go back to writing about endangered snail darters and Alaskan caribou." He waited for the reporter to say something in return, but the reporter tried to appear busy writing notes and didn't return Lewars's glare, so he turned to the other side of the press briefing room. "You. Go."

"Would President Martindale ever send any military forces into Iran to assist any opposition or insurgent groups take over the clerical regime?"

"Again, I cannot comment on every hypothetical situation thrown at me. However, I can say that in my conversations with the President he has never indicated any willingness or desire to support any military opposition or insurgent groups in Iran. He has expressed his desire for peace, stability, and democracy in all nations of the world who oppress and repress their citizens, and he wants to do anything he can to help those nations fight off their oppressors and build a better society and government for their people. But it must be done pursuant to the inalienable rights of life, liberty, and the pursuit of happiness, in the context of a peaceful, democratic framework established by the people, their representatives, and the rule of law. Next."

"General, the Russian embassy called several media outlets and complained that the United States was illegally flying manned spaceplanes over their sovereign airspace without permission. Any truth to this complaint?"

"We receive hundreds of complaints every day from the Russians ranging from illegal fishing to playing music too loudly at our embassy parties," Lewars said, again without looking up and without any change or inflection in his voice—but unseen was the sweat prickling out around his collar. "No matter how many trivial or just plain bogus complaints we get, the State Department fully investigates each and every one."

"But you're not denying an illegal overflight took place?"

"Every complaint filed by any person or nation is investigated. When the investigation is over we'll reveal the results. Until then, we keep quiet about it. Thanks to you good folks in the media, sometimes mere accusations carry the weight of outright guilt if overpublicized. Don't you agree?"

"Is it the Air Force's new hypersonic bomber, General? Is the Pentagon overflying Russia with a new bomber?"

"We don't comment on the movement of any military or government vehicles. Aircraft, spacecraft, and surface vessels of all kinds transit sovereign airspace all the time. The Russians send a dozen spy satellites a day over the United . . ."

"This is the second such complaint by the Russians this month," the reporter insisted. "They claim they have proof we are conducting illegal espionage and harassment missions over their country."

"I haven't seen their proof or any formal diplomatic protests. Until I do, it's speculation. Next."

"General, rumor has been circulating for months about . . ."

"Wait one, folks," Lewars interrupted, maintaining his stiff posture and manner and trying like hell to avoid appearing too exasperated. "I know I haven't been in this job very long, but you should have all realized by now that I won't answer questions based on speculation, rumor, hypothesis, or conjecture. Are there any questions I can answer on behalf of the President, Vice President, the Cabinet, or the executive branch of government regarding any of the topics that I've already briefed?" He waited a couple heartbeats;

then: "Thank you, ladies and gentlemen. I'll be happy to take e-mailed questions and I'll be available in the press room at the usual hours." He quickly stepped off the dais as the television reporters moved to the front, ready to give on-air and taped on-camera summaries.

Lewars went to his office, answered a few phone calls, then went to the Oval Office, where the President was already meeting with the members of his national security staff: Vice President Hershel, Secretary of Defense Gardner, Secretary of State Carson, National Security Adviser Sparks, Joint Chiefs Chairman Glenbrook, and Director of Central Intelligence Gerald Vista. Chief of Staff Carl Minden looked up from his tablet PC computer as Lewars entered. "Thought you were going to lose it for a moment, Tony," he commented.

"I never 'lose it,' Mr. Minden," Lewars said sternly. "If the press corps wants to hear me say 'I won't speculate' a dozen times during these briefings, fine with me. I tried to save them a little time, that's all." He turned to the President and added, "They definitely got a strong sniff of the spaceplane overflight, sir, and it won't take long before the Russians' claim is substantiated by tracking data from some other country. I need a cover, nonspecific but enough detail to keep their editors happy for a few days. I suggest we tell the press it was an unarmed classified military spacecraft, one of many that routinely transits Russian airspace in accordance with international aviation laws, and leave it at that."

"We need a ruling from the White House counsel on exactly what the law says about spacecraft overflight," Carl Minden said.

"An official ruling is fine, but I can tell you what the Outer Space Treaty says: no one can regulate space travel or access to Earth orbit," National Security Adviser General Jonas Sparks said. "That's been the case ever since Sputnik. Besides, we have dozens of Russian spy satellites overflying us every damned day."

"True," Secretary of State Mary Carson said. She turned to President Martindale and continued, "But sir, that only applies to spacecraft in Earth *orbit*. If General McLanahan's men flew the spaceplane through the atmosphere over Russia, that's a violation."

"Hell, Doc, we flew spy planes across each other's borders for decades," Sparks said. "It was so commonplace, it became a game."

"And we're on the path to returning to the Cold War mentality that existed back then," Carson retorted. "Sir, if we continue to allow General McLanahan and his spaceplanes to just flit across the planet like that without advising anyone, sooner or later someone's going to mistake it for an intercontinental ballistic missile and fire a real missile. Overflying Russia with a satellite in a mostly fixed and predictable orbit is one thing—having an armed spaceplane suddenly appear on a Russian radar screen out of nowhere could trigger a hostile response. A simple courtesy message on the 'hotline' to Moscow or even to the Russian embassy in Washington would be sufficient."

"Frankly, Mary, I don't feel very courteous when it comes to the Russians," the President said.

"I mean, sir, that a simple advisory might prevent an international diplomatic row, a retaliatory overflight, or at worse someone getting nervous and pushing the button to start another attack."

"Okay, Mary, I get the message," the President said. He turned to the Secretary of Defense: "Joe, get together with Mary and draft up a directive for General McLanahan and anyone else using the spaceplanes to notify the State Department to issue an advisory to the Russian foreign ministry in a timely manner. That should be sufficiently ambiguous to allow us some leeway in when to report."

"Yes, Mr. President." Gardner glanced at Carson's exasperated expression but did not comment.

He could always count on Mary Carson to bring up all the negatives about each and every situation crossing his desk, Martindale thought—her comments always served to head off possible difficulties, even though he generally thought she pressed the panic button too often and too soon to suit him. "It's not the Russians I'm concerned about right now, folks—it's the Iranians," the President said. "Gerald, what do you have?"

"Not much yet, sir," Director of Central Intelligence Gerald Vista responded. "No one has heard from any of the clerics or most of the executive branch of the Iranian government for days."

"My office has been trying repeatedly to get a statement from the Iranian U.N. ambassador, but he's nowhere to be found," Secretary of State Carson added, "and some of the NATO foreign ministries who still have diplomatic ties with Iran tell us the Iranian ambassadors and consuls have dropped out of sight."

"Sounds like they're lying low," the President observed. "But is Buzhazi the reason, and if he's powerful enough to scare government officials as far way as New York City, does he have a chance of succeeding in engineering a military coup?" He turned to Joint Chiefs chairman Glenbrook. "What about the Iranian army, General?"

"The latest we have is the regular armed forces are still in their garrisons, sir," Glenbrook said. "We don't know if they're just staying in defensive positions, awaiting orders, or defying orders and not going out to hunt down Buzhazi and his insurgents. A few specialized units have mobilized—we think those units will try an assault on the Khomeini Library in Qom within forty-eight hours."

"This has been a Pasdaran fight so far," Vista said. "We haven't seen any regular army involved. Maybe the Pasdaran has been weakened to the point where they can't do the job."

"Is it possible that we haven't heard from the clerics or the president of Iran that were apparently in Qom . . . because they're dead?" Vice President Maureen Hershel asked. She turned to a video teleconference unit on the credenza beside her. "General McLanahan?"

"Unfortunately General Briggs didn't ask that question when he met up with General Buzhazi at the Khomeini Library in Qom, ma'am," Patrick McLanahan said from the command center at Elliott Air Force Base in Nevada. Instead of a business suit and tie, he was wearing his trademark Dreamland black flight suit, a wireless earpiece stuck in his left ear, surrounded by his battle staff officers. He hadn't officially taken over the High Technology Aerospace Weapons Center yet, but he was clearly the man in charge. Maureen couldn't help but smile. Patrick never looked comfortable wearing a business suit or attending meetings in the White House. He was back in his element, where he belonged. "General Briggs's objective was to degrade the Pasdaran units surrounding the library and make contact with Buzhazi if possible, all without compromising his men or the Black Stallion spaceplane."

"Is Buzhazi still in Qom?"

"It's unclear, ma'am," Patrick replied. "We should be getting a satellite image update soon. General Briggs estimated Buzhazi's force inside the library at around a thousand men, well-equipped—apparently there was a large weapons cache inside the mosque and library. If they departed, it wouldn't take them long."

"You actually think Hesarak Buzhazi would slaughter a bunch of clerics and government officials inside one of the holiest sites in Iran?" the President asked incredulously.

"Back when he was chief of staff and commander of the Pasdaran, I'd say 'never'—five thousand Americans on an aircraft carrier, yes, but a bunch of power-hungry Muslim clerics, never," Maureen replied. "But the man was dumped, disgraced, nearly assassinated, and relegated to training half-crazy volunteer fighters. He went from leading the fight for the clerical regime to nothing almost overnight. If anyone's got an axe to grind against the current regime, it's him."

"Let's say he succeeds," the President asked. "Would he be worse than the clerical regime, or would he work with us to help stabilize the region—and perhaps even assist the West in stopping the current tide of radical fundamentalist Islamists operating around the world?"

Maureen turned to the speakerphone and said, "The only two Americans who have spoken to him since his insurgency began are Generals Briggs and McLanahan. Patrick? What are your thoughts?"

"He swore up, down, and sideways that he was going to take down the theocracy or die trying, ma'am," Patrick said. "My initial gut reaction is I don't trust him, but everything he's done so far points to one thing: his objective is the destruction of the Pasdaran and elimination of the theocracy. I don't know if he wants to become the strong-armed dictator of Iran, but if he gets the support of the regular army he could certainly take over."

"But what are the chances of that?"

"He's a disgraced military chief of staff who was blamed for Iran's greatest military defeat in history," CIA director Vista said. "He tossed away a third of Iran's navy in just a few days, including the Middle East's first aircraft carrier. Not only that, but he was commander of the Pasdaran—he gave the orders that resulted in the executions of thousands of regular army soldiers, government officials, and ordinary citizens, usually on skimpy or no evidence whatsoever, on allegations they conspired against the clerical regime. The regular army would never follow him."

"I disagree, Director Vista," Patrick radioed. "Because he refused to be exiled—he was given a shit job that should have killed him and he excelled in it. He purged the Basij, the paramilitary group of volunteers, of all the radicals and fundamentalists, and he turned it into a real fighting force—and he did it with pure leadership, convincing the dedicated men and women in the Basij to get rid of the maniacs. He turned the organiation around without resorting to intimidation or violence. The grunts respect that. I think he has a very good reputation with the regular army. Combine all that with the regular army's hatred of the Pasdaran, and I think Buzhazi is lining himself up very nicely for a coup d'état."

"My information says otherwise," Vista insisted. "Buzhazi is an outsider. Besides, the regulars are too afraid of the Pasdaran to support a rebellion, especially one without any other support besides a few thousand volunteers."

"OK, folks, I need some ideas," the President said, barely masking his impatience. "Let's assume Buzhazi survives Qom. What happens next? Gerald?"

"Overall I'd say his odds are terrible, sir," the CIA chief replied. "He needs the regular army—his little group of Basij fighters can't survive against the Pasdaran. The Pasdaran is like the U.S. Marine Corps, except much larger with respect to the regular army: while our Marine Corps is one-tenth the size of the army, the Pasdaran is one-third the size of their entire armed forces, and just as well equipped; I would equate Buzhazi's Basij fighters with a well-trained Army National Guard infantry battalion."

"I agree with the DCI, Mr. President," Secretary of State Carson said. "And even if Buzhazi does succeed in destroying or disrupting the Pasdaran with help from the regular army, using some sort of magical leadership ability as General McLanahan describes, he'll have to contend with other forces as well. Every covert ops and insurgent force the Pasdaran has created over the years will return to Iran to try to topple the junta or at least cause it a lot of trouble: al-Quds in the Gulf region; Hizb'Allah in Lebanon; Hamas, Islamic Jihad, and the Popular Front to Liberate Palestine-General Command in the Gaza Strip and West Bank; Ansar-al-Islam in Iraq; and Hizb'Islami in Afghanistan, just to name a few. All of those groups are controlled and funded by Iran through the Pasdaran, and they'd undoubtedly be brought back to assist in a wide-ranging insurgency against Buzhazi. We could even see pro-Iranian military or terror groups from Chechnya, Pakistan, or North Korea fighting against Buzhazi. Then of course there is the one-third of Iran's citizens, about twenty million adults, who actively support the theocracy and who might support an Islamist insurgency against a secular military regime."

"Doesn't sound like a winner to me," the President said. "Anyone disagree with this analysis?"

The room was quiet . . . until: "I don't disagree with Dr. Carson's or Director Vista's analysis, sir," Patrick McLanahan said through the videoconference link, "but if Buzhazi survives and is actively trying to stage a coup in Iran with the help of the regular army, we should do everything possible to support him."

"Support him?" Carson asked incredulously. "If I remember correctly, he tried to kill you and your men several times. Now you want to risk your life to help him?"

"We may never get another chance for years," Patrick said. "Iran doesn't hide the fact that it actively supports insurgent groups all around the world who try to topple secular or unfriendly governments in favor of a fundamentalist theocracy—we shouldn't be afraid to support any movement, even a military coup, that tries to establish a democracy."

The President shook his head with a sardonic smile. "As usual, a solid consensus about a course of action," he deadpanned. He slumped in his chair, rubbed his temples wearily, retrieved a bottle of water from a desk drawer, and took a deep sip. "I'd be just as happy to see the two factions tear each other apart," he said. He finally turned to General Sparks: "Jonas, I asked you to come up with a plan of action for dealing with Iran. Anything yet?"

"No, sir," Sparks replied. "No real consensus from the intelligence and operations staffs. Buzhazi's insurgency is just complicating the issue worse and worse every day. We should just continue surveillance, monitor the situation carefully, and be sure to warn the Iranians that we won't tolerate any foreign offensive operations in the wake of this Buzhazi insurgency."

The President nodded. "Holding pattern—not exactly what I had in mind," he said. "Anyone else?"

"Mr. President, in my staff's opinion, Buzhazi is not the issue—the Iranian Revolutionary Guards and their control of Iran's weapons of mass destruction and their delivery systems are," Patrick McLanahan said via the videoconference link. "If the regular Iranian army keeps sitting on the sidelines, the Pasdaran will only turn up the heat even more. Eventually the army will be completely marginalized, maybe even dismantled.

Once the Pasdaran takes over, they'll tear the country apart. Then they'll start on any other neighboring countries they feel is a threat to the Islamist regime."

"So what do you propose, Patrick?"

"I'd like permission to launch a dedicated constellation of reconnaissance satellites over Iran to look for their missile sites," Patrick replied. "I'd like to forward-deploy Air Battle Force air and ground teams to Afghanistan and Uzbekistan, ready to go into Iran covertly and destroy the most dangerous missile batteries. And I'd like permission to place two of our fleet of three Black Stallion spaceplanes in orbit, armed with precision-guided weapons to react in case Iran launches any attacks that we can't reach. I've sent this proposal to Mr. Minden and General Sparks for their review."

"You're recommending putting a major strike force over Iran in the middle of their internal crisis?" Secretary of State Carson asked incredulously. "How do you think the Iranians will interpret such an action?"

"I don't intend for the Iranians to find out, Madame Secretary," Patrick said, "but if they do, they'll know we mean business."

"More gunboat diplomacy," Carson said irritably. "Makes my job all the more difficult."

"The Air Battle Force will stay out of Iran unless they lash out against the United States or our allies in the region," Patrick said. "But once they move, they move swiftly and silently, and even after they engage they leave a very small footprint. If the Iranians never threaten our interests—if they confine their reaction to Buzhazi's insurgency to their own borders—we never go in. But if they do try to launch missiles or mobilize for large-scale operations, we can hit them in vital spots while our main forces start gearing up."

"We don't need McLanahan's gizmos, sir," Secretary of Defense Gardner said. "We've got one carrier battle group in the Persian Gulf, one in the Arabian Sea, and another in the western Pacific en route to the Indian Ocean. There are twenty-five thousand NATO troops in Afghanistan, a thousand U.S. troops in Uzbekistan, fifty thousand in Iraq, and another fifty thousand ashore and afloat spread between Turkey and Diego Garcia. The Air Battle Force doesn't and never has integrated with the total force. They'll just get in the way."

"But the fact is, Joe, they can send a tremendous force out there in a real hurry," the President said. "Special Operations Command can send a small force out quickly; the army can send a big force out slowly. McLanahan's guys can send a big punch anywhere fast."

"We're getting ahead of ourselves here, ladies and gentlemen," Vice President Hershel said. "Looks to me like we're letting Buzhazi pull our strings now—he attacks, then we're forced to act when the Revolutionary Guards counterattack. Buzhazi's insurgency is an internal Iranian matter. We'd be provoking a serious and unpredictable Iranian response if anyone caught us sending covert military forces in or over Iran. Iran still commands a vital chokepoint in the Persian Gulf and is the most powerful Islamic military force in the entire region. Let's not get drawn into a fight we don't want by a disgruntled and disgraced Iranian general."

"Mr. President, I'll be happy to look over McLanahan's plan and give the staff my thoughts," General Sparks said, "but right now I'd advise against putting armed spacecraft in orbit, no matter how speedy or cool they are."

"I agree," Carson interjected. "And double goes for sending McLanahan's stealth bombers anywhere near Iran. We don't want to be seen as ratcheting up the tension. If Iran does lash out, they could claim it was our actions that led them to retaliate."

President Martindale glanced back and forth between the videoconference screen and his advisers in the Oval Office. "I agree that our primary concern should be Iran's missiles and whether Masoud Ahmadad intends to use them," the President said after a short silence. "General McLanahan has a plan for dealing with them, so I want the plan vetted right away. Patrick, be prepared to brief the national security staff as soon as the schedule permits. General Sparks and Secretary Gardner will review it and have their comments ready as well."

"Yes, sir."

"Carl will find a slot in tomorrow afternoon's schedule—be ready by then. Thanks, Patrick." He was about to motion for Minden to disconnect the videophone link, but Minden was taking a message from the White House office assistant. Minden's expression after he read the message got the President's full attention. "What now, Carl?"

"Message from Communications, sir," Minden replied. "The wire services are reporting that Russia intends to file a protest with the United Nations Security Council to halt illegal overflight of American spaceplanes over its territory."

"Oh, shit . . ."

"Several members of Congress have called for press conferences within the hour, including Senator Barbeau. General Lewars was right on—the press had wind of this already."

"General Lewars, draft up a response so we can brief the staff and get a statement out right away," the President ordered.

"Yes, Mr. President."

"This is starting to smell like a big sewer leak right here in the White House, and I will personally kick his or her butt when I find out who it is." He turned to the videophone: "Okay, Patrick, out with it. Did your guys overfly Russia? Do the Russians have a legitimate beef?"

"Our crew did overfly Russia, sir, but I don't think the Russians have a legitimate reason for a protest," Patrick replied.

"Explain—and this better be good."

"During its ascent, the spaceplane was lower than one hundred kilometers—about sixty miles—aboveg-round when it entered Russian airspace. One hundred kilometers is the altitude mentioned in the Outer Space Treaty as to where 'space,' and therefore the treaty's provisions, begin. Russian military air defense operators broadcast a warning on the international emergency frequencies, which we received. When the spaceplane did not alter course it was fired upon by Russian surface-to-air missiles. But the spaceplane was accelerating to suborbital velocity—approximately nine times the speed of sound—and it outran the SAMs."

"So the crew did violate Russian airspace. Why?"

"I gave the order to do so, sir," Patrick said. Both the President and the chief of staff nodded—they had already guessed that. "The Black Stallion had four passengers on board—the four Air Battle Force 'Tin Men'—and I wanted the spaceplane on the ground as soon as possible to prepare it for another mission. The original flight plan had the spaceplane flying in a southeasterly orbital course which would have taken it away from hostile airspace but would have meant keeping them aloft for an extra three hours or longer and would have given the crew no military alternate landing airports. Based on those factors, I uploaded a suborbital flight plan to the crew that took them directly back to Dreamland . . ."

"Over Russia."

"Yes, sir. But at all times the spaceplane was accelerating and climbing—it was not descending and decelerating like a warhead or missile would have. The spaceplane was not armed with anything more than hand-carried infantry weapons—it had no weapons of mass destruction or any kind of ground attack weapons of any kind."

"None of that makes a rat's ass of difference, General," Minden snapped. "The press is going to start a shitstorm over this, and Congress is going to jump in with both feet."

"You've done it again, General McLanahan," Secretary of Defense Gardner said bitterly. "You're starting to look as bad as Oliver North during Iran-Contra, running your own covert ops agency right out of the White House basement."

"I authorized the mission over Iran, Joe . . . with your blessing, reluctant as it was," the President reminded him.

"I judge the mission to help Buzhazi a success, sir," Gardner said. "Unfortunately, General McLanahan's decision to send the spaceplane back over Russia will quite possibly erase all the good his crew did. This is going to kill the Black Stallion project for sure." He turned to the President and added, "I recommend we ground the Black Stallion project pending an investigation as to whether or not it was necessary to send it illegally over Russia without permission. It'll be necessary for you to remove McLanahan from his White House position and definitely not consider him for commander of HAWC pending the outcome of the investigation. We should also announce a suspension of all Black Stallion spaceplane flights. We can call it a 'safety review' or 'policy review,' whatever sounds appropriate, but they stay on the ground indefinitely."

"That's the typical knee-jerk reaction to something like this, Joe—we don't need to indulge in it too," Vice President Hershel said. "All the crew did was overfly Russia—they didn't attack, and they did nothing hostile."

"That's not going to be the way it's perceived."

"We don't know how it's going to be perceived, Joe," Maureen argued. "All I'm saying is, we shouldn't hang Patrick—General McLanahan—or . . . or the spaceplane crew out to dry until we know the facts."

"I understand your feelings and admire your loyalty to McLanahan, Miss Vice President, but . . ."

"But nothing, Mr. Secretary," she snapped. "My feelings for the general have nothing to do with this. I . . ."

"That's enough, all of you," the President interjected. "Maureen, I've got no choice on this one. We know the press and the opponents of the Black Stallion spaceplane program are going to use this incident against this administration and against the project, and I don't want to give them any more ammunition to use against us." He thought for a moment; then: "I'm grounding the spaceplanes until the furor over the overflight blows over and the Senate concludes their midnight snipe-hunt. Is that clear, General McLanahan?"

"Yes, sir."

"Patrick, you will report back here to your post in the White House," the President went on. "I don't want you anywhere near Dreamland. You're still a special adviser to the President and covered by executive privilege. You let us take any comments on the spaceplane incident. And you don't step foot on a combat aircraft even if it's just flying you to Washington. You're flying a desk for a while, right here, in a suit and tie. Understood?"

"Yes, sir."

"Dr. Carson, I'd like you to send a message to the Russian embassy, apologizing for the overflight, promising them it won't happen again, assuring them the spacecraft was unarmed, not spying on Russia or any other country, and posed no threat of any kind to Russia," the President went on. "You can even offer to pay for the missiles they shot at the spaceplane . . . the ones the spaceplane outran. We'll provide no other details. Tony will mention this communiqué to the press."

"Yes, Mr. President."

"Anyone have anything else for me?" the President asked.

"Yes, sir," Patrick replied. "I'm looking at overhead imagery of the Ruhollah Khomeini library in Qom taken just moments ago, and it appears that the library has been destroyed."

"What?" the Secretary of Defense exclaimed. "Destroyed by whom? McLanahan, I swear, if you had something to do with this . . . !"

"Most likely it was done by General Buzhazi," Patrick said. "He's making good on this promise to wipe out the theocracy. I never would have expected him to assassinate them, but I believe that's what he's done."

"I haven't heard McLanahan deny he had anything to do with it!"

"Patrick? Let's hear it," the President said.

If Patrick was stung by the accusation or the President's request, he didn't show it. "We have no spaceplanes or weapons of any kind in orbit, sir," Patrick responded.

"What about the satellites that shot you that overhead imagery?" Gardner asked. "How many other satellites do you have in orbit?"

"We have a constellation of four NIRTSats in a circular orbit, initially providing surveillance and communications support for the Black Stallion mission and now providing surveillance on northern and central Iran," Patrick replied. "Those satellites will cease operations in about six days. We are in the process of launching another constellation of more persistent reconnaissance satellites in an elliptical orbit over eastern Russia, maintaining a longer-term watch over the Kavaznya ground-based anti-satellite laser site. We have no other spacecraft in orbit."

"Kavaznya? Why in hell would you watch Kavaznya?" Vice President Hershel remarked. "That place was destroyed decades ago . . . by you."

"We believe the Black Stallion spaceplane was hit by a high-powered laser from the vicinity of Kavaznya," Patrick said.

"What . . . ?"

"You have proof of this, Patrick?"

"No, ma'am. That's why we're going to launch the surveillance satellites as soon as possible."

"If the Russians want to complain about spaceplane overflights, maybe we should complain about our aircraft being shot at by their laser!"

"I'd rather not, ma'am," Patrick said. "I'd like time to get some photos and gather more intel first."

"Why—so you can plan and carry out another sneak attack on Russia?" Secretary of Defense Gardner asked derisively. "That's your style, isn't it, McLanahan—keep all the intel you gather for yourself and lash out without getting permission? You follow the old saying: better to ask forgiveness than ask permission. Right, General?"

"Enough, Joe," the President said. "I was in the White House when the Russians first fired that thing, and it was the most terrifying weapon we've ever encountered except for their nuclear missiles. We rely on spacecraft a lot more than we did twenty years ago. If it was Kavaznya, the Russians must shut it down immediately, or we'll destroy it again."

"You sure you want to restrict the spaceplane fleet now, in light of this new development, Kevin?" Maureen Hershel asked sotto voce. "If we had to move against that laser, the spaceplanes might be the only weapon system short of a sub-launched ballistic missile that can take it."

"The spaceplanes stay restricted," the President said, loud enough for everyone in the room to hear. "We'll deal with Kavaznya diplomatically. Got that, Patrick?"

"Yes, sir."

"Jonas, I want to know everything about that laser site as soon as possible," the President said. "General McLanahan, cancel your plans to insert that new satellite constellation to watch over Kavaznya. Let General Sparks coordinate intel work with the National Reconnaissance Office and the NSA—the Air Battle Force does have a habit of giving out information only after the fact."

"That's not our intention, sir," Patrick argued, in a more defensive tone of voice than he'd intended. "We share all our information in a timely . . ."

"General."

"Yes, Mr. President, we'll cancel our constellation setup immediately."

"Thank you." The President nodded to his chief of staff, who immediately hit the "OFF" button on the videophone device.

"I accept that you're bringing McLanahan back to the White House, sir," National Security Adviser Sparks commented after the videophone terminal had gone dark, "but I will not take any more reports or requests of any kind from him unless I ask for them first. He can sit in the basement and twiddle his thumbs all day for all I care."

"I'll have plenty for him to do," the President said.

"That'll be important if we intend on protecting him under executive privilege," chief of staff Minden pointed out. He accepted a folder from an aide that had hurried into the Oval Office. "The various legal advisers to whatever Congressional committee who wants to subpoena him will surely find out if he's just taking up space in a basement office. If they believe we're just hiding him here, they'll pierce the executive privilege veil easily." He paused, then said, "And here's the first subpoena: the Senate Armed Services Committee, naming all the usual players in the White House, including McLanahan. Requested by Senator Barbeau as ranking member but signed off by the chairman."

"Hand it over to the counsel's office and winnow the list down."

"Yes, sir," Minden said.

"It might help if you spoke with Senator Barbeau yourself, Mr. President," Secretary of Defense Gardner suggested. "Privately."

The President glanced over at Minden, noticed the conspiratorial smile on his face, and scowled at both of them. "Are you pimping for me now, Joe?"

"We know exactly what the woman wants, what motivates her, and what tantalizes her," Minden said seriously, yet the smile remained. "She's as hard to read as a *Playboy* centerfold."

"Stick to the issues, Carl."

"What she wants, other than ever-increasing doses of power and influence, is a strong long-range attack force based on manned and unmanned bombers—built and based in Louisiana, of course," Gardner said. "The Pentagon wants a balanced, powerful, flexible, effective force, composed of land-based bombers, sea-based attack aircraft, and ballistic missile submarines. Spaceplanes might be thrown into the mix, but they'll take at least ten and perhaps twenty years to develop. If we put them on the back burner and rebudget the money, we can have a robust force of bombers and attack planes on the line in five years—less than half the time it'll take to build McLanahan's gadgets."

"It's McLanahan's contention that the bombers and carrier-based aircraft represent outdated twentieth century technology," Vice President Hershel said. "The spaceplanes represent the twenty-first century. They've proven they can do the job, even in this initial phase of operational testing."

"Employed properly that may be so, Miss Vice President," Gardner said. "But right now only one man knows how to use the damned things."

"You mean, because that one man is Patrick McLanahan, you want to put the entire program on the back burner?"

"I just don't trust the guy, that's all, Miss Vice President," Gardner said, spreading his arms resignedly. "Any other general would have requested permission to fly those spaceplanes over Russia, or at least notified us ahead of time. Not McLanahan. And it's not the first time he's sprung a surprise on the White House or Pentagon."

"He gets the job done . . ."

"He's not the guru everyone thinks he is," Gardner argued. "Not long ago, McLanahan was clamoring for more money for his robot bombers, hypersonic missiles, and fancy airborne lasers . . ."

"That was before the American Holocaust, Joe."

"Exactly. Now we have no bombers in the inventory, except for a handful of those robot planes. That's the force that needs to be rebuilt again, not spaceplanes. McLanahan is delusional. He has this inflated ego that makes him think he's got all the answers . . ."

"This is not about the man, but the weapon system . . ."

"Unfortunately they seem to be one and the same right now, ma'am," General Sparks said. He turned to the President and added, "I agree with SECDEF, sir: if we place all our trust and funding into these spaceplanes, we may not see a return on our investment for twenty years—if at all."

"But the alternative is bombers that take twelve hours and a half-dozen support aircraft to reach a target, or ships that can be sunk with one torpedo or cruise missile?" the President asked. "Is that the best the United States can do?"

"We're not talking about propeller-driven bombers and wooden sailing ships," Gardner argued. "We're talking about several wings of unmanned stealth bombers carrying long-range standoff weapons, modern aircraft carriers, and the latest carrier-based aircraft and weaponry, all assembled and deployed within five years. It may not be the latest and greatest technology, but it's years better than the enemy's."

"And we'd have it on the line sooner rather than later and have the manpower, education, and infrastructure to support it all," Sparks added. "I do believe that's a better choice than putting the bulk of the budget into unproven technology."

"And it would avoid a lot of political wrangling in Congress," chief of staff Minden interjected, "which because of McLanahan we cannot afford to indulge in now."

"That's called 'appeasement,' Carl—attempting to stop complaints or reduce difficulties by making concessions or abandoning desires or goals," Maureen said. "There's no reason to avoid confrontation, in Congress or anywhere else. The President knows what he wants. It's up to us to support him."

"Hold on, hold on," the President said. "This is not about forcing agreement or browbeating one another to get our own way. We all want the same thing: security for the United States of America. Even in her most outspoken partisan political scheming, I believe even firebrand operatives like Stacy Anne Barbeau want the exact same thing."

Kevin Martindale affixed each of them with a direct, stern expression, then said, "This is the way it's going to work, folks: you will give me all your input, pro or con, whichever way you see it, without hesitation or personal attacks; I will take it all into consideration and come up with a decision. My expectation is that you will support whatever plan I come up with. If you can't support me, tender your resignation and it'll be reluctantly but quickly accepted."

He scanned the faces of his national security staff once again, then added, "There's no reason why this decision has to be a test of political will, but somehow it's become that. I'm sure it's because of the money—two hundred, three hundred billion dollars over the next ten years is hard to ignore. I don't want to fight, and I don't think we need to fight over this. But I've been in the White House for sixteen years and in Washington for twice that—I know political turf wars start over much less. If it's a battle they want, they'll get a good one.

"But I don't want any battles in the White House or in public between the people in this room or anyone else that reports to me—McLanahan included," the President went on. "My door is open to all of you any time. Tell me what you think; tell me what you fear. I'll listen. Otherwise, you keep your traps shut unless it's something you've been briefed you can say. If you can't abide by that simple rule, I'll show you the door. Got it?" There was a murmur of "Yes, Mr. President" all around the Oval Office. "Good. Now get the hell out so I can do something about this headache."

CHAPTER 4

OFFICE OF THE DIRECTOR OF THE SUPREME NATIONAL SECURITY DEPUTATE, TEHRAN, ISLAMIC REPUBLIC OF IRAN

The Next Morning

"This is an absolute abomination!" screamed the Ayatollah Hassan Mohtaz, director of the Supreme National Security Directorate, a conglomeration of military, civilian, and religious leaders who advised Iran's Supreme Leader on military matters. "That this should happen in the holiest of places in the Islamic Republic is nothing short of criminal bestiality!"

"General Yassini should be arrested and charged with treason for his unauthorized meeting with Buzhazi and for criminal conspiracy in the attack on

Qom," Colonel Zolqadr said. "I shall prosecute him personally. He and all his outgoing communications from the Defense Ministry will be monitored carefully in case he attempts to contact Buzhazi. He should be removed from office and placed in solitary confinement to prevent him from using his staff or privileges of office to act against us."

"I think that is a wise precaution, but we will need permission from the Supreme Leadership Council or the Faqih himself to authorize such a move against the chief of staff," Mohtaz said. "Although I do not believe Yassini would betray the government and the people like Buzhazi has done, their friendship muddles the equation greatly. If Yassini was in Qom actually meeting with Buzhazi when the library was destroyed, and he had the slightest hint of what was about to happen, it is most certainly a case of conspiracy to commit high treason, and he must be dealt with accordingly."

"Yes, Excellency," Zolqadr responded.

"What is your plan for dealing with Buzhazi and his murderous criminals, Colonel?"

"Certainly not the 'wait and then give amnesty' tactic, Excellency, as Yassini advocates," the Pasdaran commander said. "Buzhazi has many more men to feed, equip, and move, and so he will be desperate for resupply—contrary to what Yassini believes, Buzhazi can't equip a battalion-sized force off the land or begging from civilians. He will certainly be targeting supply bases—he has no choice. That is how I propose to destroy him."

He spread a map out on the conference table for the ayatollah to examine. "The Pasdaran supply warehouses at Arān were evacuated and abandoned because of the chemical gas attack Buzhazi staged," Zolqadr went on, "but the gas has since dissipated. If it appears that we do not know this, and Buzhazi returns to loot the rest of the warehouses, we can surround him."

Ayatollah Mohtaz looked at the map, but he wasn't thinking about the plan—he was thinking about whom to support in this conflict—it was a much more pressing issue for his own safety and future well-being than whatever Buzhazi had in mind.

It was generally believed that the regular armed forces were more secular than the Pasdaran, and so were less likely to support the clerical regime. But so far the Pasdaran hadn't captured Buzhazi—in fact, the insurgency had steadily grown into a serious fighting force now despite the Pasdaran's pursuit. Yassini's plan was to deal with Buzhazi logically and rationally, appealing to his soldier's sense of honor and duty to his country and his men. Zolqadr simply wanted to lure him into a trap, and Buzhazi appeared to be well prepared to wiggle out of any trap, especially one set by Zolqadr. Which was most likely to succeed?

Well, he thought, there really wasn't any choice to make. If Mohtaz even hinted at supporting the regular army over the Pasdaran, he would be immediately arrested, imprisoned, and probably executed. Buzhazi represented the regular army, and he had killed a great many politicians and leaders already—anyone even remotely appearing as if they supported him was doomed . . .

. . . like Yassini, if it was shown that he actually was in Qom meeting with Buzhazi before the library was destroyed.

"I will present your proposal to the entire acting Security Council, Colonel," Mohtaz said, "but you should expect approval in very short order, so you should be prepared to act."

"Yes, Excellency. All will be ready."

"Very good." Mohtaz thought for a moment; then: "One more thing."

"Yes, Excellency?"

The cleric turned away from Zolqadr, as if distancing himself from his own words, then said, "You are sure that Yassini was in Qom meeting with Buzhazi, without a shadow of doubt . . ."

"I have many witnesses who will testify to it, Excellency, as well as testify about the intercepted radio transmissions picked up between them just before the library was destroyed." Zolqadr hoped all that was true—his actual information had come from gossip and rumors about Yassini possibly going to Qom to check out the situation at the Khomeini Library and personally take charge of a rescue mission.

Mohtaz nodded, still turned away from Zolqadr, then said, "Then his guilt is beyond doubt. Deal with it as you see fit . . . General Zolqadr."

HIGH TECHNOLOGY AEROSPACE WEAPONS CENTER, ELLIOTT AFB, NEVADA

A Short Time Later

"You told them we weren't in orbit yet when we flew over Russia, sir?" Captain Hunter Noble asked incredulously. He was meeting with Patrick McLanahan, Dave Luger, Ann Page, Hal Briggs, and Chris Wohl in the Battle Staff briefing area at Elliott Air Force Base.

"What did you expect the general to say, Boomer?" Dave asked.

"Lie, of course," Hunter replied matter-of-factly. "The only guys that could have tracked us were the Russians, and nobody believes what they say any more."

"You need a little more experience talking with the President of the United States before you go around giving tips on lying to the national security staff, Boomer," Patrick suggested. "If I recall correctly, you had a tough time saying anything when we visited the Oval Office."

"Touché. I'll be quiet now, sir."

"Thank you."

"So we're grounded now?" Ann Page asked. "I just got here! I love those little Studs! Can't we do something? You're the special adviser to the President and a three-star general, General—pull some strings, throw some weight around."

Patrick was silent for a few moments, adopting his infamous "thousand-yard stare" as his mind turned over possibilities. "Look out, everyone—the 'Rubik's Cube' is in motion," Dave Luger commented.

Patrick winked at Dave. "The spaceplanes are grounded, we can't launch any more NIRTSats, and the ones we have monitoring Iran will fall out of the sky in less than six days," he summarized. "What else do we have?"

"Squat," Boomer said. "We're shut down."

"Maybe not," Patrick said. "We still have one asset we can bring online to help us—we just need someone who can fly the thing over to where we need it."

Ann Page noticed Patrick and Dave Luger looking . . . at her. "What?" she asked. "I'm grounded, same as you guys. Get me permission to fly the Stud again and I'll take her anywhere you want."

"I'm not thinking about the Stud," Patrick said. "I'm thinking about bringing Armstrong Space Station online again."

"Silver Tower!" Ann exclaimed. "You serious?"

"It's the greatest surveillance platform in existence," Patrick said. "It can scan every square foot of the entire Middle East or Siberia in one pass, including underwater and underground. If we want to find out what's happening in Iran—or Kavaznya, if we have to go up against that thing again—that's what we need."

"Sounds fine with me, Patrick—I love going up to that thing and turning it on," Ann said happily, so excited she could hardly keep her seat. "But the only way we have to get up there is with the Shuttle, and it takes at least two months—more like six—to get it ready for a mission."

"We have access to Ares," Dave Luger said. "We've been involved in testing from the beginning, and we can put together a launch in no time."

"The new Crew Launch Vehicle?" Ann remarked. Ares was the next generation of low-cost, highly reliable, reusable heavy rocket launchers. Its first stage was a five-segment solid-rocket booster similar to the Shuttle's Solid Rocket Boosters; its second stage was a liquid-fueled booster uprated and improved from the Saturn-V's J-2 engine. "Cool. But what about Orion?"

Dave shook his head. "We never got to play with the Crew Exploration Vehicle, only the booster," he said. Orion was the name of the new series of manned space vehicles destined to replace the Shuttle Transportation System. Resembling the Apollo spacecraft, Orion could carry as many as six astronauts and was designed to be configurable for any space mission from low Earth orbit to a trip to Mars. "But we do have a cargo stage that we used to test the Meteor weapon dispenser."

Ann shook her head. "Ares won't help if the cargo stage can't carry passengers," Ann said. "We need at least two persons aboard Silver Tower to bring it online again and operate the surveillance systems." She paused, smiled, and said, "And me to command it, of course. We need a Shuttle mission. We hitch a ride on the next Shuttle flight, get on board, restart the environmental systems, and reactivate the station's sensors and datalinks," Ann Page said. "When's the next flight?"

Dave queried the "Duty Officer," the electronic virtual assistant at Dreamland, and got the answer moments later. "Four months," Dave Luger replied.

"Too long. Whatever's going to happen in Iran will happen in four days."

"Well, let's put together an earlier one."

"Are we talking about the same National Aeronautical and Space Administration as I am?" Patrick asked. "NASA is so ultra-cautious that if we make a simple five-pound payload change they will either cancel the flight or slip it six months to study all the possible ramifications. If it was an Air Force program, like the Black Stallion, we might have a chance."

"What about the America spaceplane?"

"Canceled years ago."

"The Stud can make it," Boomer said.

"No way," Ann said. "Last I knew, the Silver Tower was in a two-hundred-mile-plus orbit. How high can you take the Stud? I didn't think it could go higher than one hundred miles or so."

"It can do two hundred easily—if it was a one-way mission," Boomer said matter-of-factly.

"A one-way mission?" Patrick asked.

"I haven't computed the exact fuel requirement, sir, but I'd guess the Stud would use just about all of its fuel to get up to two hundred miles," Boomer said. "Since I assume we'd be using the cargo bay for passengers, some supplies, and the docking system, there's no room for extra fuel for the return, even for a ballistic

Shuttle-like re-entry. It would have to be refueled on the station to return."

"Which means if you can't reach the station or fail to dock . . ."

"We'd be stranded in orbit until we were rescued," Boomer said. "But we'd just have to make sure we got it right the first time."

"The passenger module is ready to go?"

"Sure. We can fit a docking adapter and airlock onto the passenger module. We can carry two passengers plus the Stud's crew and still transfer everyone to the station. We'd have to bring jet fuel and 'boom' up on a Shuttle or on the Ares booster with the cargo stage. Can that be done?"

"The station has a Soyuz- and Agena-compatible cargo dock and a universal crew docking adapter, so we can dock and resupply at the same time," Ann said. The unmanned Russian Soyuz modules resupplied the Russian and International Space Stations, while the Agena modules resupplied the American Skylab station. "We refueled America on the station several times."

"We can use the cargo stage of Ares to bring jet fuel and BOHM to the station to refuel the XR-A9," Dave said. "It has plenty of room to carry that, and the stuff is stable enough to handle a launch. We would just need to be sure that Silver Tower has the gear necessary to service the Stud."

"You've got the exact same gear the America spaceplane used for servicing," Ann said. "It'll work. You get the Stud and the Ares cargo stage to Silver Tower, and we can fill 'er up."

"I've never docked the Black Stallion before," Boomer said. "I mean, I know I can do it—I can fly that thing anywhere you want—but . . ."

"If he can't do it, the crew is stranded," Dave said.

"Can't you just park the spaceplane near the station and then just spacewalk from the spaceplane to the station?" Patrick asked.

"You can, but a spacewalk is by far the most dangerous activity in all of space flight," Ann said. "It takes training and practice to get the movements just right. Push when you're not supposed to, miss a leap or a grasp, activate the wrong switch, and you could go flying off into Neverland in the blink of an eye—or fall to Earth and burn up like a meteorite. Get a tether or umbilical tangled and you could be like Captain Ahab lassoed to Moby Dick for all eternity. The longer the distance between spacecraft, the greater the danger. Twenty feet will seem like twenty miles up there." She looked at Hunter. "I don't even think we can fit a Shuttle-style EVA getup in the Black Stallion. We'll have to use Gemini- or Skylab-style spacesuit setups—pressure suits and emergency oxygen bottles only, with simple tethers. I don't even think the Black Stallion is set up for umbilicals, is it?"

"We never intended to do spacewalks from the Stud," Boomer said. "Heck, we'll have to modify the safety squat switches to allow us to open the canopies with the landing gear retracted."

"But it can be done?" Patrick asked. "We can fly the Black Stallion to Armstrong Space Station, dock or climb out, and space-walk over to the station?"

"Sure," Ann said. "There are a million things that can go wrong, but that's typical for any space mission. I don't see why we can't do it."

"Shuttle astronauts did tethered spacewalks quite a bit," Dave said. "Even Gemini and Apollo astronauts did little spacewalks all the time. Every Skylab mission had several spacewalks to service the experiments they were running."

"But each spacewalk was preceded by months of training and years of design study and testing," Ann said. "We're trying to put all this together in hours. We need some experienced crewmen to send up there. I volunteer. Got any ideas for another?"

Patrick smiled and nodded. "Dave, get Kai Raydon on the phone for me," he said. Dave smiled, nodded, then picked up the telephone.

"Raydon, the Shuttle pilot?" Ann asked. "Haven't seen him at the bar in quite awhile—I'm sure he owes me a few rounds. Is he still with NASA?"

"Was," Patrick said. "He was reassigned to Los Angeles Air Force Base and put in charge of a program that just got canceled, and he came to me recently looking for a flying job. You may have heard of the program, Ann: Hermes."

"The European Space Agency spaceplane project? It was canceled years ago. Raydon's not that old."

"The name was deliberately used to throw people off the track," Patrick said. "Kai's been involved in another project using that name. You knew it as 'Skybolt.' "

"Skybolt!" Ann Page exclaimed. "That's my project! What in hell's going on, sir?"

"Skybolt, the space-based laser?" Boomer asked. "It's still up there?"

"Did you really believe the U.S. would spend two billion dollars and five years to launch a massive space station into orbit and then just leave it up there, Ann?" Dave Luger asked. "When Raydon was getting his Ph.D. in the Air Force Institute of Technology program his dissertation was on the reactivation of Skybolt."

"I know, I know, General—I was on his doctorate panel," Ann said. "The guy's brilliant. But the proposal never went anywhere. I was in the Senate committee overseeing funding for military space programs, and I pushed several budget cycles for the money to reactivate it. It never happened."

"Skybolt went on life support funding under HAWC's advanced technology research budget," Patrick explained. "Officially the money went toward refueling and servicing the Armstrong Space Station to keep it aloft, and to use the station's systems as a risk reducer for the SpaceBased Radar and SpaceBased Infrared System programs. Unofficially, we funneled some money over to Skybolt. The money runs out at the end of this fiscal year. After that, there's enough money for a maximum of three Shuttle flights over the following twelve months to strip whatever useful stuff we could off the station before it re-enters the atmosphere."

"They don't want to spend a few measly million a year to save a space station worth more than three billion?" Ann asked. "The characters in Congress can be real jerks sometimes—I should know. So Raydon's been to Silver Tower?"

"A few times. That's classified."

"That's good," Ann said. "And he's an experienced Shuttle jockey, so he can handle the docking chores. So we got me and Raydon to turn the station on—all we need is for young Hunter Noble to give us a ride up there."

STURGEON RIVER STATE FOREST, NEAR VERMILLION LAKE, MINNESOTA

The Next Afternoon

"Okay, cadets, listen up," Civil Air Patrol Captain Ed Harlow, commander of the Grand Rapids Composite Squadron of the Civil Air Patrol, said. He and a group of thirty-six cadets surrounding him were in a grassy clearing in the middle of a large forest in the Sturgeon River State Forest, about fifty miles northeast of Grand Rapids in northeast Minnesota. The cadets, wearing camouflaged fatigues, baseball caps, and combat boots, ranged in age from fourteen to seventeen years old. "This is our final exercise for this encampment, but it's also the most important, so pay attention.

"We've concentrated on a lot of the search, rescue, first aid, communications, and critical support functions of the Civil Air Patrol mission. But all of our procedures deal with using our equipment, technology, and skills to help others in distress. But what if we get in trouble while on a mission? What if you become lost or crash-land while on a flight? How do we even understand what it's like to be in a search, survival, or escape-and-evasion situation? Our final exercise will be to see how well you can help yourself if you become involved in a difficult situation.

"This exercise is a confidence-builder rather than a procedural evolution," the CAP commander went on. "Your objective is simple: collect as many different objective markers as you can in four hours and return your entire flight to the starting point in the center of the exercise area. The flight with the most markers collected in the shortest time wins.

"We're located in a wooded area of about ten square kilometers, bordered by Vermillion Lake to the north and east, the state park highway to the east, and Highway Twenty-four to the south and west—if you come across any of these major landmarks, you'll know which way to travel to get re-oriented and headed back to the objective. We'll drive you to starting points on different sections of the exercise area and set you loose at the same time. The markers are located in camouflaged metal ammo boxes marked on your maps. When you find the can, each flight takes one marker only from the can and leaves the rest.

"To make it more interesting, you have the capability to capture another flight's markers," the CAP commander went on. "You are all wearing laser targets and carrying eye-safe laser guns. If you come across another flight, and if you can hit the flight leader before he hits you, you capture his markers. The guns have a range of only thirty feet or less, so you need to be fairly close to your target to hit him. You can return to a previously discovered can to get another marker, but remember, only one marker from each can per flight." He answered a few questions, made sure his four flights of nine cadets each were equipped and ready, then split them up into vans that took them to their starting points.

The exercise proceeded throughout the afternoon. The terrain was flat and rolling, with numerous hiking trails, outhouses, signs, and other landmarks to make the test challenging without letting anyone get lost. Harlow's staff acted as referees and would assist any cadet flights who were having real difficulty, but most of these cadets, all from northern Minnesota and the Upper Peninsula of Michigan, were experienced outdoors enthusiasts, and Harlow didn't expect any emergencies.

In fact, the flights were so evenly matched that as they approached the four-hour cutoff time, three of the four flights were approaching the objective point in the middle of the exercise area all at once. Harlow had set out each flight's guidon in the clearing, and as the cadets got closer they started running through the woods toward their flag. "Once you enter the clearing, no more laser guns," Harlow announced over a bullhorn as he saw the three groups converging on the objective point. "C'mon in and let's count 'em up."

This was strange, he thought as the three groups ran in—the fourth flight, Delta Flight, nicknamed "Red Dogs," was nowhere to be seen. All of the flights were evenly matched; Delta Flight was perhaps slightly less "outdoorsy" and more intellectual than the others, but this was rather surprising—with only a few minutes left to go, the Red Dogs still were not anywhere in sight. Usually they were able to keep up with whatever else the rest of the cadet squadron did, but it didn't appear to be the case today. Harlow raised his walkie-talkie and clicked the mike button: "Anyone seen Delta?" he asked. The answers all came back negative.

Well, Harlow thought, perhaps this will take a little steam out of Delta Flight's fiery commander, fifteen-year-old Cadet Lieutenant Katelyn VanWie. She had this annoying air about her. She was cocky but wasn't a braggard; she was smart but not a know-it-all; quiet but not shy; self-confident but not pretentious. It was as if she knew she was better than everyone else but simply chose not to prove it. She had infused the other eight members of Delta Flight with the same assuredness to the point that the team took on the same personality as its commander, which didn't exactly endear them to the rest of the squadron.

To be honest, Harlow thought, Katelyn wasn't an annoying kid—but she was different. He could sense it. It was as if she had some sort of magnetic attraction that drew people to her side somehow. That kind of personality turned some people off. Moreover, she knew she was different, that she had this power, but she chose not to exercise it for some reason—even though she did employ it. Frequently.

Harlow scanned the treeline once more, shook his head in confusion, then keyed the mike button: "Let's bring the rest of the flight in, then we'll organize a search," he radioed. "We'll concentrate our search on Route Twenty-four and the forest service road. If they somehow crossed the service road without realizing it, they could be outside the park in . . ."

At that moment he heard a cacophony of high-pitched buzzers. The cadets heading in from the forest slapped their hands over the laser sensors, trying to block the incoming laser beams, but it was too late—in seconds, every flight leaders' target alarm was sounding. "Hey, I said, no more lasers!" he shouted. "Who is doing that?"

As he watched, members of Delta Flight appeared out of nowhere—out of trees, from behind bushes, even from underground. They tapped the flight commanders and held out their hands. Each flight commander looked up at Harlow imploringly, asking if this was real. He could do nothing but shrug his shoulders, and the flight commanders handed over their marker buttons. The members of Delta Flight marched in triumphantly with their prizes. "Red Dog Delta reporting as directed, sir," the flight's senior noncommissioned cadet officer, Cadet Master Sergeant Doug Lenz, said, saluting. He held out his hand. "Here's our tally, sir."

"Every member of your flight needs to be present by the expiration time to claim the win, Cadet Master Sergeant," Harlow said perturbedly, confused as to what exactly just happened here. He looked at his watch. "Lieutenant VanWie has fifteen seconds to report here before I'll . . ."

"All of Red Dog Delta reporting as directed, sir," came a girl's voice. Harlow spun—and saw Katelyn VanWie standing directly behind him, saluting, appearing as if out of nowhere. She was shorter than most of her other teammates, thin, with a darker complexion than most Scandinavian-bred Minnesotans had. Her red hair was tucked up under her cap, and her hazel eyes flashed, giving away her glee in shocking her squadron commander . . .

. . . and his eyes were drawn to the hand raised to the brim of her cap. He knew he shouldn't be distracted by it, knew it really wasn't a big deal. But every time he saw it, it was as if it was for the first time. Could that be part of the pervasive uneasiness he always felt around her?

Harlow had to blink and take a deep breath to rinse away the surprise before returning the salute. "Jesus, VanWie, how long have you been there?"

"On this particular spot, sir? About two hours."

"Two hours? What is going on here?" he snapped.

"Red Dog Delta reporting as ordered, sir," Katelyn said, dropping her hand. "We claim the victory."

"Where have you been? No one has seen you in the exercise area all afternoon!"

"We didn't go to the exercise area, sir," Katelyn admitted.

"What? Where did you go then?"

"We came directly here, sir."

"Here? Where's 'here?' "

"Here, to the objective point, sir."

"Did you not understand the instructions, VanWie?"

"I believe we understood the directions perfectly, sir."

"But you didn't go to the exercise area? How many markers did you collect?"

Katelyn quickly counted the markers her NCOIC had given her. "We collected twenty-five, sir."

"No, I mean, how many did you collect?" He could see that Katelyn was about to give the same answer, so he interjected: "I mean, how many ammo boxes did your flight find out of the ten on the course?"

"We didn't find any of them, sir."

"None of them?"

"No, sir." Katelyn started to look confused—Harlow couldn't tell if it was playacting or genuine.

"Then how can you claim to be the winner if you didn't find any of the markers you set out to find?"

"We didn't set out to find anything, sir."

"You said that. But the purpose of the exercise was to use land navigation skills to locate the ammo cans, retrieve as many markers as possible from those cans, then return here as quickly as possible before the end of the exercise period. Am I correct, Lieutenant?"

"No, sir."

"No?"

"You said the objective was to rendezvous at the objective point with as many markers as possible before the end of the exercise," Katelyn said. "The flight with the most markers wins. We have twenty-five markers. I believe that makes us the winner, sir."

It was finally starting to dawn on Harlow what was going on, and he felt the anger rising in his temples. "You mean to tell me that you didn't actually go out to find markers, but you took the four hours allotted for this exercise to set up an ambush on your fellow cadets to take their markers after they returned here to the rendezvous point?"

"Sir, the objective was to collect the markers and . . ."

"The purpose of the exercise, Lieutenant, was for you and your flight members to practice land navigation techniques and participate in a friendly competition on the last day of our encampment, not to ambush your fellow squadron members!"

Katelyn snapped to attention. "Perhaps I did misunderstand the objectives of the exercise, sir," she said. "I apologize." She waited a few moments; then, just as Harlow thought the argument was over, asked, "Pardon me, sir, but . . . who won the exercise, if Red Dog Delta flight did not?"

He had been wondering the very same thing—and he didn't have an answer. "This was not about 'winning' anything, Lieutenant—it's about practicing land navigation, evasion, and teamwork techniques, plus having a little fun in the outdoors on the last day of our encampment."

"Yes, sir."

It was a wishy-washy answer—he knew it, she knew it, and he knew that she knew that he knew it too.

He looked at the eager, exhausted, and happy faces of Red Dog Delta around him, and then at the disappointed, angry, and confused faces of the other squadron members, and realized he had better just leave it at that. "Good job, all of you," he said. He checked his watch. "The Minnesota National Guard will be at the parking lot in about two hours to fly us out in the Chinook. Police the area and get some water. We'll march back in fifteen minutes." Harlow stepped away from the cadets, feeling the disappointment of VanWie's flight on the back of his neck.

"Sergeant, organize a site cleanup detail," Katelyn said to Doug Lenz, her cadet NCOIC. She picked out two landmarks to the north and west of the center of the clearing they were in. "We'll take this quadrant and police the area out toward the treeline and one hundred meters beyond. Let me know when you're ready and I'll join you."

"But what about the exercise?" Lenz asked. "Do we get any recognition for winning the exercise?"

"You heard the captain—the prize was the successful completion of the exercise," she replied. She stepped closer to him, smiled, and added, "Besides, we all know who won."

"Yes, ma'am!"

"Now get going. Be ready to move out in one minute." Lenz saluted and trotted away.

"I suppose you think you're clever, don't you, VanWie?" one of the other flight leaders, a seventeen-year-old boy named Johansson, who looked closer to twenty-seven, said. The other flight leaders had been talking together and had turned defensively toward Katelyn as she approached them. "You knew damned well that we were supposed to find those markers ourselves, not ambush one another and steal theirs!"

"Sure I knew it," Katelyn said, "but the captain made it clear what the objective was, and I made my plan based on the objectives of the exercise, not what I assumed we were supposed to do."

"You didn't win, and you just showed everyone again what a little red-headed weirdo you are."

"I'm going to take this quadrant of the clearing for cleanup," Katelyn said, ignoring the remark. Her cadet NCOIC trotted up to her and told her the flight was ready to move out. "You guys decide what areas you're going to take."

"Why don't you just take you and your ET hands out into the woods and stay there, freak," Johansson said.

Katelyn ignored the remark—she was accustomed to it—but her friend and cadet NCOIC, Doug Lenz, didn't. Before she could stop him, Lenz—who wasn't that much bigger than Katelyn, even though he was a year older—shouted, "Shut up, asshole!" then charged at the other flight leader. He got one good punch in to the side of the flight leader's chest, and Lenz's head butted the other boy's chin and opened a slight cut, but that was all.

Johansson pushed Lenz's head down and aside, then wiped blood from his chin. "Motherfucker . . . !" he muttered, then punched Lenz once, hard, on the back of his neck, and the younger boy went down. The flight leader turned, knelt on Lenz's back, and raised a fist. "I'm gonna waste you, you piece of . . . !"

Suddenly he felt a boot strike his chest, and he stumbled back off the young cadet. Unhurt but confused, he looked around to find where the blow had come from . . . and he found Katelyn VanWie standing between him and Lenz, jumping slightly from foot to foot, her hands raised defensively . . . her hands, those hands, showing just four fingers on each hand. "Hey!" he shouted, getting to his feet. "You butt out, freak!"

"It's over," Katelyn said. "I apologize for Doug, and it won't happen again."

"I'm gonna kick his ass!" Johansson said. He took one of the other flight leaders by the arm and pushed him toward Katelyn. "Keep the freak away from me while I teach this a-hole not to mess with Bravo Flight."

It was obvious the second cadet, a younger kid named Swanson, didn't want to have anything to do with this, but he put up his hands and stood in front of Katelyn, determined to keep her away from his flight leader until the squadron commander came back. As he approached Katelyn, though, all he could look at was those hands and the weirdness of what looked like a finger in place of her thumbs . . .

. . . and he didn't see her left leg sweep out and trip him. Swanson landed hard on his back and decided he was going to stay right there—he'd had enough of the girl with the ET fingers already . . .

"What is going on over here?" Captain Harlow thundered from several yards away.

"Group, ten-hut!" Katelyn shouted. She snapped to attention but kept her eyes on the flight leader, making sure he didn't make a move toward her.

"I said, what's going on here?" Harlow shouted again. "VanWie, did I see you just trip that cadet?"

"Yes, sir."

"Why?"

"Cadets Swanson and Johansson wanted a demonstration of muay thai, sir."

" 'Muay thai?' What's that?"

"Kickboxing, sir."

"Is that true, Swanson?"

The second cadet had just gotten to his feet, trying to get to attention while rubbing the back of his head. "Uh, I . . . yes, sir . . . I mean . . ."

"Johansson, what's going on here?" Harlow demanded. He noticed the dust and dirt on Lenz's uniform and the cut on Johansson's chin—the only person here not dirty or bloody was VanWie, by far the smallest kid in this group. "Well?"

"We're just . . . playing around, sir," Johansson said. "We were demoing some martial arts moves."

"I thought I told you guys to police this area and get ready to move out," Harlow said. "I only see Delta out there. Now get busy." The cadets saluted and ran off. "VanWie." Katelyn trotted back and stood at attention. "Okay, Lieutenant, tell me what really happened."

"It's just like Lieutenant Johansson said, sir."

"You don't think I saw what happened, Lieutenant? Do you think I'm blind? Cadet Lenz attacked and struck Johansson, he defended himself and was preparing to hit back, you stepped in and kicked him, then stepped in between him and Lenz and knocked over Swanson. That makes you and Lenz the instigators and liable for disciplinary action. Now do you mind telling me what happened?"

"It was a misunderstanding, sir, that's all."

"A 'misunderstanding?' Explain."

"Cadet Lenz misunderstood a comment made and overreacted. It was a failure in leadership on my part, so I'm responsible. If there's any disciplinary action, it should be directed at myself."

"I'll be the judge of that, Lieutenant. What comment was made?" Katelyn remained silent. "I asked you a question, Lieutenant."

"I'd rather not say, sir."

Harlow stepped back, crossed his arms, and took a breath. This was not the first time he'd heard about such comments, but it was the first time he'd ever seen VanWie react to it.

React, hell . . . Katelyn kicked his ass. Johansson easily had twenty-five pounds on her, and she made it look easy. As much as Johansson probably deserved it, the use of physical force instead of ignoring or reporting such comments was a dangerous change that had to be nipped in the bud right away.

"Lieutenant . . . Katelyn, listen: I strongly advise you not to resort to violence to solve problems, even if a friend or colleague is in danger," Harlow said. "Striking a fellow officer is not permitted, and you could face some serious repercussions no matter what the circumstances are; but more importantly, violence in the heat of emotion is the most dangerous and non-productive kind. It makes you weaker, not stronger. Do you understand me?"

"Yes, sir."

"I'm saying this as your friend, Katelyn, not just your CO," Harlow went on. "You've obviously got some martial arts skills, which I didn't know you had. Nothing wrong with that, as long as it's used for self-defense—otherwise, you should be smart, avoid confrontation, and notify the proper authorities first before things get out of hand, whether it's myself, a teacher, your parents, or the police, if you're in a situation where your friends or family are getting hurt." Harlow could see Katelyn's eyes briefly turn away when he mentioned her parents, but they quickly returned to his. "If you start acting like the enforcer, you turn into nothing but a bully. Am I making myself clear?"

"Yes, sir."

"Was Johansson's comments about your hands, Katelyn?"

He could see her eyebrows droop a bit under the brim of her fatigue cap, but she replied, "I'd rather not say, sir."

"You know that hypoplastic thumb is one of the most common congenital birth defects of the limbs, don't you?" Harlow asked. Katelyn had received special permission from the Air Force to join the Civil Air

Patrol because she was born with bilateral hypoplastic thumb—missing thumbs from both hands. At the age of one year she had pollicization surgery to position her index fingers in place of her missing thumbs, so she only had four fingers on each hand. But the results were excellent: despite her handicap, Katelyn was an accomplished student, pianist, typist, outdoorsperson, marksman—and apparently a martial artist, especially with her feet, which made perfect sense for someone with deformed hands. There was no skill or challenge in the Civil Air Patrol that she couldn't master.

But her greatest skill wasn't what she could do with only four fingers on each hand, but in the realm of leadership. Perhaps because most others expected less of the diminutive red-haired girl with the "ET hands," she inspired others by her actions and distinguished herself as a natural-born leader. Her "Red Dog Delta" flight was consistently tops in required exams, dress and appearance, and field exercise performance in the squadron, and she often beat out flights all across the state that had far more physically capable members.

Yet she never stayed in the spotlight for very long, was annoyingly camera-shy, and had no other hobbies or interests outside her little northern Minnesota school other than Civil Air Patrol. She was a standout performer—especially so in an organization composed mostly of boys—but preferred not to stand out at all. It was the same with her parents: older, rather formal, bankers or some sort of financial consultants, always well-dressed but modestly so, not particularly demonstrative or affectionate. Like Katelyn, the parents looked as if they liked a challenge and craved a little action but preferred to be quiet and stay out of the spotlight.

"I did a little checking on the subject when you joined the squadron," Harlow went on. "Although double hypoplastic thumb is rare, the condition is . . ."

"May I go back and supervise my flight, sir?" Katelyn interjected.

Harlow kicked himself for his insensitive babbling and nodded. "Just remember what we talked about, okay, Katelyn? Don't try to be the hero. Being a good leader doesn't mean kicking butt."

"Yes, sir. May I go, sir?"

Harlow wasn't sure how much he had said sunk in, but his clumsy way of trying to act empathetic toward her and her affliction probably ruined any chance he had of reaching her today. "Of course, Lieutenant. Carry on."

"Thank you, sir," she responded immediately, then saluted and headed off toward the clearing.

Katelyn had taken just a few steps when Harlow heard the beat of helicopter rotors approaching. He was a former Army finance officer and didn't know very much about helicopters before joining the Civil Air Patrol, but he did know that wasn't a Chinook—besides, it was arriving too early for their scheduled pickup, and it was in the wrong place.

Then he saw it—it was a UH-60 Black Hawk military helicopter with Minnesota Army National Guard markings on it—and it looked like it was maneuvering to land in the clearing! "Flight commanders, helicopter landing zone procedures, now!" he shouted. "Clear a zone for the helicopter!" His troops were very accustomed to working with helicopters, so the clearing was made ready in very short order. Moments after touchdown, two men stepped out of the helicopter—one in civilian clothing, and one in green battle dress uniform.

Harlow saluted the man in the BDUs, a lieutenant colonel, who returned his salute. "Captain Harlow? Grand Rapids CAP?" the man asked, shouting over the roar of the Black Hawk's idling turbines.

"Yes, sir, that's me."

"I'm Lieutenant Colonel Clay Lawson, commander of the Second of the One-forty-seventh Guard Aviation Brigade out of St. Paul," the man said. "My unit's been asked to provide support for the U.S. State Department.

Because this request was . . . rather unusual, I decided to do it myself."

"The State Department, sir?"

Lawson turned to the man in civilian clothes. "This is Special Agent Bruce Hamilton of the Protective Liaison Division of the U.S. State Department's Bureau of Diplomatic Security," Lawson said. "He's here to retrieve one of your cadets."

"Retrieve one of my cadets, sir?"

"Son, you're going to have to get it together and work with me or we're going to be out here all day," Lawson said patiently. "This man wants to take one of your cadets with him. Now I don't know your procedures, so I need you to tell me exactly what you need to do or who you need to call to accomplish this."

"Y-yes, sir. Which cadet?" But he thought he already knew who . . .

"VanWie. Katelyn VanWie."

Harlow opened his mouth, then closed it, looked away, then began to collect his thoughts. "I . . . I can only turn a cadet over to his or her parents, sir."

"We thought so." Lawson turned back to the National Guard officer. A crewmember opened the right side door, revealing two individuals strapped into web seats and wearing headsets. "Are those VanWie's parents? Do you recognize them?"

Harlow stepped toward the helicopter and looked at them carefully, then waved at them. They did not wave back. He turned back toward the National Guard officer. "I want them out of the helicopter so I can speak to them directly."

"I appreciate your concern, Captain, but we should make this quick," Lawson said. He waved, and the flight engineer helped the two out of the harnesses and out of the helicopter. Harlow escorted them away from the helicopter. Hamilton began following them, but Lawson held him back. "He's doing his job, Hamilton—let him," he said.

Now several dozen yards away from everyone else, Harlow pulled the VanWies closer to him. "Richard? Linda? What's going on? Are you two okay?"

"Where's Katelyn?" Linda asked.

"I said, are you two okay?"

"We're fine, Ed," Richard said. "But we need to leave right away. Where's Katelyn?"

Harlow turned and saw the squadron together around the periphery of the clearing, in front of the helicopter in full view of the pilot, as they were taught. As usual, Katelyn was mostly hidden in the back, almost out of sight. "She's right there. She's fine." He thought for a moment, then said, "I thought you guys were at your mother's place in Duluth during the encampment."

"It's Duquette, not Duluth, and it's Richard's brother's place, not his mother's," Linda said. "We invited you there last spring but you came down with the flu."

"I appreciate your caution here, Ed, testing us like that," Richard said, "but this is urgent. We need to leave right away."

"What's going on here?"

"We . . . we need to take her with us," Richard said.

"In a military helicopter?" He motioned to the National Guard officer and civilian. "Who are those guys? Do you know them?"

"We know Hamilton, but not the military officer."

"Hamilton's from the Defense Department?"

"State Department. Protective Liaison Division."

Another test passed—Harlow was beginning to become convinced. "What's this about? Are you in some kind of trouble?" They didn't answer right away. "Listen, if you're under some kind of duress—if these guys aren't who they say they are—I can try to get you and Katelyn out of here. I have a satellite phone, and Katelyn and her flight are familiar with these woods and they have good escape and evasion skills. I can call for help . . ."

"No," Richard said. "Those men are who they say they are." He paused, then added, "But we're not who we said we were."

"What? What are you saying?"

"We're not Katelyn's parents—we're her khataris, her bodyguards," Richard said. He looked around nervously. "Something has happened, and we feel the shahdokht's life is in danger, so she needs to be evacuated immediately."

"The who?"

"Please, Ed, can we get out of here?" Linda said, desperate pleading in her voice. "Maybe we can talk on the helicopter . . ."

"I've got the whole squadron out here—I can't leave!" Harlow said. "And I can't let Katelyn leave until I'm satisfied she'll be safe. If you're not the VanWies, who in hell are you?"

"I am Major Parviz Najar, and this is Lieutenant Mara Saidi," Richard said. "We are security officers assigned to His Highness King Mohammed Hassan Qagev, pretender to the Peacock Throne of Iran."

"What?"

"It is true, Ed," the one who called himself Najar said. "Katelyn's real name is Princess Azar Assiyeh Qagev, eldest surviving child of the true king of Iran, may God bless him and all true believers."

Harlow's mouth dropped open in shock. "You . . . are you kidding me? Is this for real? Is this some kind of *Candid Camera* crap?"

"I know it's hard to believe, Ed, but we're telling you the truth," Linda said. "The princess's family has been in protective custody of the U.S. State Department since Reza Khan Pahlavi took power in Iran in 1925 from the princess's great-grandfather. The princess is the last of her siblings alive—the rest have been hunted down and killed by the Iranian Revolutionary Guards, the Pasdaran."

"But if she's safe here, why take her away?"

"Because we have lost contact with the king, the princess's father, and his court," Najar said. "Until we can contact them, Princess Azar is the heir apparent to the Peacock Throne—the Malika, the queen of Iran."

"Katelyn is . . . a friggin' queen?"

"She must make contact with her countrymen as soon as possible to assure her followers that the dynasty is intact and ready to take power should God and events in Iran allow it," Najar said.

Harlow put a hand on his temple and shook his head, trying to make sense of all this. "I need some sort of verification," Harlow said. "I don't know those two, and now I don't know you. I'm not going to let Katelyn or any of my cadets out of my sight until I'm satisfied everything is in order."

"Ed, it's us—it's still us, the people you know, even though our names have changed," Lieutenant

Saidi said. "We still love and care for Katelyn as if she is really our child. She learned as a youngster not to expect to be treated like a princess while in the United States, and she never has. But now we have to become her guardians again. Her safety is the most important thing now."

"We appreciate all you've done with Katelyn over the years, Ed," Major Najar went on, "but the charade is over. We have to move to a new location for the princess's safety."

"What if I don't let you take her?" Harlow asked.

Najar looked at Saidi, then grimly at the Civil Air Patrol commander. "We have two men aboard the helicopter, Ed," he said darkly. "We surrendered our primary weapons to the lieutenant colonel before he agreed to take us to you, but we all have hidden backup weapons which they did not discover. We are prepared to kill every one of you and take the helicopter if you resist." Harlow was afraid that was going to be his response. He carried a Beretta pistol—loaded but not chambered—and he noticed that both Najar and Saidi glanced to his hip and had probably already decided how they were going to take it away from him. He had no doubt they could do it, too.

"If this is some kind of joke, you two, you just threatened me and all of these children who are on a required training exercise for the U.S. Air Force Auxiliary," Harlow said seriously. "I'll see to it that you're thrown in prison for twenty years if this turns out to be a gag."

"Ed, call anyone you need to call—but please, do it quickly," Saidi pleaded. "We brought our State Department liaison and the National Guard unit commander with us—we would've brought another helicopter filled with officials if we had the time."

"Ed, listen to me—we need to go, so you have to make a decision," Najar said. "The only other fact I can tell you is that if we meant the princess any harm . . ."

"Stop calling her that," Harlow protested. "She's Katelyn, my friend, my subordinate, and out here, my responsibility."

". . . I guarantee you, we would not have hesitated to kill you and all these children to accomplish our mission. We're out in the middle of nowhere—we could kill all of you right now and we'd be in Canada and halfway to safety before anyone discovered your bodies. That's what the Pasdaran would have done if they found the princess first."

"I said, stop calling her that!"

"It's who she is, Ed," Najar said. "I think you've known that for a long time now yourself, haven't you?" Harlow said nothing, but he was perfectly correct—he had noticed she was different, and now he knew why. "You've seen there is something special about her. She has the courage, the intelligence, and the compassion of a princess—you've seen it, as have we and a handful of insightful American teachers we've encountered since living in protective custody in the United States."

Harlow thought for a moment. He looked toward the Black Hawk helicopter and saw one of the two men inside peering back at him, and he knew he had to think of something to verify all this. After a moment, he withdrew his satellite phone from his pocket and dialed his home number—very relieved when he realized that Najar and Saidi, the Iranian bodyguards, allowed him to use the phone. If they were here to harm any of them, that's the last thing they would have wanted.

"Hello?" Harlow's wife answered.

"Hi hon, it's me."

"Hey. How's it going out there? Any problems?"

"Nothing too out of the ordinary," he replied, hoping his wife wouldn't pick up the tension in his voice—and then again, hoping she would. "Can you do me a favor, sweetie?"

"It'll cost you tonight, stud." When he didn't respond, she turned serious. "Sure, babe. Go ahead."

"Hop on the Internet and Google something for me, would you?"

"Hold on a sec." A moment later: "Okay, shoot."

"We're discussing the recent stuff happening in Iran, you know, about the military insurgency they've been talking about?"

"Yeah."

"We got to talking about who was in charge of Iran before the clerics. Can you look that up?"

"Sure. One sec." It did not take long at all: "You mean the Shah? Reza Khan Pahlavi."

Najar was writing something down on a notepad even before Harlow asked: "How about before him?"

"Hold on." A moment later: "Got it. Before the Pahlavi dynasty it was the Qagev dynasty, seventeen eighty to nineteen twenty-five. Before them it was the Zand dynasty, seventeen fifty to seventeen sixty-four. Before that . . ."

"That's what I was looking for, hon, the Qagev dynasty," Harlow interrupted. "We were discussing anyone still alive from the Qagev dynasty. Anything on that?"

Najar held up his notepad. It read: "Mohammed Hassan Qagev II, Dallas, Texas, 3 sons, 4 daughters."

"Hold on," Harlow's wife said. "This is fun. Are you still out in the field?"

"Yes."

"On the satellite phone? Must be costing a fortune."

"Babe . . ."

"I got it right here, Mr. Impatient. Yes, there is a guy still alive from that dynasty. His name is Mohammed Hassan Qagev. And how about this? He lives in the United States—in Addison, Texas. He has a Web site where he blogs on what's happening in Iran."

"Anything else about him?"

"Lots. His wife looks like Angelina Jolie, big lips, big tits—you'd like her. He has seven kids . . . no, wait, it says here that all of them were killed by Iranian secret agents in Europe and Asia. How sad."

"Does it say when?"

"No."

"Anything else?"

"Wait, I'm reading . . . no, nothing much else . . . hey, this is interesting."

"What?"

"There's a picture of him and his wife, from several years ago, and guess what? He's only got four fingers on each hand!"

"He what? Are you sure?"

"That's what it looks like . . . yep, definitely, just four fingers. He's not even trying to hide it. I think that's brave of him. Hey, doesn't one of your cadets, the red-haired girl, have only four fingers on each of her hands?"

"Katelyn. Yes. It's called bilateral hypoplastic thumb."

"Well, I'll take your word for it—it doesn't mention it here. It's like . . . hey, they have a picture of Mohammed's father, in a British World War Two uniform, and guess what?"

"He has only four fingers too."

"It's a little hard to be sure in this photo, but it looks like his right thumb is real short and fused to his index finger. So it must be hereditary, like a royal birthmark thing, huh?"

"I guess."

"Hey, wouldn't it be funny if your cadet, Katelyn, was secretly related to this Mohammed, and living in exile in the United States, hiding out from the Iranian secret police? She'd be, like . . ."

"An Iranian princess," Harlow muttered.

"Exactly. How cool would that be?" No response. "Hon, you still there?"

"Thanks for the info." He thought for a moment; then: "Stay on the line for a minute or two, sweetie, just in case anyone else has any questions."

"Sure, babe. As long as we're not paying that satphone bill."

"It'll be taken care of, don't worry. Hold on. Don't hang up until I tell you to, okay?"

"What's going on, Ed?" his wife asked, but he had already lowered the phone. Najar and Saidi looked at his stunned expression, then looked at the phone but made no move to take it away from him.

This is insane, Harlow thought, completely unbelievable—but he was beginning to believe it. He turned toward his waiting cadets and shouted, "VanWie! Over here."

Katelyn trotted over, smiled at Najar and Saidi, snapped to attention, then saluted. "Reporting as ordered, sir," she said.

"At ease, Lieutenant. With me." Harlow stepped several paces away from the others.

"Why are my parents here, sir?"

"No questions now, Katelyn," Harlow said. He turned toward the helicopter and pointed at Hamilton. "Do you know that man over there?"

"He's a friend of my dad. They work together at the finance company, I think."

"His name?"

"Mr. Hamilton. I'm not sure of his first name."

"How about the guy looking out the door of the helicopter?"

Katelyn looked, swallowed hard, then looked at Harlow. "He's a friend of my dad's too," she said nervously.

"A 'friend?' "

Katelyn looked a little anguished. "What's happening, sir? Why are my parents here?"

"Katelyn, this is very important," Harlow said, studying her eyes carefully. "What you tell me next will determine what I'm about to do in the next few seconds, but you have to be completely honest with me or I could do the wrong thing and . . . and put you in very great danger."

"Danger?" The apprehension in her face melted away, replaced by concern and steely determination. "What's happened, sir?" Her voice had changed—markedly so.

"Katelyn, yes or no, and be honest with me: are those two people really your parents?"

"What's happened, sir?" she repeated, almost a demand now.

"Answer me, Katelyn, or I'm going to grab you and take you and the rest of the squadron back into the woods and call for help."

"Something's happened to my parents," Katelyn breathed. "Hasn't it, sir?"

"Are these your parents, Katelyn? Yes or no. Tell me."

Katelyn realized she wasn't going to get the answers she wanted unless she changed her tactics. "No, they're not," she replied. "They are Major Najar and Lieutenant Saidi."

"What do they do?"

"They are specially chosen members of the King's Palace Guards, assigned to protect me," Katelyn said. Harlow's mouth dropped open, and a roaring sound unrelated to the Black Hawk's idling turbines began in his ears. "Now tell me what's happened, sir. My father . . . ?"

"Is missing. They said they've come to take you away from here. They . . ."

"Na baba!" Katelyn shouted in a voice Harlow had never heard from her before except in instances of extreme excitement or tension. "Fori-ei! I've got to do something!" She dashed off toward Najar and Saidi, who snapped to attention as she approached.

"Katelyn!"

The girl turned, then stood at attention and saluted. "Pardon me, sir, but I must leave. Thank you for all the precautions you've taken on my behalf, and thank you for your leadership and dedication. I won't forget it." She dropped her salute, then ran for the helicopter, with Najar and Saidi close behind. The two men inside the helicopter scrambled out and snapped to attention on either side of the Black Hawk's right door. The last Harlow saw of her, she was pulling a headset over her fatigue cap, gesturing for Hamilton and Lawson to get inside, and pulling the Black Hawk helicopter's door closed herself.

After the helicopter lifted off, Harlow raised the satphone. "It's okay, babe," he said. "I'm heading home now."

"Ed, I heard some of that," his wife said anxiously. "What's going on out there?"

"I'll explain everything when I get home—or someone will."

"What do you mean? Ed . . . ?"

"I'll be home in a few hours, babe. See you," then reluctantly pressed the red button on the phone.

He was never certain, he thought as he turned and headed toward the other completely stunned cadets, exactly where Katelyn VanWie belonged . . . until now.

"What can you tell me about my parents, Agent Hamilton?" Azar Qagev asked as soon as she donned her headset.

"The Protective Liaison Division agents assigned to your mother and father found your parents' home empty early this morning, Your Highness," Hamilton said. "There's been no word on any of our message lines. We executed the recovery network established for them but they have not made contact with anyone in the system." Every foreign dignitary in the United States had a plan established where they would go to a particular city and make contact with a certain individual, usually at a hotel, airport, restaurant, or other such public place in a large metropolitan area, in case of danger. In the meantime, the area would be flooded by agents of the Diplomatic Security Services, Federal Bureau of Investigation, U.S. Secret Service, U.S. Marshals, and other federal law enforcement agencies. Unfortunately, foreign dignitaries who stayed in the United States for long periods of time rarely updated or exercised their plans until it was too late to respond to an attack. "It's still very early, but we decided to make contact with you and take you to a safe location."

"Thank you, Agent Hamilton," Azar said.

"Unfortunately, because your father runs his Internet blog and frequently comments on happenings in Iran, the media is all over this development," Hamilton went on. "It was only a matter of time before they tracked you down to Grand Rapids. And now that your parents have disappeared, you'll be the focus of their attention. There's already been a leak to the wire services that Iranian royalty is being protected in the United States, and the FBI and State Department have already received inquiries. I hope you understand how hectic it's going to be. The State Department will do all it can to shield your movements from the media, but they are very persistent."

"I understand, Agent Hamilton." She thought for a moment, then said to Major Najar in perfect Farsi, "Major, I need to contact the Court immediately."

"Of course, Malika," Najar said. "I will . . ."

"Do not call me that yet, Major," Azar said. "I am Shahdokht to all until the whereabouts of the King and Queen are positively determined."

"I apologize, Shahdokht," Najar said. "Agent Hamilton, when is the first chance we will have to access a secure telephone or Internet connection?"

"We'll return to Grand Rapids, then take a chartered flight to Minneapolis," Hamilton said. "The FBI office has loaned us armored vehicles, which will take you to a safe house outside the city. They should have secure communications capability in the vehicles. We'll arrange a secure satellite Internet link in the safe house if it doesn't already have it."

"Very well. Thank you," Azar said. To Najar, she asked in Farsi, "What's the latest about the insurgency back home?"

"Confused and sketchy information, Shahdokht," Najar replied, "but it appears that General Hesarak al-Kan Buzhazi has launched a major attack on a mosque in Qom that may have been a safe house for a good number of clerics and government officials. Speculation is that he destroyed the Khomeini Library with his captives inside."

"Bavar nakardani!" Azar exclaimed. "Buzhazi is either completely insane or utterly ruthless—we need to find out which it is. Major, I need the latest information on Buzhazi, the Pasdaran deployments, and our resistance and intelligence networks in-country."

"Yes, Shahdokht."

"Buzhazi is blind with rage and power-lust, Shahdokht," Lieutenant Saidi said. "He and his followers have narrowly managed to avoid complete destruction by the skin of their teeth. They are outnumbered at least ten to one. The Pasdaran will crush them soon enough."

"No insurgency of any kind has had this much success—and Buzhazi has taken on the Pasdaran directly," Azar said. "If he succeeds, or even if he ignites the passion of freedom in the people, we can use it to our advantage. We must learn everything we can about Buzhazi's goals and plans and see if we can join forces with him."

"Join forces?" Najar asked. "Princess, Buzhazi was the Faqih's chief executioner not too long ago—he and his minions killed most of your family and drove us out of Europe and the Middle East. He can't be trusted. It would be better to bide our time and see what happens with this insurgency."

"If Buzhazi is crushed, the Pasdaran will only grow in power and status, perhaps eclipsing the army," Azar said. "If the regular army or the people will follow

Buzhazi in destroying the clerics, we must be sure we have a seat at the table for whatever else may happen. But we must know what is going on, up to the second." She fell silent for a moment, then said, "I want you to activate the rud-khaneh immediately."

Najar's eyes widened in surprise. "Are you certain, Princess?" he asked. "The underground network is secure and has been growing for a decade. If we activate the network and the Revolutionary Guards destroy Buzhazi and discover it . . ."

"We must know," Azar said. "It must be done. Our people will just need to take extraordinary precautions and be prepared to go back to ground if the insurgency fails and the Pasdaran start a new purge."

Najar looked at the princess carefully, then said in a low voice, "Should you not wait to hear from the King, Princess?"

Azar looked at her long-time bodyguard, considering not only his words but the tone. "They're alive, Major. I would have felt their passing."

"Then wait a while longer before committing to activating the intelligence network, *Shahdokht,*" Najar said. He smiled at her. "I'm happy to see you are so ready to take charge, Princess—the lessons we taught you were not lost in the thick mud of Western decadence that you have subjected yourself to for all these years. But use caution. The situation is dangerous for you, but to our friends and supporters back home, it is deadly. When we rise up, we should do it in concert."

"We will, Major," Azar said. "But in order to decide when to rise, we need information. If my parents are alive, it is my responsibility to assist them in making the decisions that affect our future." She squinted back tears, then said, "If they are dead, I'll need the advice of the network to assess the situation and decide a course of action—whether we support Buzhazi, conduct our own insurgency alongside his, or go back into hiding and await the will of God."

"Insh'Allah," Najar and Saidi said together.

"Insh'Allah," Azar echoed. She thought for a moment, then took out a notepad from her Civil Air Patrol battle dress uniform, wrote a note, and passed it to Najar. He took a deep breath as he read it, then passed it to Saidi, whose expression was even more incredulous. "Can you do it, Major?" she asked.

Najar passed the note to the men in the back of the Black Hawk, who looked at each other in surprise, then nodded warily. Najar made a few notes of his own, showed them to Azar and Saidi, then to the men. They all nodded in assent. "It will be done, Shahdokht . . . insh'Allah," Najar said. "If it is the will of God."

In just a few minutes they were making an approach to Grand Rapids–Itasca County Airport and parked just outside AirWays Aviation, the lone fixed-base operator on the field. Just a few yards away was a Falcon business jet, with a Jet-A refueling truck just pulling away. The jet's crewmembers watched the helicopter touch down, then moved to the boarding door to help the passengers aboard. Katelyn shook hands with Lawson. "Thank you for all you've done, Colonel," she said.

"Good luck to you, Lieutenant—or whoever you are," Lawson responded.

"Salam aleikom, agha," Katelyn said, then shoved open the door and scrambled out.

"The jet's fueled up and ready," Special Agent Hamilton said after speaking with the pilot and escorting Katelyn to the boarding door. "Weather is favorable in Minneapolis but traffic is heavy, so we'll use Flying Cloud Airport instead of the international airport. The FBI is standing by."

"Wouldn't it look less conspicuous to go to the bigger airport, Agent Hamilton?"

"Flying Cloud is a pretty busy airport—most bizjets go there," Hamilton replied. "The FBI thinks it'll be safer, and you should have less interference from the media." Within moments they were aboard, the door closed, and they were taxiing to the end of runway 16 for takeoff. With no traffic in the pattern, the jet was airborne within minutes. "Less than a hundred and fifty miles to Flying Cloud, Your Highness—no more than twenty minutes," Hamilton said. "Are you all right?"

"Yes, Agent Hamilton," Azar said. "And I wanted to thank you again for all you've done for me. Your service is very much appreciated."

"My pleasure, Your Highness."

"So I hope you don't take offense by what we are going to do." Azar made a motion with her hands, and her four bodyguards leapt to their feet, guns drawn. Two headed immediately to the cockpit while Najar and Saidi stayed with Azar, their guns drawn.

"What in hell is this?" Hamilton exclaimed. "What are you doing?"

"No offense to you or the American State Department, Agent Hamilton," Azar said, "but putting us into protective custody in Minneapolis is not what we need to do right now for the people of Iran." She took Hamilton's sidearm and backup weapon away from him, then turned to Najar and said in Farsi, "Make sure the pilots don't make any radio calls or change the transponder codes to report a hijacking, Major. Can we file an international flight plan inflight?"

"No, Highness," Najar said. "We'll have to fly low over the border and try to go under radar coverage.

We risk a military pursuit, but they will not be able to respond quickly enough to find us. We will contact our agents in Canada and arrange for them to meet us at the alternate landing site."

"Very well." The plane started turning, and soon the two charter pilots were heading back to the cabin, hands over their heads.

"If you wanted to get out of the United States, Highness, why not just request that?" Hamilton asked angrily. "We would have complied."

"We want to avoid the media as much as possible and shield our movements from everyone," Azar said. "Going into protective custody in Minneapolis, with the media all around us, would have wasted time and put my parents in even greater danger."

"Where are we going?"

"Canada," Azar replied. "We have agents throughout Canada waiting for precisely this moment. After we're safely away, we'll release you and your aircraft."

"This is completely unnecessary, Highness . . ."

"Again, Agent Hamilton, I thank you for your concern and dedication," Azar said sincerely. "But we have been guests of the American government for too long. It's time the royal family went back to Iran and took our place among our people again." Hamilton shook his head and sat back. Azar looked at Najar and Saidi and asked in Farsi, "Am I insane for doing this, Major? Lieutenant?"

"Once we place ourselves in the hands of the Americans and their out-of-control media, Highness, we would be at their mercy," Najar said. "We would be trusting our lives to someone else's political agenda."

"What if Buzhazi made a deal for him to cooperate with Washington in forming a government favorable to them—in exchange for turning over you and your family to him, or having us placed in permanent 'protective custody?' " Saidi asked. "The point is, Highness, that with us in the hands of the Americans, our fate is not our own—it belongs to them and whatever agenda they may have. It will be difficult for us, but at least our fate is in our hands and the hands of your loyal subjects."

"We are proud of you, Highness," Najar said. "It took extraordinary courage to do this. It would have been far easier and more comfortable and perhaps safer for you to simply go along with the Americans, but you instead decided to take the initiative and plan your own escape. Now whatever happens is up to God and ourselves. That is the way it should be."

Azar smiled, nodded, and sat back in her seat. She looked out the window at the flat lake-strewn landscape of northern Minnesota. It was the only place she ever remembered, the only home she ever knew—and now she was leaving it, perhaps forever.

"Are you sad to leave here, Shahdokht?" Saidi asked gently. "It is truly a beautiful land."

"You have grown strong and wise here, Princess," Najar added. "There will always be a part of this land in you."

Azar took one last look, then resolutely closed the window shade and shook her head. "As soon as we can," she said by way of response, removing her fatigue cap, touching her hair, and holding it out for them to see, "I want some hair coloring so I can get back to my natural-born hair color. I enjoyed being a redhead, Lieutenant, but I'm ready to be a dark-haired Persian again—now, and forever."

CHAPTER 5

ARĀN, IRAN

The Next Evening

As the old line went: It was quiet . . . too quiet.

General Mansour Sattari and his task force had captured or eliminated almost three full platoons of guards on their way to the Pasdaran warehouses outside Arān. So far the operation was going precisely as planned . . .

. . . which made the general very, very nervous indeed. Even though the objective was in sight and so far they had suffered no casualties and met numerous but weak resistance, Sattari couldn't suppress the feeling that something bad was going to happen.

"I don't like it, Babak," Sattari said to his aide, Master Sergeant Babak Khordad, as they received the final report from the scouts. Khordad was an old crusty veteran when Sattari picked him over fifteen years ago to run his staff, and he hadn't changed much—which was exactly the way the general preferred it. Even his name, which meant "little father" in Farsi, still accurately described him. "The reports were completely accurate: the warehouses are virtually unguarded. That has me worried—rumors and unverified reports from the field are never that accurate, unless they're planted by the enemy."

"They have a large number of guards, sir," Khordad said, "but they look to me like children. It's as if they emptied out the conscripts' training centers before they barely began, gave them a weapon and uniform, and put them to work guarding these warehouses."

"I agree," Sattari said. "Where are the front-line Pasdaran forces, Babak?"

"We do have reports stating that the Pasdaran is concentrating forces in the capital," Khordad said. "Maybe the new government is pulling in all the well-trained troops to protect them at home."

"Maybe," Sattari mused.

"If you don't feel right about this one, sir, let's pull everyone out," Khordad said. "If it smells like a trap, it probably is."

"But we've got two hundred men surrounding this area checking in every three minutes, and no one has spotted any sign of the front-line Pasdaran forces," Sattari said. "Not even one helicopter in the past hour. From where we are now, we could completely empty three warehouses and be on the rail line heading into the system before the outer perimeter scouts spotted anything."

"I don't know, sir," Khordad said. "I still say, let's withdraw and continue monitoring."

"Our intel says the Pasdaran is going to start emptying these warehouses in the next two days," Sattari said. "They have the trucks and locomotives waiting—it's going to happen soon. So far our intel has been spot-on. Besides, we're running low on everything back at the base. We've got to do this tonight or it'll be too late."

"That's when it's the worst time to do something, sir," Khordad said.

Sattari peered through his low-light binoculars again, scanning for any sign of a trap, but he saw and heard absolutely nothing. He had to press on. With a dozen heavy cargo trucks filled, they had enough supplies to keep their insurgency going for another month. That could spell the difference between success and failure.

But the "little father" was worried—there was danger here. Why couldn't he see it? "Maybe the Pasdaran has suffered so many losses, captures, and defections that soft targets like these warehouses were being lightly guarded?" he suggested. "Maybe they really are afraid of lingering chemical weapons effects . . ."

"They know as well as we do what the persistence time of those chemical agents are, sir," Khordad said. "And their detection equipment is better than ours. If it was safe, they'd be here. Something's happening that we don't know about."

"Could the warehouses be booby-trapped?"

"Very likely, sir, although we saw a lot of those guards going in and out rather freely," Khordad said. "It's usually dangerous to turn initiators on and off whenever someone walks in and out like that—you'll soon forget if you shut it off or not."

Sattari swore to himself, then picked up his radio. "Spider to Wolf."

"Go," General Hesarak al-Kan Buzhazi responded.

"We've arrived at point 'Kangaroo.' 'Bedroom' in sight, but I'm recommending we head back to the 'nursery.' Our 'album' is incomplete. Over."

"Understood. Bring it on back. We'll take better pictures later. Wolf out."

"Okay, Master Sergeant," Sattari said, putting away his command radio, "let's set up the patrols and position for exfiltration before . . ."

"Shit, what is he doing?" Khordad swore. Sattari lifted his night-vision binoculars. A squad of men had broken from cover and had bolted for their assigned warehouse, while another squad was commandeering trucks.

"Call them back, damnit!"

Khordad was already raising his radio to his lips: "Shark, Shark, this is Spider, get back! We're heading back to 'nursery.' Acknowledge right now."

"Spider, we're in, we're in!" came the reply. "It's all here, Spider, lined up and ready to load. We can have a truck loaded in two minutes."

"I said get out of there!" Khordad growled through clenched teeth, trying to communicate the urgency without raising his voice. "Acknowledge!"

"Spider, this is Bear," another squad leader radioed. "We're in too. We've started loading two carriages already and the others are moving inside. We've already filled our baby bottles all the way. Recommend we proceed. Over."

"Sir?" Khordad asked.

"Let's get out of here, Babak," Sattari said. "There will be other targets. This one looks poisonous. Bring them out now."

"Negative! Negative! Withdraw!" Khordad radioed. "Spider's orders. All squads, acknowledge!"

"Spider, this is Pony, we're in too," yet another squad leader radioed. "Let us play for just a few minutes more. This is the real party, and we want to stay for the cake."

Sattari grabbed Khordad's radio and mashed the mike button: "All squads, this is Spider, I ordered you to withdraw, and that means right now! Get your asses moving and report at point Parlor. Do not acknowledge, just move out!" He tossed the radio back to Khordad and began scrambling out of their hiding place toward the perimeter fence. "Damn them! What a time for a discipline breakdown! I know they're hungry and running low on everything, but they should know better than to . . ."

"Sir, wait!" Khordad interrupted, holding his radio close to his ear. "I thought I heard another call."

Sattari raised his own radio to his ear and listened intently. "Another squad?"

"I think it was one of the scouts, sir . . ."

And at that moment they heard over their radios: "Spider, Spider, this is Sparrow, reporting in the blind, I say again, warning, warning, lightning storm, lightning storm, call the children in, repeat, call the children in!"

"Ridan!" Sattari cursed. On his radio, he and Khordad both frantically called, "All Spider units, all Spider units, lightning storm, lightning storm, take cover!"

Sattari then leaped to his feet, pulling Khordad and their security guard up onto their feet and pushing them toward the hole in the outer perimeter fence about fifty meters away. "Move it, move it!" he shouted. "Shoot anyone that gets in your . . . !"

Sattari didn't hear the rest . . . because the entire warehouse complex erupted in a brilliant tidal wave of fire seconds later.

From a dozen launch sites—some as far as fifteen kilometers away—multiple volleys of artillery, rockets, and guided missiles bombarded the warehouse complex all at once. Not only was every warehouse building individually targeted and completely obliterated, but the entire complex—parking lots, storage bins, loading ramps, fences, barracks, offices, and service buildings—were bracketed. Within two minutes, every square centimeter of the entire twenty-acre complex was hit multiple times.

In moments, it was over—and not one thing was left standing in or around the complex.

IMAM ALI MILITARY ACADEMY, TEHRAN, IRAN

Several Days Later

After checking in with his supervisors by telephone, commander-in-chief of the Iranian armed forces General

Hoseyn Yassini emerged from his quarters on the campus of the Imam Ali Military Academy in Tehran and began his early evening stroll across the grounds. He immediately identified at least one shadow, a young man dressed as a first-year cadet. He was far too young to be Pasdaran. More likely he was a komiteh officer, a religious-political functionary whose job it was to observe and report on any activities that might be considered a threat to the clerical regime. Like the zampolit political officers in the old Soviet Union, komiteh officers pervaded every level of Iranian life, watching and reporting on everyone from ordinary citizens on the streets to the highest levels of government. They were an abomination in a place like this military academy, but under the theocratic regime their presence was as demoralizing as it was pervasive.

Yassini's usual evening stroll while on restriction was down the wide sidewalks of the main cluster of buildings to the parade grounds, a couple kilometers of mostly well-lit, open areas. Formerly known as the Shah Reza Pahlavi Military Academy when Yassini attended here, it was changed to the Imam Ali Academy after the revolution. A few cadets were still on the streets. Yassini enjoyed stopping them and, after the initial shock of meeting the chief of staff wore off, speaking with them and learning about their studies and training while attending the school. For the most part, the cadets were eager, respectful, proud to be wearing the uniform, and determined to spend the next twenty to thirty years in service to the Faqih and their country. Thankfully, none of them seemed to know that he was here on house arrest or why, or if they did they didn't show any signs of displeasure.

After passing the main cluster of classroom buildings, Yassini came upon a large square courtyard, surrounded by the cadets' barracks buildings. This was the Esplanade, or brigade assembly area, where the cadet units would gather and form up before marching off to class, functions, drills, or parades. At other times, the assembly area was used in that age-old custom familiar to cadets from all over the world for eons—marching off demerit points. Before any cadet could graduate from the Academy, he had to spend one hour marching back and forth in the assembly area for every point he had accumulated, dressed in full uniform and carrying an assault rifle. While marching, he could be grilled by any upperclassman on the Koran, any knowledge item, or critiqued on the condition of his uniform, and additional demerit points could be awarded. Cadets marched off points at any time of the day or night, in any weather, sometimes for an entire weekend if necessary to clear away demerits before graduation.

Hoseyn Yassini was a good student and leader, but he was a terrible cadet, and he spent many, many hours on this dark marble square, either marching the demerits off or scrubbing it clean, which was another acceptable way of working off demerits. Being out here as a young officer gave him a clearer sense of duty and honor, and also sharpened his mind in preparation for the grilling he knew he would get.

But he was not out here because of some nostalgic wish to visit, or coming here restored his soul of any lost humility or discipline.

The assembly area had a small booth where a cadet officer was assigned to take down the name and unit of any cadet who arrived to march off demerits and to make sure the cadets performed properly while out here, and Yassini strolled over to the booth to chat with the cadet officer on duty. The cadet snapped to his feet and saluted as soon as he saw the general approach. "Cadet Sergeant Beheshi, Company Joqd, sir."

Yassini returned his salute. "Good evening, Cadet Sergeant," he said. "How are you this evening?"

"Very well, sir, thank you," the cadet responded. "I hope you are well tonight, sir."

"I am, thank you."

"May I serve you in any way, General?"

"I was wondering, Cadet Sergeant: are you happy here at the Academy?"

The question took the cadet by surprise, but as expected he recovered very quickly: "I am proud and honored to serve the Supreme Leader and the people of the Islamic Republic, sir," he replied, reciting the typical Academy mantra taught to every cadet from the moment they stepped foot on campus.

"I can see you are, Cadet Sergeant, but I'm asking you: are you happy here?"

Obviously the cadet didn't like the question or its implications, because he uncharacteristically stammered: "I . . . I . . . yes, sir, I am very happy here."

"What field do you wish to serve in upon graduation?"

"I will serve at the pleasure of the Supreme Leader and the people . . ."

"No, Cadet, I mean, what service do you want? Surely you have a particular desire? A specific specialty?"

The cadet still looked flustered, but he smiled and nodded. "Yes, sir. I wish to be a Special Forces commando, possibly even a Revolutionary Guards Corps brigade commander."

"Oh? Why?"

"Because I believe it is vital to pursue the enemy beyond our own borders," the cadet responded. "I do not wish to wait for the enemy to be upon us before we fight back—I want to destroy the enemy before he even leaves his base. Even better, destroy him before he leaves his home—destroy him while he's in his home!"

Yassini was taken aback by this show of utter ruthlessness. "So you wish to kill noncombatants even if no war is declared?"

The cadet's eyes looked a little panic-stricken. "I hope I haven't offended you, sir," he said.

"No, not at all. Anything we say here is between us soldiers." He could see the relief in the cadet's eyes even in the dim light. "So, killing the enemy's family in their homes is how you wish to fight?"

"Yes, sir. I wish to see the terror in their faces as I dispatch them. I wish to see the faces of their neighbors, families, and friends when they find their slashed corpses lying in their beds. The horror of such an attack multiplies the power of the state a thousandfold."

"Is that what they teach you here, Cadet?"

"Absolutely, sir. Concepts of asymmetric warfare, commando operations, guerrilla warfare, psychological combat . . . it is my favorite area of study. We take lessons from all of the guerrilla armies around the world throughout recent history—Hizb'Allah, Islamic Jihad, Fatah, Hamas, Mehdi Army, al-Qaeda, the Viet Cong, the Tamil Tigers—study them, and adapt them to modern-day scenarios and equipment."

"Interesting. But what about areas such as air defense, border security, the submarine service, or land warfare?"

"Those are fine areas of study, sir—for women," the cadet responded. "Fear is the great multiplier, sir. You can detect and pursue a submarine, tank, or aircraft—but no one has yet developed a sensor or defense against fear. Create fear in the mind and heart of the enemy, and you almost don't need a bullet or bomb to kill him."

"But attacking noncombatants . . . ?"

"All the better, sir. A soldier will not think about his unit or duty if he feels his family is in danger. That gives us the advantage."

My God, Yassini thought, is this really what the Academy is teaching its students these days? In his day, the Academy taught leadership, history, and tactics, not murder.

"I must do my rounds and report to my superior officer, sir," the cadet said. "Please stay here if you wish. I will have some tea brought from the mess."

"Thank you, Cadet. I think I will stay awhile longer. It was a pleasure speaking with you, Cadet Sergeant."

"The pleasure was mine, sir. Good evening." He saluted and departed.

A few minutes later, just as Yassini was thinking about heading back to his quarters for the evening, an orderly arrived with a large copper pot of tea and a basket of cups, sugar, and cinnamon sticks. "Thank you, sir," Yassini said as the orderly poured.

"So, you old fart, the new generation has you a little bewildered and flustered, eh?" the orderly asked. Yassini looked at him in surprise . . . and saw none other than General Hesarak Buzhazi smiling back at him. He was dressed in servants' robes and pants, but he could see his combat boots under his robe and perhaps the bulge of a weapon underneath. "Disappointed no one wants to fly helicopters or go up against stealth bombers and smart missiles anymore?"

"What in hell are you doing here, you crazy idiot? The entire country is out looking for you."

"The Academy is the last place they'd look, Hoseyn," Buzhazi said. He looked at Yassini seriously. "I told you they were going to retaliate against you, Hoseyn, and now here you are, on house arrest. Why are you just standing around like some pea-brained sheep waiting for the slaughter? You should get out of here now, before you have more than just one brainless snot-nosed komiteh goon on your ass."

"Did you kill him too?"

"I didn't have to. He is gone beating off or something—he thought you were just going out on your evening constitutional and left. That's the kind of idiots Zolqadr has working for him. Why the hell don't you get away from here, Hoseyn? They think you're just a scared tottering old man. Save yourself while you can."

"I should take career management advice from you, the most wanted man in the entire damned country? That would be hilarious if it wasn't so tragic. What in the world are you doing here?"

"You invited me, remember? 'Let's march off a few'—that's what you said. I've been waiting for you ever since."

"No, I mean, what are you still doing in Iran?" Yassini asked. "Haven't you done enough damage to the country?"

"I'm not finished, Hoseyn," Buzhazi said. The Pasdaran is like a typhoon—as long as it's unopposed, even by the smallest hill or tree, it will grow stronger, its path will become more unpredictable, and it will destroy more and more lives. I plan to stop it."

"You have about as much chance of doing that as stopping a real typhoon," Yassini said. "Can't you see that?"

"Some things are worth dying for, Hoseyn: freedom from betrayal, freedom from persecution, freedom to live our lives with dignity and honor. I'm doing something about it. What I don't understand is how you can even stand the stench of being around Pasdaran butchers after what happened last night."

"I heard," Yassini said gloomily. "Typical Pasdaran tactics—disregard friendly forces in the target area, disregard taking prisoners, and kill everyone in the area. Monstrous."

" 'Monstrous?' That's all you have to say? There was an entire company of security guards in that warehouse complex, some just teenage conscripts with barely any training! They're all dead! They were obliterated in a massive artillery attack designed to kill every living thing in the entire area!"

"I had nothing to do with planning, authorizing, or executing that attack."

"I never thought you did, Hoseyn, but the question is: what are you going to do now?"

"What can I do about it?"

"You're the damned chief of staff, Hoseyn!" Buzhazi retorted. "Call out the army, disperse them to operational areas outside the cities, and tell Zolqadr and whoever else is in charge that you will send them into the cities and crush the Pasdaran if they don't lay down their arms and stop this madness!"

"They will never lay down their weapons," Yassini said. "The fact is, Hesarak, that you have driven them to execute such extreme operations! They would never have done it if you and your insurgent forces had just gotten out of the country instead of embarking on this insane plot."

"Hoseyn, this is only the beginning," Buzhazi said. "They will stop at nothing now. They won't just be chasing me—they'll be going after every soldier and soon every civilian that doesn't toe the fundamentalist line just so. You've condemned millions of Iranians to death because of your inaction. And when they're done in Iran, they'll spread out over the entire region, perhaps the entire planet."

"Don't blame this on me, Buzhazi! It's you who started this, not me! The deaths of the innocents will be on your head, not mine!"

"At least I'm doing something about it, Hoseyn. My death won't be as horrible as the one you are condemning Iran and the world to with your silence and inaction." Yassini didn't—couldn't—answer that. "Do it, Hoseyn—now, tonight, before it's too late. Call out the army and disperse them to the countryside. The Pasdaran is too involved in hunting me down to guard every base across the country. You'll only get one chance at this. Do it tonight."

"That's treason, Hesarak," Yassini said. "That's a crime, punishable by public beheading."

"The people and the armed forces will suffer much worse if the ayatollahs unleash the Pasdaran on the cities," Buzhazi said. "Do it, now."

Yassini paused . . . then shook his head, and Buzhazi's shoulders slumped in disappointment. "You realize that I have to report this contact, don't you?" Yassini said instead. "I have no choice. I could be executed just for the very thought of being seen with you."

"Then why did you want to meet here, Hoseyn?" Buzhazi asked. "I know the reason—you're unsure of what to do. I'll tell you what you should do, my friend—get out and come with me, now. I have a squad with me standing by that can get us all out safely. I have more men ready to get your family out of the capital as well."

Yassini turned and looked away, out onto the assembly area. "You know I can't do that, Hesarak," he said after a long, quiet moment.

"You're a fool, Hoseyn."

"I'm not like you, Hesarak. I believe in my country and its leaders, right or wrong. They may not be perfect—they may not even be right. But I'm a soldier, and I'm sworn to live by my oath and defend this nation. You may think I'm crazy or suicidal, but that's what I have to do." He took a deep breath, turned, then said, "And part of my duty is to call for the guards and . . ."

But it was too late—when he turned to look at his old friend, he was gone—most certainly for the last time.

General Yassini took his time walking back to his quarters, but upon arriving he immediately picked up the phone. He didn't have to dial any numbers—he knew someone was listening and would inform Zolqadr right away. He probably didn't even need to pick up the phone—the entire apartment was probably bugged, like the phone.

"This is General Yassini," he spoke. "I would like to report contact with a known wanted criminal, General Hesarak al-Kan Buzhazi, near the assembly yard duty officer's station on the Imam Ali Military Academy campus, just a few minutes ago. He said he was here with a squad of men. He was dressed as an orderly or kitchen laborer. He did not appear armed, but he should be considered armed and dangerous."

General Yassini shook his head as he hung up the phone. Poor bastard, he thought—Buzhazi doesn't have a chance, and he still doesn't realize it.

ELLIOTT AIR FORCE BASE, GROOM LAKE, NEVADA

The Next Morning

"I hope everyone realizes that we're not going to be making this a regular thing," Hunter Noble said, squirming uncomfortably in his seat. He had already bumped his helmet on the canopy a dozen times, and he dreaded having to touch any switch in the cockpit. Not only was he bumping into things, but he wasn't even in his seat—he had been relegated to the mission commander's seat, the dreaded "Guy in Back," for the second time.

"Quit your complaining, Boomer—I think this is very cool," "Nano" Benneton said, strapped into the passenger module of the XR-A9 Black Stallion spaceplane. "I think making you ride bitch every now and then keeps you humble."

"I let the general fly his mission in the front seat," Boomer said. "I'm still trying to live that one down too." It was also the first time he had ever worn a spacesuit in the cockpit of the XR-A9 Black Stallion spaceplane, so he was feeling doubly uncomfortable. It was an older-style Skylab-type spacesuit, a design at least thirty years old, the first series of spacesuits not custom-fitted for a particular astronaut—and it felt like it too. Underneath the suit was a thin mesh garment with fluids circulating through tubes to help keep the wearer comfortable, and under the helmet he wore the classic "Mickey Mouse" cap–style headset. The suit was not yet pressurized, and Boomer still had complete mobility in it, but he still groused.

He had to put it on hours earlier and seal it up so he could pre-breathe pure oxygen, and then he had to suffer the indignation of having to be helped into the cockpit by Nano and the smiling, laughing ground crew. "I can't see or feel a thing, it's noisy, I can't hear the radios, and it smells. The cockpit pressurization system is just fine."

"Boomer, if I hear you complain about the suit one more time, you're staying on the ground," Lieutenant-General Patrick McLanahan radioed from the Dreamland command center.

"I know, sir, I know," Boomer responded.

"Poor baby's got to wear a spacesuit," Ann Page said, chuckling. She was seated with Nano in the passenger module. "Get over it, Boomer."

"Hey, you old farts had to wear them all the time," Boomer argued. "This is the twenty-first century. Our stuff works."

"Captain, you are about to experience the thrill of a lifetime—enjoy it," Colonel Kai Raydon said. He was in the front seat as pilot of the XR-A9. Raydon was a little over average height—which meant tall for an astronaut—with short blond hair and quick, piercing blue eyes. Everyone found it amusing that Raydon's fingers were always in motion, as if he couldn't wait to start flipping switches or entering instructions into a computer. "We are going to knock your socks off this morning, I guarantee it."

Although designed for six passengers, the Black Stallion's passenger module was loaded to capacity with supplies and equipment, so Benneton and Page had absolutely no room to move about even if they wanted to do so. The rear of the module contained all their supplies, and they were seated in the middle row. The front of the module was mostly occupied by a large flexible tube attached to the top of the module. This was the docking adapter and transfer tunnel. Like many of the systems and procedures they would use on this flight, the adapter had never been operationally tested either. It was definitely going to be a day full of firsts.

"I can't wait, sir," Boomer said moodily. "Really, I can't." He checked his readouts when an alert tone sounded. "Computer's started the pre-engine start checklist, crew," he announced. Things happened quickly after that, and before long the Black Stallion was airborne.

Because this was going to be a different kind of mission, the insertion into orbit was anything but typical. After refueling over the Pacific Ocean as normal, Boomer flew the Black Stallion on a steep climb and descent across the North Pole, then over the Norwegian Sea and North Sea just off the coast of Scotland, where they rendezvoused with another modified KC-77 tanker and refueled once again. They then turned north and cruised off the coast of Norway as directed by the flight computers, awaiting the proper time for orbital insertion. At the proper moment, the Laser Pulse Detonation Rocket System engines flared to life, and the Black Stallion propelled itself once again into space.

It was soon obvious that this was not another typical orbital insertion mission—the boost burn lasted several minutes longer than normal, and the view from the cockpit was completely different. The difference in altitude was striking. "Well, this looks weird," was all Boomer could say. The sense of altitude and the sight of so much more of the Earth was unnerving, like looking down from a very tall bridge while standing on the edge of a very narrow catwalk.

"Coming up on the last normal orbital abort point," Dave Luger said.

"Everyone okay?" Boomer asked, forgetting for the umpteenth time that the aircraft commander called for checklists to be completed, not the "Guy In Back." "Station check and give me a green light to continue." At this point if there was some sort of problem they could execute a deorbit burn, come out of orbit, and still have enough fuel to make a normal landing at a good variety of airports. If they went past this point with the main engines still boosting them higher, their options quickly decreased. But everyone reported all systems normal, so they continued.

It happened with amazing speed: five minutes past a normal burn period, Boomer got a flashing warning message on his supercockpit display. "Cripes, just fifteen minutes to bingo fuel," he muttered. "Normally we'd be getting ready to land by now—we haven't even completed our insertion burn yet."

"It's going to be a close one, crew," Dave Luger said. "We're watching the burn curve carefully, and so far we're just a few percent under it. About ten minutes to the emergency abort point."

"Too much information, General," Raydon said. "We're committed—there's no emergency abort." Everyone knew he was correct: they could make it back to Earth intact, but exactly which runway they'd land on—or even if there was a runway nearby—was unknown. Their best—and soon their only—hope was to make the trip as planned.

It seemed to take forever, but soon the "leopards" engines shut down, and the ship went from a sustained, loud roar to complete silence within milliseconds. "Two hundred and fifteen miles up," Boomer breathed.

"I didn't think it would make that big a difference, but it does." He looked at the fuel readings, then told himself not to bother looking any longer—they were dismal. Their fuel was nearly exhausted, and they still had one large LPDRS burn to do to slow the Black Stallion down from its current "chase" speed to a speed slow enough for the crew to use maneuvering thrusters to position the spaceplane.

The telemetry readouts showed them exactly how far they had to go and how long it would take to get there, so there were absolutely no surprises, but Boomer found himself staring out the canopy side windscreens for their objective. The glare of the Earth against the darkness of space made scanning the horizon difficult. "Man, it's easy to see the station at night—I've even seen it at late afternoon," he said, "but I can't see it now."

"Be patient, Boomer," Raydon said. "Don't anticipate. If we start chasing it, even subconsciously, we'll run out of fuel. Relax." It was easier said than done, but Boomer forced himself to close his eyes and recite his Transcendental Meditation mantra to help calm him down.

It obviously helped, because Boomer found himself awakened by the warning tone that the computer was beginning the pre-rendezvous checklist. Moments later the thrusters activated to flip the Black Stallion around so it was flying tail-first, and shortly afterward the LPDRS engines flared briefly to life. Soon the speed of the station and the spaceplane were just a few miles an hour different. "Okay, Colonel, she's all yours," Patrick radioed.

"Roger that," Raydon said. Using the opposite set of thrusters in order not to deplete too much propellant from one set of maneuvering engines, Raydon carefully nudged the Black Stallion up and around until they were facing the direction of flight again . . .

. . . and Boomer felt himself take a deep, excited breath as their objective came into sight. My God, he breathed, it's beautiful . . . !

At magnitude minus-6, the Armstrong Space Station was fifty percent brighter than the planet Venus in the night sky—only the sun and moon were brighter. It was so bright that quite often the light reflecting off its solar panels, radar arrays, antennae, and reflective anti-laser outer skin cast shadows on Earth. Boomer knew all that and had studied and even photographed "Silver Tower" through a telescope as a kid. But seeing it this close was breathtaking.

The main cluster of four large habitats was arranged perpendicular to Earth's horizon, which gave it its "Tower" nickname, with a short service, storage, and mechanical spar horizontal. It had four rows of solar power–generating panels on the upper half, each over four hundred feet long and forty feet wide. Two large remote manipulator arms were visible, ready to assist loading and unloading cargo and inspecting all of the modules.

The lower half of the station below the keel had two rows of electronically scanned phased-array radar antennae each over a thousand feet long and fifty feet wide, resembling a delicate ribbon floating in mid-air. This radar, the largest ever built, could detect and track thousands of stationary and moving targets as small as an automobile on land, in the sky, in space, and even hundreds of feet underwater and dozens of feet underground. A number of smaller antennae for signals collection, datalinks, and station self-defense surveillance were mounted on arms connected to the keel. Atop the tower was another device Boomer knew was the station self-defense system, nicknamed "Thor," but it had been destroyed and had been mostly removed.

"Can you see it, Boomer?" Ann Page asked. "How does it look?"

"It looks . . . lonely," Boomer replied. He knew exactly what Ann was asking about—and it wasn't the space station.

At the very "bottom" of the station below the keel and radar arrays was a single module almost as long as the upper "tower" of the station itself. It was actually four separate modules that had been lofted up to the station by the Shuttle Transportation System over a period of three years. This was Skybolt, the world's first space-based anti-missile laser, designed and engineered by Ann Page and a team of over a hundred scientists.

Skybolt was a large free-electron laser, powered by a small nuclear-fueled generator called a magnetohydrodynamic generator, or MHD, that produced massive amounts of power for short periods of time. The generator cranked an electrostatic turbine that shot an electron beam—a focused, intense bolt of lightning—through to the laser chamber. Inside the laser chamber a bank of powerful electromagnets "wiggled" the electron beam, thereby producing the lasing effect. The resultant laser beam was millions of times more powerful than the energy generated by the MHD, creating a tunable and extremely powerful beam in the megawatt range that could easily destroy objects in space for thousands of miles and, as Ann and her crew soon discovered, even damage targets as large as a warship on Earth's surface, or aircraft flying through Earth's atmosphere.

"Good. That's good," Ann cooed. "What are we waiting for, Kai? Let's hook up and get aboard."

"Hold your water, Senator," Raydon said. "I don't like distractions when I'm flying, so everyone pipe down. That's an order." He flexed his fingers one more time, then unstowed the thruster controls and carefully placed his hands on them. Resembling small bathtub faucet knobs, the controls could be twisted, pushed, pulled, and jockeyed sideways or up and down to activate the small hydrazine thrusters arrayed around the Black Stallion. The controls were "standardized," meaning that the same manual controls had been used in manned spacecraft since Mercury and extending all the way to the Black Stallion.

With the closure rate now less than five miles an hour between the spaceplane and the station, Raydon activated the exterior cameras and began his approach. Armstrong Station had two docking points, one designed for manned spacecraft such as the Shuttle and USS *America* spaceplane, and one for unmanned cargo modules such as Agena. The docking port for manned spacecraft was on the side of the upper "tower," about halfway between the top of the tower and the keel.

Raydon began by flying the Black Stallion beside the tower directly opposite from the docking port, then gently stopping the spaceplane so the port was slightly behind his left shoulder but clearly visible out the side windscreen. There was an electronic positioning device straight ahead, but several pieces were missing and the indicators were dark. "Looks like the positioning target has been damaged," Raydon said.

"Thank the Russians for that," Ann said. "Their 'Elektron' spaceplanes did a lot . . ."

"I said, be quiet," Raydon interrupted. "I didn't want to chat, Senator. Button it." Ann shook her head and snorted her frustration so hard it briefly fogged the inside of her helmet. "I'll just have to line it up by feel and guide it in after I translate." Raydon made a few more barely perceptible adjustments with the controls. The only sound anyone heard was the briefest of puffs from the thrusters. Then slowly, ever so slowly, the Black Stallion started a roll to the left so the top of the spaceplane was pointed at the station.

Just then, they heard a strange humming noise. Boomer checked his readouts—everything was normal. "Crew, station check," he ordered.

"Quiet, Captain."

"I hear a funny sound."

"That's me, Noble. Now be quiet." Sure enough, a moment later the humming sound came back, getting louder and louder as Raydon nudged the Black Stallion ever so slowly toward the tower. "Clear the docking tunnel, Senator," he said.

"Tunnel's clear."

"I asked you to clear it, not talk!" Raydon snapped. "What part of 'be quiet' don't you jokers understand?" Ann had to bite her tongue to keep silent. "Okay, Captain, extend the tunnel . . . slowly." Boomer hit a switch, and the docking tunnel extended out the top of the spaceplane. "Stop." Raydon made a few more imperceptible adjustments. "Okay, extend . . . stop." Another nudge of the controls; then they heard a deep "CLUUNK!" and four sharp snaps. "Contact, locks engaged," Raydon said. "Senator, double-check your suit status lights, and tell me what they say." Silence. Raydon waited a moment longer, then said irritably, "You can talk now, all of you."

"Four green, no red," Ann Page said. "My, Colonel, what a fart you are."

"Thank you, Senator. I'm just doing my job. Lieutenant?"

"Four green, no red. I've double-checked Ann's controls—she's ready."

"I've checked Nano's controls," Ann said. "She's good to go."

"Roger. Captain?"

"I've got four green, no red," Boomer responded. "I'm ready."

"Roger. I'm showing four green, no red. Flight crew is ready for cabin depressurization, and passenger module is ready for equalization with the transfer module. Senator, Lieutenant, ready to go?"

"We're ready, Colonel."

"Ready."

"Very good. Captain?"

Boomer checked the status readouts being transmitted via an encoded datalink from the station. "Transfer module showing pressurized to nine point nine psid," he reported.

"Good. Clear to match cabin pressure."

"Roger. Bringing the passenger module pressure down to nine point nine." Boomer hit a control. "Passing fourteen psid . . . twelve . . . ten . . . nine point nine pressure differential in both station transfer module and Stud passenger module."

"Very good. Okay, Senator, Lieutenant, you're cleared to unstrap, enter the tunnel, and open the hatch. Be sure to check the visual indicators first. Good luck."

"We're on our way," Ann said. "And you still owe me a shot for every time you called me 'Senator,' Kai." She and Nano carefully removed their seat restraints and floated free. Ann moved to the tunnel first and pulled herself up inside. At the top of the tunnel she opened a small shutter over an observation window, which lined up exactly with a similar window on the station's transfer module. She flicked a switch, and a tiny LED light illuminated a pressure gauge inside the transfer module. "Transfer module shows nine point five on the gauge," she said. "Close enough for government work. Here we go." Ann twisted two recessed levers in the tunnel's hatch, and the hatch unlatched. She floated back and swung the hatch in, then locked it in place. She then reached up to the hatch visible just a few inches away, double-checked the pressure differential gauge again, then twisted two handles and swung the hatch open. "Hatches are open. I'm going inside. See you when I see you."

"We did it," Boomer breathed.

"We've still got a long way to go, Captain," Raydon said. "But we've cleared one incredible hurdle."

Nano began by unstrapping several equipment cases and boxes inside the passenger module, floated them through the tunnel to Ann, then followed them inside. In a few minutes she was inside the station's transfer module, and she secured the hatches behind her. "The hatches are closed and latched," she reported from the transfer module. "Tunnel and module are pressurized and secure. This is so cool. Can't believe all the room in this thing!"

"The transfer module is the smallest on Silver Tower," Ann said. "Wait till you see the rest of the place. You might want to move up here permanently."

"Awesome!"

Inside the station, Ann floated into an adjacent tunnel, turning on lights as she went, then entered the adjacent crew sleeping quarters. She had stayed on the station a few times in the past several years, and she was pleased to see many of her "womanly" touches still in place—some artificial silk flowers, a few pictures, and even a magnetic chess board floating in the middle of the module.

"Wow, this is huge!" Nano remarked. "You can sleep a dozen people in this thing with room to spare! And there's a shower, closets, TVs, and desks—how cool! I thought it'd be all cramped like the Shuttle orbiter."

"I told you you'd like it," Ann said. She floated "down" to another connecting tunnel and checked the pressure gauges. "The cargo module is depressurized and checked, guys. Come on over."

"Ready, Captain?" Raydon asked.

"As ready as I'll ever be, I guess," Boomer said.

"I'll go over first," Raydon said. "Follow me and do what I do. There's nothing to it."

"Easy for you to say."

"Your readouts look okay?"

"Four green, no red, reading nine point eight psid."

"Me too. Check your tether."

Boomer opened a hatch on his side of his seat and pulled out a length of shielded nylon cable. "It's ready."

"Mine too. Here we go." Raydon hit a control, and the forward cockpit cabin began to depressurize. "Fourteen psid . . . twelve . . . ten . . ." But this time it didn't stop at ten psid, but went all the way to zero. "Forward cabin depressurized. Canopy coming open." As Boomer watched in amazement, the forward canopy motored open, and moments later Raydon floated free of his seat and was outside the spaceplane. My God, Boomer thought, he's walking in space! "How you doing back there, Captain? You look like you seen a ghost."

"I . . . I'm okay."

"This is my fifth space walk, and I'm still nervous and excited every time I go out," Raydon admitted. "But we don't have all day. Let's go." Without appearing to push or even touch anything, Raydon gently moved away from the spaceplane so he was floating in space several yards away. As Boomer watched, the remote manipulator arm began to move toward him. Raydon reached up, and Ann steered the grapple at the end of the arm precisely into his grasp and towed him toward the cargo module on the station. Moments later he was inside the module, and he motioned for Boomer to follow him.

His stomach was knotted with flocks of butterflies, but he was holding up the show, and the remote manipulator arm was waiting for him. He touched the controls and slowly depressurized the rear cockpit cabin . . . done. With a finger that he noticed was shaking slightly, he hit the canopy switch . . . and it motored up. Holy Jesus . . . he was in space! Not just flying through space, but in space!

"Let's move out, Captain."

Boomer undid his seat straps, being careful to keep the metal buckles under control as they snaked around him, then pushed himself out of his seat . . . too hard, and his helmet banged up against the inside of the canopy overhead.

"Easy does it, Captain," Raydon said. "Use just enough force to overcome inertia and that's it, and remember you have to counteract inertia on the other side—nothing stops by itself up here. Remember that. Otherwise you'll be making like a pinball all day. Don't even think about moving and you'll find you can move just fine. Keep an eye on your tethers and those locking teeth on the edge of the canopy—rip your suit and your blood will boil away in seconds."

Slowly, carefully, Boomer eased himself away from the canopy and floated across the sill. Unconsciously he swung his legs out of the cockpit and almost succeeded in spinning himself around like a top. But before he knew it, he was outside the spaceplane, floating between it and the space station. God, he was space walking! He remembered watching videos of the Gemini astronauts doing their spacewalks, stepping outside their tiny capsules to float around at the end of an umbilical cord while millions on Earth watched on TV, and now he was doing it! He looked around and got a hint of vertigo as he saw Earth over two hundred miles below him, and he realized only then that he wasn't floating—he was falling around the Earth at over seventeen thousand miles an hour! It was an absolutely incredible feeling.

"Sightseeing time is over, Captain," Raydon prompted him. "Let's get going. Ann, bring the arm down."

But Boomer had other ideas. Without waiting for the remote manipulator arm, Boomer gently pushed against the Black Stallion and propelled himself across the distance between the spaceplane and the open cargo module. Somehow he measured that push just right, because he gently floated through space and glided like a falling leaf directly inside the open module's hatch. Raydon barely had to stop him before the magnets on Boomer's boots engaged and he stood proudly and excitedly on the cargo module's deck.

"Well, well, look at the newbie," Raydon said. "Thinks he's Buzz Aldrin all of a sudden. Very impressive, rookie."

"Like he's been space-walking all his life," Ann said.

"Enough showing off for the ladies, Captain," Raydon said with a smile. "Let's get this cargo module ready to dock the Ares cargo stage and to refuel the Black Stallion, and we can get you on your way. After that, we've got a space station to run!"

ASHKHABAD, TURKMENISTAN

A Few Days Later

She was almost home. She could feel her strength increasing with every step she took in the direction of her real homeland.

Azar Assiyeh Qagev waited patiently in her seat in the Turkmenistan Airlines Boeing 737 for the other passengers to deplane. Major Najar sat across the aisle from her watching the departing passengers; Lieutenant Saidi sat beside Azar, appearing to flip through her carry-on bag but was actually scanning the passengers and crew as well for any sign of trouble. Although certainly not required on this airline, but to avoid any complications or undue attention, both Azar and Saidi wore thick medium-colored scarves and plain brown dresses that covered every part of their bodies except for face and hands.

Although Turkmenistan was predominantly Sunni Muslim, and in recent years under new president Jalaluddin Turabi, the former Afghan Taliban fighter who helped defend Turkmenistan from a Russian invasion, Islam was undergoing a resurgence in an attempt by the government to quiet religious unrest, religious expression was still generally not encouraged and anyone flaunting their religious beliefs or customs was viewed with suspicion or sometimes outward aggression. It was a tactical decision to dress conservatively on this flight from Istanbul, Turkey, to the capital of Turkmenistan. According to strict Muslim practices it was not allowed for a man to stare at a woman in public who was not his wife, and Azar and her bodyguards hoped that practice would be followed even in this former Stalinist country.

It had been a long, harrowing trip so far since hijacking the jet chartered by the U.S. State Department. American and Canadian radars along the border had improved markedly since the American Holocaust, and after commandeering the plane and crossing into Canada they were approached immediately by Royal Canadian Air Force patrol jets. Fortunately the jets didn't attack, but instead shadowed them as they flew northward. Major Najar's plan was to land, force the airport to give them fuel, then try to make it to an isolated American airport, refuel again, and try to make it to the Caribbean or Bahamas. But stuck almost directly in the middle of North America, their chance of fighting their way out safely was quickly diminishing.

Finally Azar herself got on the jet's telephone and contacted the Canadian foreign ministry office in Winnipeg, proclaimed they were political refugees, and promised to land the jet there. Upon landing they were immediately placed under arrest. Fortunately the American Department of State only wanted the jet and crew back and didn't want to press charges, so Canadian officials promised they would not prosecute if they left the country immediately.

The three carried two sets of passports, American and Turkish. The Canadian officials confiscated the American passports on behalf of the United States—another condition of release—but allowed the group to use their Turkish passports to exit the country. They purchased Lufthansa airline tickets from Winnipeg to Istanbul. While in Istanbul they received a required letter of introduction from a former Turkmeni consular officer—price, one thousand dollars U.S.

for the three of them—then purchased tickets on Turkmenistan Airlines to Ashkhabad.

Thirty grueling hours later after departing Minnesota, they were finally just a few miles from Iran. All they had to do was get safely past Turkmeni customs and immigration, and the Qagev security network would take them across the border. Unfortunately they did not have visas to enter Turkmenistan, and the Turkmeni government disliked foreigners who didn't bother getting visas before trying to enter the country.

Najar tried to steer them toward a customs officer who looked like he might be Muslim, but soon they couldn't hesitate any longer, and they queued up before an agent who unfortunately looked anything but Muslim. "Your papers, please," the customs officer ordered in Turkmen, holding out his hand without looking up. Najar handed over their passports and letter of introduction. Azar and Saidi had pulled their scarves low, obscuring their faces, and kept their heads bowed.

The customs officer looked at the passports carefully, eyeing Najar suspiciously. "You have no visa to enter Turkmenistan," he said. When Najar's narrowed eyes told him he didn't understand, the officer switched to Arabic and repeated his statement.

"I was assured I could get a short-term visa here, at the airport," Najar said.

"Only under very unusual circumstances—very unusual circumstances," the customs officer said. "Is this an urgent trip or some sort of family emergency?"

"No. Just business."

"I see." He scowled, looked past Najar at the two females, then flipped open their passport photo pages and motioned. "Take off the scarves."

"It is not permitted," Najar said sternly.

"In your society it is not permitted—here, on my order, it is," the customs officer said perturbedly. Najar hesitated again. The customs officer closed the passports and shuffled some papers as if getting ready to write a report. "Very well, sir. With all deference to your religious preferences and your women's frail and unassailable femininity, we will send your wife and young daughter to a segregated area where a female officer will continue inprocessing. It should take no longer than . . . oh, I'd say a few hours, perhaps tomorrow morning, depending on availability of suitable personnel. All of you will have to sleep here in the airport security office's holding cell—along with all the drunks, pickpockets, and other reprobates we catch preying on honest visitors and residents of Turkmenistan. Now tell me, sir, which would you prefer to do?"

Najar sized up the officer, considering whether he should challenge this affrontery, then deciding to relent. He turned and told the females to take off their scarves, and they did.

"I am relieved to see that God has not turned anyone to slabs of salt before my eyes," the customs officer said dryly. He studied the photos carefully, taking his time, then shaking his head to indicate to the females that they could cover themselves again. "So. You are from Turkey but come from Winnipeg, Canada. What do you do, Mr. Najar?"

"Telecommunications software engineer."

"What is your business in Turkmenistan?"

"I am to enter discussions to upgrade your country's wireless phone system and provide service to every part of your country."

"I see. Very impressive, very impressive." He peered at the letter of introduction. "I assume you deal with the government ministry of energy and industry for this project?"

"No, I would deal with His Honor Matkarim Ashirov, minister of communications," Najar corrected him, thankful he had taken the time to carefully study his own cover's background. "But we are in negotiations with RuTel for some of their infrastructure and land leases—that is the purpose of my visit. Hopefully we will be meeting with His Honor Ashirov soon afterward."

"I see," the customs officer said. But he impaled Najar with an icy stare, held up the letter of introduction with disdain, then said, "But what confuses me, sir, is why you would need to go through this particular person in Istanbul for a letter of introduction when you could have just as easily obtained a visa from the ministry of communications or a letter of introduction from RuTel—if you are indeed working with these agencies? This person in Istanbul is well-known to us as a letter-writing hack—he would give Satan himself a letter of introduction for a thousand dollars. Can you please explain this to me, sir?"

"Of course," Najar said. "If I would have requested a letter from Mr. Saparov at RuTel, I would be beholden to him, and that is no way to begin any business negotiations. And I have not spoken to the minister about my deal because it has not been formalized to my shareholders' satisfaction. We wish to go to His Honor Ashirov at the very least as equal partners with RuTel in this venture, preferably as majority partners. So the ministry was not obligated to grant us a visa since we have not been dealing with them at all yet."

"I see," the customs officer said. "I do not understand all this business psychology and maneuverings, but what you say makes a certain amount of sense to me." He stamped something on the letter of introduction. "So you will be meeting with this Mr. Saparov at RuTel soon?"

"After I complete my due diligence and business proposal, I will," Najar said. "But I wish to be fully prepared before I ask for a meeting. That may take a few days. That is why I requested only a ten-day business visa, with no re-entry privileges." He withdrew and opened his wallet, letting the customs officer peek inside the billfold, revealing it fat with American dollars and Turkish new lira. "I am prepared to pay the expedited visa fee, in cash—it is four times the normal fee, is it not?" Najar knew the expedited fee was only twice the normal fee—he hoped the extra "incentive" would cause this guy to back off. He undoubtedly had most of this guy's entire annual wages in his wallet right now.

"I see," the customs officer intoned. He looked through the passports again, imperceptibly nodding his head. "Just so." He got up from his chair and ordered, "Follow me." Najar's heart sank.

They were taken into a very small office just behind the service counter. Najar and Saidi could see no surveillance cameras—that was good. There was a long steel table in the center of the room, along with a telephone on a rickety wooden desk and inspection devices such as flashlights and rubber gloves. "Well," the agent said after he locked the door behind them, "I think we shall have to meet with my supervisor for some additional information. We shall undoubtedly have to speak with Mr. Saparov and someone at the ministry's office to confirm your story."

"It is no story, sir—it is the truth," Najar said, trying to remain calm. "But I will be happy to meet with the unit supervisor here, and I should like to inform the trade and commerce consul at the Turkish embassy of this exchange as well. I think he should be apprised at how unfairly one of its citizens is treated by Turkmenistan customs."

The customs officer's eyes flared. "Are you threatening me, sir? I assure you, that is most unwise."

"Please, sir," Azar said in crude but passable Turkmen, removing her scarf and affixing the customs officer with an imploring, desperate look, "please let my father, mother, and I come into your country."

"Azar, no . . . !"

"Look, the China doll speaks!" the customs officer laughed.

Najar's mouth tightened and his fists balled, but Azar touched his hand under the counter, ordering him to be calm. "Please, sir. My father has . . . he has sold everything to come here and make this deal—our home, our farm, his inheritance, everything," Azar said. "My father is very smart and has many ways to help the people of your country, but no one at the Russian phone company or in your government minister's office will talk to him while he is in Turkey, so we came here together. My father brought us all here to Turkmenistan as a sign of his commitment to this project—this will be our home for many years if this deal is concluded. We have no place else to go and no money other than what my father carries with him. This is our last hope. Will you please help us, sir?"

The customs officer scowled at Najar. "So, you let your female child do the pleading for you, eh, Mister Telecommunications Engineer?" he scoffed. "That is a true Turkish businessman for you. And why does she learn Turkmeni when her father does not?" Najar forced himself to lower his eyes contritely. The customs officer chuckled. "Have you declared that foreign currency yet, sir?" Najar shook his head and handed him all the money out of his wallet—he noticed how quickly the customs officer hid it from sight with his hands and with the letter of introduction. "Any more to declare?" Najar turned, and Saidi withdrew another wad of bills from a pocket inside her robes.

"Ah, just so. As I thought. Not so delicate and feminine as to stop her from hiding foreign currency from a customs agent, eh?" The customs officer counted it all, separated all of the American dollars from the rest, slipped the greenbacks into his pants pocket, counted out a thousand dollars' worth of Turkish new lira for the visa fees, logged the remainder, handed it over to Najar, and stamped the passports. "Five days tourist visa, no re-entry," he said. "You must apply for a business visa before you contact the ministry of communications or anyone at RuTel—if you fail to do so, you could spend six months in jail for the violation, unless of course you have your lovely daughter talk them out of arresting you. You must check in at a hotel in the capital and surrender your passport to the manager within four hours or be in violation of the terms of your tourist visa."

He handed back the passports, then looked at Azar, smiled evilly at Najar, pursed his lips as if giving her a kiss, and added, "What pretty eyes she has. I'll bet she drives all the boys wild." He grinned at Najar's suppressed anger, laughed, then shook his head toward the exit. "Welcome to Turkmenistan." Najar again forced himself to control his anger as he took his passports, bowed politely at the laughing customs officer, and turned to go.

They collected their bags at the inspection station. No one said a word outside. They tried to flag down a taxi, but a private citizen stopped first and offered them a ride. After a few moments of haggling, they settled on a price and piled into the broken-down, dilapidated Russian sedan.

The driver took them to the Tolkuchka Bazaar at the outskirts of Ashkhabad, which looked like the gaudiest Hollywood B-movie set of a bazaar they had ever seen—thousands of shoppers circulating around hundreds of merchants, some in multi-colored tents but most just sitting on colorful carpets with their wares spread out before them. The sights and sounds were rich and varied, and Azar found her eyes wandering to the beautiful silks, silver, jewelry, and rugs on display.

But they had a job to do. Job one: make sure they were not being followed. They dared not look behind them in the car or speak except in conversational Turkish, fearing the driver to be a Turkmenistan National Committee for Security agent, so they didn't know if they were being tailed and so assumed they were. They did several switchbacks, quick dodges, and reversals to try to spot any shadows, but didn't spot any tails. Still not satisfied they were safe, they bought some lamb kebabs and tea and sat outside a camel corral with other visitors taking a break from the crush of people in the bazaar, safe from everyone except an occasional herder or vendor peddling something.

"Thank you for helping me at the airport, Shahdokht," Najar said in a low voice.

"I'm sorry if it embarrassed you, but we did not want to be confronted by a superior officer—the more eyes around, the lesser chances we'd have of bribing our way into the country," Azar said. "Thankfully you showed him your money—he was just looking for the right opportunity to be able to take it from you. What is our situation, Major?"

"We have just two hours before we'll be reported for not surrendering our passports," Najar said. "Hopefully that customs officer won't be so efficient . . ."

"We have to assume he'll be more efficient," Azar said.

"Agreed, Shahdokht. Our network contact is supposed to meet us here at the bazaar, but I don't know what he or she looks like or who it is, so they'll have to make contact with us."

"We'll wait here and finish our wonderful meal, then lose ourselves in the crowd again until nightfall," Azar said. She was serious about the food—she was afraid that the spicy, chewy meat would be too much for her stomach, but she enjoyed every bite. She looked toward the south. "Those must be the Kopetdag Mountains. I've read about them and seen pictures. They are beautiful."

"That's Mount Shahshah there," Saidi said, pointing a bit to the west. "The Turkmenis claim it's on their side of the border—based on Soviet surveyors' claims, naturally—but it's really in Iran. But wait until you see the Alborz Mountains north of Tehran and the volcano Mount Damavand. It's almost twice as high as Shahshah, and it's the largest volcano in Eurasia west of the Hindu Kush."

"I can't wait to see it, Lieutenant," Azar said. "I can't wait to see the Caspian Sea—I only caught a glimpse of it from the air—and the Persian Gulf, and even the Great Salt Desert. Minnesota is nothing like my Iran."

Another vendor wearing colorful robes and sashes, a red turban, and white skull cap wandered over, carrying a cart full of bags of hot pistachios, and Azar's mouth watered again. The vendor saw this immediately and smiled a crooked, yellow-toothed smile. "Peace and happiness to you, my child," he said in Turkmeni, bowing to Najar as a way of asking permission to address the girl. "Would you like some warm, satisfying pistachios? Just six thousand manat, freshly picked this morning and roasted right here just minutes ago, the best bargain in the whole bazaar!"

"Thank you, sir, and peace to you and your family as well," Azar said in her best Turkmeni. She looked at Najar, and he nodded, keeping a careful eye on the vendor's hands and the men behind him. A few other hawkers had started to cluster around nearby, waiting to see how much money these pilgrims would pull out. "All I have is Turkish new lira, sir."

"Turkish lira! Even better, my child! But because that is not official currency here in Turkmenistan, I must ask for eight thousand manat, still a very great bargain for you, a pittance really if you consider the exchange rate between our currencies. I will be sure to give you more than enough of my succulent pistachios for all three of you."

"That is generous of you, sir, but my father says I have spent enough and can only give you one thousand manat—fifty kurus."

"Your father is wise and must be respected, child, but I have children of my own to feed," the vendor said. "But in respect for your father and mother, I will sell an extra large bag to you for the original price—six thousand."

"I'm afraid my blessed father will disapprove of any more than two thousand manat."

The vendor bowed his head to Najar, who only scowled back. "I would not like to be the cause of any ill feelings whatsoever between such a powerful-looking gentleman and such a sweet child," the pistachio seller said, "but I have a father, mother, six brothers, a wife, and four children to answer to as well—and a girlfriend or two, of course, but don't tell my wife, please!" His chuckle subsided when he saw Najar's scowl deepen. "I will tell you what, my child, in reward for being so good with me and for speaking our native tongue so well." He brushed his hands together as if anticipating closing this deal immediately. "Four thousand manat for you, and not a tennesi more. The rest I shall receive when I see the pleasure in your faces as you enjoy my pistachios."

"You are generous and patient, sir." She counted out coins in her hand. "I have seventy kurus here, and I dare not ask my father for more—I have been too much of a burden to him already on this trip. You will become the most generous man we have met in Turkmenistan if you accept."

The vendor smiled, bit his index finger, then bowed. "Done, child, and may God smile on you." Azar gave the coins to Najar, who gave them to the vendor. He indeed did portion out a very large bag of steaming pistachios and handed them over to Najar, who gave them to Azar without taking his eyes off the vendor. "Thank you, thank you, a thousand times thank you, and may God continue to smile on you. Is there any other way I can serve you, child?"

"Like how?" Najar growled in Farsi.

"Like taking the Shahdokht and her royal bodyguards to her home," the man replied in Farsi. He bowed slightly, taking a peek over his shoulder at the slowly growing number of vendors starting to move closer. "I'm sorry, Shahdokht, but it's not every day you get to haggle over the price of a bag of pistachios with a member of the Persian royal family. Now, allow me to take you into the waiting arms of your loyal followers in your homeland. God be praised, our salvation is at hand! The blessed and powerful Qagev have returned!"

"You wasted a lot of time," Saidi said.

"I decided that simply approaching you without at least trying to make a sale would look bad," he said. "I've been here at the bazaar for three years, waiting for this blessed day for the true rulers of Persia's return, God be praised. I know the bazaar well."

"The transaction attracted too much attention," Najar said perturbedly. "Where can we meet?"

"My truck is parked at the far northwest vendor lot, beside the bicycles," the man replied. "I suggest . . ."

But suddenly there was a commotion behind him, and moments later two Soviet-era light infantry vehicles and a sedan burst toward the corral. Three Turkmeni soldiers jumped out of the vehicle, and a man in a plain dark business suit emerged from the sedan. Najar and Saidi were on their feet faster than Azar had ever seen them move before.

"No one move!" the sergeant in charge of the military forces shouted in Russian. "Hands where I can see them!" The other soldiers carried rusty-looking AK-47s and sidearms in worn, rotting leather holsters. Azar had no doubt that Najar and Saidi could take them out within seconds . . . if they had weapons or were within reach of them. Najar, Saidi, Azar, and the vendor open their hands to their sides in plain sight.

The man in the suit approached them, smiling—and then, to everyone's surprise, bowed. "Salam aleikom, Miss Qagev," he said in Farsi. "Welcome to Turkmenistan. I am Colonel Jamal Fattah, deputy chief of mission and chief political officer of the Iranian embassy in Ashkhabad." He looked at Najar and Saidi. "You must be Miss Qagev's bodyguards . . . Richard and Linda VanWie, or is it Major Najar and Lieutenant Saidi now?"

"Salam aleikom, sir," Azar replied, bowing slightly in return. Fattah was obviously pleased at that response, though he kept his eye carefully on Najar and Saidi. "What brings the Iranian deputy consul here?"

"Why, a member of the Qagev royal family, here, in Turkmenistan—it's practically a cause for yet another national week of celebration, just like the Turkmenis award themselves just about every other week of the year for some reason or another," Fattah said.

"How did you know we were here?"

"I would be revealing important state secrets if I . . ."

"The Russian embassy intercepted communications between Canada and the United States about the arrest and deportment of three persons who were under protective custody of the U.S. State Department, Shahdokht," Saidi said. "They obviously passed the information to their friends the Iranians."

Fattah nodded and smiled. "Lieutenant Saidi is as smart as she is beautiful," he said. "Rumor had it that you actually stole the plane sent to evacuate you to a safe place? Extraordinary. Anyway, the report said the trio was in quite a rush and headed to Istanbul via Frankfurt. A message was put out to all embassies to watch for you. After you left Istanbul, a very resourceful researcher at the Federal Security Service in Moscow guessed who you might be, based on recent events in Iran, and the word was put out to be on the lookout for you and your parents . . ."

"What of my parents?" Azar interjected.

"I'm afraid I can't tell you that, Miss Qagev," the Iranian said. "Once the word was out it was not difficult tracking down two adults and a female teenager traveling together through eastern and central Asia. We made positive identification shortly thereafter, pulled up your files, and then put all known pro-monarchy individuals and Iranian expatriates in Turkmenistan under surveillance, knowing you'd make contact with your underground network."

"We do not have any quarrel with the Turkmeni government," Azar said, "and we have broken no laws here . . ."

"I am sure you entered the country using false papers . . ."

"We were legally admitted into this country and we have valid visas . . ."

"That will be thoroughly investigated," Fattah said. "While that investigation is underway, Iran will file extradition papers with the Turkmeni courts, and I have no doubt you will be turned over to us in a very short time."

"On what charges?"

"Sedition, conspiracy, terrorism, murder—the list is very long and horrible," Fattah said. "I am sure the Turkmeni government will be anxious to cooperate. These soldiers will take you into custody and take you to the Niyazov jail in Ashkhabad, where you'll stay awaiting extradition to Iran. The wheels of justice move slowly in Turkmenistan, but you will eventually return home . . . as the guest of the ayatollah." He lowered his voice, turning his back to the Turkmeni soldiers, and went on: "Now, you don't want to die in a hail of gunfire outside a filthy camel corral in Ashkhabad at the hands of those mostly bored-looking, undertrained, and underpaid soldiers over there, so I'm asking you to come along quietly. I know your bodyguards are well trained and could probably twist those soldiers' heads right off their shoulders, and mine as well, but I'd hate for anyone to die out here like common criminals, especially a royal princess. If you resist, I can't be responsible for what happens next." He motioned to his sedan. "Shall we, Miss Qagev?"

Najar stepped forward, the menace clear in his eyes and body—so palpable was it that the Turkmeni soldiers sensed it immediately and stiffened. Azar scanned the growing crowd around them, but she didn't see any sympathetic faces. They might scatter and confuse the crowd if her bodyguards could get their hands on those rifles, and they could probably lose themselves in the bazaar easily . . .

. . . but then Azar noticed other men in the crowd . . . and they didn't look like Turkmeni vendors or shoppers. They looked military but wore civilian clothes, they were less Central Asian–looking, their gazes were sure and steady, and their hands were free, hovering near open coats. They were Iranians, Azar thought, surely Pasdaran—she was positive of it. She turned to Saidi and motioned toward the men she spotted, and Saidi saw him right away too.

"Major, no," she said softly. "Pasdaran."

Najar's eyes darted around the crowd and soon spotted the very same subjects. He looked accusingly at Fattah, then let his body relax and opened his palms. "I wonder what the Turkmeni government would think about Iran bringing in Revolutionary Guard assassins into their country," Najar said.

"They probably wouldn't like it very much," Fattah admitted, "but by the time they found out about him they'd be long gone, and you'd still be dead. Now come along quietly, please."

CHAPTER 6

HIGH TECHNOLOGY AEROSPACE WEAPONS CENTER, ELLIOTT AFB, NEVADA

A Short Time Later

"Here's the latest update, ladies and gentlemen," Brigadier-General David Luger said in the Dreamland battle staff room. He was standing before Patrick McLanahan; Brigadier-General Rebecca Furness, commander of the Air Battle Force based at Battle Mountain Air Reserve Base, and Brigadier-General Hal Briggs, commander of the Air Battle Force's ground forces; and Captain Hunter Noble and First Lieutenant Dorothea Benneton, representing the XR-A9 Black Stallion spaceplane crews.

"Armstrong Space Station will take another day and a half to get settled into its new orbit to start detailed reconnaissance and surveillance of Iran," Luger went on. "We're getting a few oblique images but nothing tactically useful yet. We've increased NIRTSat overflights and we've narrowed the search for Iran's mobile medium- and long-range missiles to a dozen different sites."

"One dozen? Doesn't sound too narrow to me, Dave," Hal commented.

"Once the station gets in place, it'll be able to discriminate between real missiles and decoys and even look inside bunkers and storage buildings," Dave said. "We've got the best eyes out there on it now."

"Anything on Buzhazi's whereabouts?" Patrick asked.

"Negative," Dave replied. "He's hiding deep. No recent attacks except for very low-level insurgent activities. He might be gearing up for some big operation—the attacks lately have been small raids, collecting nothing more than uniforms and small-arms ammunition, but this could be a prelude to something much bigger."

"The White House won't even consider our plan to attack the Iranian missile sites until we've narrowed the field down," Patrick said, "so we're on hold until then." He turned to the Air Battle Force commander. "Rebecca, status of your forces?"

"Same—three EB-52 Megafortresses, all manned; four EB-1C Vampires, two unmanned; and one AL-52

Dragon anti-missile aircraft," Furness replied. One of the first female combat pilots in the U.S. Air Force, Furness was also the first woman in charge of a tactical bombing wing. Her Air Force Reserve B-1B Lancer bomber wing was selected by Patrick McLanahan to be converted to strategic flying battleships, capable of carrying an extensive array of weaponry. Most of her aircraft had been destroyed by the Russians at Yakutsk—her little force of bombers represented virtually all of America's air-breathing long-range strike aircraft. "I think we have access to one or two B-2A bombers and six KC-10 tankers as well."

Rebecca's EB-1C Vampire bombers, EB-52 Megafortress battleships, and AL-52 Dragon anti-missile aircraft were the most sophisticated attack planes in the world. The EB-1C Vampire was a modified version of the Air Force's B-1B Lancer, with the addition of stealth technology, advanced computers, avionics, aircraft systems, and flight controls. But the real power of the Vampire bomber was its weapons. Every air-launched weapon in the American military arsenal could be utilized on the Vampire, and most weapons others in the American military had never heard of.

The EB-52 Megafortress was a highly modified version of the venerable B-52 Stratofortress bomber, so much so that it could hardly be called a B-52 any more at all. Instead of five or six crewmembers, it had just two pilots—all other functions and crew positions were automated. The skin and structure of the original B-52 had been changed, using composite fibersteel, radar-absorbing materials, and unconventional mission-adaptive flight controls, to turn it into a real stealth bomber. The avionics and systems on board had all been changed to make the aircraft more precise, more connected, lighter, faster, and more efficient. Only a handful of EB-52s and its other even more highly modified brothers and sisters still existed after the American Holocaust, but the remaining few planes were the cutting-edge of long-range air attack.

"Updates on Iran's defenses?"

"The Revolutionary Guards and Iranian air defense forces are on full alert," Rebecca replied, "and we're seeing every kind of Russian, French, Chinese, and even some American air defense weapons from the seventies to the present operating out there. Tehran, the Turkish border, and the Persian Gulf, Gulf of Oman, and Arabian Sea coastlines are the heaviest defended, with multiple layers of very sophisticated surface-to-air missiles sites—many of them mobile and harder to pinpoint. They've obviously learned some lessons from their last encounter with you guys. Very few fighter patrols. We're looking at possible missile launch sites but so far all of them have similar numbers of defensive batteries installed around them. So far we can't tell which are decoys, so it's hard to tell which are real.

"We've had to modify our original plan to reflect the denser and more sophisticated order of battle," she went on. "We'll need to use a lot of resources to punch through both their outer as well as terminal defenses. Once our bombers get through the outer defenses they can roam over the countryside fairly freely until they get within fifty miles of the target area, and then they run the gauntlet again. Each plane may have just a couple big precision-guided munitions left to attack by the time they make it through." She looked at Hal. "Our attacks need to be finely coordinated both for ingress and egress, and even if everything works perfectly our guys will be in for a very rough ride at best."

"But it's still doable?"

Rebecca hesitated just long enough for many of their throats to go dry, then replied, "Yes, we can do it. We'll need as much intel as we can scrape together, better than average aircraft and weapon reliability, perfect timing, perfect aiming, and a lot of luck . . . but yes, sir, we can do it."

"Thanks, Rebecca." Patrick knew that Rebecca Furness's assessment was as brutally honest as possible—she wouldn't hesitate to tell them if she didn't think her bombers could make it. "Boomer?"

"We've got two Black Stallion spaceplanes ready to go," Hunter Noble replied. "Both can be configured for attack, satellite launch, or passengers. The third spaceplane hasn't gone into orbit or carried any cargo but we can use it if necessary—we'll be testing as we go. Nano?"

"I wanted to bring up the new gear General Briggs mentioned we might be bringing along," "Nano" Benneton said, smiling enticingly at Hal just as she had been since returning from Las Vegas. "I took a look at some of that new gear we acquired. The problem is not with weight, but volume. The unit itself folds up fairly small, but we need to remove two crew seats to accommodate it. That means we can carry one unit, two or three mission backpacks, two spare power cells, and three passengers in the module. It's impressive technology, but my question for you is: is it worth losing two Tin Man commandos?"

"Can we fit two units in the passenger module, Lieutenant?" Dave Luger asked.

"Yes, sir, but with spare power cells only, not with any of those mission backpacks," Nano replied. "Again, it's volume, not weight. Obviously those units can carry a big load, and they were designed to be carried into battle aboard large cargo-sized aircraft or those cool Humvees we got, so there was never any attempt to miniaturize the mission backpacks. Once they're redesigned, they'll be much more useful."

"We'll adjust the mix depending on the mission and the tactical situation," Patrick said, "but for now I want to be able to bring one unit with as many mission backpacks as possible together with two Tin Men."

"Yes, sir. We can do that."

"Good," Patrick said. "All right, folks: the plan still stands, and we're just awaiting approval and a warning order. The primary objective is to locate, track, and destroy Iran's tactical and strategic missiles, so whoever's in charge out there won't destroy half a city again like they did with Arān. It'll take Ann and Raydon another day or so to reposition Silver Tower so we can do a detailed ISAR search on the spots we've identified so far with the NIRTSats. With thirty-six suspected storage, garrison, and launch sites, we're going to need every person and every weapon system pulling together to make it work."

"I'm hoping at least half of those are decoys that Silver Tower can identify—otherwise we're going to need a lot more boots on the ground," Dave said.

"We need to start getting the boots over there now," Patrick said. "As soon as we locate those missile sites we need to take them down." He looked up and spoke, "Duty Officer, conference Colonel Raydon in for me." The computerized "Duty Officer" made the connection just moments later. "How's it going up there, Colonel?" Patrick McLanahan asked on the secure video communications datalink from his command center at Dreamland. "Ready to come home yet?"

"Not on your life, sir," Kai Raydon responded. "I feel like a kid again. I might just retire up here. Glad you called. I have something for you. Got a minute?"

"Sure, Kai," Patrick replied. "What do you have?"

"As you know, sir, we're repositioning the station to cover Iran better," Raydon said. "It'll take another day or two to complete the orbit change. But as we're moving I decided to poke around eastern Iran and its neighbors with the sensors and electromagnetic sniffers Ann's got up here to see if anyone else is getting as worried as the Iranians over this insurgency. I've been picking up an awful lot of uncoded chatter between Turkmeni border patrols and Iranian Revolutionary Guard units right around Ashkhabad, Turkmenistan. It doesn't appear to be routine—something's going down."

Patrick's stomach tightened at the double mention of both the Iranians and Turkmenistan—his experiences with both had mostly been very unpleasant. Moreover, he considered the president of Turkmenistan, Jalaluddin

Turabi, a friend, and if the Iranians were becoming active again in that country, his life was definitely in jeopardy. "Moving border security units in response to what happened in Qom?"

"Maybe, but there's something else," Raydon said. "We ran a lot of the uncoded chatter through our translators, and we keep on picking up the word 'princess.' There's only two of us up here, and Ann is pretty much working on setting up the station and placing us in our new orbit, so we don't have time to check the intelligence dispatches on anything pertaining to 'princess.'

"At first I thought it was a glitch in the decoder, and then I thought it was a code-name for a weapon or vehicle, but I think they're talking about a person. Can you look around and see what you can find?"

"Sure. Did you send me the intercepts you're referring to?"

"Should be sitting in your in-box already, sir."

"I'll call you back as soon as I find anything."

"I'm standing by." Patrick gave the information he had to his Plans and Intelligence office, who had access to all classified reports submitted to various agencies in the U.S. government, including the State Department and Pentagon.

Less than an hour later, Dave Luger read over the report. "It's not a code-name as far as we can tell,

Muck," he said. "We can't detect any attempts to use code-words in any of the transmissions Raydon pulled down—the Iranians and Turkmenis are both chatting away in the clear. We think they're talking about a real princess they may have captured. What do you suspect up there, Kai? What are you seeing out there in Ashkhabad?"

"Nothing specific," Raydon replied. "But we can track and triangulate the transmissions, coded and uncoded, and we traced activity to a big bazaar outside Ashkhabad."

"The Tolkuchka bazaar. I've been there," Patrick said. "One of the biggest in Central Asia."

"We can't pick out faces or anything like that, but we did get ultra-wideband synthetic aperture pictures of a confrontation between some Turkmeni military units and the source of some of the uncoded transmissions—namely, a car in which radio transmissions were being sent and received in Farsi."

"Not unusual. The border area is pretty heavily traveled, and the Iranians have a significant presence there."

Patrick was indeed very familiar with the country. After the U.S. invasion of Afghanistan, some fleeing Taliban forces crossed the border into Turkmenistan. The insurgent force had grown as it moved westward into a fighting force big enough to threaten the pro-Russian Turkmeni government, and the Russians moved in to crush the rebellion. Patrick McLanahan's fledgling Air Battle Force was ordered into Turkmenistan to covertly monitor the situation, and a low-scale but fierce shooting conflict erupted between American and Russian air and ground forces to prevent a slaughter in that oil-rich but underdeveloped country.

Patrick had been severely reprimanded for his actions against the Russians, but his Air Battle Force ground teams did succeed in rescuing the ex-Taliban fighter turned Turkmeni armed forces commander Jalaluddin Turabi from the Russians. Turabi returned to his adopted country and later became president of Turkmenistan. Although protected by the United Nations and slowly transforming into an Islamic republic similar to Turkey, most of the educated, elites, petroleum industries, urban areas, and government were heavily Russian or Russian-sympathetic, and Turabi was under constant pressure to return Turkmenistan to the Russian sphere of influence.

"Well, maybe so," Raydon replied, "but it looks like the military guys and the ones in the Iranian vehicle were confronting a group of three persons sitting near a horse pen or corral."

"Three persons, you say?" Dave Luger asked.

"You got something on that?"

"The State Department put out a bulletin a few days ago that said that a group of three political refugees under their protection had fled the country by stealing a jet and flying it to Canada, presumably heading toward Iran," Dave said. "They were accompanied by two guards apparently assigned to assist, but there were three in protective custody. Can you send me some of those images?"

Raydon already had his finger poised on the button. "Done," he said. "The timing works out correct if they traveled from Canada to Central Asia by air." There was no response. "Genesis, how do you copy Armstrong?"

"Sorry, Kai, I was reading here," Patrick said, paging through more of the dispatches presented in his search. "There's another report uploaded from the Minnesota Civil Air Patrol to the Air Force and copied to Air National Guard headquarters and the U.S. Department of State. Seems that a unit commander reports that one of his cadets was taken by an Air National Guard unit, claiming that he was supporting a State Department mission to recover the cadet who is purported to be a female descendant of Iranian royalty . . ."

"In other words, a 'princess,' " Raydon interjected.

"The Air National Guard crew had two persons that the unit commander recognized as the cadet's parents but apparently were in reality the cadet's bodyguards, along with two more individuals who were security forces accompanying the bodyguards."

"No shit!" Raydon exclaimed. "You don't suppose . . . ?"

"It's quite a stretch from here on out, Kai," Patrick said. "The State Department can give us more information."

"Now that you mention them, it's way above my pay grade," Raydon said. "I'll leave it up to you from here on out, sir. Let me know if there's anything else I can do."

"One question: can you track the three subjects?"

"Sure—for now," Raydon replied. "Armstrong is tied into several other surveillance satellites, and we can pull information from them. Now if they transfer them to another car or if they stay off the air I'll probably lose them, but they're not practicing any COMSEC or OPSEC at all. I think I can track them no sweat."

"Great, Kai. Keep me posted."

"Roger that. Armstrong clear."

Patrick dismissed everyone from the meeting except Dave Luger, then sat back to think. It wasn't just a stretch to link the persons apparently being apprehended in Ashkhabad with three political refugees from Minnesota . . . it was almost science fiction. But what if it was true? He wasn't going to just sit on the information.

Patrick phoned the Secretary of State's office. No one was available to speak with him—no surprise there—until he drilled all the way down the hierarchy to the assistant undersecretary of state for Central Asian affairs, Norman Moller. "Mr. Moller, good morning, this is General McLanahan, calling from Elliott Air Force Base in Nevada, secure."

"Norman Moller, assistant undersecretary for Central Asian affairs, secure," Moller recited for the benefit of the dozens of overt and covert listening and recording systems monitoring all government calls these days.

"How are you today, sir?"

"*The* Patrick McLanahan? The guy who bombed Russia after the Holocaust?"

"Yes, sir. I have a question I'm hoping you can answer."

"I'll try."

"I received information from my intelligence sources that indicate that three foreign persons under the State Department's protection, ones who recently left Minnesota, were spotted in Ashkhabad, Turkmenistan, and may have been picked up by the Iranians. Can you confirm this for me?"

There was a considerable silence on the phone, long enough to confirm in Patrick's mind that his and Raydon's guesses were correct. Finally: "I'll have to call you back to confirm your identity, General," Moller said. "I'll be in touch shortly. Good-bye. Moller clear."

In Washington-speak "shortly" could means five minutes or five days, Patrick knew. He let out a breath . . . loud enough to get everyone's attention. "You stirring up more shit, Muck?" he asked. "What are you thinking about?"

"I want to find out who the Iranians and Turkmenis captured at that bazaar in Turkmenistan," Patrick said.

"That station's sensors are really incredible, and the technology is twenty years old," Dave said. "Just wait till we start upgrading the processors. But I digress. Why do you care about this particular contact—you have a thing about princesses? Maybe the troops captured a good-looking female nomad and that's their pet nickname for her."

"It's not just about the princess—it's about what to do about Iran," Patrick said. "Buzhazi is going to need a lot more help if he hopes to battle the Pasdaran for control of the Iranian government. Remember all the stuff in the news lately about former Persian monarchs and their families living in the United States?"

"Yeah—I thought it was just fluff pieces," Dave said. "Some royal family wishing to return in case the fundamentalist government is brought down—not the most recent royal family, but one from before the Shah. I can't remember his name. The guy has a blog on the Internet. I think he uses it to send secret instructions to his loyalists in Iran or something." He logged into his computer at his console beside Patrick and punched in instructions.

"Well, Ashkhabad is very close to the Iranian border," Patrick said. "If someone was going to sneak across, that would be a good place to do it."

"Says here that all the children of the heir presumptive of the Qagev dynasty, the last true monarchy in power in Iran before the revolution, were killed by the Iranian Revolutionary Guards after Khomeini took power," Dave said. "So the 'princess' thing might be going nowhere." He surfed a few more sites. "There are kids still around from the Pahlavi dynasty living in America."

"In Minnesota?"

"Doesn't say. The previous dynasty's heir lives near Dallas. Want me to call the State Department and ask?"

"Already did—they hung up on me. I left a message for Carson and CCed Sparks—they can't ignore me forever."

"Sounds like you're right on the mark, or really really warm, and that's taking the rest of the White House and State Department by surprise," Dave said.

"What if there were not just a few old monarchs still alive, but they had a following, maybe even an army?" Patrick said. "What if they were all waiting for a time just like now to rise up and try to overthrow the Islamist government?"

"A sleeper army, underground since before the fall of the Shah, big and strong enough to take on the Iranian Revolutionary Guards?" Dave asked. "So what if there is?"

"Then if the princess is part of this sleeper army, maybe even the leader, she needs to be rescued so she can lead her army against the Pasdaran."

Dave laughed. "Sounds like your space flight has restricted blood flow to your brain, sir," he said. "So you're thinking of sending in a Battle Force squad to snatch this princess—if she really is a princess and not just an endearing term used by the soldiers for a hooker they found in the bazaar—and set her on the path of revolution?"

"We're planning on sending in the Battle Force to hunt for Iranian missiles—this would be a good reason to go in and probe Iran's northeastern frontier," Patrick said. "If there is an Iranian princess, and she has followers, they can help our guys get into the country."

"I don't think we need help getting into the country, Muck," Dave said. But his mind was beginning to churn now as well. "We can certainly use all the local support we can get. But we're not fighting Turkmenistan. If we drop a squad in there, aren't we stirring up more trouble rather than trying to contain trouble? We should try to get some kind of cooperation from the Turkmenis—if that's even possible."

Patrick thought for another moment; then: "Then why not ask the guy in charge?" he remarked. He picked up the phone and spoke, "Duty Officer, call President Jalaluddin Turabi in Ashkhabad, Turkmenistan. Private line."

"Yes, General McLanahan," the computerized ever-present voice of Dreamland's virtual information and access service responded. "Please stand by." Patrick hung up the phone.

"Assuming he knows anything," Dave said. "He may be the president, but the Russians still have their boots on his neck pretty well."

"We'll find out." A few minutes later the phone rang, and Patrick picked it up. "General McLanahan."

"This is Rejep Aydogdijev, assistant deputy chief of staff to President Turabi of Turkmenistan," a heavily accented voice said in halting English. "All communications with the president from overseas must originate from our embassy in Washington. Good night." And the call was abruptly terminated.

"Ever get tired of being hung up on, Muck?" Dave deadpanned.

"Yes—but hopefully this won't be one of them," Patrick said calmly. He surfed a bit around the Internet, mostly on sites regarding the Qagev dynasty of Iran and its surviving members. "Where's Hal?"

Dave summoned Hal Briggs to the command center via the "Duty Officer." "What do you have in mind, Muck?" he asked after Hal acknowledged the order.

"It depends on what Jalaluddin says."

"You going to call the State Department and ask . . . ?"

Just then the phone beeped. Patrick smiled, shook his head, held up a finger, and spoke: "McLanahan here." He noted the line was secure—he must have been working late in the office.

"My old friend the troublemaker," Jalaluddin Turabi greeted him. "I hope you and your son are well."

"We are very well, Jala," Patrick replied. "How is your new wife?"

"She drinks like a Russian, spends money like a Saudi—but fortunately makes love like a Californian. She has already honored me with two healthy sons."

"Congratulations."

"Why do you call, my friend?"

"I want to ask about a certain incident in the Tolkuchka Bazaar yesterday. I'll ask plainly—did the Iranians capture an Iranian princess and her family?"

Patrick heard a loud commotion in the background—it was Turabi, obviously chastising someone, loudly trying to chase them out of earshot. A few moments later: "So. Are your eyes on the ground or still in the sky?"

"In the sky—for now."

"We see your big space station over us almost every night now, and I tell my men, the Americans will be critiquing everyone's lovemaking skills, so be diligent," Turabi said with a laugh. "Well, my friend, all of your eyes are very good—as I well know. Yes, it is true: the Shahdokht Azar Assiyeh Qagev, the youngest daughter of the surviving heir to the Qagev royal dynasty, was captured in the bazaar shortly after she arrived from a flight from Canada via Istanbul."

"I thought all the king's children were murdered by the Iranian Revolutionary Guards."

"Apparently not, my friend."

"The Iranians have her?"

"One of my military police battalion commanders, more loyal to the Iranians than to their own people—or paid off better—assisted the deputy chief of mission Fattah to place several pro-monarchy loyalists under surveillance and capture them once they were found," Turabi said. "But it was only the daughter, Azar, not the mother and father. The daughter was accompanied by two bodyguards. I believe they were taken to the federal jail here in the capital."

"I would rather not assault your jail, Jala," Patrick said, "so if it's possible to sneak her out, I can snatch her. Can you do that?"

"Of course," Turabi said. "I can advise you when we have her, and then you can, as you put it, 'snatch' her."

"Thank you, Jala. You can loudly and publicly protest any actions that may take place in your country in the next few days," Patrick said.

"That I can do very easily, my friend—you can be assured of that," Turabi said. "We have spoken long enough, and I do not want to hear any more anyway. Peace be with you, my friend." And the connection was broken.

Hal Briggs and Chris Wohl returned to the command center when Patrick hung up, and Hal had someone with him that Patrick did not recognize. "Sir, I'd like to introduce you to Captain Charlie Turlock," Hal said.

Patrick got to his feet, confusion evident in his face. "Charlie Turlock?" The more confused he looked the broader the smile became on Hal's face.

"Problem, sir?" Turlock asked.

Patrick glanced at Hal's smile, nodded knowingly, and shook Turlock's hand. "Sorry, Captain," Patrick said. "General Briggs failed to inform me that Charlie Turlock was a woman. Is that your real name, a nickname, or a call-sign?"

"Unfortunately 'Charlie' is my real first name, sir," the newcomer replied. "My dad wanted a son and thought I'd need a boy's name to make it in the world, and out of respect for him I never changed it."

"And I suppose you like seeing the confused faces of the men who make incorrect assumptions about you and don't do their homework."

Turlock smiled. "Something like that, sir."

"I'll deal with General Briggs later. Welcome to Dreamland."

"Thank you, sir," Charlie said. She was a little over average height, with strawberry-blond hair pulled up and off her shoulders, revealing a long, graceful, athletically tanned neck. Other than her dancing green eyes it was hard to make out any distinguishing features about her, dressed as she was in her army combat uniform, but the one thing Patrick did notice was her supreme air of confidence. Most junior officers and enlisted personnel withered and shriveled in the presence of so many stars and stripes in one room, but Turlock definitely wasn't one of them. "I've heard all the stories and rumors about this place, and I've always wanted to visit. I assume there's a lot more to this place than what you see when you drive on post?"

"Sure is, Captain," Patrick said. "General Briggs will show you around. I'm looking forward to seeing a demonstration of your Cybernetic Infantry Devices. I've seen their aftermath on TV, of course, but I'd like to get an up-close and personal tour."

"The CID units, sir?" Charlie asked, confused. "I assumed you were interested in the National Guard's next-generation airships—that's what I'm prepared to demonstrate for you."

"I am, Charlie, but my primary interest right now is the CID units," Patrick said.

"I don't have access to any of the CID units any more," Charlie admitted. "The program was canceled and I've since lost track of the CIDs. I don't even know if the Infantry Transformational Battlelab at Fort Polk assigned anyone else to the project—I wouldn't even know whom to refer you to."

"We know all about the CID program—in fact, we *bought* it," Patrick said.

"You *bought* the Cybernetic Infantry Device program? All of it?"

"It seems the Army was rather anxious to get rid of the four CID units they had. They didn't let them go cheaply, but they gave us everything—almost your entire lab at Fort Polk. The units, your computers, files, and equipment are in your new facility. We don't have anything plugged in or set up, but we have guys ready to help you, and we can get more technical or specialized help fairly quickly."

"'Help me?' Help me do what, sir?"

"Help you set up your lab here at Dreamland and develop them for the Air Battle Force ground forces, under my command," Hal Briggs said.

"What does the Air Force want with manned robots?"

"The Air Battle Force combines both air and ground strike forces into one integrated unit, Charlie," Hal said. "Our specialty is sending small, high-tech, highly mobile forces anywhere in the world in less than a day, and we're working on technology that will get them there even quicker."

"Like a Marine Recon force?" Charlie asked, looking at Chris Wohl.

"Think half the size, three times the speed, and four times the firepower," Hal said. "But your CID units have capabilities that even our Tin Men don't have."

"'Tin Men'?"

"Our version of CID," Dave said. "Not as armored or strong as CID, but ten times as capable as an infantry soldier in the field."

"You're offering me a job out here?"

"Your official base of operations will be Battle Mountain Air Reserve Base up in northern Nevada," Patrick said, "but you'll test and evaluate your systems down here in Dreamland. You'll be deployed quite often with the Air Battle Force and with other agencies. If you don't mind moving out to the high desert and working in a place where everything you do is monitored twenty-four-seven, we'd be thrilled to have you."

"Moving to Vegas sounds cool, sir—the monitoring thing, not so cool," Charlie admitted. "Is that nece ssary?"

"Unfortunately, yes," Patrick said. "You get used to it. Dave, Hal, and I have all been wired for sound for almost twenty years."

"'Wired for sound . . . ?'"

"I can't get into details yet," Patrick said. "Hal can explain more after the necessary waivers and disclosures are signed. If you don't agree it's the place for you, we'll send you back to the Guard training center in Los Alamitos, and we'll get to work on the CIDs ourselves."

That seemed to change Charlie's attitude. "Frankly, sir, I'd rather the CIDs stayed in storage than have anyone else messing with them," she said. "I'll listen to General Briggs . . . I can't promise you anything else."

"I'll tell you right now up front, it's not the kind of posting you can just walk away from in a year or two," Patrick warned her. "It's one of those lifelong commitments that go way beyond just getting a security clearance and special access. It's intense. It'll affect you and everyone you come in contact with for the rest of your life."

Charlie smiled a tomboyish, mischievous grin at that last statement. "If that was meant to talk me out of it, sir, it failed," she said. "I'll make up my mind after I talk with General Briggs, but I think I'll do just fine here."

"Good," Patrick said. "I'll need your CIDs up and running as soon as possible."

"Meaning . . . ?"

"Tomorrow."

"*Tomorrow?* I haven't even agreed to come here yet!"

"You'll find that everything we do here at Dreamland needs to be done by tomorrow . . . or, better, later the same day, Captain," Dave Luger said seriously. "But we have a lot of tools and gadgets of our own that help facilitate that."

That seemed to pique Turlock's interest even more. "Yes, sir," was all she could say.

"We're pretty informal around here, Charlie," Patrick said. "The uniform of the day is always utility uniform; your work hours are your own; we keep mandatory formations, inspections, and functions to a bare minimum except for security purposes. Most of all, we encourage thinking outside the box, and we do everything we can to get you what you need or want. No request or idea is too outlandish—tell us what you want to do and we'll move mountains to get it for you. Literally."

Charlie looked at each of the men around her—from the scowling, impatient, pent-up energy of the Marine Corps master sergeant to the smiling, animated one-star general that brought him here, to the infamous three-star general leading this group—and liked what she saw. The Army was always so serious and regimented, and these guys were a definite departure from that. "Let me see the CID units, sir," she said, "and I'll tell you how soon I can get them ready for action."

"Excellent," Patrick said. He shook Charlie's hand again. "Welcome aboard."

"Thank you, sir. I'll need volunteers to pilot the CIDs."

"Count me out," Chris Wohl growled.

"You're too tall anyway, Master Sergeant," Charlie said. Wohl nodded imperceptibly—that seemed to suit him just fine.

"I'll be the first volunteer," Hal said. "I've wanted to check one out ever since I saw 'em on TV. I think we'll have plenty of volunteers for the other units. BERP is good, but I think CIDs are way cooler."

"On your way, Captain," Patrick said. "Hal, report back in one hour and let me know what we're looking at. Let Dave know if you're having any trouble detaching Charlie from the Guard."

"You got it."

Patrick could see Charlie shaking her head in amazement and excitement at the whirlwind of activity and the close personal camaraderie that existed in this place—he knew that she knew she was signing onto something truly extraordinary. "*That's* the expression I like seeing in the newcomer's faces around here," he said to Dave Luger as she was led away.

"Sorry I didn't brief you on her, Muck," Dave said. "I should have known Hal wouldn't have told you—he'd want to see your expression." He noticed Patrick looking in the direction she and Hal had gone. "What do you think, Muck?"

" 'Think'? About what? About Turlock? She hasn't done anything yet. Her record is impressive, and if that robot thing is half of what it's cracked up to be . . ."

"No, I mean . . ."

"Mean what, Dave?" Patrick admonished his friend, perhaps a little more harshly than he wanted. He scowled first at Dave, then at himself when he realized he was still standing and still turned in the direction she had left. "We'll need to get those robot things ready to go ASAP," he said gruffly as he took his seat again. "From what Hal said, those robots take up a lot of room, even folded up, and they're way too big to be worn while inside the Black Stallion's passenger module. We'll need spacesuits for whoever rides in the passenger modules that will be piloting the CIDs. We'll need those right away."

"No problem," Dave said. "But we may not get clearance to go in to look for missiles for a few days."

"I want to go in tomorrow, as soon as we've installed the thermal blanketing in the modules."

"Tomorrow?"

"I thought you just told the captain that we always want things done tomorrow!" Patrick said with a smile. "Well, you were absolutely right."

"Where do you want to take the Black Stallions, Muck?"

"I want a ground force to go into Turkmenistan, rescue this princess, turn her over to her followers, then travel into Iran with her and stand by to move against the Iranian missile sites."

"Why waste time with this princess, Muck?" Dave asked, his head shaking in confusion. "If our mission is to find and neutralize the Iranian missiles, let's send the entire ground force out there."

"I can't explain it any further, Dave, but I think that princess . . ."

"If she's who Turabi says she is!"

". . . is an important key to whatever happens in Iran—even as much as Buzhazi. If we can track her, I want to try to rescue her. If we lose contact for whatever reason, we'll send the entire force after the Iranian missiles."

"I think it's pretty damned risky to send a squad after this unknown person, Muck," Dave said seriously. "I'd be very surprised if the President authorizes it."

"Until we find those Iranian missiles and plan a way to neutralize them," Patrick said, "I think the only way we'll get any Battle Force ground units into the region is through Turkmenistan. Once Jalaluddin gives us a location, we swoop in, snatch the girl, and get out."

"To tell you the truth, Muck, I don't trust your friend Turabi," Dave said. "He may be a swashbuckling hero to the Turkmenis, but to me he's just an opportunistic Taliban fighter who does whatever he needs to do to survive. I find it a little suspicious when a guy who has ambushed and disrupted the Russians as much as he has in the past few years is still surviving in that country, literally surrounded shoulder-to-shoulder by Russians and Iranians."

"He's our best contact inside the country, Dave," Patrick said. "We have pretty good eyes over Turkmenistan now, so if he comes through we can be on the lookout for trouble when we move in. Besides, he owes us for saving his neck—twice."

The concern on Dave Luger's face bothered him, but Patrick held firm. "I need Hal to draw up a plan to infiltrate into Turkmenistan with a Black Stallion and a combined CID and Tin Man squad," he said, "assault wherever Jalaluddin manages to transfer this Qagev princess to, spring her, take her to wherever she was going to contact her underground network, set her on the path, and follow her in to Iran."

"You're making an awful lot of assumptions here, Muck," Dave said, trying one more time to dissuade his old friend from this plan. "My recommendation would be to go to the National Security Council and the President with a plan to assault the most likely locations of Iran's medium- and long-range missiles capable of carrying weapons of mass destruction. The list will be refined as we move in. Once we nail down the locations, we attack with everything we've got—orbital weapons, ground forces, and air-launched weapons from the Megafortresses. We punch Iran's missile threat off the board in one night. The Revolutionary Guards now need to deal with threats on multiple fronts—Buzhazi's insurgency, us, and possible action from the regular army. We'll have them back on their heels."

Patrick thought for a moment. "Dave, yours is a good plan," Patrick said, "but my gut still tells me that this princess is important. I don't know how I know, but I think she's the key to a non-Islamist future for Iran. But I'll pitch your plan as well. Either way, we'll get our forces moving in the right direction. I think they'll buy my plan only because it doesn't immediately put the Battle Force on the ground in Iran."

"But you have to trust Turabi."

Patrick hesitated again, but shook his head. "I know, but I think the reward is worth the risk," he said. "Help Hal and Chris draw up both plans and have them ready for me as soon as possible."

"Roger that," Dave said. "What about Buzhazi? Are we done trying to help him?"

"We'll re-evaluate once he surfaces or makes contact with us," Patrick said, "but Buzhazi has to sink or swim on his own. He should be enlisting the help of the regular army if they have any hope for stopping the Pasdaran—otherwise a hundred squads of Tin Men or

CIDs won't do much good against a hundred thousand Iranian Revolutionary Guards."

Dave sat down at his console in the command center and began to outline his thoughts for the mission into Turkmenistan. They were very familiar with the military situation in Turkmenistan. Most of the country's small police and self-defense forces were used for just one thing: maintaining a strong government presence in the capital city of Ashkhabad to control the spread and growth of radical Islamist groups. The Russian military and private security firms handled security for their own oil executives, refineries, storage facilities, and pipelines—and they did so with such utter brutality that attacks were rare. Border security was almost nonexistent—in fact, the country generally encouraged foreign workers to come to work in the arid, barren country, documented or not.

About an hour later, Hal Briggs rejoined them in the battle staff area. "I think Turlock's in," he told Patrick and Dave. "We impressed the hell out of her with having all her CID gear in a lab ready for her. She even activated one of the robots and had me get inside."

"What's it like?" Patrick asked.

"Awesome!" Hal exclaimed. "The thing unfolds itself in less than thirty seconds and it stands about nine feet tall, like an Erector Set–looking robot with skin.

It sort of crouches down, and you climb up the legs and slide inside, and you're wrapped in this snug scratchy Neoprene-like stuff. The back closes up and you feel like you're going to suffocate for a few seconds . . . and then you feel like you're standing naked in the middle of the room. You have absolutely no sensation that you're inside a machine. The hydraulics actuate a hundred times faster than the Tin Man exoskeleton, and they're far stronger."

"Downsides?"

"Other than the size, not much," Hal said. "Turlock says the CIDs are equivalent in speed and firepower to a Humvee missile or machine gun squad, and I'd agree. It's not a sneak-and-peek system like the Tin Men—it's definitely a break-the-door-down-and-kick-ass system. It's not that heavy, but it's bulky. The things suck a lot of power, and I'd say bringing spare power cells for any missions longer than an hour or so is a must. Good thing is, those things can carry a lot of stuff on a mission—a spare backpack and a spare power cell are easy, along with the mission backpack it wears. It definitely has a very high coolness factor."

"Are they ready to go?"

"Two of them appear to be. One looks like it's damaged; not sure about the fourth. Turlock says we definitely have two CIDs, two twenty-millimeter machine gun backpacks, two forty-millimeter missile backpacks, one 'Goose' mini-UAV launcher backpack—another very cool gadget that launches these bowling-pin–sized UAVs out that sends pictures back to the CIDs—and five spare power cells. I think we're good to go."

"Good, because we're planning a mission to Turkmenistan for tomorrow night," Dave said.

"Turkmenistan? Jala Turabi? Is he in trouble? Wouldn't surprise me."

"The general wants to rescue an Iranian princess before she's sent back to Iran, probably to be executed."

"A princess? Is she cute?"

"She's fifteen years old, you letch."

"Still cool. Doesn't give us much time to train in the CIDs, though."

"Do you need more time?"

"I could sure use it," Hal admitted. "I recommend we send Chris and three Tin Men to Turkmenistan in the Black Stallion—that way I can spend more time in the CIDs. It won't take long to get up to speed on them, but one day is not enough time. I'll be studying the manual on the electronic visor graphics and controls all night as it is."

"All right—I'll pitch that to General Sparks and see how they like it," Patrick said. "Get it ready to go ASAP."

BANQUET HALL, IMAM ALI MILITARY ACADEMY, TEHRAN, IRAN

The Next Evening

"I am privileged to speak to you tonight on the eve of your commissioning ceremony," Chief of Staff of the Armed Forces General Hoseyn Yassini said. He was standing before an audience of three hundred senior classmen of the Imam Ali Military Academy, after hosting their pre-commissioning dinner. Although he was still a virtual prisoner in his residence at the Academy, he was permitted to carry out ceremonial and VIP functions, and he did so with enthusiasm. As always, if the students knew he was there under house arrest, as they certainly must have by now, they showed no signs of any displeasure. "This is one of my many official tasks that I am pleased and genuinely happy to perform.

"For two years now you have been immersed in the important tasks of training and disciplining your minds and bodies for the challenges that lay ahead. You may indeed believe that your reward for two years of Hell in his place is a lifetime of Hell on the battlefield.

Well, my soon-to-be fellow officers, that is not just a cute saying—it's the truth. But as your chief of staff, I want to be the first to thank you for your courage and dedication to such a life. I thank you, and your country thanks you. I encourage you to use the knowledge and skills you have learned here to broaden your minds to the world and the challenges that lay ahead. Do not shrink from these challenges, but embrace them."

Yassini raised a large ornate golden flask, with a winged lion's head and shoulders in front and a funnel-shaped cup in back. "Allow me the honor of toasting the republic's newest officers in the ancient traditions. This is the rhython, a batu flask dating back to the Achemenid Empire of five hundred B.C., used by the kings of ancient Persia to toast to victory before sending his generals off to battle. Whenever the rhython was used, the generals of Persia were never defeated in battle." He raised the gleaming gold flask. "Gentlemen, to our republic's future military leaders, the prayers and thanks of a grateful and proud nation. May you continue to grow in knowledge, courage, and strength."

He took a sip from the cup, then passed it to the cadet commander, who immediately passed it to his deputy commander without drinking. The deputy touched the rim to his lips but did not drink. He passed it to the cadet operations officer, who also touched it to his lips, then passed it to the commander of the honor battalion. Most of the cadets did not drink from the cup; a few did, and received warning glares and stern expressions from the others.

"And now, my soon-to-be fellow officers, the table and the evening are yours—I have spoken far too much already," Yassini said. "Enjoy yourselves tonight, but be ready for the parade at dawn. Congratulations again. Allah akbar. Cadet Commander, take charge of your corps." The cadet commander called the cadets to attention, and Yassini left the dais.

The cadet corps deputy commander escorted Yassini out of the hall and waited until his car was brought around, but Yassini waved the car away, preferring to walk back to his quarters. As he turned and headed off, several men alighted from the car and quickly caught up to the chief of staff. "Well, well, General, that was quite a surprise," Islamic Revolutionary Guards Corps commander Brigadier-General Ali Zolqadr said as he strode beside Yassini. "Is this a new tradition you're starting tonight? Where did you get the rhython?"

"I requested it from the Museum of Ancient Cultures. Don't worry—the museum will see to it that it's returned safely tonight."

"I'm not worried about the flask, General, but the spirit in which it was used tonight," Zolqadr said. "Toasting the cadet corps with alcohol? Such things are strictly forbidden by the Prophet, blessed be his name, and the Faqih has expressly prohibited alcohol of any kind and for any purpose on all official government or religious property."

"Toasting success and courage with the rhython is a Persian tradition dating back over two thousand years, Zolqadr," Yassini said. "The only time it hasn't been used is in the past thirty years, since the revolution. I'm not starting anything new, Zolqadr, just restoring a long-employed honor. The cadets will never forget this night, believe me, even the ones who did not drink."

"I was relieved to see that most refused to drink, unlike yourself," Zolqadr said. "They know that alcohol is a corrupting and unholy vice that stains and perverses body, mind, and soul. Pity you fail to recognize that same truth."

"It's not a truth, Zolqadr—it's a belief," Yassini said.

"No, General, it's the law, based on teachings and commands handed down to us from God through the Prophet and codified by the Faqih," Zolqadr said. "That should be simple enough for you to understand."

Yassini knew he was never going to win any argument with a zealot—no, make that a fanatic—like Zolqadr, even if his beliefs were based solely on his thirst for power and not true personal faith. "You didn't come here to lecture me, General. What do you want?"

"No, General, I did not. I'm here to place you under arrest for crimes against the Islamic Republic and for conspiracy to aid the enemies of the republic."

Yassini stopped, and only then noticed the three armed soldiers walking behind him. "You can't arrest me, Zolqadr," Yassini said. "I report only to the minister of defense or the Supreme National Security Deputate, not to the Pasdaran."

"Wrong again, Yassini," Zolqadr said gleefully. "As of tonight, the Pasdaran has once again been detached from its subordinate position in the Ministry of Defense and has been placed directly in the hands of the Director of the Supreme National Security Deputate, where the blessed Ayatollah Khomeini first assigned it and where it properly belongs as an instrument of divine retribution. My orders come directly from the Ayatollah Mohtaz. The Supreme National Security Deputate has charged you with treason and conspiracy to commit treason, and you are hereby ordered to be placed under arrest and confinement pending summary court-martial."

SAPAMURAD NIYAZOV CENTER FOR PUBLIC LAW AND ORDER, ASHKHABAD, TURKMENISTAN

That Same Time

A line of three vehicles, two sedans and one armored troop transport, pulled up to the front of the Sapamurad Niyazov Center for Public Law and Order criminal justice building in the center of the Turkmeni capital. A squad of soldiers ran out of the building and took up defensive positions around the vehicles, scanning the streets and surrounding buildings for any sign of trouble. Moments later a door on the armored vehicle swung open, followed by the doors to the building, and three persons in handcuffs and leg restraints were led from the building into the armored vehicles. As soon as they were inside, the guards were recalled and the armored vehicle and their escorts sped away.

Unseen by anyone who might be watching the operation—unlikely, since the police enforced a strict dawn-to-dusk curfew in the capital district of the city, punishable by caning—was a second armored vehicle that had slipped in to a fenced official parking lot in the rear of the building. A single guard opened the barbed-wire-topped gate and let the armored car through.

The vehicle drove to a dark rear corner of the lot and parked near several other similar vehicles, and moments later the driver alighted and walked away, exiting the lot without turning back. Except for the occasional squawk of a peacock—used in Turkmenistan like a watchdog—the place quickly fell silent once again.

Several minutes later a sedan was admitted through the gate, and it parked a few yards away from the armored vehicle. Two security guards, with AKS-74 assault rifles at the ready, emerged from the sedan and took up guard positions. Moments later, a man in a long coat emerged, went around to the other side of the sedan, and opened the door for Turkmeni president Jalaluddin Turabi.

"Everything is clear, sir," the chief of Turabi's security detail said. "No sign of them."

Turabi looked into the darkness outside the floodlit walls and chuckled. "They're here, don't worry," he said. "They've probably been here for a while." He walked over to the armored vehicle and rapped on the side door, and a guard inside opened it up. "How are you tonight, Princess?"

Azar Assiyeh Qagev leaned forward in her seat, squinting in the darkness. "Very well, thank you," she said in passable Turkmeni, her tone of voice suspicious yet pleasant. "I presume I have the honor of addressing President Jalaluddin Turabi?"

"My staff informed me that you are observant and smart—I see they were not exaggerating," Turabi said after shaking off his surprise.

"Do you intend on turning me over to the Iranian government without benefit of legal process?" Azar asked.

"As far as Turkmenistan is concerned, you are a citizen of the United States and Turkey, and you have broken no laws in Turkmenistan," Turabi said. "If Iran has charged you with serious crimes, according to treaty you must be taken before a judge who will hear their arguments. But we have reason to believe your life is in danger, so you will be taken someplace safe until your extradition hearing."

"I am forever in your debt, Mr. President," Azar said.

"Why are you in Turkmenistan, Princess?" Turabi asked. "Certainly not to upgrade our cellular phone system."

"I hope I don't appear ungrateful, sir," Azar said, "but I don't wish to discuss this without benefit of legal counsel. I'm sure you understand."

"Of course," Turabi said, checking his watch. "I was hoping there was some other way I could help, that's all."

ON THE OUTSKIRTS OF ASHKHABAD, TURKMENISTAN

That Same Time

"Things look quiet out here, One," Master Sergeant Chris Wohl radioed via the Tin Man battle armor's built-in satellite transceiver. Wohl was hidden at the rendezvous point suggested by Jalaluddin Turabi, observing the area for any signs of danger. "Turabi just showed up. You copy, Genesis?"

"Roger that," Dave Luger radioed from the Dreamland Battle Management area. "Sorry, but it looks like the drone you launched isn't sending any video, just stills every few minutes. You copy us, Stud Five?"

"Roger," Hunter Noble responded. He was patrolling the southern section of their landing spot outside of the capital, carrying a Heckler & Koch MP-5 submachine gun. "We lost the video too, so we're all out patrolling the area." He looked over to where his copilot and mission commander, Captain Wil Lefferts, was nervously pacing, another H&K MP-5 submachine gun cradled awkwardly in his arms. "Six's about ready to have a cow, I think."

"What's wrong, Five?"

"Nothing—it's just quiet as hell out here," Boomer replied. "Wil—er, I mean, Six—jumps at every little sound." He peered out through the darkness. His eyes were finally getting night-adapted, and he could see more and more details of their surroundings. "This is a great landing site, guys—a road plenty long for us to land on, lots of cover, far from any major highways, and open space for Stud Four to run around." Boomer had landed the XR-A9 Black Stallion spaceplane outside a large truck parking area several miles outside the capital city of Ashkhabad. The facility appeared to be abandoned—it was easy to find from the air, easy to approach, and easy to touch down. There was a long, wide access road to the west of the complex, and that's where Boomer landed the XR-A9.

"Just keep your eyes open, guys," Dave said. He didn't voice his main concerns again—the fact that Jalaluddin Turabi had recommended this spot for an insertion—because Dave had already expressed his doubts several times already. He had insisted on, and Patrick had approved, several methods to ensure that their crews weren't walking into a trap:

The powerful sensors on Armstrong Space Station had swept the area twice in three hours prior to landing and cleared the Black Stallion to land, which made everyone feel better. There was a constellation of small NIRTSats supporting surveillance operations over Iran, and one of those satellites passed over the area every few hours to update the strategic picture of the target area.

In addition, the second XR-A9 spaceplane, launched shortly after Boomer's, had released a Meteor payload re-entry module which seeded four surveillance drones over the area and beamed streaming video images to the Air Battle Force commandos on the ground and back to Dreamland. The drones were positioned over the landing zone and three other key places in the area: central Ashkhabad, including the government center, Hall of Justice, and the Russian embassy; the Turkmeni army barracks south of the city; and Ashkhabad-Berzien Military Airfield west of the city.

Unfortunately two of the drones malfunctioned—one crashed someplace in the desert shortly after release, and the second was still aloft but not sending any video. Dave had carefully considered requesting that they abort the mission because of the lack of timely intelligence data on the target and the area defenses. But he knew Patrick wanted this mission to happen. So after scanning the Turkmeni air base for any sign of movement that might suggest the ground team had been discovered, Dave ordered that drone moved to the Black Stallion landing site. The drone had to fly south around the city, well away from Niyazov International Airport, to avoid discovery, so it would not be on station for several minutes—meaning the Black Stallion and its crew were on their own until the drone arrived.

"Stud Four is shifting to the south—I thought I saw headlights," Army Sergeant Maxwell Dolan in Tin Man battle armor and powered exoskeleton radioed. "Genesis, are you receiving my video?"

"Affirmative, Four," Dave Luger responded. Video and sensor images received by any of the Tin Men in the Air Battle Force ground team were uplinked via satellite back to the Battle Management Area at Dreamland, where they could be shared by any other member in almost real-time. "We didn't see the lights, but proceed"—then he added—"with caution."

That kind of chatter made Boomer very nervous—and at that moment he found himself unconsciously flicking the mode selector on his MP-5 up and down. Shit, he thought, he forgot which way the switch went for the "SAFE" position, and he didn't want to radio the others to remind him—again—which was correct. He designed high-performance jet and rocket engines, he admonished himself, but for some damned reason he could never remember if flipping the switch up was "SAFE," or the other way around.

Boomer moved toward a small concrete pump building a few dozen yards away from the Black Stallion, crouched down on the far side of the building, pulled a small LED flashlight from a flight suit pocket, covered the bulb as much as he could with his hand to avoid spoiling his night vision and startling Wil Lefferts, then shined it on the left side of the little submachine gun. Oh shit, he swore to himself, he had switched it to the three-round burst mode. For safety reasons there was no full-automatic mode on these weapons, just a SAFE, semi-automatic, and three-round semi-automatic mode.

OK, OK, he yelled at himself, pushing the switch down is bad—flipping it up is good. Push down to get down . . . that's what the weapon instructor from Battle Mountain said when he . . .

Suddenly there was a tremendous burst of red and orange light, followed moments later by a tremendous "BOOOM!" so powerful that it knocked Boomer on his butt. "Stud Four, Stud Four . . . Max, how do you copy?" Dave Luger radioed frantically. "Come in!"

"Bastards!" Dolan radioed back. "I just got hit by a damned RPG round!" Boomer's skin and fingers instantly turned cold. Were they under attack . . . ?

"Are you OK?" Luger radioed.

"I'm going to blast those motherfuckers into the next century!" Dolan shouted. Boomer heard two or three sharp "CRAACK!" reports and knew that Dolan was firing his electromagnetic rail gun. "I see four armored personnel carriers and maybe one light tank approaching the area. I want . . ." Suddenly his audio report cut out.

"Stud Four, how do you copy?" Luger radioed. "Stud Four?" Still no response. "Stud Five and Six, Four is still on the move but I've lost his audio. I need you to . . ." At that moment the audio channel was completely blocked by loud squealing, hissing, and popping sounds so loud that Boomer found it hard to concentrate.

Wil Lefferts suddenly came into view, running over between Boomer and the Black Stallion, his MP-5 submachine gun upraised. "Boomer! Where are you?" he shouted.

"Over here!" Lefferts whirled around at the sound, aiming his gun at the voice. "Don't shoot, you idiot!" Boomer ran over to him, then pulled him down to the ground and shoved the muzzle of the submachine gun away in a safe direction. "Are you all right? Are you hurt?"

"What's happening?" Lefferts yelled. His voice, and indeed his entire body, was shaking.

"We're under attack! Let's get the Stud ready for takeoff!"

"Shouldn't we wait for the ground force?"

"I'm not going to lose the Stud to whoever's attacking us," Boomer said. "Our safest place is in the air. We'll come back for the ground forces once the attack is over. Let's go!" Crouching low, Boomer ran over to the spaceplane and climbed aboard, hoping Wil was right behind him. He pulled on his helmet and his lap restraints, flipped on the battery switch, and motored the canopy closed. As soon as he sensed that Wil was aboard, he commanded, "Engine start procedures."

"Stand by for engine start procedures," the computer responded. "Beginning before power on checklist."

"Override," Boomer ordered. "Begin engine start procedures."

"Override before engine start checklist. Beginning power on . . ."

"Override. Begin engine start procedures." Boomer had to repeat the override command for each of the checklists he wanted to skip, having to wait for the computer's warning and verification messages each time. It seemed to take forever, but finally the computer was on the right page.

The first human interaction step wasn't for almost another twenty seconds, so Boomer securely strapped himself into his seat and made sure Wil was doing the same—and then he looked out to his right, and his jaw dropped. Sergeant Max—Boomer wasn't sure of his last name—was standing less than fifty yards away from the Black Stallion's right wingtip, the electromagnetic rail gun in his arm, firing into the darkness. Every few seconds he would shift positions, darting back and forth with amazing speed, occasionally going out of sight as he moved away from the XR-A9 or back toward it to block a round fired at it. Seconds after he'd fire there was a tremendous explosion off in the distance, and often several secondary explosions as well. Boomer couldn't believe he was moving like that after already being hit by a rocket-propelled grenade round!

The sergeant turned toward the Stud and gestured frantically down the road, urging them to take off. The checklist was proceeding normally—still ten seconds to the first hold. Finally Boomer spoke the "Acknowledge" command, verifying that the crew was ready for engine start, and the auxiliary power unit spun up and began shunting compressed air into the number two engine. The big engine took a long time to spin up, but finally it reached twenty-five percent RPMs and the fuel began injecting . . .

Boomer happened to glance up right before light-off . . . just in time to see a heavy explosive round hit the sergeant square in the chest, then instantly disappear in a blinding globe of fire. "Oh, shit," Wil exclaimed. "My God . . . !"

"Get ready for takeoff—we're going as soon as we got the power," Boomer said. He already pre-loaded "Override" commands to the computer—it might not accept any of them except the first one, but he had to do something while he was waiting for the computer to catch up. Finally the first engine was started. Boomer's first order to simultaneously run the "Before Taxi," "Taxi," and "Before Takeoff" checklists while the other three engines were being started were accepted, and Boomer instantly took manual control of the steering switch and . . .

At that moment a streak of fire raced out of the darkness, and they felt a massive shudder and heard a deafening "BOOM!" A small explosive round, probably an RPG, hit the Black Stallion's right main landing gear. The right wing immediately flew upward a few feet, then came crashing down all the way to the ground. "Evacuate! Now!" Boomer cried. He ordered the computer to perform the "Emergency Shut Down" checklist, but it was already being done. He knew the Stud wasn't going to be flying anytime soon—if ever—so instead of motoring the canopy up, he hit the yellow and black striped "EMER CANOPY" button to blow the cockpit canopy off the aircraft. He hurriedly unstrapped and waited for the canopy behind him to blow before standing up in his seat.

To his shock, Boomer found the aft canopy gone, but Wil was nowhere to be seen. Boomer jumped down off the spaceplane and found his copilot and mission commander lying facefirst on the hard sandy ground. "C'mon, Wil, we gotta get out of here," he said.

"I'm hit," Wil muttered, barely audible over the gunfire just on the other side of the plane, getting closer by the second. Boomer couldn't see any of his wounds, but he could feel the blood covering him everywhere he touched. "Jeez, Boomer, I'm hit . . ."

"We're outta here." Boomer began dragging Lefferts away . . .

. . . just as another explosive ripped across the Black Stallion, sending pieces of composite skin flying in the air atop a column of fire. Boomer, egged on by the feeling that the entire front of his body was afire, kept on going as fast as he could. He knew that the concrete pump house was the only bit of cover nearby, so he pulled and pulled as fast as he . . .

Just then it appeared as if the entire fuselage of the XR-A9 Black Stallion erupted and burst apart like a child's balloon. Boomer had a brief sensation of floating in mid-air before hitting something behind him. The cloud of fire and smoke enveloped him, as did several pieces of his beloved spaceplane, and then everything went dark . . .

SAPAMURAD NIYAZOV CENTER FOR LAW AND ORDER, ASHKHABAD, TURKMENISTAN

That Same Time

"I hope I didn't offend you, Mr. President," Azar said. "I am thankful and more than a little surprised to be under the supervision of the president of Turkmenistan himself." She paused, then asked, "Whom are we waiting for, Mr. President?"

"Your benefactors, Princess," Turabi said. "I wish I could take all the credit for this event, but I'm doing this as a favor to an old friend."

"I am still grateful for any assistance you might provide us, Mr. President."

"Not at all." Turabi looked at his watch impatiently. "But if your benefactors don't show up soon, there might be . . . how shall I say it . . . unexpected complications."

"Like what, Turabi?" an electronically synthesized voice said in Turkmeni. The ex–Afghan fighter whirled around. Perched atop a nearby lamppost, completely hidden in the shadows and glare, was a figure in a dark outfit. "What are you doing here?"

Those on the ground could make out no other details—but despite that, Turabi smiled. "Judging by your size and gruff tone of voice, I would say I am speaking to the infamous Master Sergeant Christopher

Wohl," he said. Azar strained to see who Turabi was talking to, but that was impossible. "I am here to make sure this transfer goes smoothly."

"That was not smart, Turabi," the voice of Chris Wohl said. "You should get out of here, now."

"Where is your comrade General Briggs?"

"Never mind the chit-chat, Turabi," Wohl said. "Turn that armored car around and head for the airport as planned."

"Very well, very well," Turabi said. "I will leave the rest in your very capable hands, Master Sergeant." He shouted orders to the drivers and guards, who closed the doors and boarded the armored car, then motioned to his guards. "Open the gates and let the vehicles pass." He got into his sedan and, with his guards flanking the vehicle, it motored in reverse toward the gate.

Chris jumped down from his hiding place and approached the armored vehicle. The guards fearfully stepped back away from the menacing figure, their weapons upraised. Parviz Najar and Mara Saidi pushed Azar behind them protectively when they saw the gray-clad helmeted figure in the door of the vehicle. "Stop where you are!" Najar shouted in Farsi.

"I am here to take the princess and you out of here," Chris spoke in electronically synthesized Farsi. "Get in the driver's seat."

"Who are you?"

"Does it matter?" Chris responded through his electronic translator. "Use the vehicle radio or telephone to contact your network and let's get out of here."

"What network? What princess? What are you talking about?"

"Listen carefully," the unearthly apparition said angrily, leaning into the vehicle menacingly to emphasize his point. "I don't know you, and I don't care one bit about you, but I've been ordered to get you out of the city and in the hands of your escape network into Iran. If you deny you're the Iranian princess and her bodyguards who escaped from protective custody in the United States and are trying to return to Iran, then I've made a mistake. In that case, I'll be happy to leave you here in the custody of the Turkmenis and the Iranians. Now which will it be?"

Azar elbowed her way between Najar and Saidi. "I am Azar Qagev, sir, heir to the Peacock Throne of Persia," she said in perfect English, "and I am grateful for your help. Major, take the wheel. Lieutenant, get those weapons from the guards, then call the secondary blind drop number as soon as we're on our way. We'll proceed to the secondary contact point as planned."

"Glad to see someone's taking charge and not playing games," Chris said. "Move out."

"Where will you be, sir?"

"Not far. Move." And in the blink of an eye, he disappeared.

But just as they got turned around and started heading out of the parking lot, several military vehicles swarmed down the street outside. Suddenly every floodlight in the lot snapped on, bathing them all in a harsh, inescapable glare. The exit was quickly blocked by three armored vehicles with machine gunners ready in their gun turrets. "Nobody move!" a voice on a loudspeaker blared in English. "By order of the Turkmenistan Capital District Federal Police, you are all under arrest!" But it was soon obvious that these soldiers were not the same casual, ill-outfitted soldiers from the bazaar: they wore civilian clothes like the locals, but they did not look like Turkmenis. In moments about two dozen men armed with AK-74 assault rifles surrounded Azar's armored vehicle. One of them yanked open the door, disarmed Najar and Saidi, and pulled all three of them out of the vehicle.

Jalaluddin Turabi got out of his sedan. "I am sorry to do this, Master Sergeant Wohl," he shouted in halting English, looking carefully around him for any sign of trouble, knowing the American could hear him, "but the Iranians were most insistent on keeping custody of the princess and having her reveal her network. But what they would really like is you. Apparently they were impressed by your performance in Qom not long ago, and they wish to inspect your armor technology up close. If you don't want to see the girl and her bodyguards slaughtered before your eyes, come out here, now." No response, only the sounds of more Iranian Revolutionary Guards swarming the area. "You have no chance of escape, Master Sergeant. You've come an awfully long way just to see the princess die and your missions fail. The Iranians don't want you—they want your armor, weapons, and aircraft technology. You will be saving lives if you cooperate. I have received their assurances that they will let you and your men, here and at the truck farm, leave the country unharmed if you drop your weapons and remove your armor. Surrender now and . . ."

At that moment there were three simultaneous explosions right in front of Turabi as the three Iranian armored vehicles blocking the entrance to the parking lot disappeared in massive clouds of fire and smoke. Turabi was knocked off his feet by the triple blasts. After finding himself dazed but unhurt on the ground, he picked himself up and took cover behind his sedan, away from the burning vehicles.

Through the sounds of burning and popping metal, Turabi heard another series of noises, ones he had heard a long time ago but remembered as clearly as yesterday—brief screams, occasional gunshots, followed by a sickening, gory crunching sound and a loud THUD! somewhere off in the distance. He didn't hesitate, but immediately whirled and started running down the street . . .

. . . only to be stopped after just a few strides by what felt and looked like a steel wall that suddenly appeared directly in front of him. Turabi ran headlong into the obstruction and fell flat-out backward, semiconscious.

When he could see straight again, he was staring up at Qagev, Najar, and Saidi looking down at him—and standing beside them was one of the American Tin Men, its helmeted face, smooth armor, and massive tank-killing weapon making it look even more the wraithlike avenger he knew it was. The armored figure knelt beside him. "Kill me, Wohl," Turabi said, coughing up blood from a smashed nose. "Get it over with."

"Why, Turabi?" Chris Wohl asked. "Why did you cooperate with the damned Iranians? McLanahan was your friend."

" 'Friend?' He abandoned me in this hell-hole, surrounded by thousands of damned Iranians," Turabi said weakly. "I barely escape one assassination attempt by those bastards every week. Half my government has been paid off by Iran, and the suburbs outside the capital are swarming with Iranian-trained insurgents all waiting to sweep in and take over. The only way I could survive after becoming part of this damned government was to cooperate with them."

"You told them about us, about the Air Battle Force?"

"I told them you would be rescuing the princess, and they thought they could capture you and your spacecraft," Turabi said.

"Shit," Chris swore, rising to his feet. He spoke through the Tin Man battlesuit's built-in satellite transceiver: "Stud Four." No response. "Stud Four, how do you copy?" Still no response. He cursed himself for not checking in more often with the XR-A9 Black Stallion crew. "All Stud units, report back to the landing zone on the double and assist Stud Four. Prepare to engage hostile forces." He received two acknowledgments. He knelt down again and stuck his helmeted face close to the stricken Turkmeni president's. "Why didn't you ask for our help, Turabi? The general would have sent an entire army to help you. He would have taken you out of here if that's what you wanted."

"I'm an Afghan and a soldier, Wohl, not a charity case," Turabi said. "The Iranians offered me a life back in Afghanistan—money, weapons, and assistance in raising an army again in my own homeland. All I had to do was help them capture you, then turn over control of the government to their hand-picked Islamist puppet. McLanahan offered me a pat on the head and nothing else except virtual captivity here in this miserable dustbowl." He spat out another mouthful of blood. "What are you going to offer me now, Master Sergeant?"

"Just this, you fucking coward," Chris Wohl said darkly . . . then delivered a single blow to the Afghan's face that penetrated all the way down hard enough to crack the pavement below his head. Azar and her bodyguards watched as Turabi's head exploded like a ripe tomato under a sledgehammer. Wohl wiped his left fist off on Turabi's robes, then stood and faced the three Iranians. "I'll escort you to the outskirts of the city," he said, "then I have to see to my troops."

"No," Azar said. "Tell us where your forces are, and I will send my people to help."

Chris thought about that for a moment, then nodded. "Outside an abandoned truck farm fourteen kilometers east of Niyazov Airport," he said.

"How soon can you get there?" Azar asked.

"Faster than you," Chris said.

"Then go—do not worry about us," Azar said. "We will make contact with our network, then dispatch someone to help."

"My mission was to be sure you got safely out of the country."

"Your mission has changed, Master Sergeant," Azar said. "Go." Chris needed no more convincing. In the blink of an eye he had leaped into the night sky and was gone from view. "Extraordinary," Azar said to Najar and Saidi. "Whoever neutralized weapon systems such as that much be extremely powerful."

"The Pasdaran want you very badly, Shahdokht," Najar said. "We must get out of this city as quickly as possible."

"Not before we help the Americans," Azar said. "Contact the network immediately."

Azar and her bodyguards took Turabi's sedan, and they encountered absolutely no difficulties traveling through the city—the vehicle was instantly recognized by the police on patrol, who did nothing more than salute the vehicle as it drove past. Ten minutes later, easily negotiating the nearly deserted streets of Ashkhabad, they came to the Niyazov Thirtieth Anniversary Racetrack on the eastern side of the capital, and made their way to the stables, where they met up with dozens of members of the Qagev monarchy's underground support network.

"Any news of my parents?" Azar asked.

"None, Shahdokht," the network leader replied. "Some reports said they were intercepted in Paris by the Pasdaran. We simply do not have any first-hand information."

"We must proceed on our own, assemble the Court and the war council, organize the militia, and prepare to take action should the opportunity present itself," Azar said. "But first we have a debt to repay."

They found the truck farm about ten kilometers east of the racetrack. The entire area was deserted, but it did not take long for Azar and her entourage to notice the smell of burning jet fuel, metal . . . and human bodies. Their vehicles bumped across craters made by high-explosive detonations, and small fires were still burning everywhere. The underground fighters drew their weapons as they approached the worst of the battle-ravaged area. "No," Azar ordered, sensing danger nearby. "Lower your weapons. The enemy has already left . . . or has been dispatched." She got out of the sedan and approached the center of the devastated truck parking lot. "Master Sergeant? Are you here?"

"Yes," an electronic voice replied. Chris Wohl emerged from his hiding spot atop a forty-foot trailer and lowered his electromagnetic rail gun. "You came after all."

"I said I would," Azar said softly. "I would not abandon you after you rescued us from the Iranians.

I have two squads of fighters and transportation with me. What happened here?"

"Turabi told the Iranians where we'd land," Chris said. "They waited until my advance team left the area, then attacked. They captured one of my commandos and several pieces of our aircraft. My man destroyed several of their vehicles and at least a platoon of Pasdaran, but he's missing now. The aircraft crew is missing."

"Shahdokht, inja, inja!" one of the monarchists cried out in a low voice. "Here! Here!" Chris Wohl moved in a flash. The Iranian partisan pulled bits of flaming wreckage and heavily burned and blackened bodies out of a shallow crater beside a concrete pump house, revealing two men lying together, smoke still curling from their bodies. "Baz-mandeh! Nafas-e rahat!"

"A survivor!" Azar said. She dashed over behind the tall figure in gray. It was a young man, holding another young man in a protective embrace. The second man's body was riddled with bullet holes.

The tall armored commando removed his helmet, revealing a lean, craggy face filled with concern. "Captain! Can you hear me?" Chris asked.

The younger man opened his eyes, blinking away dirt and blood encrusting his vision. The man began to push Chris away in wide-eyed panic, and Azar knelt before him, scooped him up, and held him closely. "It's okay, Captain, it's okay," she whispered. "You're safe now." She looked at Chris. "What's his name?"

"Hunter," he replied. "Everyone calls him 'Boomer.' "

"Boomer. I like that name," Azar said. She held him tighter until he stopped struggling, then started to probe for wounds. "It's okay, Boomer. The master sergeant is here. We're going to take you to safety."

"Ch-Chris?" Boomer asked. His wits were quickly returning. "You okay?"

"I'm fine, sir. Can you tell us what happened?"

"They clobbered us before we could do anything," Boomer said. "Just when you reported in position at the pickup point, they swooped in. Your guy Sergeant Max—sorry, I don't know his full name—fought like a berserker, man. He was moving so fast, I thought there was three of him. He shot up most of the attacking vehicles, then started mowing down the ground forces, but . . . Jesus, there were too many of them." He looked at his arms and saw the corpse he was still cradling. "Whoever they were, they blasted the Stud apart. I got Wil out in time, but they got him too."

"Enough, Captain," Chris said. "You're safe now."

"But I think they got the Stud—or whatever they didn't blow apart . . ."

"Don't worry about it, Boomer," Azar said. "We'll see to it that your comrade and yourself are safe."

Boomer looked at the girl holding him. "The princess, I presume?" he asked. "At least your mission was successful, Master Sergeant. I like your accent, Princess. Wisconsin?"

"Minnesota," Azar said. She motioned to the partisans, who took the dead crewmember from Boomer's arms. "Can you walk, Boomer?"

"I think so." He struggled to his feet, steadied himself for a moment, then nodded. "I'm okay."

"Then let's get out of here," Azar said. "The Pasdaran will be after us."

"Where are we going?"

"Iran," Azar said. "We'll make contact with our freedom fighters and the Court. Once we're inside the network again, we'll get you back to the United States right away."

"The captain will go back," Chris Wohl said. "My men and I are staying with you."

"You don't need to do that, Master Sergeant . . ."

"Those are my orders, ma'am," Chris said. "Until I'm relieved or given further orders, I'm staying with you."

"You would abandon your superior officer . . . ?"

"He's a pilot, ma'am," Chris Wohl said flatly. "He may be a very good pilot, but he's still just a pilot. My orders did not include baby-sitting the pilot . . ."

"Jeez, thanks, Master Sergeant," Boomer moaned.

". . . but to accompany you and your men to Iran, collect intelligence data, report back to my headquarters, and await further orders."

"Your men are injured and captured, Master Sergeant," Azar said, confused. "Why do you want to stay with me?"

"My commanding officer believes you're the key to the future of Iran, Princess," Chris said. "He does not support General Buzhazi's military insurgency, and he wants more information on you and your monarchist movement. My mission is to give him the information he wants and to stand by with you in case he has further orders."

"Who is your commanding officer?"

"I'd rather not give you that information, Princess," Chris said. "He's a powerful man, but no one else believes that either the military insurgency or an underground monarchy will survive the Pasdaran's rampages. My mission is to give him the information he needs to convince my government to support you . . . or not."

Azar smiled and nodded. "That's fair, I think," she said. "My mission is to get us to safety inside Iran, convene the Court and the council of war, assemble the army, and march on to Tehran. Hopefully we can make contact with General Buzhazi and find out what he has in mind. Perhaps our forces can work together . . . perhaps not. We shall find out together, won't we?"

CHAPTER 7

THE WHITE HOUSE SITUATION ROOM, WASHINGTON, D.C.

A Short Time Later

"So, you got your wanker slammed in the drawer, eh, McLanahan?" Secretary of Defense Joseph Gardner said as he took his seat in the White House Situation Room. Patrick McLanahan was on a secure video-conference connection from the Battle Management Room at Battle Mountain Air Reserve Base, Nevada. "I guess your Tin Men aren't as tough as we all thought if a bunch of ragheads with RPGs can take them down."

"Sergeant Dolan took on four squads of mechanized infantry and destroyed three of them before they finally got him, sir," Patrick said. "He died saving two of our crewmen."

"Of course, of course—no disrespect to the sergeant or to the copilot that perished," Gardner said quickly. "What I was trying to say, McLanahan, is that you should have known that your Tin Men aren't supermen. You should have realized that leaving just one to guard a three-billion-dollar jet wasn't going to hack it, and you should have called on more special ops forces to assist."

"There wasn't time, sir."

"That's getting to be a very tired old album, McLanahan," Gardner sighed wearily, "and I for one am starting to get tired of listening to it. There's never enough time when it comes to you and your operations, is there?"

At that moment a staffer in the room noticed a flurry of movement outside the room. National Security Adviser Sparks entered the Situation Room, followed by Chief of Staff Minden, Vice President Hershel, and then by President Martindale. The staffer called the room to attention. "Seats," the President said immediately. He turned to the videoconference screen. "Sorry to hear about your loss, Patrick. What do you think the Iranians got?"

"They got Sergeant Dolan, one Tin Man battle armor system with the exoskeleton probably mostly intact, plus plenty of photographs, maybe a few composite material samples, and some electronic gear and computer modules, sir," Patrick responded. "The communications, transponders, and computers are programmed to auto-erase whenever the emergency shutdown order is given or initiated by the computer in case of an accident or attack, but it's not foolproof."

"Is there any kind of self-destruct mechanism?"

"No, sir—that's too dangerous in a spacecraft normally subject to very high heat and stresses. Master Sergeant Wohl destroyed any electronic components by hand that he could find or that were pointed out to him by Captain Noble; wearing the Tin Man suit, that would have been done very quickly and effectively. But the Iranians may still be able to recover any data or programming stored in the components they seized."

"What about Sergeant Dolan and the suit he was wearing?"

Patrick looked uncomfortable, almost pained, but he kept his head and shoulders straight as he replied, "We're hoping that the RPG rounds and the 105-millimeter tank round that killed Sergeant Dolan destroyed most of the armor and electronics in the suit. But the Iranians have taken a very valuable piece of hardware along with the body of a U.S. soldier. They need to give all of it back immediately or face the most severe consequences."

"That's not your call, McLanahan!" Jonas Sparks retorted loudly. "We're in this mess because you didn't plan properly, and you're not going to even think about doing anything to recover what was taken without full presidential authority!" He rubbed his eyes wearily. "Jesus, this could be the worst compromise of highly classified technology since John Walker or Robert Hanssen."

"Those guys were spies and traitors—the Black Stallion was attacked by Iranians inside Turkmenistan," Vice President Maureen Hershel said. "There's a big difference."

"What I meant was, the damage done due to the loss of our most sensitive and cutting-edge technology is much worse, Miss Vice President," Sparks said. Maureen scowled at the national security adviser but said nothing.

"Sir, I wanted to update you and the national security staff on developments in Iran," Patrick said. "We'll have to deal with the loss of the Black Stallion and Tin Man technology later." The President looked perturbed and grim, but nodded.

"First, we've located about a dozen forward-deployed launch sites or hiding spots for as many as a hundred medium- and long-range Iranian missiles," Patrick said. "The Iranians have deployed a large number of decoys but we've been able to separate most of them out. We believe they might have another six to ten more launch sites in other locations. We discover at least one new site per day so I feel confident we can find the rest soon.

"The Air Battle Force has the capability of neutralizing the Iranian missiles in three ways: by destroying as many launchers as possible with air and ground strikes; by hitting missiles in the boost phase with our AL-52 Dragon airborne laser; and by hitting more in the cruise phase of flight with air-launch anti-ballistic missiles," Patrick went on. "Although we can have the ground units in place quickly, it'll take two days at least for the full force to get set up over Iran and ready to strike."

"How many of the dozen sites do you think you can take out, McLanahan?" National Security Adviser Sparks asked.

"Conservatively, with our full force in place: fifty percent," Patrick replied. "We coordinate the space-borne, air-breathing, and ground attacks, and make sure our anti-ballistic missile aircraft are over the likely launch and target areas when the attacks begin."

"Fifty percent? I don't think that's good enough to risk a larger-scale war in the Persian Gulf, Patrick," Vice President Hershel said.

"We'd limit our attacks to the heaviest missiles we can find, the ones that can threaten our forces or our allies in Iraq, the Middle East, or Central Asia," McLanahan said. "Thanks to Colonel Raydon in Armstrong Space Station and the NIRTSat constellation we launched in support of our ground operations, we've located a half-dozen possible missile launch sites in the western and southern sections of the country, containing approximately a hundred medium- and long-range rockets and missiles, including the Shahab-2, Shahab-3, and possibly the Shahab-4 and -5 long-range missiles.

"However, although the recon data is updated regularly, we might not know in time if a mobile launcher missile has been moved," Patrick went on, "so we would need to place some eyes in the sky to keep constant watch on the known or suspected launch sites. We would use the Black Stallion spaceplanes and the Megafortress bombers to launch small unmanned aerial vehicles over the launcher sites. These drones can stay aloft for almost two days and send back real-time videos of the launch sites. If they move, we'll know about it. Once the Black Stallions and Megafortresses are on station, they can destroy any Iranian missiles within minutes."

"So now we're sending manned and unmanned aircraft and armed spaceplanes over Iran," Maureen

Hershel summarized, "and attacking Iranian missiles, all without a declaration of war or even a certain threat to any American or allied forces? Are we sure we want to be doing this?"

"Miss Vice President, that's a decision for the national security staff," Patrick said, his eyes narrowing a bit at Maureen's question. "But all the intel and information we're receiving tells me that the Iranian leadership will order the Revolutionary Guards to use their missiles again if Buzhazi stages another attack, which if he survived the attack on Arān he will most certainly do . . ."

"That's my point, Patrick: should we attack the Revolutionary Guards, or even have strike aircraft over Iran in the first place, if we think Tehran will just attack insurgent forces inside its own borders?" Maureen asked. "My opinion is, we should not. Iranians killing Iranians is tragic and despicable, but it's not a reason for us to go to war. Theirs is not an act of war . . . ours most certainly would be."

"Maureen . . . er, ma'am, I'm informing the national security staff that I have forces in place that I think have a very good chance of taking out Iran's long-range missile force," Patrick said, painfully aware that he was speaking much more sharply at Maureen than he liked. "I'm not guaranteeing that I can neutralize Iran's Revolutionary Guards or even neutralize all their missiles—all I'm saying is, I can send my forces into action in hours and reduce Iran's ability to threaten its neighbors or attack its own people. All I need is a decision from this group whether or not to send me in and do it."

President Martindale looked at his vice president, then over at Patrick quizzically. "I thought you two would have a closer meeting of the minds," he said in a quiet voice. He turned to the Secretary of State. "Mary, get in contact with someone in charge in Tehran. I want to impress on them the seriousness of the situation here. And prepare a statement for the allies, informing them of the capture of one of our commandos and that we are contemplating a military response."

"Yes, sir," Secretary of State Mary Carson said. She picked up her phone on the conference table, gave instructions to the Signals officer and then to her staff at the State Department, then hung up to wait for a callback. "The U.S. affairs office in the Swiss embassy in Tehran informed us that they have been dealing with an Ayatollah Hassan Mohtaz, who is the chief military adviser to President Ahmadad, similar to our national security adviser—he's apparently the senior leader in the government, or the one picked to stay in public view. I asked to speak with him directly. My staff is drafting an urgent flash e-mail to NATO and the Gulf Cooperative Council states."

"Who do you have inside Iran right now, Patrick?" Maureen asked.

"Master Sergeant Wohl is still in Iran, traveling with the Qagev princess," Patrick said. "Captain Noble and the body of Captain Lefferts are somewhere in Khorāsān province with Qagev partisans, awaiting exfiltration."

"What? You left Noble with a bunch of unknown Iranian revolutionaries?" Gardner retorted. "Why didn't the master sergeant go with him?"

"It was Master Sergeant Wohl's decision, and I reluctantly authorized it," Patrick said. "Wohl's mission was to rescue the Qagev leadership from the Iranians, return them to their underground network, stay with them, and report back on their capabilities, organization, and progress. Captain Hunter is needed back at Dreamland to fly the Black Stallion spaceplanes—they're headed in opposite directions. We decided the best course of action was to trust Boomer with the partisans."

"You trust the Qagevs so much that you'd risk Noble's life with those Iranians?" Maureen asked. "Noble would fetch a hefty bounty if they decided to turn him over to Ahmodod."

"It was a risk we had to take, ma'am," Patrick explained. "We're in constant communications with Captain Noble, and we know exactly where he is through his hypodermal transceiver. An Air Force Special Operations team is en route from Afghanistan to meet up with them—they should rendezvous in less than two hours from now. He'll be flown from Herat, Afghanistan back to the United States aboard a Black Stallion spaceplane. He'll be home about six hours from now." The President and most of his advisers in the Oval Office shook their heads at that news, hardly believing that someone could be taken from the middle of nowhere in western Asia back to the United States so quickly.

Secretary of Defense Gardner, however, was not impressed. "Any more forces in Iran?" he asked accusingly. "What about in the region? Who else have you sent out that way, other than a ten-billion-dollar space station and several dozen mini-satellites?"

"I deployed exactly what I briefed the national security staff earlier, Mr. Secretary," Patrick said. "I ordered two EB-1C Vampire flying battleships deployed to Diego Garcia. They should arrive in about fourteen hours. They are carrying Condor special ops transport aircraft, each with a force of two Tin Man and CID ground units. They can be armed for suppression of enemy air defense, ground attack, or anti-air missions after they deploy the Condor transports. I have one AL-52 Dragon anti-missile laser aircraft deployed to Diego Garcia as well."

"So you propose to locate and destroy all of the Iranian ballistic missile sites with four commandos, three bombers, and two spaceplanes?" Gardner asked incredulously. "It's not possible. And do you expect to do all this without the Iranians finding out about it and screaming bloody murder? What if they discover your guys or your stealth bombers, fear we're executing an all-out attack, panic, and decide to launch every biochem and nuke they have at Israel, Bahrain, Qatar, the United Arab Emirates, Saudi Arabia, or Kuwait? Will your toys stop them? If one nuke gets through and hits just one city like Tel Aviv or Doha, an entire nation ceases to exist. A dozen supertankers pass within Iranian anti-ship missile range every day. Are you going to take all those missile sites out as well too?"

"My concern is with Iran's ballistic missiles . . ."

"Why are they more important than Iran's anti-ship missiles or weapons of mass destruction, General?" Gardner retorted. "You've lost perspective here, General." He turned to the President and went on, "Mr. President, McLanahan's plan is impressive and very high-tech, and we've all seen his weapons' effectiveness over the years, but unless we take the time to mobilize follow-on and defensive forces, we're leaving ourselves wide open to disaster. An Iranian counterattack could be devastating."

"But if we do nothing, and the Iranian Revolutionary Guards strike . . ."

"Then they'll have the blood of their own people on their hands," Maureen said. "But if we strike, and the Iranians retaliate, we could possibly lose millions of friendly forces and allies. It's too big of a gamble, Patrick."

"But if we do nothing, we may be passing up our best chance of assisting a people's revolution in Iran," Patrick said. "Master Sergeant Wohl is traveling with the Qagev princess, and according to his reports the Qagev have a sizable political, civil, and military infrastructure in place . . ."

"Enough to defeat the Revolutionary Guards? I don't think so," Director of Central Intelligence Gerald Vista said.

"It's another important factor in the array of forces opposing the Pasdaran and the theocratic regime . . ." McLanahan said.

"And it could be another complicating factor too, McLanahan," Vista pointed out. "There's absolutely no indication whatsoever that the military would accept another monarchy—especially a Qagev, a dynasty that was bloodlessly overthrown almost eighty years ago. Recent surveys indicate that only 30 percent of the population might accept another monarchy."

"I'm familiar with those polls—they were taken either in secret during the current regime, or the respondents were Iranian expatriates," Patrick said. "It's not representative . . ."

"We're not going to base our foreign policy or military response on surveys and polls, Patrick," Maureen commented.

"I agree, ma'am," Patrick said. "Nevertheless, the monarchists are viable, organized, well-funded, and on the move, and the regular army still hasn't supported the Pasdaran's efforts to shut down Buzhazi's insurgency. We should make every attempt to support any uprisings in Iran."

"Now you want to support this Azar Qagev instead of Buzhazi?" the President asked. "Which is it, Patrick?"

"Both, sir," Patrick said. "We support both insurgencies and we try to steer the outcome in our favor."

"Which is what?" Gardner interjected. "A military junta led by Buzhazi, who at one time was one of the biggest Islamist enforcers of them all? Another monarchy that lavishes itself with palaces and gold while repressing their people?"

"Neither, Mr. Secretary," Patrick said. "As flawed as we believe it is, Iran is a democracy, and an overwhelming majority of the people want a democracy. Frankly, I don't think it matters if the people rally behind a general that uses his power to destroy the Pasdaran and strip the theocrats from their grip on the government, or a historical monarchy that brought that country into the twentieth century and made it an important Western ally. What we care about is that Iran becomes a stable, open, representative society, able to defend itself and its government against hostile and repressive forces." He looked at each one of the presidential advisers, then said, "Or we can just pull our guys out, then sit back and simply watch what happens next."

Most of the advisers and Cabinet officials shook their heads at Patrick's speech-making but fell silent and looked at the President, not offering any more arguments. The President looked at them knowingly. He knew that McLanahan's arguments made sense to them—they were just miffed that McLanahan was making them.

Secretary of State Carson's computer terminal beeped, and she scrolled through the messages. "Response from the Iranian government through the Swiss embassy, sir," she said as she read. "Looks like it might be going out over the news wires and Middle East news outlets soon too."

The President could see the consternation growing on her face. "What did they say, Mary?"

"They say, 'The Iranian Revolutionary Guards have captured a spy that killed several of their embassy staff just outside Ashkhabad, Turkmenistan, who were out on cooperative security maneuver exercises with their Turkmeni counterparts,'" Carson read. "'The Americans have claimed responsibility for the attacks, making President Martindale completely and personally liable for the murders. The captured spy and other evidence recovered at the scene of the murders is being held and analyzed for the upcoming trial.'"

"Bastards," the President muttered.

"The message further states, 'The Iranian government believes that the American military spy was assisting anti-Iranian terrorist and insurgent forces to illegally infiltrate into Iran, recruit and train anti-government rebel forces, attack Iranian military, civilian, and government targets, work with the insurgents to disrupt or destroy the democratically elected government, and attack Muslim holy sites and supply centers that help the poor and underprivileged, such as what occurred in Qom and Arān,'" Carson went on. "'The Iranian government condemns this irrational and unprovoked hostile action, and it calls upon the peaceful law-abiding nations of the world to join the Islamic Republic in indicting the United States and President Martindale for committing these atrocious acts.

" 'If the United States continues its illegal covert war, sends military forces within striking range of Iran, sends spy planes, spacecraft, space weapons, military space platforms, and satellites over our territory to pick targets to strike, or continues to foment and support terrorist and separatist actions, the Islamic Republic of Iran has no choice but to retaliate massively and with all means available at a time and place of our choosing against the United States and all of its allies, supporters, client states, and interests around the world.' There is a bunch of religious citations and the usual call for all devout and loyal Muslims to holy war against America, Israel, and anyone aligned with us. End of message."

"Carl, get General Lewars in here and let's draft up a statement for immediate release to the press," the President said. Chief of staff Minden was already on the phone to the rest of his people. "Let's schedule a meeting with the leadership and we'll get them briefed up too. Mary and I will field the calls from overseas that I expect will start coming in . . ."

The computer on the President's desk beeped, and he glanced at the display. "First up, President Zevitin of Russia," he said resignedly. Since the American

Holocaust, President Martindale had a policy of always taking calls that came directly from a handful of world leaders, and President Leonid Zevitin of Russia was one of them. Martindale got along with Zevitin and usually had productive and open talks with him, but he was dreading this call.

Zevitin, one of the youngest presidents of Russia at age forty-nine, was the second president of Russia since the American Holocaust just four years ago. He didn't come from the Party apparatus, government, or the military, but from Russia's rapidly growing oil, gas, and nuclear energy industry. He was educated in America and Britain and headed several large multinational energy companies in postings around the world before being chosen to head Russia's energy ministry. His wealth, good looks, charm, and international presence made him popular in Russia as well as around the world, and when the interim military president of Russia suddenly died at the surprisingly young age of sixty-one, Zevitin was elected president in a landslide.

President Martindale scanned his computer display briefly. Every phone call prompted an automatic page on the computer that offered interesting and sometimes extremely useful and insightful information pertinent to the caller: as well as verifying the caller's identity and origin, it gave the local time, weather, some headlines, facts on the caller's family's names—Zevitin had never been married—recent decisions and legislation supported or rejected by the caller, recent decisions made by the President regarding the caller, and names of the caller's key advisers and their recent activities. He picked up the phone, and the other advisers in the room picked up theirs so they could listen in. "Mr. President, this is President Martindale, how are you today, sir?"

"Very well, very well, Mr. President," Zevitin replied in very good English with a curious mix of Russian, American, and English accents. "Thank you for taking my call."

"Not at all, Leonid," Martindale responded, hoping that using the Russian president's first name would signal an end to their use of titles. "My national security advisers are listening in as well; I hope that's all right with you."

"It is, sir, and thank you for so advising me," Zevitin said. "Unfortunately for me, there is only my dog Sashi with me tonight."

That was contrary to the usual rumors concerning the playboy antics of the Russian president, but Martindale didn't feel like calling him on it. "How can I be of service today?"

"I'm calling about the incident in Ashkhabad, Mr. President," Zevitin said. Damn, the President thought, he's keeping with the titles—this was not a good sign. "I was advised of it through our embassy there. First of all, I want to say I'm sorry for the loss of your men."

"Thank you, Leonid. Which embassy told you of this incident—the Turkmeni or the Iranian embassy?"

There was a very slight pause; then: "Both, actually," he replied. "We also received the general notice from Iran a short time ago. I expect the Iranians to release your man right away, and if you go to the United Nations about it, Russia will join you in calling for the body to be released immediately. The incident happened on Turkmeni soil, not Iranian. They have no right to do what they did."

"We'll go to the United Nations as a matter of routine and diplomatic protocol, Leonid," the President said, "but we'll send a message directly to the Iranian government through the Swiss embassy informing them that they have created a serious and dangerous international incident, bordering on an act of war, and that we demand the immediate return of our man and all his equipment and supplies taken in Turkmenistan. If we don't receive them within twenty-four hours of notification, we'll take all steps necessary to recover them."

"Mr. President, I strongly urge you to play this one carefully and quietly," Zevitin said. "There is a major societal upheaval going on right now in Iran. Most of the government has been wiped out—murdered—by this nutcase Buzhazi. The Revolutionary Guards are being spurred on by the surviving ultra-conservative theocrats that must crack down on the insurgency or find themselves either blown up by insurgents, crushed by the army, or rejected by the people. They'll toss law, civil rights, and basic human decency out the window to save their own hides."

"Leonid, I wouldn't be sad to see the end of the theocracy if it meant a more moderate Iran," the President said. "What they do to their own people is none of my concern. If they cooperate with us and give us the property they stole while in Turkmenistan, we'd be happy to step aside and let events in Iran take their course."

"Then you would not interfere with further events in Iran if you got your man and your property back?"

"Leonid, I'm not going to tie future events in with the current crisis. Iran has to return our man they murdered and the property they stole . . . period. I have no other quarrels with Iran presently."

"Then why the attack on Iran's missiles recently, Mr. President?" Zevitin asked. "We know you have sent your secret Dreamland spaceplanes over Iran at least twice and perhaps more than that; we detected an object being launched by the first spaceplane that could have easily been an orbital or suborbital weapon that could have struck inside Iran. The second spaceplane you flew right over Russia without asking permission or even notifying us ahead of time."

"That was an error, Leonid, and we acknowledged that and apologized . . ."

"I know, I know, Mr. President, and I'm not going to dwell on it," Zevitin said in a surprisingly conciliatory tone. "I would like you to punish the officer that sent that craft over our country . . . General Patrick McLanahan, no doubt." The President said nothing, only glanced at Patrick. "But that can wait for another day.

"We also know that you have sent several microsatellites into orbits to cover Iran and have even moved your Armstrong Space Station into a sun-synchronous orbit in order to carefully surveille Iran at specific times of day," Zevitin went on. "And we have recently received reports that several of your stealth warplanes have been moved to Diego Garcia, just a few hours' flying time from Iran. It looks like preparation for an invasion to me, Mr. President."

"We have to forward-deploy many of our strategic air assets because our numbers have been almost eliminated," Martindale pointed out.

"It pains me that you bring that up, Kevin," Zevitin said, and he really sounded as if he meant it too. Five years earlier, General Anatoliy Gryzlov, the former chief of staff of the Russian military, successfully overthrew the elected Russian government and began a large-scale buildup of the Russian military. When Patrick McLanahan and the Air Battle Force preempted a Russian invasion of Turkmenistan's vast oil and natural gas fields, Gryzlov responded by attacking American air and ground-launched intercontinental ballistic missile sites and bomber bases with nuclear cruise missiles. Over thirty thousand Americans died and another seventy thousand injured in what became known as the "American Holocaust."

"President Gryzlov acted irresponsibly and foolishly, and I have denounced and condemned his actions in each and every venue that opportunity affords," Zevitin went on. "But you can well understand our concern as we watch these moves, sir: they appear to be directed toward an invasion of Iran to support a takeover of the legitimately elected government by force of arms.

"And we also know that most of your remaining stealth warplanes are commanded by General McLanahan," Zevitin continued. "Frankly, Mr. President, Russia considers McLanahan to be quite dangerous, and any time we think he may be involved in some conflict or action, we expect and must prepare for the worst. We're surprised he is still an integral part of your pool of military advisers, and he is considered a highly destabilizing element—on a par with Gryzlov himself."

"Let's get back to the issue of Iran, Leonid," Martindale said. "I'll acknowledge to you that the United States is keeping a careful watch over events in Iran, not because we want or support a violent overthrow of the government, but because Buzhazi's actions or the reactions of the Revolutionary Guards could cause a ripple effect of violence throughout the entire region. We certainly retain the right to set up surveillance of any nation we fear could harm America's interests and to forward-deploy all necessary assets to try to halt any spread of violence."

"That's fair, Mr. President," Zevitin said. "But I know you understand that Russia has interests in the region as well, and American military actions directed against Iran may interfere with Russia's interests. That's why I urge restraint and caution, Mr. President: your forces may harm Russia just as easily as McLanahan's spaceplanes violated Russian airspace."

"I pledge to you that America will not intentionally do anything that violates Russia's sovereignty or national interests," Martindale went on. "But America considers Iran's actions in Turkmenistan a serious violation of international law and of America's sovereign right to operate in non-aligned territories. We respect and appreciate Russia's call for restraint and caution, but we won't sit back patiently while Iran kills and captures Americans and steals our property. Russia is cautioned that if they are in harm's way when America responds, we are not responsible for what happens."

"Kevin, that sounds like a prepared message—I thought we could talk to each other man to man," Zevitin said.

"It's not a prepared speech, Leonid. That's how I feel, and that's my position. Our problem right now is with Iran. We know you have economic and military ties with Iran. We know . . ."

"Our only ties to Iran are economic, Kevin, as well as diplomatic," Zevitin said. "But Iran is a friend and a recognized strategic partner of Russia. Any military action against Iran would be of very great concern to us."

"Leonid, Russia has sold over five billion dollars' worth of advanced military hardware to Iran in just the past few years," Martindale said. "We know you have advisers and instructors on the ground throughout Iran. You may consider that purely economic, but the United States considers that military support. Russia has in the past tried to assert the 1987 Russo-Iranian Mutual Defense Treaty . . ."

"That treaty was signed only because of American support for Iraq during the Iran-Iraq War," Zevitin said. "Russia does not station any troops in Iran, as you do in Iraq. We have occasionally conducted joint exercises and participated in training and officer exchange programs, as does the United States with many of their friends and allies." He paused for a moment, and when he spoke again his voice was considerably lighter. "Come come, Kevin, we can argue like this to the end of time. Why bother? Let's let the diplomats with their rose-colored language squabble over this and that. We can deal with this issue like leaders.

"I called to offer Russia's sympathy and assistance in getting your man and your property back," Zevitin went on. "As I said, Kevin, if you go to the Security Council, file a protest, and draft a resolution condemning Iran and demanding immediate return of all American property, Russia will stand with you. We will use all of our influence to see to it that the resolution is unanimously passed, and we will support any actions, short of war, to enforce the resolution. But if you decide not to take that path, Russia will not support you, and will vigorously protect and defend our own interests in the region."

"Now who sounds like he's reading from a prepared statement, Leonid?" Martindale asked, trying to keep his own tone light.

"As you know, Kevin, we Russians do not like to have breakfast each morning unless it has been planned five years ahead of time," Zevitin said in an equally light tone, "but this time it is not from a prepared statement—it is from me." His tone darkened considerably, and his Russian accent abruptly overshadowed the Western ones. "Step lightly in Iran, Mr. President. Use the United Nations, your allies, and Russia, and have patience. America has been wronged here, but America is not an innocent party in Iran either—we both know this to be true. Ask for support and you will get it, especially from Russia. Ask for trouble and violence, and you will get that as well."

"Especially from Russia, Leonid?" Martindale asked.

There was a long, ominous pause on the line; then: "Good-bye, Mr. President," Zevitin said. "May you be well. Good night to all your advisers listening in as well."

"Good-bye, Mr. President. Take care." He hung up the phone, and the others did as well. "That went better than I expected," he said sarcastically.

"I wouldn't trust him as far as I could throw him, Mr. President," National Security Adviser Sparks said.

"He's telling us what he knows, sir," Secretary of State Mary Carson offered, "and he knows a lot. The Iranians must be feeding the Russians all their intel."

"We've known the Russians have had military advisers in Iran for years, as the President told Zevitin," Patrick McLanahan said. "But this level of cooperation is a serious development. Zevitin was issuing us a warning."

"A warning? What warning?"

"I think Russia will intervene if we go into Iran," Patrick replied. "He's giving us a way to save face by going to the United Nations; by doing that, he can also give the Iranians more time to deal with the insurgency without resorting to more heavy-handed tactics. Whatever the reason, there's no doubt that Russia and Iran are assisting each other now."

"Why would Russia help Iran?" Vice President Hershel asked. "Just to sell them more military hardware?"

"Not only that, ma'am, but a powerful Iran that distracts attention and commits resources toward the Middle East takes attention and pressure away from Russia, which allows it to continue its own military buildup and reassert itself in Europe and Asia," Patrick said. "Iran will take bolder steps toward regional hegemony if they know Russia is behind them. And even a few Russian so-called 'advisers' and 'instructors' in Iran is a good tripwire in case we do act. If we kill Russians, it'll be seen as an overt act of aggression."

"Which is precisely why we can't escalate this crisis by planning any more actions in Iran, Mr. President," Carson said pointedly. "How would we even know if Russians were on the ground if we struck an Iranian target? We'd have to assume every Iranian missile site had a Russian nearby. They might even put a Russian uniform on one of theirs and call it an act of war."

"Enough already," the President said, exasperation in his voice. "You all heard what I told Zevitin: I'll be relieved and happy to start de-escalating tensions with Iran, but only after our man and our equipment are returned to us. Until then, Iran stays in the crosshairs. I think Zevitin will communicate that plainly enough to the Iranians, but in case he doesn't, I want to start moving toward direct action."

He rose, and his advisers got to their feet as well. Martindale clasped Patrick on the shoulder as he departed. "Patrick, as usual, you're the tip of the spear—again. Keep me and General Sparks posted on your team's progress, and be prepared to move as soon as possible."

"Yes, sir."

"Mary, when we talk to the allies, we'll have to notify them that we've already begun plans for direct action against Iran."

"They're not going to like it, sir," Carson said. "Should I give them details?"

"Of course not . . . and I don't give a damn if they don't like it," the President said. "If they want to talk to me about it, fine, but I'll tell them the same thing."

"Yes, Mr. President."

"Joe, I need you to build a plan that protects all the assets you mentioned that Iran could strike—shipping in the Persian Gulf, allied nations, and our forces stationed in the region. Let's notify the theater commanders and MAJCOMs of what's going on and what we intend to do about it."

"But those plans can't work together with McLanahan's, sir, if he's already got bombers, spaceplanes, and those armored commando gizmos already there," Gardner protested. "It'll take us days, perhaps weeks, to surge enough assets to the Gulf region to protect our allies who might be in danger from an Iranian retaliatory strike. The Iranians have a big head start. McLanahan's guys will have to pull back."

"No one's pulling back," the President insisted. "Maybe if the Iranians see more American ships and planes deploying to the area, they'll back off."

"Or they might move faster and more aggressively, sir," Gardner warned.

"Then they'll be on the defensive and have to decide if they want to start a shooting war or pull back," the President said. "Up until now, they've been calling the shots, and I want that to stop. Push all the forces you can into the Persian Gulf, Gulf of Oman, and Iraq. Have everyone keep their fingers off the triggers unless the Iranians fire first, but have them ready to fight if they're needed."

"Yes, Mr. President," Gardner said. He shook his head at Patrick as the commander-in-chief departed. "I hope your guys do better this time, McLanahan. Thank God I don't know what in hell you're doing."

Maureen Hershel came over to Patrick after everyone had left. "Don't listen to Gardner," she said softly. "All he's been doing around here lately is railing against you. I haven't seen any plans from his office on how to deal with the insurgency or what the Iranian Revolutionary Guards might do. I don't even think he believes it's real or of any concern for the United States. Now that Iran has got your guys, he thinks everyone will be coming to him for answers. Watch out for him—he still has the President's ear, even more than you or I."

DOSHAN TAPPEH AIR BASE, TEHRAN, IRAN

Three Days Later

"Allah akbar, allah akbar!" the loudspeaker announcement began. "There is no God but God, blessed be his name, and Mohammed is his prophet! May God keep the faithful safe and protected, and may he bring unspeakable wrath upon all infidels and the unfaithful! All true believers gather before me and heed the commands of the Faqih, the voice of God on Earth."

A large crowd of about a thousand men, mostly older men and teenagers, began to move toward the loudspeakers, carrying simple construction tools, tool boxes, and bags of food and water. "Upon the command of the Faqih, may he stand at the right hand of God, to all the faithful, the Jihad-e Sazandegi Ministry of Construction Crusades announces a construction jihad this day on behalf of the Islamic Republic of Iran's Revolutionary Guards Corps. Our mission is to rebuild the gates and outer walls of this installation. The rewards for the faithful and hard-working citizens who help will be the thanks of Allah, your government, and the Revolutionary Guards Corps for whom you will serve.

"Along with the blessings of the Almighty, any man who serves with the Jihad-e Sazandegi will receive relief from tithe for one year for himself, as well as relief for himself, one son, or one grandson from compulsory military service once the project is complete. Step forward, sign your name to the register, swear your oath to work diligently on behalf of the Faqih and the state, and let us begin, under the watchful eyes of God the generous."

As commanded, the men stepped forward in several lines to sign up for work. The construction jihad was a popular way to get workers for a project. Although there was no pay, the workers were fed and housed at least as well as a soldier, were generally treated well, and received not only the benefits mentioned but consideration for other transgressions or wishes: a student wishing to get into a good college or madrasa might get a second look after he or his father participated in a construction jihad, or a man falling behind in his rent or utility payments might get part of his debts erased by volunteering.

The workers' belongings were checked as they filed through the entryway to the base, and their persons were subjected to pat-down searches, but it was soon obvious that it was more important to get workers busy than it was to do thorough searches. Each worker signed his name and filled out a short form detailing where he was from, his skills, and his training. The names were cross-checked on a computer to scan for convicted criminals or wanted men. But a construction jihad was a way for convicted men to reduce their parole or probation period, so the computer usually turned up many hits on convicts. Those men were typically assigned to duties outside the base, on the wall or close by.

"These are all old men and children—we'll never get this project done," the commanding officer of the work detail, Pasdaran Major Abdul Kamail, said to his noncommissioned officer in charge. "I need workers, Sergeant, not drunks, kids, and handicap cases."

"Best we could get, sir," the NCOIC, Sergeant Qolam Loshato, said. "Putting out the word for a work detail without pre-screening individuals usually results in this type of turnout. Besides, they're working in a Pasdaran facility—who in their right mind wants to voluntarily step within grasping distance of the Pasdaran?"

"If the people are innocent, they have nothing to worry about from the Pasdaran," Kamail said dismissively. Loshato suppressed a chuckle—he knew no one ever wanted to cross the Pasdaran, innocent or guilty. "Anyway, I don't care about the people's paranoia—the priority is still to get that outer fence up. That shouldn't take more than one or two days. Work them through the night if you need to, but I want that outer fence up."

"Sir, may I suggest bringing some of the jihadis that do not have criminal records in to begin work on the training center and repairs on the security building?" Loshato said. "If we're going to be asked to bring the Pasdaran force up to two hundred thousand in six months, we're going to need those buildings repaired, wired, and ready for recruits and cadre."

"I'm not worried about offices for cadre or barracks for training more recruits, Sergeant—I'm worried about insurgents getting into this base," Kamail said.

"Our orders were to get the base ready at all costs . . ."

"And what about security while we repair and outfit this base, Sergeant?" Kamail asked. "Reports are that over two hundred insurgents were killed at Arān. Two hundred! They could have caused a lot of havoc if they attacked here instead."

"Buzhazi's total force is estimated at less than two thousand, sir," Loshato said. "If the reports are true, we killed over ten percent of their entire force in one strike. Not only that, but their objective to steal supplies to keep themselves going failed. They sustained heavy losses and have fewer resources than they did. It was a great victory."

"Sergeant, we still lost several dozen men and we blew up our own warehouses, which were filled with real supplies," Kamail said. "What kind of asinine plan was that? Why didn't we lay a trap for them outside Arān instead of right inside the damned warehouse complex itself?" He shook his head. "No. I want the perimeter secure before we bring in any more men and supplies. And I want as many of those jihadis checked as possible, especially any assigned inside the base itself. I don't want any of Buzhazi's men waltzing in to my base free and clear."

"Buzhazi wouldn't dare attack Doshan Tappeh again," Loshato said. "There are over five thousand men here. He'd be crazy to commit the rest of his troops to the strongest Pasdaran base in the country."

"If the man was smart, he'd be high-tailing it to Turkmenistan or Turkey right now," Kamail said. He thought for a moment; then: "Very well, Sergeant. Pick the best of the ones not convicted of any felonies and assign them to work inside the base on the barracks and headquarters building. All others remain on the perimeter work details. Notify the security officer on duty that I'm bringing men into the base. Tell him to call me if he has any questions."

"Yes, sir," Loshato said. He saluted, then turned to his radio to issue the new orders.

Shortly thereafter the clerks in charge of doing background checks on volunteers pulled up a list of about thirty men who had no felony convictions, were between the ages of sixteen and fifty, and who were not infirmed, and Loshato had these men marched over to the foreman in charge of rebuilding the headquarters building that was assaulted by Sattari when he and a hundred other armed insurgents rescued Buzhazi from custody.

"These are the best of this group, Sergeant?" the foreman asked when the men were assembled before him. Loshato had to agree that they were a grungy-looking crew—filthy louse-ridden clothes, decrepit shoes, and most with some kind of injury and many with missing ears and bandaged limbs.

"They were all able to get here under their own steam," Sergeant Loshato said, "and they all appear to be free of felony convictions as far as we can tell after a cursory check. What you see is what you get."

"And who takes the blame for shoddy work, stolen equipment and tools, or inoperable systems? I do, that's who! How am I expected to work under conditions like this?"

"You're under contract to the Iranian Revolutionary Guards Corps to complete rebuilding the base on time and on budget," Loshato reminded him sternly. "It's not our fault that you didn't hire enough skilled laborers for the job. The IRGC is reimbursing the government for the cost of issuing a jihad to help your company—if it's not done on time and on budget, you might find yourself liable for that cost as well as any penalties in the contract and whatever else the commander-in-chief wants to hit you with. So stop complaining and get busy."

The foreman muttered a curse word after the NCO departed, then turned to the men assembled before him, suppressing a disgusted sneer. "All right you men, listen up," he said, speaking slowly and deliberately in case they had trouble understanding him. "Our task is simplicity itself. We are fishing fiber-optic, telephone, audio-visual, electrical, and Category-5 network cable through the new walls. This is not brain surgery, but you must pay attention and do as ordered or else we'll waste valuable time and even more valuable equipment. The fiber-optic cable is especially delicate—it cannot be bent like ordinary cable, and it has to be placed just so in its conduit. Do you understand?" There was a murmur of assent from the men—it was impossible to tell if they understood a word he had said. "Very well. If you remember nothing else, remember this: do not touch anything unless I tell you, and if you're unsure of any of our instructions, stop what you're doing and ask. Let's get to work."

It was going to be slow going. After the security guards performed another search of the men and their belongings and issued them ID badges, the men shuffled toward the new headquarters building as if in a fog. The foreman knew he was going to be in big trouble if he didn't find some way to get these guys organized. He spotted an older man who seemed to be the erstwhile leader of this group. "You. Over here." The old man came over to him. He had several cuts and bruises on his face, head, and neck as if he had been beat up—probably on the street or in jail. "What is your name?"

"Orum, sir," the old man said. He straightened painfully, then added, "Orum, Abdul, Volunteer Group Leader, reporting as ordered, sir."

"Volunt . . . ?" And then the foreman realized who he was: a former Basij volunteer from the Iran-Iraq War in the early 1980s, one of the hundreds of thousands of men, women, and children used as "human shields" to waste Iraqi ammunition before sending in the main fighting forces. "You were a Basij . . . ?"

"I was a group leader of the Muhammad Corps, sir, and proud of it," the man named Orum said, a hint of steel rising in his voice. "I had the best volunteer group in the entire Fish Lake front."

"Muhamm . . . you were in the battle of Fish Lake?" The campaign known as Operation Karbala-5, the operation to try to take the Iraqi port city of Basrah which began in January of 1987, was one of the bloodiest in the Iran-Iraq War—over sixty-five thousand Iranians, mostly Basij volunteers, were slaughtered in six weeks of intense fighting and artillery and rocket battles. The worst battle of Karbala-5 was known as Fish Lake, referring to the artificial river over thirty kilometers long and two kilometers wide which the Iraqis had constructed to keep Iranian forces from sweeping into Baghdad. The Iranians outnumbered the Iraqis ten to one. Most of the Iranian fighters were conscripts and Basij volunteers like this old man—ordinary citizens who had received little or no military training. Fish Lake was protected by mine fields, barbed wire, trenches, and interlocking fields of machine gun and artillery fire—some even thought that Saddam had electrified the water itself.

When artillery barrages failed to break down the defenses around Fish Lake, the Pasdaran decided to send in the Basij. Over a quarter-million men, women, and children were marched forward against Fish Lake's defenses with little more than a rifle and one clip of ammunition, and the Iraqis ruthlessly cut them down. The casualties were so staggeringly high that it was believed that the sheer mass of corpses in Fish Lake would allow the Iranian Revolutionary Guards to simply walk across without getting their feet wet.

The Battle of Fish Lake was still re-enacted every year in Iran and the participants celebrated as heroes, but the foreman could never understand what could drive a man to march against machine guns, artillery, and barbed-wire fences like that. "Yes, sir, and I fought proudly and may I say, sir, like a lion," the old man said. "I firmly believe that the apostate Saddam was assisted by the Americans and the Zionists to destroy the Islamic republic, and it was completely necessary to send in the citizens of Iran en masse to win a great victory." In fact, Operation Karbala-5 was a tremendous failure—Iran withdrew from Iraq and sued for peace just a few months later. "So you may place your complete trust in me and call upon me any time for any purpose whatsoever, sir."

"I see that some of the men follow you," the foreman said. "Are you their leader?"

"I suppose I am, sir," the old man said, "since I appear to be the senior officer of this particular group of proud and able veterans, but I assure you, sir, that I had no intention of taking command or control of these men from yourself, sir."

"Of course not—I assumed you all might be veterans or served together, and it is quite natural for old ties to hold," the foreman said. He winced at the word "able" to describe them—none of them looked capable of carrying anything heavier than a hammer. "You can be a great help to me by organizing your men into three groups for the three sections of wall where we must install the cables, then further dividing them into threes for each segment of the wall. Do you understand?"

The old man looked as if the foreman had just told him that he was about to meet his seventy virgins promised to him in Heaven. "Why, I . . . I am honored, sir!" the old man squealed. "I will do as you wish immediately, sir! To whom should the details report when they are formed, sir?" The foreman pointed out the team chiefs, who were supervising as large spools of cable were being unloaded and brought to the site, and the old man hobbled off on battered thin legs, croaking orders in a battle- and cigarette-scarred voice. The others, some in even worse shape than he, at first did not appear to believe that the old man was their new supervisor, but after pointing and gesturing at the foreman and snapping orders, he quickly made the others get in a ragged line and started splitting them up.

To the foreman's surprise, the three little details of old and battered-looking men were in a rough but presentable formation in short order, and the old man had them marching off to report to their team leaders. They then began hauling the big spools of wiring and cables into the headquarters building. Not bad, the foreman thought. They looked like they might work out well after all. He might even consider hiring the old guy for . . .

"Excuse me, sir." The foreman jumped. The old man was beside him, standing almost at attention on unsteady legs.

"What is it?" the foreman asked impatiently. God, he thought, the old man moved like a cat despite his rickety appearance.

"There appears to be a problem with the detail's security clearance. The guards are not allowing the men to enter the security center of the building without your authorization."

"They have all been properly cleared," the foreman groused. "Are you all wearing your new badges? I'll straighten this out." The foreman strode into the temporary doorway to the headquarters building. Even though the security center was the most secretive room being rebuilt, sometimes the guards got a little too . . .

. . . and then the foreman realized that the old man was right beside him, matching his gait step for step. At first he didn't think anything of it . . . until he wondered how the old man knew that they were working on the new security center? The guards would not have told him which room they were working in—they just would have prohibited them from going inside. And why was the old man walking right behind him like . . . ?

Suddenly the foreman was pushed inside the room, and his site radio was taken away from him. "What is going on h—?" He was pushed against several men sitting on the floor, gagged, their hands and feet secured—and only then did he realize that they were the building's Pasdaran security guards. "What do you think you're doing here?"

"Beefing up your construction jihad," the old man, Orum, said. His entire demeanor had completely changed—he didn't appear to be disabled or confused at all, and neither did any of the jihadis in the room. "Believe me, the repairs to the outer wall will go a lot faster now."

"Who are you?" the foreman asked. Orum ignored the question, but the foreman soon realized who it was: he was all the Pasdaran soldiers could talk about. "General Buzhazi? *Here?* What in hell do you think you're doing? This is a Pasdaran assignment! You'll be beheaded for interfering with . . . !"

"I suggest you make that the last comment about my future you say aloud if you like to keep your tongue attached to your throat, friend," General Hesarak al-Kan Buzhazi said. "I need you to round up as many trucks as possible and have them driven over to the Pasdaran supply warehouses near the flight line. My men will be waiting to load them up."

"I can't cooperate with you—I'll be executed the minute they find out . . ."

"Cooperate with me and at least you'll have a chance to live," Buzhazi said. "If you help us, I promise you won't be harmed by my men or myself. Otherwise I'll kill you and find another way to get supplies without starting a firefight."

"I'm just a simple worker doing my job. I have no argument with you . . ."

"Your owners picked the wrong time to contract out to the Pasdaran, friend—like it or not, you have an argument with me," Buzhazi said. "At least now you have a chance to do something for the right side for a change. What do you say?" The foreman had no choice but to comply, and he got on the phone and ordered trucks moved to the warehouses. "Next, I want you to cut power, natural gas, and communications to the entire base when I give you the word. You can tell the Pasdaran battalion duty officers that workers accidentally cut the lines and everything will be restored right away, and no you don't need any assistance."

"Their backup generators will automatically kick on . . ."

"Most of the backup generators run on natural gas, so if you cut off the gas the generators won't stay on," Buzhazi said. "For the generators that run on their own diesel supplies, it'll take several minutes for their surveillance equipment to reboot, and by then we'll be set up and waiting for their response.

"Finally, you will move every piece of heavy equipment you have to locations General Zhoram will direct—most on the perimeter, but a few in some key intersections and battalion entrances. Once they're in place, have the drivers cut the battery cables to disable them. After that's done, you and your men can get out."

Brigadier-General Kamal Zhoram, the former Pasdaran rocket brigade commander who escaped from prison at the same time as Buzhazi, gave the foreman back his portable radio and directed him on exactly what to say and where to move his heavy equipment, then found Buzhazi watching the deployment of his men on the perimeter wall. The contractors were nowhere to be seen; some of his men were now dressed like the contractors, ordering Buzhazi's soldiers into key defensive positions on the wall but making them appear as if they were still working. "Fifteen minutes and we should be ready to cut power, sir," Zhoram reported. "The trucks are in position and ready to assault the warehouses."

"Very well, Kamal. Get them moving, and make sure they work fast."

"Yes, sir." Zhoram issued the orders, and almost five hundred men began opening up Pasdaran supply warehouses and loading up stolen vehicles with ammunition, food, and other supplies. "No opposition yet," Zhoram said a few minutes later, "but this was a very risky move, sir, assaulting the headquarters of the Pasdaran in broad daylight."

"I suppose so."

"You have spoken many times of the fact that every insurgency has their moment of greatest desperation," Zhoram said. "Is this yours, General?"

Buzhazi took a deep breath, then replied, "I think it was the moment I learned Mansour and every man in his detail was dead at Arān. I knew then that we couldn't run, and that the fight would take us back to this place." He looked at the former Rocket Brigade commander. "But I'm not here to have my final pitched battle to the death with the Pasdaran—I'm here to gather supplies so we can fight another day. If this turns out to be our Tet Offensive or our Al-Fallujah, then so be it. Maybe today will be the beginning of the end of the Pasdaran . . ."

"Even if it's the end of us?"

"Even so," Buzhazi said.

Zhoram swallowed hard, then raised his radio when he felt it vibrate, silently alerting him of a call. He listened for a moment, then reported, "Problem, sir. A Pasdaran officer was behind one of the earthmoving vehicles when it stopped in an intersection. When the officer approached, the driver ran off. The Pasdaran brigade headquarters has probably been alerted."

"Have the power and natural gas cut immediately, redeploy the warehouse teams as planned, and order all units to prepare to repel attackers," Buzhazi ordered. "Looks like we've run out of time already."

Buzhazi and several of his men hurried through the security center, heading down two flights of stairs to the stockade. His men had already captured the guards and staff and were surrounding the security center's most important prisoner, former chief of staff General Hoseyn Yassini. The general was standing, dressed in a simple white and black prisoner's shirt, trousers, and sandals. Amazingly, the lights were already off, and the corridors lit only with battery emergency lamps. "Well, well, sir, looks like your new office is not quite as luxurious as your old one," he said.

"Hesarak! I should have known this was your doing!" Yassini remarked when he saw Buzhazi before him. Buzhazi motioned to the guard, who opened the cell door. "What in hell is going on here?"

"Shut up and listen for a moment, will you, Hoseyn?" Buzhazi said. "Any minute now the entire Revolutionary Guards Corps will be swarming in on us. We're taking as many supplies as we can and getting out, but I came here to release you so . . ."

"Release me? On whose orders?"

"That's a funny way to say 'thank-you,' Hoseyn," Buzhazi snorted. He tossed Yassini a radio. "I want only one thing from you in return, General: order the army to deploy into the cities and confront the Pasdaran."

"You mean, start a war between Iranian armies in the capital?" Yassini asked incredulously. "Why in the hell would I even consider that? The Revolutionary Guards Corps are committed to the defense of the nation just as the regular army. Why would I order the army to do battle with the Pasdaran? We are all Iranians . . ."

"Damn your eyes, Hoseyn, I'm telling you, the clerics and the Pasdaran will destroy the army—starting with you—because they represent a threat to their regime and to their goal of a regional theocratic Islamist state," Buzhazi said. "After that, they'll round up and execute any man, woman, or child who is even suspected of opposing the regime. If they need to launch a full-scale attack with their missiles, bombers, bio-chem weapons, or even nuclear weapons, they'll do it. And when they're done with the opposition here in Iran, they'll go after any opponents anywhere else in the region. They don't care if that means a world war—they'll use an Israeli or Western counterattack as proof that the rest of the world just wants to kill Muslims, and they'll emerge stronger than ever. They won't care that hundreds of thousands of citizens will die in the process. Can't you see all that?"

Yassini looked at the radio in his hands as if it was a serpent ready to strike—but he did not give it back. "You want me to start a civil war just to save your own hide," Yassini said. "You're desperate, out of supplies, and you're stuck in a corner facing total annihilation. Your best way to escape is to hope the regular army engages the Pasdaran. Why should I listen to you, Hesarak? You've been condemned by the leadership for high crimes and treason against the faith, the state, and the people of Iran. You face death by public hanging. You'll do or say anything to save yourself."

At that moment there was a huge explosion somewhere above them, and Buzhazi's own radio squawked. He shook his head at the chief of staff. "Glad to see you're alive, Hoseyn," he said acidly. "Now you can go to hell. I'm sure I'll see you there soon." He motioned to his soldiers, and they followed him down the hall and upstairs, leaving a confused and frightened general officer alone in the dark cell behind them.

Buzhazi and his men drove over to the flight line and climbed up to the top of the largest aircraft hangar, which was the spot they chose for their observation position. He found Kamal Zhoram waiting for him. "I was afraid I'd have to take charge of our Tet Offensive here, sir," he said with a weak smile. "Glad to see you're still alive. Where's Yassini?"

"Crawling down a sewer pipe to save himself—or informing Zolqadr of our presence," Buzhazi said. "Forget him—he's on his own. Situation?"

"Pasdaran guards came across one warehouse team and set off a booby trap, sir," Zhoram said. "Survivors are being suppressed by our forces, but we've picked up general alerts on the base emergency frequency. The scouts report perhaps one battalion still in their barracks." He motioned behind them toward the flight line. "Aviation units are still quiet—no patrol or attack helicopters spinning up. Surely they issued the alert already. What are they waiting for?"

"Maybe Zolqadr doesn't want to blast his own base to smithereens with his rockets—at least not yet," Buzhazi said. "Let's not wait to find out. What about our scroungers?"

"They're still loading up trucks as fast as they can," Zhoram said. "I told them to get ready to move out at any moment."

"The moment is now," Buzhazi said. "Everyone out. If the men have to drop them to escape, so be it."

"Yes, sir." As he issued the evacuation orders, they heard sounds of turbine engines spooling up. They turned toward the flight line and saw pilots and crew chiefs running toward the attack helicopters parked below. "Fire in the hole!" Zhoram said, and he activated the remote-control detonators for the explosives they had planted on the choppers. But only two of the six detonators activated. After a few moments of confusion, the Pasdaran crewmembers started heading back to the undamaged helicopters, with security forces frantically scanning the area with assault rifles, looking for the source of the attack.

"Damn it, four detonators didn't go off," Zhoram swore. "My men picked the wrong time to screw up." Buzhazi wondered about that: his saboteurs had been nothing short of miraculous up until now, planting devices in the most unreachable yet vital spots with very little apparent difficulty. Now with this, their most important mission, four crucial explosives fail to operate . . . ? "You'd better get out of here, sir." Zhoram signaled to his security man, who lifted a grenade launcher, loaded a 30-millimeter anti-personnel round, and fired one at the closest helicopter. He managed to scatter the crewmembers for that chopper only, but the other three helicopters still made preparations for takeoff.

"Don't stay up here too long, Kamal," Buzhazi said, scrambling for the ladder.

"Don't worry, Hesarak—I'll be right behind you," Zhoram said.

Security forces on the flight line were already returning fire, forcing Zhoram's guard to scramble for cover.

Zhoram picked up his own grenade launcher and fired a round at the Pasdaran guards, but more defenders were on the way and returning fire, and the helicopters were almost ready for takeoff. He adjusted the grenade launcher's sight for maximum range, aiming for the helicopter that seemed the most ready for takeoff, and fired. But he was a missileer, not an infantryman. It had been years—no, decades—since he had fired a grenade launcher, and he had never fired one like this, and his round flew far from the mark. Moments later the helicopter, a Russian-made Mil Mi-24 attack helicopter, lifted off.

Damn, he swore at himself, they were too late. Zhoram could see the quad 12.7-millimeter machine gun in its remote-controlled chin turret turning back and forth, active and looking for targets—namely, whoever had been lobbing grenades onto the flight line. Zhoram couldn't tell what kind of weapons were on its stubby weapon pod wings, but he assumed they were even nastier than that machine gun. Time to get off this roof and out of this area. He shouted, "Get going! Get off the roof! Now!" His guard wasted absolutely no time—he was across the roof and sliding down the ladder in the blink of an eye. Zhoram slung his grenade launcher over one shoulder, looped the bandolier of grenades over the other, and ran as fast as he could toward the . . .

From less than a kilometer away, the machine gun's bullets arrived before the sound did, and with an extremely accurate eye-pointing telescopic sight slaved to the pilot's helmet, he could not miss. Over four dozen rounds pierced Zhoram's body in less than half a second, killing him before his body fell to the hangar roof. A bullet then hit one of the grenades Zhoram was carrying, obliterating whatever was left of his body.

Buzhazi knew that he had probably lost Zhoram the second he heard the smooth, deep-throated "BRRRRRR!" sound of that attack helicopter's cannon behind him and the blast that followed. He turned and saw the big attack helicopter hovering over the hangar, pedal-turning and looking for more targets, then lining up directly on him. There was no time to run, no place to hide . . .

But seconds later a grenade round came out of nowhere, exploding right on the helicopter's tail rotor. Smoke started pouring from the chopper's transmission, and it turned, wobbling back toward the flight line for an emergency landing. Buzhazi turned and saw Zhoram's security officer running toward the flight line, his smoking grenade launcher in his hands. They waved at each other, and the security officer took cover behind a concrete guard shack and motioned to the general that there was no sign of pursuit.

Buzhazi nodded and put his radio up to his lips: "Rat units, report."

The voice on the channel made a cold chill zip up and down Buzhazi's spine: "R . . . Rat One, Rat One . . . sir, they're gone, they're all gone . . . sir," someone from the first warehouse raiding team radioed frantically, "sir, help me, help me, I've lost my right leg, it's gone, sir, help me . . ."

"Hold on, son, hold on," Buzhazi said. "Help is on the way. Rat Two, report." No response. "Rat Three."

"Three is almost out, heading to rendezvous point Beta," someone responded. Buzhazi heard the sounds of gunfire and men screaming in the background.

"Acknowledged, Rat Three," Buzhazi responded. "Sing out if you need any help. Protect yourselves at all costs. Dump the supplies and fight your way to safety if you have to." No response. He received reports from just one more of the seven scrounger teams he had sent in. Just two teams out of seven were on their way; he didn't recognize any of the voices that responded, meaning the team leaders were dead or captured; and no one said how many in each team were left. He probably wouldn't find out until they all met at the rendezvous point . . . if then.

Buzhazi was about to head back to the security building, but stopped and dropped to the ground when he heard a shot ring out. Following the direction of the gunshot, he turned and saw one of his company commanders, Flight Captain Ali-Reza Kazemi, dragging the body of one of the security officers—he realized it was the security officer that had just saved him from getting mowed down by that same attack chopper!—to the side of a small concrete block guard shack outside the flight line fence. He quickly scanned the area, looking for any sign of attack. The security officer had just signaled that the area was clear—where had that shot come from?

He was sorry to see Zhoram's officer dead, but relieved that Kazemi was still functioning. Kazemi—the former Revolutionary Guards Corps transport pilot he had taken with him from this very facility when Mansour Sattari rescued him, what seemed like decades ago but was only a few days—had proved to be a very valuable individual. He could fly anything with wings, rotary or fixed-wing, and no situation was too much for him—he was just as comfortable flying an overweight helicopter over the mountains at night and in a sandstorm as he was in perfect daylight conditions. Kazemi had managed to fly in supplies and fly out wounded even in disastrous situations where the Pasdaran seemed to have them pinned down. "Kazemi . . . !"

"Get down, sir, get down!" Kazemi shouted, waving frantically. "There's a sniper around here somewhere!"

Buzhazi crouched low and dashed off toward Kazemi, flattening himself against the concrete guard shack. "Any idea where he is?"

"No, sir." Kazemi drew his pistol. "Somewhere inside the flight line fence, firing out, but I couldn't see him." There were several large towed power carts and fire extinguishers on the flight line—plenty of places for snipers to hide—and much of the parking ramp was still obscured by smoke from the two burning helicopters. "Is General Zhoram with you?" Kazemi asked.

"I think he's dead." Buzhazi motioned to the dead security officer. He had been shot in the back of the head, a remarkably accurate shot—the sniper must have incredible skills. "Zhoram ordered this man off the roof just before the Mi-24 opened up on him. He shot down that attack helicopter just before it got a bead on me." He looked at Kazemi. "Can you give me a report on the situation, Ali?" he asked.

"There's a lot of confusion on the radio, sir, but I think I put together a reasonable picture," Kazemi replied. He pulled out a fairly detailed handmade map of Doshan Tappeh Air Base with the positions of their insurgent forces and their current manpower and ammunition situation marked on it. "It looks like we're facing three concentrations of Pasdaran soldiers right now: the barracks to the west, the main gate area to the southwest, and the northeast aviation command headquarters. We count two helicopters airborne and two more ready to go on the airfield. The good news, sir, is that our scrounger security teams have engaged the units sent to the warehouse area to the north, and although we took some heavy losses it appears the Pasdaran concentration there has been broken up."

"Your recommendation?"

Kazemi looked at Buzhazi carefully. "Two of our scrounger teams made it out, sir—we lost the rest, except for a few stragglers," he replied. "You made contact with General Yassini, and he's not helping us. Two of the three mission objectives have been completed. The third objective is to get out safely and withdraw. That is what we should do."

Buzhazi nodded. "Well thought out, Ali."

"I recommend we disengage and get out before the Pasdaran organize and flood in," Kazemi continued. He pointed toward the warehouse area. "The defenders have disengaged and fled the warehouse area, but I think they'll send in counterattack forces shortly, so the north and northwest escape routes will soon be cut off. The only other alternative is to the southeast, between the main part of the base and the flight operations area. Once outside the base, we have just two kilometers to go until we're outside the capital province, and then we're in open terrain and can move out quicker. We'll be traveling in the opposite direction of the scrounger units, which will give them a better chance of escaping, and we'll be heading away from the residential areas north of the base, so there'll be less danger of having civilians caught in the crossfire."

"But we'll have to cross the runway and taxiways," Buzhazi said. "We could be caught in the open."

"It's a risk, sir," Kazemi said honestly. "But they won't expect us to go in that direction." He indicated two dashed lines than ran across the runway complex approximately mid-field. "Men on foot and in smaller vehicles can cross via this tunnel that goes under the runway; the rest have to go across the runway. But we'll be heading away from the counterattack vector. We can have a platoon set up booby traps and ambush sites to make it appear that's where we're headed and to slow down the Pasdaran advance, while the rest of the force heads south."

Buzhazi thought for a moment, then nodded. "Very well, Ali. I agree with your plan." He put a hand on his shoulder. "I hate to do this, Ali, but you're the most senior officer surviving, so I'm going to have you organize and lead the diversion team." He pointed to Kazemi's map. "I'll have you set up ambushes here, at the security center entrance gate. You set up booby-traps along the main road that will funnel responders toward your ambush zone. Will you do that, Ali?"

Kazemi's eyes widened, but after a moment he lowered his head and nodded solemnly. "Of course, General. Who should I take with me?"

"General Zhoram's company is scattered across the northern warehouse area in overwatch positions," Buzhazi said. "You'll have to find them and get them organized." He handed Kazemi the radio from the dead security officer's belt. "They should be monitoring Zhoram's channel. I'll check on you before we depart."

"I'll get as many as I can, but I won't waste time—I can set up booby-traps as well as the next guy."

"Good," Buzhazi said. "Remember, you're just a diversion, not a suicide squad. Once the attackers pull back from the ambush zone to regroup and re-evaluate, your job is complete. Head out immediately and we'll meet up at rendezvous point Delta to the south. No heroics, understand?"

"Yes, sir. You know me: I'm no hero."

"If you aren't one today, Ali, I don't know what else to call you." The two men shook hands. "Thank you, Ali. You've done well."

"Thank you, General. I won't let them past me, don't worry." He hurried off.

The radios were very quiet in the next fifteen minutes, and only sporatic gunshots were reported around the base. Buzhazi found Kazemi in the second floor of an administration building, just a few dozen meters from the security center entrance. "Are you all right, Ali?" he asked.

"I'm fine, sir," Kazemi said. He looked over Buzhazi's shoulder—the general was alone. "Shouldn't you be leading the battalion off the base, sir?"

"I wanted to check on you first. The rest of the battalion is ready to move. Report."

"I could only locate a couple of General Zhoram's men—the rest have been captured, killed, or fled," Kazemi said. "But we have set up roadside bombs in several places along the road." He motioned outside. "We've got two machine gun squads set up either side of the gate, and two men with a grenade 'blooper' that can suppress counterfire out to about a hundred meters. Best I could do on short notice. What's our situation, sir? I haven't heard anything on the radios."

"We've been beaten up pretty badly," Buzhazi said plainly. "We're going to try to move out along three routes." He motioned to them on Kazemi's map, which had already been extensively updated in a very short time. "I want to thank you again for all you've done, Ali."

"It was my duty as well as my pleasure, sir. I'll be ready for them if they try to rush us, and then we'll be hightailing it right after you." He looked at the map. "How many do you think you can take through the tunnel under the runway, sir? I would think most of the battalion can get on the other side that way before the Pasdaran would even be alerted."

"Ah yes, the tunnel," Buzhazi said. "We decided not to take the tunnel, Ali."

"Why, sir?"

"Because frankly we didn't know it existed," Buzhazi said. He quickly drew his sidearm and pointed it at Kazemi's face. "We found it, of course—and we found the Pasdaran ambush platoons covering it too."

Kazemi's eyes widened in surprise. "What are you doing, sir . . . ?"

"As soon as I saw the size of the bullet hole in Zhoram's man's head, Ali, I knew it wasn't from a sniper rifle—it had to be from your sidearm," Buzhazi said, taking Kazemi's rifle away from him. Two infantrymen came in and pulled Kazemi to his feet. "And I couldn't figure out why you were drawing such a detailed map of our deployment and cataloging our supply situation so carefully . . . unless I considered that you were passing all that information along to the Pasdaran. And when you didn't seem to have any trepidation about guarding the north part of the base, I knew that the Pasdaran had to be waiting for us on the south—the direction you urged us to go." Kazemi made no attempt to rebuff any of those arguments. "Why, Kazemi?"

"Because this revolution of yours is doomed, Buzhazi," Kazemi said. "You can't stop the Revolutionary Guards from crushing you—you can't even stop Zolqadr's men from infiltrating your ranks at will and inciting defections and sabotage. General Zolqadr promised that all charges against me would be erased forever and I would be promoted if I set you up."

"And you believed him? That's the last and biggest mistake you'll ever make." Buzhazi pressed his pistol into Kazemi's abdomen, feeling for any body armor under his clothing with the muzzle, then pulled the trigger three times. The guards let the corpse fall forward in a pool of blood. He pulled his radio from its pounch on his web belt. "All Lion units, *jangal, jangal.*"

As Buzhazi and his guards left the building they heard several explosions behind them as the insurgents launched grenades and fired on vehicles, fuel trucks, aircraft, and anything else that might catch on fire, and several bigger explosions that destroyed remaining vital parts of the security building. When they exited the administration building, Buzhazi could see several columns of smoke rising from the south. It wasn't much, but it would have to do.

From a half-dozen spots along the northern wall surrounding the base, Buzhazi's men emerged from the base and onto Setam-Gari Avenue. Much of the traffic on this busy thoroughfare had stopped or slowed to see what the smoke on the base was about, and Buzhazi's men used that opportunity to their advantage. They picked out several large trucks, motioned with upraised weapons for the driver to get out, then blasted it with grenade and rifle fire. Soon the boulevard was a mass of confusion, blocked off in both directions, clogged with fleeing drivers escaping the smoke and gunfire.

But the smoke and explosions caught the attention of two Mi-24 attack helicopter crews orbiting over the runway and the southern part of the base, waiting for the insurgents to flee in that direction. They immediately swooped in over the avenue and began firing at anyone with a gun in his or her hands—and when there was a larger concentration of individuals, the helicopter weapons officers opened fire with fifty millimeter rocket launchers, spraying high-explosive, fragmentary, and flechette-tipped projectiles into the terrified crowds.

The carnage was unimaginable, and the completely indiscriminate slaughter enraged Hesarak Buzhazi. But he knew he could not stand out here in the open and fight. He hated the idea of rushing across the avenue into the dense shops and homes north of the airbase, but he had no choice—soon the troops set to ambush them from the south part of the base would be rushing north to engage. The attack helicopters had set up a slow orbit over the avenue, their slower rate of fire showing that they finally decided they had better start conserving their ammunition until the rest of the Revolutionary Guards entered the battle. If he was going to make an escape, now was the time.

"All units, take cover inside the strongest looking buildings you can find!" Buzhazi radioed. "Tell anyone you find inside to get out as fast as they can! Once they're away, get away from the area and rendezvous at point Gazelle as planned. Out." He turned to the dozen men surrounding him. "This way. Keep down and keep your weapons out of sight—those helicopter gunners are firing at anyone who looks like they're carrying weapons." He then dashed off into the most modern-looking building he saw in front of him, a branch of the Bank Sepah.

It was a good defensible spot—unfortunately it was also a good place to get trapped in, since access was limited in any other direction except out the front door. Buzhazi immediately radioed for other platoons to spread out around the bank building to help defend it from different directions and to provide cover fire in case they needed to escape. Setam-Gari Avenue was choked with cars and obscured with smoke, with people running in all directions trying to cover their mouths with belongings, scarves, or hankerchiefs. Every few moments he would see another horrifying sight of a woman carrying a bag of groceries or a child holding a soccer ball get gunned down by the attack helicopter's cannons. He swore loudly, trying desperately to squeeze the images out of his consciousness. He lifted his radio: "All Lion units, Lion One, report! Lion . . ."

Suddenly the entire front of the bank office was blasted apart by rocket fire, sending clouds of brick, stone, and glass inside. One soldier standing beside Buzhazi caught the full brunt of the explosion, his lifeless body plowing into the Iranian general. Buzhazi's vision was gone—the only thing that told him he was still alive was the terrible ringing in his ears from the blast and the feel of the young soldier's blood and tissue covering his face. Someone lifted him free of the wreckage and body parts. The soldier asked something, but Buzhazi couldn't hear him, so he just nodded and patted his arm to tell him he was okay.

A few minutes later, with the volume on the radio turned up all the way, Buzhazi was able to hear the reports coming in from his battalion: "Lion Two is about a half-block away. Are you all right, One? Anyone there?"

"I'm okay, Two," Buzhazi radioed. "One casualty so far. Lion Three, report."

"Lion Three doesn't have you in sight, but . . . stand by . . ." There was another loud explosion not far away, with more screaming and panicked citizens running in every direction.

"Lion Three, what's your status?" No reply.

"This is Two. Looks like Three got hit pretty bad."

"Copy. Lion Four." No reply. "Lion Four, report." Still no reply. "Lion Five." Again, no response. "Lion Four and Five, key your mikes if you can hear me." Buzhazi thought he heard the coded clicks on his radio, but he wasn't sure if it was real or just wishful thinking.

"One, this is Two, armored personnel carriers advancing from the west," the leader of Second Company reported. "I see one . . . no, two, two of them. Traffic is slowing them now . . . One, I see dismounts! Six . . . eight . . . ten dismounts, approaching each side of the street."

"Copy, Two." Buzhazi turned to the men behind him. "Listen up, men. Who do I have behind me?"

"Lieutenant al-Tabas, sir," a terrified, high-pitched voice responded. "I've got Sergeant Ardakan and most of the members of Kush platoon with me."

"Weapon status, Lieutenant? Anyone with a grenade launcher and some HE rounds?"

There was a long, uncomfortable silence; then, Tabas and Ardakan moved beside him, crouching low. The sergeant was carrying an AK-47 assault rifle along with a "blooper," a thirty-millimeter grenade launcher, and he wore a bandolier of grenades. The lieutenant carried an AK-74 assault rifle. "What do you need, sir?" Tabas asked.

"I need that launcher and your grenades, Sergeant," Buzhazi said. Ardakan looked confused, but gave the general his "blooper" and grenades. Buzhazi loaded a smoke round into the launcher.

"Sergeant, I need some cover fire."

"Are you all right, sir?"

Buzhazi's vision was still a bit blurry but there was no time to wait any longer. "I'm fine, Sergeant. Lieutenant, there are two armored personnel carriers off to the right down the street, with dismounts heading our way on the sidewalk on both sides of the street. I'm going to lay down some smoke, and then you and I are going to head down the street in between the cars and trucks and see if we can get close to those armored vehicles. They may be our way out of here."

"I'll go, General," Ardakan said. "When was the last time you led such an assault?"

"Negative, Sergeant, I'm doing this," Buzhazi insisted. "When we pop the smoke, I need you and your men to engage the dismounts and get them before they get us, then follow us down the street so we can take those vehicles. If we don't make it, I need you to link up with Lion Two—I think he's a half-block to the east." He handed the sergeant his radio. "After that, try to link up with as many of the battalion as you can and get out. Understand?"

"Yes, sir."

"Good. Lieutenant, stay down and under cover in between the disabled cars as much as you can. I'll be firing the grenade launcher, so you cover me the best you can. When we get to the armored vehicles, keep an eye out for security gunners in the turret or on the passenger side. I'll pop smoke and frags on them, and then we'll try to take them. Ready?" The lieutenant gurgled something that vaguely sounded like a "yes."

There were a hundred other things to think about, a thousand other things to consider, and he hadn't asked anyone for their advice—there was simply no time.

The lieutenant looked young enough to be his grandson. He knew he shouldn't think about that, but he still said, "Let's go, son," as he raised his grenade launcher and headed off toward the exit.

He almost instantly regretted not getting more advice on a plan. The second Buzhazi stuck his head out to look for the Pasdaran dismounts, he was met with a hail of gunfire that made him cry out in surprise and nearly fall over backward into the bank lobby, thankful he wasn't hit. They were a lot closer than he anticipated! He heard more gunfire and saw a few of his men, probably from Second Company, advancing across the avenue, trying to distract the Pasdaran infantrymen.

Buzhazi motioned to Ardakan, and the sergeant stuck his AK-74 out the doorway without aiming it and fired down the street at the approaching Revolutionary Guards. The return gunfire abruptly stopped. "Now!" Buzhazi yelled, and he and Tabas scurried out of the bank building and into the street, hiding behind disabled and abandoned cars. Buzhazi took aim and fired at the first squad he saw, nearly hitting the squad leader in the forehead with the smoke grenade. The exploding grenade burst right in the midst of the Pasdaran infantrymen, knocking one unconscious and scattering the others. Buzhazi quickly loaded another smoke round, tracked the direction Tabas was shooting, and found the second squad. His second grenade round sailed over their heads and exploded behind them, but it frightened and confused them long enough for Tabas, Ardakan, and the soldiers from Second Company to dispatch them.

Buzhazi loaded a high-explosive grenade into his "blooper" and fired at the first armored vehicle he saw, a Russian-made BMP infantry combat vehicle—with the driver and vehicle commander sitting up in their seats, heads poking out of their hatches, watching the gunfight like a couple of spectators! Buzhazi fired his grenade launcher. The round struck the steeply angled front deck of the APC, deflected upward off the engine compartment exhaust louvers, and exploded on the 73-millimeter smooth-bore cannon barrel, killing the crew instantly and starting a small fire atop the engine compartment. Moments later, hatches opened up on the second APC, and the crew jumped out and ran off.

Allah be praised, Buzhazi rejoiced to himself as he loaded another HE round in his grenade launcher, the damn plan might actually work! "First Company, move out and take those BMPs!" Buzhazi shouted over his shoulder to his men in the bank. "Let's go, let's . . . !"

He heard a roar of rotor blades behind him and turned, raising the blooper . . . but it was too late.

Before he could fire, an Mi-24 attack helicopter raced in from the south, stopped just south of the avenue a few hundred meters away, then unleashed its entire load of one hundred and twenty-eight 57-millimeter rockets point-blank on the bank building before any of his men could get out. The entire building and both buildings on either side of it disappeared in a terrific cloud of fire, smoke, and debris. Buzhazi ducked behind the cars clogging the avenue just before the shock wave, searing heat, and hurricane-force blast of flying stone, steel, and glass plowed into him.

"Don't move!" he heard above him. A Revolutionary Guards soldier was aiming his rifle at him. The air was thick with dust, debris, and smoke, and Buzhazi found it difficult to catch his breath. He could hardly hear because the roar of the Mi-24 hovering less than a hundred meters away was deafening. Buzhazi raised his left hand, trying to hide the "blooper" in his right hand, and another soldier yanked him up by it, nearly breaking his fingers in the process. "Allah akbar, it is him! It's Buzhazi!" the first soldier shouted gleefully. "The old man himself led this raid! The general will be very pleased." His sidearm, ammo, and grenade launcher were stripped away from him. "Take him to . . ."

The soldier was interrupted by the crash of some small object against the windshield of a nearby car.

Buzhazi hardly noticed it in all the other confusion of sounds and smells around them, but the Pasdaran soldiers were suddenly distracted. When Buzhazi could see clearly, he saw a very loud crowd of citizens marching up Setam-Gari Avenue toward them, less than a block away now. He couldn't hear what they were shouting, but they didn't look one bit happy.

"Take him!" the first Pasdaran soldier shouted, and the second soldier pinned Buzhazi's arms behind him. The first soldier lifted his AK-74 rifle and fired two shots over the crowd's head, waving at them to get back. No dice—the crowd, at least a couple hundred people and growing larger by the second, kept coming. More rocks, bottles, and pieces of blown-apart buildings started to rain down on them. Fear filling his eyes, the first soldier fumbled for his portable radio. "Susmar air unit, Susmar air unit, this is Gavasn Seven-One, I am at your ten o'clock position, approximately one hundred meters. I have General Buzhazi in custody. Requesting fire support on that mob heading toward me! We are outnumbered! Acknowledge!"

"Acknowledged, Gavasn," the reply came. "We have you in sight. Stay where you are." The big helicopter gunship pedal-turned to the left, hovering just a few dozen meters in the air near the air base boundary fence across the avenue. The 12.7-millimeter cannon slewed downward, zeroing in on the advancing crowd, and then . . .

. . . a laser-straight streak of orange-yellow fire zipped across the sky directly on, then directly through the gunship's engine compartment. Buzhazi at first thought he had imagined it, because the gunship didn't seem to be affected at all, even though he thought the fire had hit the helicopter. But seconds later the entire engine compartment ripped apart like an overfilled balloon and exploded in a cloud of fire, and the stricken helicopter—minus its entire engine compartment, main rotor, and most of the top of its fuselage—simply dropped straight down out of the sky and exploded in a brilliant burst of flames, showering them with still more smoke and burning debris.

Buzhazi remembered seeing those exact same streaks of light at Qom and knew who his unseen benefactors were. "The angel of death has come to Doshan Tappeh, my friends," he told the horrified Pasdaran soldiers holding him. "Better get out while you still can." He found he didn't have to break the Pasdaran soldier's grip—he and his comrade were already running off toward Doshan Tappeh Air Base as fast as they could negotiate the stranded cars and burning debris all around them. The crowd cheered as the soldiers ran off.

About a hundred eager hands steadied him as the crowd surrounded him, thumping his back happily. "Who are you people?" Buzhazi shouted. "Where did you come from?" But he couldn't make himself understood from the cheering and celebrating. "Everyone, get out of here, now!" he yelled. "There are more Pasdaran troops on the way! They'll mow everyone down if you don't get away now!"

And just as he shouted that warning, he looked south toward the airbase and saw exactly what he feared—all of the Revolutionary Guards that had been waiting for his battalion to try to escape to the south were now streaming north across the double runways of Doshan Tappeh Air Base right toward them! There were at least four companies of infantry heading his way, probably less than two kilometers away now, along with scores of armored vehicles. Farther to the east, he could see three more Mi-24 helicopter gunships flying in echelon formation, slowly advancing toward them as well. They were sending over a thousand troops out to mop up what was left of Buzhazi's insurgents, and they would undoubtedly cut down these protesters too because they had helped him. There was going to be another bloodbath . . .

. . . or worse. As he scanned the area farther east, he could see three tiny fast-moving dots on the horizon, rolling in and lining up right down the middle of Setam-Gari Avenue—Pasdaran attack jets! They looked like Russian-made Sukhoi-24 close air-support bombers, laden with bombs on both wings. The bastard Zolqadr was actually going to bomb the city from fast-movers! There would be nothing left of this entire avenue for the Pasdaran infantry to clean up after this attack was over! He looked to the west and saw another attack formation, this time of two more Su-24 bombers. "Run!" Buzhazi shouted. "Get out! Get away from here! The Pasdaran will attack any moment . . . !"

Seconds later, the jets attacked . . . but not on Setam-Gari Avenue. At the last second the jets peeled away, banking hard . . . and lining up on the advancing Pasdaran forces.

The jets to the east attacked first, launching radar-guided air-to-air missiles on the helicopters and shooting them down nearly simultaneously before peeling away. In a precisely coordinated attack which left almost no time for the men on the ground to react, seconds later the jets to the west swept over the Pasdaran infantry formations, dropping anti-personnel clusterbomb canisters. It appeared the entire air base lit up with thousands of flashbulbs, but Buzhazi knew that each "flashbulb" was a half-kilogram explosive charge that sent metal fragments out in all directions, killing or maiming anyone within ten meters.

"Hoseyn, you bastard," Buzhazi said aloud as he watched in relieved fascination at the scene of destruction right before him, "you finally got off your ass and decided to do something."

Just as quickly as it began, it was over. The airbase was obscured with thick smoke from the clusterbomb explosions, exploding vehicles, and from the burning wreckage of the attack choppers. Soon the terrifying sounds of injured and dying soldiers reached the crowd's ears, and they turned away and started to quickly leave the area.

"Who are you people?" Buzhazi asked anyone within earshot. "Where did you come from?" But the jubilant masses said little that he could understand.

Buzhazi returned to the Bank Sepah building to look for survivors, where he found members of Second Company already searching the rubble. "Not much left, sir," the sergeant in charge of Lion Two reported. "I guess the air force decided to get into the fight after all, sir?"

"Looks that way," Buzhazi said. "General Yassini finally came to his senses—or his service commanders did. I think they'll have the Pasdaran on the run. I hope they took out the Pasdaran's missiles, though, or we could be attacked again at any moment."

"Those people that marched down the street? They said they were organized by a member of the Qagev royal family, a girl no less, to rise up and throw out the Pasdaran. Do you believe that, sir?"

"Qagev? I haven't heard that name since history class in grade school—ancient history. I didn't know there were any still around." Buzhazi shook his head in disbelief. "Now we have to contend with a damned monarchy? Well, it can't be any worse than the theocrats and Islamists. If they are, we'll be picking up guns and fighting all over again."

"What hit the first gunship, sir? It didn't look like a missile."

"Just call it a lightning bolt from heaven," Buzhazi said, scanning around to look for his unseen but very powerful armored savior. "Let's finish searching this area for survivors, then let's head off to the rendezvous point to join up with the rest of the battalion. Then we'll find out what in hell is going on around here."

CHAPTER 8

PASDARAN-I-ENGELAB HEADQUARTERS, DOSHAN TAPPEH AIR BASE, TEHRAN

That Same Time

"Zolqadr? Are you there?" the voice of Ayatollah Hassan Mohtaz thundered over the wireless phone. "Answer me, damn you! What's happening out there?"

General Ali Zolqadr, commander of the Iranian Revolutionary Guards Corps, was standing open-mouthed on the roof of the Pasdaran-i-Engelab headquarters on the western side of Doshan Tappeh Air Base. He lowered his pair of field glasses as if looking at the horrific scene with his own eyes would somehow change the situation. Just seconds ago he was gleefully watching his plan to crush Buzhazi and his insurgency unfold exactly as planned—he was so confident in victory that he decided to call Mohtaz and tell him the good news himself. Then, just as abruptly, everything completely collapsed. He had just watched the utter elimination of an entire battalion of elite Shock Troops and a company of attack helicopters!

"Uh . . . I . . . Your Excellency, I will have to call you back," Zolqadr stammered. "I . . . I . . . must . . ."

"You will explain what is happening out there now!" Mohtaz ordered. "I am watching the television news, and they are reporting several helicopters down and large multiple explosions on the base! What's going on?"

"I . . . Your Excellency, just now, several attack and interceptor fighters attacked my troops as they were about to begin mopping-up operations," Zolqadr explained.

"Fighters? Whose fighters?"

"They were our fighters, sir!" Zolqadr exclaimed. "I don't know where they came from!"

"Who gave the orders to launch fighters? Yassini? Where is Yassini?"

"He's in my jail, sir," Zolqadr said. He turned his binoculars toward the security and interrogation building . . . and saw it on fire. "There is . . . I see smoke coming from the security building . . ."

"Never mind that! Did you get Buzhazi? Did your men attack? Damn you, answer me! What's happening?"

"My men . . . yes, they did attack, but . . . but the jet attack fighters, they came out of nowhere . . . we had no warning . . . they're all . . . all . . ."

"Your entire force . . . dead?" Mohtaz asked incredulously. "I thought you sent an entire battalion, almost half of the entire force based at Doshan Tappeh! You're telling me they were all killed?"

"Excellency, I need to get a report from my staff," Zolqadr said. He finally noticed his chief of staff standing before him with a piece of paper in his hands. "Wait, I have a report now. Stand by, please." He accepted the field report, his mouth and throat running dry as he read in complete astonishment and fear. "We . . . we are evacuating the base, sir," he muttered.

"What did you say, Zolqadr?" Mohtaj screamed over the radio.

"The insurgents are overrunning the base, collecting weapons and supplies and releasing prisoners," Zolqadr said in a shaking voice. "Thousands of regular army troops and civilians are with them. Security forces are engaging, but they are outnumbered, and some are joining them. I don't have all the details yet. I'm at least a kilometer from the fighting and . . ."

"Destroy Buzhazi at all costs," Mohtaz said angrily. "Don't let him escape."

"I'll assemble an entire brigade if I have to, Excellency, but I'll . . ."

"No, Zolqadr," Mohtaz said. "After Buzhazi is done slaughtering the Pasdaran, he will come after the government ministers and the clerics. You must stop him before he can assault the executive branch, the Majlis, the Assembly of Experts, or the Council of Guardians. And if the military is conspiring with Buzhazi to bring down the government, they must be destroyed as well."

"I'll get a status report on my forces and send them immediately to do everything in my power to . . ."

"You're not hearing what I'm saying, Zolqadr," Mohtaz said. "I want you to destroy Buzhazi before he gets away from Doshan Tappeh and escapes again."

"But Excellency, we don't have the forces here to oppose him," Zolqadr said. "It'll take us several hours, perhaps days, to assemble a force large enough to crush him. And if the regular army supports his insurgency as the report claims, he may be unstoppable. I will . . ."

"I'll tell you what you will do, General," Mohtaj said. "Destroy Buzhazi, now. Launch an attack immediately and blanket the entire base."

"But sir, I just told you, it will take hours to assemble . . ."

"I don't mean with ground forces, Zolqadr. Use the same forces you used against the insurgents in Arān."

"Arān? But we didn't . . ." And then Zolqadr finally realized what Mohtaj was telling him to do. "You mean . . . ?"

"It is the only way, Zolqadr," Mohtaj said. "I don't want this insurgency to go on one more hour. Destroy them all."

"But Excellency, the civilians . . . we'll be launching against our own people!"

"If they didn't expect to encounter resistance from the Pasdaran before participating in this uprising, they don't deserve to live—in fact, we're doing our country a favor by not allowing such stupid persons to breed any longer," Mohtaj said. "Give the order, General. Destroy them, before they get away. Do it, now."

"But sir, what if the Israelis and the Westerners detect our missile launches with their spy satellites?" Zolqadr asked. "What if they launch a pre-emptive strike against us?"

There was silence on the line for a few moments; then: "You make a good point, General," Mohtaj said. Zolqadr silently breathed a sigh of relief—Mohtaj would have no choice but to rescind his crazy order now. Everyone knew that the Americans used sophisticated heat-seeking satellites that could detect even a small missile launch anywhere on planet Earth, as they did with the missile attack on Arān. If they detected another, even larger missile barrage, they would likely order a counterattack. Mohtaj certainly couldn't risk a . . .

"You are correct, General—an attack against the insurgents at Doshan Tappeh would certainly alert the Americans, who would in turn alert the Israelis and other pro-Western Arab nations," Mohtaj said calmly. "Therefore, you will plan a pre-emptive missile attack against Western command-and-control facilities in Iraq, the Gulf, and Israel, to be carried out simultaneously with the attack on Doshan Tappeh. You will order the attacks immediately."

"What?" Zolqadr exclaimed. "You want me to attack Israel and all of the other nations in the Persian Gulf region?"

"Are you questioning my orders, General?"

"I'm . . . I'm seeking clarification, that's all," Zolqadr stammered. "A massive ballistic missile attack against the West? We aren't ready for the assault that is sure to follow . . ."

"Neither are the Americans," Mohtaj said confidently. "Days from now they may put together some sort of retaliatory air attack, but by then the damage against them will be done, our armed forces and reserves will be mobilizing, and we will enter into negotiations with them for a cease-fire. Our objectives will have been achieved while the West is hurt.

"The Americans are weak and they don't want war. This is the perfect opportunity to strike. They will never expect us to attack if they haven't detected a general mobilization. Besides, we can argue that Buzhazi's attack on Doshan Tappeh and the American captured in Turkmenistan prompted us to act. We will tell the world it's their fault!"

There was a slight pause; then: "I recall the briefing we were given by our friends on the Americans' bomber buildup on the island of Diego Garcia," Mohtaj went on. "Our friends seem to think that the Americans will try to launch another stealth bomber attack against us. This time, they won't get the opportunity. I want you to initiate an attack against the American bomber base on Diego Garcia as well, using the longer-range ballistic missiles in Kermān."

"Diego Garcia!" Zolqadr exclaimed. "That is one of America's most vital air bases in the whole world! That . . . that will be akin to attacking American soil, like the Russians did! I . . . Excellency, I think you should reconsider . . ."

"I will reconsider nothing, General!" Mohtaj thundered. "My battle staff is preparing the coded execution orders as we speak. You will transmit those orders to the appropriate missile brigades without delay, and you will ensure that the orders are carried out to the letter, or I will personally sink a knife into your weak cowardly heart and find another officer who is not stupid enough to question orders. Do I make myself clear, Zolqadr? Attack immediately!"

NORTH OF THE CITY OF HAMADAN, 180 MILES SOUTHWEST OF TEHRAN, IRAN

That Same Time

The northern reaches of the Zagros Mountain range in west-central Iran is a rugged, windswept region, pleasant most of the year but dreadfully cold and snowy in winter. The Qezel-Owzan River originates in the steep mountains near the provincial capital of Hamadan and cuts steep cliffs, caves, and rock spires as it flows north toward the Caspian Sea. Some of the tallest peaks in this area rise to over ten thousand feet above sea level.

During the Iran-Iraq War, hundreds of thousands of Kurds fled Saddam Hussein's Iraq into western Iran, and the Revolutionary Guards were sent in to try to keep them out. The lucky ones escaped into the Zagros Mountains—the others were slaughtered and left in the ravines and streams to rot. The families that survived the winters in the mountains remained, grew, and eventually prospered, out of reach of Pasdaran persecution. It was not a comfortable or idyllic environment, but living mostly unmolested in the harsh mountains was better than being slaughtered like dogs by Saddam's Republican Guards or Iran's Revolutionary Guards. As John Milton wrote, "Better to reign in Hell than serve in Heav'n."

Despite being known for its bountiful raisin harvests and the spectacular Ali-Sadr Caves north of Hamadan, the inhospitable terrain, heavy Pasdaran presence, and the suspicious, mostly secretive Kurdish population keeps visitors and tourists to a minimum—exactly what the Kurds, and eventually the Pasdaran, desired.

The Ali-Sadr Caves, one of western Iran's few popular natural attractions, were first discovered in the sixth century and used as a source of drinking water, but when the water ran low the caves were abandoned. But they were rediscovered in the mid-1960s quite by accident by a young boy looking for a lost goat. Although the caves and the surrounding area were developed by the Shah Pahlavi into a well-known tourist destination, it was not until after the Iran-Iraq War that more exploration in the area was undertaken. It was quickly determined that the Ali-Sadr Caves were not the only long, soaring caverns in the area. While the Ali-Sadr Caves were being developed and built by the government, secretly the Pasdaran began rebuilding many of the other caves to their own specifications.

The result was the Gav-Sandoq Khameini, or Khameini Strongbox, named after the Supreme Leader who commissioned the construction of the military complex in the early twenty-first century. The Strongbox ran for almost four miles through the east and northeast side of the Zagros Mountains near the town of Gol Tappeh, about ten miles southwest of the Ali-Sadr Caves, with six entrances and dozens of tunnels connecting forty-three caverns strewn throughout the mountain. While most of the caverns were just house-sized, several were building-sized, and a few of them were massive warehouse-sized halls that took thousands of lights, massive generators, and a ventilation system large enough to air-condition a fifty-story skyscraper to keep it habitable.

Originally built as a weapons of mass destruction shelter and military weapon and equipment stockpile to protect and then retaliate against another invasion by Iraq, the Strongbox was situated perfectly to strike at Iraq by Iran's medium-range ballistic missile fleet. Most of the three hundred missiles stored in the Strongbox were the Shahab-2 ("Meteor" in English) series of road-mobile ballistic missiles, which were locally modified versions of the Russian SCUD-C missile, with a range of about three hundred miles.

The missile's accuracy was not very good—perhaps a quarter-mile circular error—but with a fifteen-hundred-pound nuclear, chemical, or biological warhead, accuracy wasn't that important. The missiles could be brought out of the Strongbox, driven just a few miles away to pre-surveyed launch points, fueled, erected, aligned, programmed, and launched in just a matter of hours. They had plenty of range to hit Baghdad and most large cities in Iraq east of the Euphrates River. Launched from the Strongbox, the rockets could devastate Iraqi targets with ease, almost without warning.

But as Iran's missile fleet got more sophisticated and the targets changed from Iraq to Israel and Western military forces stationed in the Middle East and Central Asia, the mix of missiles garrisoned at the Strongbox changed. The new weapon of choice was the Shahab-3. Built in North Korea with Iranian financial assistance, and known to the world as the Nodong-1 medium-range ballistic missile, approximately a dozen Shahab-3 missiles were shipped to Iran beginning in 1996, and three successful test launches were conducted.

Because of pressure by China and the United States on North Korea to stop shipping missiles to "rogue states," Iran announced in 2000 that it would start to build the missile itself at its new Shahid Hemat Industrial Facility south of Tehran. The first missile was test-fired in 2001, and the weapon system declared operational in 2002. By 2006 thirty indigenously built missiles had been completed and secretly deployed to the Strongbox, where they could be fired quickly and accurately and could easily reach targets in Israel and Western military bases in Iraq, Turkey, Kuwait, Bahrain, and Qatar. Like the Shahab-2, it was road-mobile and could be deployed and set up to launch within hours.

The duty officer in charge of the Seventh Rocket Brigade of the Iranian Revolutionary Guards Corps received the radio message from headquarters. Because the call came in on the direct emergency-only channel, he immediately hit the alarm button, which sent an "Action Stations" alert throughout the entire complex. Each of the three missile regiments inside the Strongbox—two Shahab-2 regiments and one Shahab-3 regiment, plus security and support companies—immediately began preparing their units to deploy to pre-assigned launch points, all within thirty miles.

The coded message copied by the communications officer and verified by the duty officer gave the actual order—and it was a "prepare to attack" order. The duty officer immediately radioed the brigade commander, Major-General Muhammad Sardaq. The commander was already hurrying to the command post by the time the message was decoded and verified. "We have received an actual 'prepare to attack' order, sir," the duty officer reported.

"An 'actual' message, you say?" Sardaq queried. The brigade ran numerous exercises every week, so "exercise" messages were common, not "actuals." "Verify it again." The general watched as the two officers decoded the message—again it authenticated as an "actual" message. He swore to himself, then picked up the direct secure telephone line to Pasdaran headquarters at Doshan Tappeh Air Base in Tehran.

"That's not the procedure, sir . . ."

"I'm not going against procedure, Major," Sardaq told the duty officer. "Continue the checklist and have the brigade prepare to attack. Never mind what I'm doing."

As he waited for someone at headquarters to answer the phone, the general watched carefully as the command post team began tracking the progress of each regiment as it prepared to deploy the missiles. After sending their own coded message acknowledging receipt of their orders, headquarters would then send another short coded message with either the preplanned strike package for each unit, or a very lengthy message with target coordinates and a force launch timing matrix. The longer message had to be verified, decoded, verified again, and compared to a catalog of possible targets chosen in advance by the National Security Directorate, then broadcast as a coded document to the regiment. After receipt, the launch crews would have to verify, decode, and check the target coordinates again, then enter the coordinates and the launch timing matrix into their launch computers. The launch timing matrix was critical to ensure that each of the brigade's missiles didn't interfere with one another at launch, inflight, or at impact.

The commander and duty officer gasped in astonishment as they read the decoded attack orders. The first verified target set was a short "canned" message for the Shahab-3 regiment, ordering strikes against military air bases in Israel, Kuwait, Bahrain, Turkey, and Qatar, designed to destroy known command-and-control facilities and alert strike aircraft bases with high-explosive warheads before they could send an alert or launch their aircraft and counterattack. These missiles would launch second. The target set for the first Shahab-2 regiment and two squadrons of the second Shahab-2 regiment was also a short message, ordering strikes against Western command-and-control, air defense, air bases, armored, infantry, and supply bases inside Iraq, scheduled to launch first so they might have a chance to destroy some of the American Patriot anti-ballistic missile sites set up in Iraq.

"Finally we're striking out against the Israelis and Americans!" the duty officer exclaimed happily. "They've been threatening us for long enough—I'm glad we're getting our punches in first!"

"Shut up, you idiot," the general said. "This will work only if the damned politicians somehow convince the Americans not to bomb us into oblivion after our missiles fall. What do you think the chances of that are?"

The last message gave the third squadron of the second Shahab-2 regiment a lengthy target list . . . with a notice saying that none of the target coordinates would be found in the National Security Directorate's catalog. That was unusual—in fact, it was a major breach of command and control policy. The order was properly authenticated, but it was still against safe operational policy.

It took several minutes for the connection to go through, and another few minutes for someone in authority to get on the line, but finally Sardaq was connected to the senior controller, a colonel Sardaq did not recognize, at Revolutionary Guards Corps headquarters. "What is the meaning of this call, General?" the senior controller thundered as soon as he got on the line. "You're not supposed to call unless it's an emergency and you are unable to comply with your orders. Are you calling to tell me you cannot follow our orders?"

"I'm calling because you issued me an inappropriate order, Colonel, and I'm calling to verify it," Sardaq said.

"Is the order not valid? Did it not properly authenticate?"

"It did, but the target coordinates are not found in the target catalog," Sardaq said. "Long-form target sets are supposed to be checked against the target catalog for verification."

"The targets are not in the catalog, General. I explained that in the message. The attack order still stands. You have a valid execution code—launch the attack."

The duty officer ran over to Sardaq with the decoded message in his trembling hand and stared at his commanding general with wide, unbelieving eyes. "The target coordinates for Third Squadron—they're on Doshan Tappeh Air Base!" he cried. "They want us to attack our own headquarters!"

"What in hell is going on, Colonel?" Sardaq shouted. "You gave us the wrong coordinates!"

"The coordinates are correct, General," the senior controller said. "Haven't you been reading the FLASH message traffic? Doshan Tappeh is being overrun by insurgents and the regular army . . ."

"The last message I read said that the Revolutionary Guards are about to launch a raid on insurgents in Tehran near the air base."

"Well, get your head out of your ass and keep reading, General," the controller said.

"Watch your language, Colonel! Maintain discipline!" But he snapped his fingers at the duty officer, urgently motioning for him to retrieve the stack of obviously unread message traffic reports on his desk.

"Fuck you and discipline, General!" the controller shouted. "They've bombed one of our infantry battalions, killed thousands, and shot down almost a dozen attack helicopters . . ."

"Who? Who is doing all this?"

"It's Buzhazi, General . . . he's here, and he's got the army, the air force, and large numbers of civilians with him and his insurgents," the controller responded. "Over fifty thousand insurgents, regular army, and civilians are on the base right now, grabbing everything they can carry and smashing anything they can't. We're evacuating the headquarters . . ."

"Evacuating . . . !"

"My last task before trying to get out of here is to send you the attack message, and here I still am, with an angry mob less than five hundred meters away ready to twist my head off, arguing with you! It might be too late to get out of here already."

The duty officer quickly read through the dispatches, and the shock and fear in his eyes told Sardaq that what the frantic, terrified Pasdaran command center senior controller was telling him was the truth. "The army? The army is helping the insurgents?"

"Don't waste time asking stupid questions, General," the senior controller said, the fear rattling his voice now. "The base will fall into rebel hands soon, and then the capital and the government will fall along with it unless they are stopped. The order to attack comes from the Pasdaran commanding general himself, and he received the orders from the chief of the national security directorate. If you don't believe me, take it up with them. I'm getting out of here. You have your orders. Kill the bastards before they take over the whole damned country." And the connection went dead.

Sardaq was completely dumbfounded as he dropped the phone to the desk. "I don't believe it," he finally muttered after a long, stunned silence. "Insurgents are overrunning Doshan Tappeh . . . and the fucking army is helping them!" He turned to the duty officer. "I want the battle staff in here in five minutes with a complete briefing on the status of our attack preparations." Before the duty officer could pick up the phone to issue the orders, General Sardaq grabbed him by his tunic. "And I want you to warn the regimental commanders that if I learn even one member of their organization is dragging his feet, I'll personally shoot him in the head. Now move!"

ARMSTRONG SPACE STATION

A Short Time Later

"Contact, sir!" one of the new sensor operators aboard Armstrong Space Station crowed. The technician was dressed in a simple blue jump suit and wore Velcro sneakers and Velcro patches on his knees and forearms to help keep himself attached to various places in the main operations section of the station. Three other sensor and computer operators, all newly arrived at Silver Tower to operate its reactivated sensors, were similarly dressed and similarly attached to various parts of the module, studying multi-function touch-screen displays of satellite imagery all around Iran. "Target area two has activity!"

"About damned time," Colonel Kai Raydon snorted. "Okay, gang, let's get ready to rumble." He switched his console's display to that operator's screen. It showed a real-time NIRTSat ultra-wideband radar image of what appeared to be tractor-trailer rigs suddenly appearing out of nowhere in the middle of the mountains of western Iran. The radar image was precisely tuned by computer to squelch out terrain and forest returns and only show moving metallic returns. "Yep, we've got the cockroaches coming out of the woodwork for sure." He flipped on the secure satellite communications channel. "Genesis, this is Odin, you got a copy on our Polaroid?"

"Roger, Odin," Patrick McLanahan responded from the White House Situation Room. The high-definition television monitors in the White House conference room had been set up to display images from not only Silver Tower's sensors but from hundreds of other aircraft, satellite, and surface ship sensors as well, or a mosaic of all sensor data put together.

"Right where you said they'd be, General," Raydon remarked. He watched as the station's computers, networked in with the computers on the ground at the High Technology Aerospace Weapons Center's operations center, started calculating the proper orbital mechanics to intercept the mobile missile launchers. "Odin to Stud One-Three, how are you doing down there?"

"Happy to be back and ready to go, Odin," Captain Hunter "Boomer" Noble responded. He was on the ground at the High Technology Aerospace Weapons

Center in Nevada, pulling "cockpit alert" in the second of two remaining XR-A9 Black Stallion spacecraft. Noble had been back in the United States for less than a day before being tasked for another mission, but he didn't hesitate to accept the assignment. "Thanks again for not grounding me, Genesis."

"No problem, One-Three," Patrick replied. "Glad you feel up to it."

"We need all the swinging dicks we can to fly, kid," Raydon said. "Are you getting the pictures and the orbital insertion data?"

"Roger," Hunter replied. A fiber-optic data cable connected to the spaceplane was busy feeding orbital information, weapon ballistics data, and precise position updates to the Black Stallion's flight and payload computers. As he read, the computer beeped at him, warning him that the "BEFORE POWER ON" checklist was underway. He acknowledged the built-in countdown hold. "Looks like I'm counting down, guys," he said. "I'll talk to you once I'm airborne."

"Contact, sir!" another sensor operator shouted. "Target area five!"

"Looks like we've got another fish on, Genesis," Raydon said. He switched to the new target. This one was the most unlikely area they had under surveillance, but if they did detect activity it would be one of the most important ones to address. "Got bad news for you, Genesis: your old friend the Shahab-5 launch site is active." He studied the latest images from the launch site. "I don't see any rockets on the launch pad—you took care of the last one very nicely—but the latest ultra-wideband radar scans we took from the Tower tell us they have three occupied silos out there. It's fair to say they're all Shahab-5s, and some might have nuclear warheads."

"Any chance they could be decoys, Odin?" Patrick asked.

"You're the ex intel guru, sir," Raydon said, peering at the radar images even more closely. "The ultra-wideband radar system installed on Armstrong Space Station has the capability of seeing underground, but atmospheric, angle of sight, and target composition conditions have to be perfect, and with our eighties-era computers we can't always get a good detailed image even if we are lucky enough to get the perfect shot. The underground missile silos at Kermān are obviously Russian-designed hardened suckers. I just can't call it for sure, Genesis. The Iranians claim the Shahab-5s are just satellite boosters, and the silos are just secure storage facilities. I don't buy that for a second."

"Neither do I, Kai," Patrick said. "But we don't have many assets out in-theater, and I need an assessment of the threat."

"Sir, if Iran has issued this alert because of what's happening in Tehran right now," Raydon said, "there's no reason I can think of for them to be warming up a space launch vehicle. I think they're going to launch their big boys. And we know what the target will be."

"Diego Garcia," Patrick said.

"It's the only logical target, sir," Raydon said. "They can hit Israel, Egypt, Turkey, and all our bases in the Middle East with their Shahab-3s. Most of the bombers that hit Iran back in '97 came from Diego—the Iranians know that, or if they don't they're not as smart as we give them credit for. And if our 'good friends' the Russians are sharing intel with them, which we definitely think they are, the Iranians would know that we've got stealth bombers out there. They're going after Diego, sir—I'm positive. Almost."

"Almost?"

"As positive as I'm ever going to be, General," Raydon said. "If I thought the Iranians had the know-how, or got it from the Russians, the only other logical target for the Shahab-5 would be Silver Tower."

"And unfortunately we don't have the Thor defense systems up and running yet," Ann Page chimed in from her console in the station's anti-missile laser's control module, "so we can't protect ourselves from up here."

There was a pause on the channel; then: "Boomer, I'm going to re-task your flight. Stand by."

A few moments later: "Updates downloading, sir," Noble reported. "Genesis, are you sure you wouldn't want to send Stud One-One on this one and let me take the Strongbox?"

"I've sent you into enough hot target areas, One-Three," Patrick replied. "You're going to take out the Shahab-5s. I'll give One-One the Strongbox." Both XR-A9 spaceplanes were loaded with air-to-ground weapons—a BDU-58 Meteor re-entry carrier, carrying three 1,500-pound U.S. Air Force AGM-170D "SPAW" missiles, or Supersonic Precision Attack Weapon. The SPAW was a two-stage solid-motor and scramjet–powered missile with a range of over one hundred miles and a top sustained cruise speed of over five times the speed of sound. It used GPS and inertial en route navigation which gave it near-precision accuracy, but then its course to impact could be fine-tuned by datalinks from satellites, target designators on the ground, or by other aircraft. These D-model missiles were specially modified by the High Technology Aerospace Weapons Center with thermium nitrate high explosive warheads that gave them an effective explosive yield of ten thousand pounds of TNT.

"It's likely to be pretty hot out there near that launch area," Boomer said. "Maybe I ought to take it instead of the 'new guy.'" The "new guy" was Lieutenant Colonel Jack Olray, who was new to Dreamland and the XR-A9 project with just two orbital Black Stallion flights to his credit, but was a combat veteran and experienced test pilot.

"The 'new guy' will do just fine, One-Three," Patrick said.

"We can handle it, One-Three," radioed Benneton from the second Black Stallion, then added, "Thanks for your vote of confidence." Boomer knew enough not to try to return her snide remark over the command channel—it would only encourage her to keep on giving him grief.

Besides, his countdown seemed to be progressing faster and faster, and soon they'd be underway. His crew mission commander, U.S. Navy Lieutenant Lisette "Frenchy" Moulain, another newcomer to the unit, was impatiently prompting him to acknowledge each countdown hold within seconds of it popping up on their screens. With Frenchy's almost constant urging, it seemed only seconds later when they closed up the cockpit and were moving out. Boomer noticed Olray and Benneton closing their cockpit canopies as they taxied clear of the hangar—they would be airborne shortly afterward.

Boomer and Frenchy made their first refueling over northern Arizona, then requested and were cleared for a supersonic cruise-climb while over southern New Mexico. They cruised at eighty-five thousand feet and Mach three for just an hour, then descended just east of Puerto Rico for their second refueling. Now safely over the Atlantic Ocean northeast of Venezuela, they accelerated to Mach ten, turned slightly northeast, then began their eight-minute orbital insertion burn. By the time they had crossed the Atlantic Ocean and reached the coast of Africa near Sierra Leone, they were at seventy-seven miles altitude and traveling at twenty-five times the speed of sound.

"Everything OK back there, Frenchy?" Boomer asked after they were established in orbit.

"Of course. If it wasn't, I'd tell you. Why did you ask?"

"That's my way of calling for a station check," Boomer explained.

"Then why didn't you say that?" Boomer scowled at the rear cockpit monitor but said nothing. "I'm in the green, oxygen and pressurization good, and the payload shows safe with full connectivity and continuity. The 'Before Release' checklist is underway. Eighty-three seconds until the first countdown hold."

"Thank you," Boomer said. Sheesh, he thought, why does Dreamland attract women like these? Aren't there any . . . ?

Suddenly there was a steady "DEEDLE DEEDLE DEEDLE!" warning tone, and the message "EARLY WARNING RADAR DETECTED" flashed on the screen. "One-Three, I'm picking up a very strong long-range early-warning radar at your twelve o'clock position," Raydon radioed. "It's unidentified—it's not Iran's air defense radar."

"We'll keep an eye on it for you and analyze it as soon as possible," Patrick said. "We show you about three minutes to release."

"That checks," Boomer said. He checked his position: near the southwest corner of Sudan and Egypt in east Africa, within sight of the Red Sea. There wasn't much he could do about this new threat except perhaps turn right and get away from land, but it was equally possible that this radar was on a warship. Well, early-warning radars were meant to be large and powerful. He forced himself to relax.

"Stud One-One is safely in orbit and on track," Raydon reported. "Three minutes to release point, reporting everything in the green." Boomer knew that Olray's mission took him on a much more highly inclined track, zooming over the Baltic states and Belarus before launching their Meteor payload. The track was designed to keep them as far away from Russian airspace as possible. Fortunately the desired orbit was perfectly aligned with the optimal track for the Meteor re-entry vehicle, so it wouldn't waste too much energy having to maneuver to get into position before releasing the JSOW missiles.

"Last countdown hold," Moulain announced. "MC's release consent switch to 'CONSENT.' "

"Roger." Boomer reached for a red switch guard, broke the thin safety wire, lifted the guard, and hit the switch. "AC's consent switch to 'CONSENT.' " It was one of the high-tech Air Force's nods to the old two-person crew concept of having two mechanical safety-wired switches physically separated from one another that had to be actuated manually before any weapons could be released.

"Roger. Crew consent entered, everything's in the green, countdown is . . ."

"It's the laser fire control radar!" Patrick radioed. "The Russians installed a Kavaznya laser in southern Iran?"

"We've had the area under satellite surveillance for days, Genesis," Raydon said, "and we haven't seen a thing. There's been normal truck traffic going in and out of the missile site at Kermān. They couldn't possibly have gotten a laser set up out there in such a short time!"

The radar threat warning receiver sounded again, this time with the warning, "HEIGHT-FINDER ACTIVE." "They've got a pretty good lock on One-Three," Raydon said. "He's forty seconds to the launch point. What do you want to do, Genesis? If he releases the Meteor, I think that's when they'll fire the laser. Do you want him to withhold?"

"It's a bluff, Genesis," Boomer said. "Like Odin said, they couldn't have gotten a big laser out here quick enough. They want us to withhold."

"Zevitin warned us that Russia would act if we attacked Iran," Patrick said. "This could have been what he was talking about."

"I'm ready to withdraw consent, Cap . . ." Moulain said.

"Keep your hands away from that switch unless I tell you otherwise, Lieutenant!" Boomer shouted over the intercom. "It's a bluff, Genesis," Boomer repeated over the command channel. "Let's do this thing."

There was a long pause on the channel, going almost all the way to the end of the countdown; then, Patrick radioed: "Continue, One-Three."

"Good choice, sir," Boomer muttered. "Final release check, MC."

Moulain verbally ran through the eight steps of the checklist, then verified that the computer had already configured the system for release. "Checklist complete. Stand by on the bay doors . . . doors coming open . . . payload away . . . doors coming . . ." At that instant the threat warning receiver blared again, this time with a fast-paced "DEEDLEDEEDLEDEEDLE!" tone, and the monitor warning read "MISSILE WARNING" and "LASER ILLUM," meaning they were being hit by a laser. "They got us!" Moulain cried out. "They're firing the laser!"

"Relax, Frenchy, relax," Boomer said. He was fixated on just one readout—the exterior skin temperature. "It must be a targeting or rangefinder laser—hull temperature hasn't moved." He checked the rear cockpit monitor and saw Moulain frantically scanning her own readouts, looking for confirmation. "Just keep your protective visor down. We'll be over their horizon in a minute or two."

The Meteor re-entry vehicle fired its small retrorocket to slow itself down, then assumed a nose-high attitude as it started to descend through the atmosphere. As it slowed to below Mach ten, the mission-adaptive systems on board activated, and the craft began to do a series of S-turns to slow itself down even more. As the atmosphere got denser the mission-adaptive flight controls became more and more active, and the Meteor was able to fully maneuver.

"Meteor passing through one hundred thousand feet, range two hundred," Moulain reported. "Still in the green. Threat warning receiver has identified the target illuminator as an SA-12 'High Screen' sector scanner . . . passing through seventy-five thousand, range one-fifty . . . coming within SA-12 lethal range . . . now." The SA-12 "Giant" surface-to-air missile system was one of the most advanced anti-aircraft systems in the world. Purchased from Russia and widely publicized, the SA-12 was designed to protect Iran's most valuable nuclear weapons production facilities from stealth bomber and cruise missile launches as well as from attack aircraft.

Another threat warning tone sounded, this time with the text warning "MISSILE LAUNCH." "SA-12 in the air," she reported. "SPAW missiles powering up, and data transfer in progress . . . thirty seconds to separation . . . second SA-12 is up . . . another SA-12 in the air . . . SPAW missile data transfer complete, missiles ready to go . . . now we have an SA-10 target acquisition radar up . . . coming up on separation point . . . now."

The Meteor vehicle split apart and ejected its three weapons. The AGM-170D SPAW missiles stabilized themselves in the slipstream, took their initial GPS satellite position and velocity updates, did a fast self-check, then fired its first-stage solid-motor rocket engine. In less than twenty seconds the SPAW missiles had accelerated to Mach three and streaked across the sky toward their assigned targets. A few seconds later, the first two SA-12 missiles plowed into the empty Meteor vehicle, blowing it to bits.

When the SPAW missiles' motor casings were empty, small air intakes on the SPAW missiles' bodies extended. The interior shape of the motor casing compressed the incoming supersonic air. Fuel and a spark were introduced, and the missiles' scramjet engine flared to life. Seconds later the missiles passed Mach five. The SA-10 anti-aircraft missiles had a max speed of Mach six, but their solid-fuel rocket motors had already burned out so they were simply coasting toward a spot in space where their targeting computers predicted their quarry would be. The more they turned to chase down the SPAW missiles the slower they flew, until seconds before intercept they could no longer maintain altitude and simply fell to Earth.

The SA-12 battery had fired two more missiles at the incoming AGM-170D attack missiles, and the

SA-10 battery fired two more as well. The SA-12s destroyed the first incoming SPAW missile. But by this time the SPAWs were just seconds from impact, and their speed had increased in the descent to well over Mach six, and the SA-10s missed the other two incoming attackers. Patrick's "Need-It-Right-This-Second" micro-satellites orbiting over the target area provided the final precision steering signals to the SPAW missiles, and both of the surviving missiles made direct hits on their assigned Shahab-5 launch silos. The resulting thermium-nitrate explosions, and the massive secondary explosions caused by thousands of gallons of rocket fuel and oxidizer blowing up in their silos, were bright enough to be seen for a hundred miles away.

"Direct hits, guys and gals!" Patrick announced. "Excellent job!"

"But we still have one silo remaining," Kai Raydon said. "They'll launch the third one, sir, I know it—now that we've attacked their other babies, they know we're gunning for them."

"We'll deal with them then," Patrick said. "Right now we've got Stud One-One ready to release."

"Meteor on course and on glidepath," Benneton said, announcing her payload readouts aloud. "Carrier temps normal. Thirty seconds to weapon release."

Olray and Benneton's targets were different than Noble's and Moulain's: they only carried three AGM-170D SPAW missiles, like Stud One-Three, but they knew there were going to be many more Shahab-2 and -3s in the field than there were Shahab-5 silos, and only three SPAWs wouldn't take them all out. Someone else was going to do that job. They also knew, like Zarand, that the Strongbox would be defended by Iran's most sophisticated high-altitude, anti-missile-capable air defense weapons.

But instead of evading the SA-10 and SA-12 surface-to-air missile sites, Stud One-One's job was to attack and destroy them.

Each SA-10 and SA-12 brigade consisted of six transporter-erector-launchers (TELs) surrounding the pre-surveyed launch points in the area of the Strongbox. Each TEL had four vertically launched missiles, connected to the command post by microwave datalinks backed up by armored fiber-optic cables. The surveillance, target tracking, and missile guidance radars were also similarly linked to the command post vehicles, and each brigade's command posts were linked to each other so they could share radar data. As with the Shahab-5 launch silos near Zarand, there were two SA-10 brigades and one SA-12 brigade in the Strongbox area, with a total of seventy-two anti-aircraft missiles ready to fire, plus another ninety-six reloads that could be made ready to launch in under thirty minutes.

There was no way one Black Stallion attacker could destroy all one hundred and sixty-eight missiles—that would take an entire squadron of heavy bombers loaded with precision-guided munitions, which didn't exist any more in the United States Air Force. But there were only three command posts coordinating the surface-to-air missile defenses of the Strongbox . . . and that was precisely how many AGM-170D SPAW missiles Olray and Benneton had just launched.

"Good missile separation from the Meteor," Benneton reported. "SA-10 and SA-12 long-range surveillance . . . switching to target tracking mode . . . now I've got a new tracking radar warning! Do you see this, Genesis?"

"Roger, One-One," Patrick responded. "It's been identified as an extremely high-powered Golf-band frequency-agile phased array radar last seen on a Russian anti-ballistic missile ground-based laser."

"Anti-missile laser!"

"Stud One-Three got the same indications down south, but nothing else happened—the SA-10s and-12s came up and engaged normally," Patrick reported. "The laser system I'm familiar with used a small electronic diode laser to refine tracking and do atmospheric attenuation readings, and One-Three got hit with it too, but nothing else happened."

"What does all that mean, Genesis?" Benneton asked worriedly.

"We think it's just a target tracking radar or a decoy emitter, One-One."

"Let's hope so."

"There's not a whole lot we can do anyway except perhaps try to accelerate and boost into a higher orbit," Olray said. "We're pressing on."

"SPAWs on course, good acceleration, still reporting good connectivity," Benneton said. At that moment the warning tone sounded and a "LASER ILLUM" alert came on their multi-function screens. "There's the laser warning, Genesis."

"Roger, we see it. Continue."

"Okay." She rechecked the flight profile of the SPAW missiles, but couldn't help glancing nervously at the "LASER ILLUM" alert. "What kind of laser did you say this was, Genesis?"

"Try to ignore it, MC," Olray said. "We'll be over their horizon in four minutes."

"It'll last just a minute—they might be trying to lock onto the SPAWs," Patrick said. "Continue."

"Roger. Good track . . . looks like Odin is taking precision course guidance."

"That's affirm, One-One," Raydon said. "Last NIRTSat picture was just four minutes ago. We got 'em zeroed in. Satellite datalink is solid and the SPAWs are ridin' the rail."

"Maybe we ought to blast off on outta here, AC, now that Silver Tower has the wheel," Benneton said. "That laser warning is making me nervous."

"One-Three didn't get anything," Olray reminded her. "Less than three minutes and then we'll be out of sight. Just try to . . ."

Except for the screams, that was the last either of them uttered. At that instant the cockpit filled with a brilliant blue-orange light that quickly grew brighter and brighter and hotter and hotter, and seconds later the XR-A9 Black Stallion exploded in a massive fireball, drawing a bright line of fire across the sky clearly visible to anyone on the ground even in daylight.

ABOARD HEADBANGER SEVEN-ZERO, SEVENTY MILES EAST OF THE STRONGBOX

That Same Time

The streak of fire was not only visible to persons on the ground, but visible to some in the sky as well. "Look at that!" exclaimed U.S. Air Force Reserve Captain Mark Hours. "Somebody's on fire. That doesn't look good."

"Way too high to affect us . . . I hope," the EB-52 Megafortress's aircraft commander, U.S. Air Force Reserve Major Wyatt Cross, said. He pointed to his supercockpit display aboard the highly modified B-52 battleship. "But we got some good news: the SA-10s and -12s are down. You copy that, guys?"

"We copy," Brigadier-General Hal Briggs responded. "Definitely good news." He and one of his Air Battle Force Ground Operations teammates were inside an MQ-35 Condor air-launched special operations transport aircraft nestled in the EB-52's bomb bay. The Condor was a small stealthy aircraft powered by a turbojet engine designed to glide commandos behind enemy lines and then fly them out again a short distance after their mission was complete. Normally the Condor could carry four fully armed commandos, but the equipment Briggs and his partner, U.S. Army First Lieutenant Charlie Brakeman, carried took up a lot of space. While Briggs rode in the Condor aircraft with his standard black battle dress uniform, Brakeman wore Tin Man battle armor. "Let us go and let's get to it."

"Coordinating with the rest of the package now. Stand by."

Hours was already checking his wide-screen supercockpit display. Two other aircraft were visible on the moving-map presentation of the battle plan. He used his eye-pointing system to select the status of the nearest of the two. "Lead is showing thirty seconds to release, guys. Stand by."

Brakeman put on his helmet, locked it in place, powered up his battle armor, pulled his chest and lap belts tight, and gave Briggs a thumbs-up. Briggs put on a standard flight helmet, clipped his oxygen mask in place, pulled his straps tight, and returned the thumbs-up. "We're ready when you are."

"Here we go, guys," Cross announced. "Good luck." Briggs heard a loud rumbling and saw the bomb bay doors retracting inside the walls of the bomb bay. "Doors coming open . . . ready . . . ready . . . release . . . doors coming closed."

The Condor aircraft dropped free of the EB-52—because it was daylight, and they rarely flew daytime missions, they actually got to watch the amazing EB-52 roar overhead as they fell free. It was the part Briggs hated most because that sudden weightlessness and the seemingly uncontrollable swaying and pitching as the aircraft stabilized itself in the Megafortress's violent slipstream was hard on his stomach, but as soon as the Condor's little wings popped out and the mission-adaptive actuators throughout the craft steadied it, he felt better.

"Doing OK, Brake?" Briggs asked.

"No problem, sir," Brakeman replied. "You okay, sir?"

"I always get a little queasy at first. I'm okay."

"Welcome to the theater, Condor," Brigadier-General David Luger radioed from the High Technology Aerospace Weapons Center Battle Management Center at Elliott Air Force Base in Nevada. "This is Genesis Two. We've got you about eleven minutes to touchdown. Everyone doing OK?"

"Condor One good to go," Briggs said. "Condors, sound off."

"Condor Two, good to go," Brakeman responded.

"Condor Three, in the green," responded the first commando from the lead EB-52 battleship, Army National Guard Captain Charlie Turlock. Her partner, U.S. Army Specialist Maria Ricardo, answered a few moments later. "Sorry, Condor Four had to lose some of her breakfast," Turlock said. "We're both in the green—Four is just a little more green."

"Welcome to the club, Four," Briggs said.

"Here's the situation, guys: the Iranian Revolutionary Guards have ordered deployment, and we suspect a launch, of their ballistic missiles following the insurgent and regular army attacks on their headquarters base in Tehran," Dave said. "Stud One-Three attacked and destroyed two of three Shahab-

5 medium-range missiles in the south. We don't know what's going to happen with the third known -5 missile, but we think they're going to launch it as soon as they can.

"In the north, the situation is more dynamic," Dave went on. "The bad news first: we lost Stud One-One. We think a Russian ground-based laser got it."

"Oh, shit," Briggs murmured. He knew that "Nano" Benneton was aboard that flight and knew she would have died quickly and painlessly. "That has to be one big-ass laser to shoot down a small spaceplane in Earth orbit."

"Does the name 'Kavaznya' ring a bell, One?" Dave asked.

"You're shitting me?" Hal exclaimed. Hal knew the name well: he was the security officer in charge of the original EB-52 Megafortress project some twenty years earlier that was tasked to destroy the Russians' first ground-based anti-satellite and anti-missile laser at Kavaznya in eastern Siberia.

"I shit you not, One," Dave said. "The radar and tracking laser characteristics are the same. We haven't pinpointed the laser's location yet."

"I've got dibs on it," Hal said.

"You got it, One. Stud One-One did launch its weapons before it was hit, and all three SPAW missiles scored direct hits on the SA-10 and SA-12 command vehicles around the Strongbox. We know they have tactical battlefield optronic and infrared sensors, but we don't think they'll see you land. So far the landing zone is clear, but they know we're coming, so be ready for anything."

"They won't be ready for *us,*" Charlie Turlock said.

"We've updated your tactical charts on the current Shahab-2 and -3 TEL locations, and we'll keep you updated every time we get a new NIRTSat pass," Dave said. "They have significant numbers of security deployed out there. When their SAM command vehicles went up it appears most of their security guards ran off—whether they were redeployed back to the Strongbox, back to the ballistic missile units, or just ran off, we don't know, but we should assume that security around the Shahabs will be tighter than first briefed. That's the latest. Any questions?"

"Any chance anyone on Stud One-One ejected?" Hal asked.

"Sorry, One," Dave said. "No ejection seats."

"Damn," Hal muttered. "Find that laser, Genesis Two. I want it."

"We'll let you know, One. Six minutes to landing. Landing zone still looks clear, threat warning receivers are clear. Good luck, Condors."

The landing site was a small concrete landing strip, built during the Strongbox's construction but largely unused and unmanned since, about five miles from the southwesterly side of the cave complex. Hal was ready to take command of the Condor aircraft, but he knew it flew mostly by autopilot, even for takeoffs and landings. The aircraft flew a wide arc southwest of the Strongbox complex and between two known Shahab launch sites. The Condor's small turbojet engine was on but still at idle since their gliding descent was steep enough that they had plenty of speed. Hal knew the other Condor was coming in from a different direction but landing in the same direction on the runway. The electronic tactical display on the Condor's instrument panel showed both aircrafts' positions—and they were close, landing just a few seconds apart.

As usual, the landing was hard. Hal used the rudder pedals to keep the aircraft straight down the runway, easing off to the left side of the landing strip to give as much room as possible for Turlock's Condor. The mission-adaptive technology on the little aircraft immediately turned the entire fuselage and flight control surfaces into speed brakes, and the aircraft slowed quickly, making both crewmembers strain against their harnesses.

As soon as they stopped, Hal unstrapped and opened the hatch. "Establish security, now," he ordered, and he jumped out, followed closely by Brakeman. Hal handed Brakeman his electromagnetic rail gun, then began unpacking the rest of their gear from the back of the Condor.

Just then Brakeman heard on his battle armor's satellite transceiver: "Condor, Condor, vehicle heading your way, north side of the field!"

Brakeman immediately plugged the rail gun into the Tin Man armor power supply, activated it, and immediately used the battle armor's on-board radar and infrared sensors to sweep the area for threats. He saw the second Condor already rolling out from its landing . . .

. . . and at mid-field, still on the shoulder of the runway but just now coming onto the pavement, was a Russian-made ZSU-23/4 self-propelled anti-aircraft gun! "Contact!" he radioed. "Zeus-23-four!" He immediately leveled his rail gun, locked on, and fired, just as the quad 23-millimeter machine guns on the Iranian anti-aircraft vehicle opened fire on the second Condor. The gunfire stopped after less than a second, but Brakeman could hear crashing noises as the second Condor veered off the right side of the runway. Seconds later the ZSU-23/4 exploded in a massive ball of fire, with thousands of rounds of ammunition cooking off inside adding to the devastation.

Brakeman ran over to the second Condor and found Turlock and Ricardo climbing out. Hal Briggs joined them moments later. "You guys okay?" he asked.

"We're okay, but the cabin filled with smoke," Turlock said. "I pulled the fire handles, but the smoke is still coming out. Help us get our stuff out before this thing blows up." In seconds all four of them had emptied the second Condor and retreated back to the first aircraft.

"We're going to have company soon, so let's move out as quickly as possible," Hal said. "We'll forget about securing the Condors—this place will be crawling with security, and one man won't be able to hold them off. All four of us will go hunt down the Shahabs." He turned to the large boxy object from his aircraft. "CID Two, deploy." Immediately the device began to unfold itself . . . until it had grown into a nine-foot-tall robot, with armored skin surrounding hydraulic "muscles." "CID Two, pilot up," Hal spoke, and the robot assumed a leaning-forward stance, its arms straight back, its right leg extended backward forming a walkway. A small hatch had opened on the robot's back. Hal climbed up the leg and slid himself into the tight metallic-like fabric inside, slid his arms into the robot's "sleeves," and secured his head inside the visor and sealed breathing mask assembly.

"CID Two, activate," he spoke into the dark, suffocating mask. Seconds later he felt as if he was standing in his BDUs at the end of the runway. He looked at his hands and feet and saw the robot's mechanical fingers and feet moving, but it was his fingers and feet! "Man oh man, I love this thing!" he said.

Charlie Turlock had already boarded and activated her Cybernetic Infantry Device, and now she carried one of the weapons backpacks over to Hal and attached it onto his back. Hal didn't feel the weight one bit, but his electronic display showed him his weapon status: twenty-five rounds each of forty-millimeter armor-piercing and high-explosive grenades.

In the meantime, Brakeman had donned his battle armor's powered exoskeleton, which was a latticework of armored microhydraulic actuators that attached to his battle armor and gave him added strength, mobility, and speed. He looped two spare battery belts over Hal's shoulders, strapped ammo bags and spare battery packs to his back, and checked his electromagnetic rail gun. Hal picked up two more weapon backpacks—again, he didn't feel as if he was carrying a thing. "Ready to move out?"

"Ready," Charlie said. She too was carrying two weapons backpacks in her hands and spare battery packs on her shoulders. Ricardo had already donned her exoskeleton, loaded herself up with spare battery packs and ammo, and her rail gun was at the ready.

"Good luck, guys," Hal said. He extended an armored fist, and the others touched their fists to his. "I'll see you all at rally point Bravo." He gave an eye-point command. The barrel of his grenade launcher extended and leveled to firing position, and he chambered a high-explosive round. "Let's go kick some Iranian ass and get the hell out of here."

Their attack plan was simple: each commando had a circuit of about twenty to twenty-five miles in which to search for and attack targets. The last known location of Shahab transporter-erector-launchers was on their electronic charts, and the team followed the land navigation prompts in their visors to each launcher. Only about half of the estimated fifty to sixty missile launchers were displayed—they hoped they would come across the rest of them as they proceeded. Since one Tin Man commando didn't have a pre-planned circuit, Ricardo and Brakeman traveled together.

Using millimeter-wave radar images, visual enhancement, and datalinked images downloaded via satellite and transmitted between the other commandos, each unit was able to "see" all of the targets around them well before they approached them, and as soon as they detected new threats the rest of the team—as well as the men and women aboard Armstrong Space Station, the Megafortresses orbiting nearby, their headquarters back at Battle Mountain, and the persons watching the mission in the White House Situation Room—knew about them too. The commandos ignored dismounted security patrols and most light patrol vehicles because their weapons couldn't pentrate their armor—they just simply ran past them directly at the Shahab launchers.

Maria Ricardo found the first targets, a group of four Shahab-2 launchers arrayed about two hundred yards apart in a small gully, with their missiles already raised into launch position. "Jackpot," she crowed. "Four Shahabs ready to fire." She knew that about a dozen soldiers and at least one light vehicle was chasing her, but she didn't care. Ricardo simply lowered her electromagnetic rail gun to her hip, locked the millimeter-wave aiming emitter in with her helmet's aiming cue, and fired one round at each TEL. She didn't wait to see if her shots had any effect because she knew there were a lot to attack in a short space of time, but she didn't need to wait—shortly after leaping off, she heard four satisfyingly loud explosions behind her as each TEL detonated, ripped apart by the two-pound hypervelocity tungsten slugs she pumped into them.

"Got some too," Charlie reported. "Two Shahab-3 TELs. Look like they're fueled but not yet elevated." She fired one armor-piercing grenade at each launcher, then a high-explosive round at the maintenance and fueling vehicles still nearby. She could feel machine-gun bullets pinging off the CID's armored shell, but she ignored them. "Moving on. One, how's it going?"

"I feel like some fucking mythical avenging angel, that's how it's going, Three," Hal Briggs responded. He had come across another group of three Shahab-2s, also in firing position. He fired armor-piercing grenades at two of the launchers, causing their missiles to topple over and explode on the ground. "I'll show 'em how it's done now!" he cried out through the flaming wreckage around him. Hal ran over to the third TEL, put his spare backpacks down beside them, then stooped down, grasped the TEL, and lifted. The entire launcher and missile flopped over on its side, crumpled as if it was made out of cardboard, ruptured, and caught on fire. Hal picked up his spare backpacks and ran off before they exploded. "Come and get me, you bastards!" he shouted over the radio. He stopped, turned toward the Iranian Revolutionary Guards soldiers pursuing him, and raised the backpacks triumphantly. "Come and get me, assholes, because I'm coming to get you!"

"Condor, exfil point Bravo loks like it's compromised," Kai Raydon radioed from Armstrong Space Station.

"We're sending Dasher to point Foxtrot." "Dasher" was the MV-32 PAVE DASHER tilt-jet transport aircraft that would come in to pick up the four Condor commandos. The jet variant of the MV-22 Osprey tilt-rotor transport, the MV-32 was larger, faster, more heavily armed, and could carry more troops or equipment. It had been deployed secretly to Iraq to assist the Air Battle Force ground ops team, but now that the Condor aircraft were going to be abandoned the MV-32 was now tasked with picking up the commandos after their mission.

The four commandos all reported successful raids and clean kills so far . . . but about three-quarters of the way through their circuits, they saw Shahab missiles rising through the sky. "Faster, guys," Hal ordered. "We're letting some get away!"

"You can't get them all, One," Patrick radioed from the White House Situation Room. "Do the best you can. I want all of you back in one piece. Remember you've got an extra three miles to go to reach Foxtrot. Watch your ammo and batteries."

ABOARD HEADBANGER FIVE-ZERO, OVER EASTERN IRAQ

That Same Time

A tone sounded and a blinking icon appeared on the mission commander's supercockpit display. "Missiles airborne," Air Force Reserve Brigadier-General Daren Mace announced. Mace was the operations officer and second in command of the Air Battle Force at Battle Mountain Air Reserve Base. The twenty-four-year veteran Air Force navigator-bombardier leaned forward in his ejection seat excitedly. "Looks like Four-Zero picked up some missile launches." He quickly designated the missiles, identified as Shahab-3 ballistic missiles, on the screen. "There's your steering, Margaret. Go get 'em!"

"Got it, General," Air Force Reserve Captain Margaret "Mugs" Lewis responded. She was more than twenty years younger than her mission commander, flying her first operational mission with the Air Battle Force, but she was a veteran B-1B Lancer aircraft commander and knew how to make the big supersonic bomber dance. But every minute aboard this variant of her beloved B-1 known as the EB-1C Vampire was a delight for her.

The sleek, supersonic Vampire bomber's three bomb bays were completely loaded for this cover mission. The forward and middle bomb bays were combined into one and contained a rotary launcher with eight ABM-3 Lancelot air-launched anti-ballistic missiles. Resembling the Patriot anti-aircraft missile, the Lancelot was designed to destroy ballistic missiles in the boost, mid-course, or terminal phase. It had a range of almost one hundred miles, a top speed of Mach six, and a precision terminal seeker radar as well as guidance from the Vampire bomber's powerful attack radar.

The Vampire's aft bomb bay was loaded with four AGM-177 Wolverine cruise missiles. The 2,000-pound weapons had a small turbojet engine, a maximum speed of just 300 knots, and a maximum range of only 50 miles. But the cruise missile was special because of its three weapons bays, each containing a different type of submunition—anti-armor, anti-personnel, and area-denial cluster bombs—and its millimeter-wave and imaging infrared seekers that could locate, identify, track, attack, assess, and even re-attack its own targets. Finally, the little Wolverine cruise missile could attack one last target before its fuel ran out by kamikaziing into it and detonating its 50-pound warhead.

The laser-projection heads-up display in front of Lewis depicted a sequence of squares angling off to the right, and so she steered the EB-1C Vampire until the aircraft icon was right inside the squares. The squares represented a "highway in the sky" route computed by the attack computers to get the bomber into perfect attack position, and a graphical bar chart told her what power to set to reach the optimal launch point on time, so she pushed the throttles up until the bars matched. "Excellent, Captain," Daren said. "About ten seconds for a LADAR launch fix."

At the proper time the Vampire's LADAR, or laser radar, automatically activated. The LADAR used high-speed electronically scanned laser beams to "draw" a picture of everything in the sky, on the ground, or even in space for two hundred miles quickly and with very high precision, presenting it on their super-cockpit displays in incredible detail. "LADAR down," Daren said. "Lancelot missiles counting down . . . ten seconds . . . doors coming open . . . missile one away . . . missile two away . . . doors closed. Okay, we're shifting targets to the launchers."

The heads-up display shifted, and Lewis turned the bomber to follow. She could have easily let the computer fly the attack runs, but this was actual combat, not a test flight, and she was really enjoying herself. "Coming on release point . . . fifteen seconds . . . ten seconds, doors coming open . . . missile one away . . . missile two away, doors coming closed. Okay, Mugs, left turn back to the patrol orbit and I'll take a look at the Wolverine's target area. We'll check our fuel state once we're out of Iran."

The Lancelot missiles, similar to Patriot PAC-3 ground-launched anti-aircraft missiles, steered themselves to an intercept "basket" using course and altitude information uploaded from the Vampire bomber moments before launch. The missile received course updates during its flight from brief bursts of the Vampire's LADAR and from datalinks received from satellites and other attackers tracking the Shahab-3 missiles. Two seconds before reaching the intercept "basket," a Ka-band pulse-Doppler radar in the nose of the Lancelot missile activated, immediately detected the Shahab-3s, and steered itself to a precision kill.

The Wolverine cruise missiles similarly steered themselves to their patrol area by navigation information from the Vampire bomber. Once in its patrol orbit, the missile activated its millimeter-wave radars and imaging infrared sensors and started transmitting detailed images of the target area. The millimeter-wave radars detected, evaluated, then precisely measured any hard metallic objects in the target area and compared the objects to a catalog of objects in its internal memory.

When it found an object it thought was a Shahab rocket launcher, it reported it to the Vampire crew. "We got a couple launchers," Daren announced. He switched his supercockpit display to the imaging infrared picture. Sure enough, it was a transporter-erector-launcher, with the rocket erector cradle just being lowered and a reload vehicle maneuvering beside it, ready to load another rocket. On the other side of the launcher was a fuel truck, ready to refuel it. "Committing the Wolverine to attack."

Daren entered commands into the missile control computers, and the Wolverine missile departed its patrol orbit and headed toward the launcher. It took about six minutes for the missile to reach the spot. As it overflew the launch site, it ejected several small canisters from one of its bomb bays, stabilized by a parachute. Each canister had an infrared sensor that detected and locked onto the heat from the launcher and service vehicles. At a pre-determined altitude above the ground the canisters detonated, releasing white-hot slugs of molten copper flying at the speed of sound that easily pierced the engine compartments of each vehicle, causing explosions and fires that quickly destroyed them. The Wolverine missile then turned and headed back to its patrol orbit to wait for more attack instructions.

Back in their patrol orbit over Iraq east of Kirkuk, Mace and Lewis checked their systems and fuel status. "AC's in the green," Margaret said. She was still hand-flying the aircraft, and Daren had to admit she was good—she was able to check her switches, her oxygen, and all of her instruments and still keep the Vampire flying rock-steady.

"Everything's in the green over here," Daren said. "One of the Wolverines was shot down, but the other one is still in its patrol orbit and has about half of its submunitions. We still have two Wolverines and six Lancelots. You did good, Mugs. You handle the jet well."

"It's easier in real life than the missions we have in the simulator," Lewis commented, taking a swig of orange juice. "It's like a big video game, except I'm controlling a four-hundred-thousand-plus-pound supersonic jet worth billions of dollars instead of a little game controller. Sometimes I forget we're in a combat zone."

"Oh, it's real enough—never forget where you are or what you're doing," Daren cautioned her. "The minute you get complacent, something will jump up and bite your ass." An alert beeped in his helmet, and he immediately switched his multi-function display to a wider view of northern Iran and then zoomed in on Tehran again.

"More Shahab-3s heading west?"

"We got missiles inflight, but they're heading east-northeast toward Tehran. The bastards are shooting at their own people! Looks like Nancy will be getting some shots in today too."

OVER THE CASPIAN SEA, TWO HUNDRED MILES NORTH OF TEHRAN, IRAN

That Same Time

"Missile contact, Hamadan, heading northeast . . . second missile in flight, same heading!" Air Force Reserve First Lieutenant Greg "Huck" Dannon shouted excitedly. Dannon was an experienced B-52 copilot, but like many of the crews at Battle Mountain, this was his first operational mission. He got his nickname because he looked like all the drawings of Huckleberry Finn anyone had ever seen, and appeared just as young. "I . . . we should . . . I mean . . ."

"Relax, Huck, relax," the AL-52 Dragon's aircraft commander, Air Force Brigadier-General Nancy Cheshire, said, straightening up in her seat as if just awakening from a nap. The veteran pilot was some sort of bionic crewdog: even though crewmembers were allowed to wear headsets while in high-altitude cruise, she always wore her flight helmet, gloves, and cold-weather jacket; always kept her oxygen mask on except when drinking water (and only water) and always kept her clear visor down; never ate any meals on board, and never had to; and never took a nap on board an aircraft, and never had to. "Let the systems do the work—you need to keep calm and monitor everything carefully."

Cheshire was the commander of all of the Air Battle Force's modified B-52 bomber fleet at Battle Mountain Air Reserve Base, a grand total of six planes—all of which were involved in operations near Iran—plus a steadily growing fleet of eight QA-45C "Hunter" unmanned stealth bombers undergoing final flight tests at Dreamland before becoming fully operational. Cheshire, a soft-spoken and very laid-back test pilot turned wing commander, was the first female test pilot at Dreamland before being chosen to command the Air Battle Force's B-52 bombers at Battle Mountain.

Although she was checked out in every aircraft under her command at Battle Mountain, plus every aircraft that had been flown at Dreamland for the past ten years, her favorite aircraft was by far the AL-52 Dragon. This Dragon—the only one that survived the American Holocaust and the Air Battle Force's counterattack over Russia—was the latest variant of the B-52 bomber tested at Dreamland and deployed at Battle Mountain. Originally a test-bed aircraft only, the Dragon carried only one weapon, but it was one of the most powerful weapons ever fired from an aircraft: a three-megawatt plasma-pumped electronic laser. Steered by an adaptive-optics mirror system in the nose, the laser beam fired from the Dragon had a maximum range of about three hundred miles and could attack and destroy or disable targets in space, in the sky, and even on the ground.

"Make sure the computer has designated the targets . . . there, that's what that symbol means, remember?" Nancy prompted her mission commander. "Do a quick scan for any other threats—don't assume the computer will always pick the right targets. A fighter a hundred miles away always has priority . . ."

"A fighter? Where?"

"Just an example, Huck," Nancy said patiently. Man, this guy was skittish—he either needed a few more combat sorties under his belt, or a roll in the hay. "The targeting computer is programmed to go after ballistic missiles first, but if a fighter is nearby, even if it's a long way away, it's a bigger threat in my book. You also want to make sure it hasn't designated any friendly aircraft or missiles. The system is good, but it's not foolproof. Understand?"

"Yes, ma'am."

"A simple 'yes' is good, Huck," Nancy said. She was only in her early forties, but these young kids in the force today made her feel much older sometimes. "Okay, it looks like the coast is clear, and the Dragon has the two top priority targets. This indication"—she pointed to the upper left corner of Dannon's supercockpit display—"tells you that the targeting laser has already locked onto both missiles and has measured them and the surrounding atmosphere for attenuation compensation. Dragon does that automatically but not continuously unless you tell it to. Will it fire the main laser automatically?"

"No . . . I mean, yes, because we've given consent and . . . no, wait . . ."

"You had it right the first time, Huck: no, it will normally not fire the main laser automatically," Nancy said, starting to lose a little patience. She always insisted on flying with the most inexperienced crewmembers, but sometimes their inexperience and nervousness-induced dumbness aggravated her. "Man-in-the-loop, remember? You have to have consent, pre-attack checklist complete by both crewmembers, targeting lock either manual or auto, and give the order to fire. The only exception is with failure of both supercockpit displays or with other kinds of serious malfunctions, when the Dragon shifts to self-defense mode. The system will . . ."

"Uh, ma'am, shouldn't . . . shouldn't we attack now?"

"What's the missile flight time remaining until impact, Huck?"

Dannon checked his display. "Uh . . . one minute forty-one seconds."

"Correct. And what's our range to target?"

"One hundred ninety-three nautical miles."

"Good. And what's the speed of light?"

"One hundred eighty-six thousand miles per second."

"Correct. And how long is a typical laser engagement?"

"Six seconds on an intercontinental ballistic-missile-sized target—a little less with a tactical ballistic missile—plus turret rotation and mirror focusing time. About ten seconds total."

"Good. So how long will it take for our laser beam to hit and destroy the Shahab-2, assuming it was an ICBM-class target?"

Dannon paused, but only for a moment: Nancy was fascinated with the guy's phenomenal ability to do complex calculations in his head. "Ten-point-zero-zero-one-zero-five seconds."

"So what's your hurry, Huck?" Nancy asked. "You gotta relax, MC." She patted him playfully on the shoulder, feeling the tension in his muscles. He was hopeless. "Okay, Huck, kill the suckers."

Dannon took a deep breath and touched the green "ATTACK" soft key on his supercockpit display. "Attack commencing, stop attack," the computer spoke, and the soft key turned into a red "STOP ATTACK" button. Seconds later they could feel a slight rumbling beneath their feet as the mirror turret in the nose of the AL-52 unstowed, disrupting the airflow around the aircraft. There was no other indication that the attack was underway—no cool science-fictiony laser sounds, no beam of light slicing through the sky, just a small blinking "L" indicator on their supercockpit displays. Seconds later the "L" stopped blinking as the computer refocused on the second missile, and then the "L" began to blink once again. Finally they heard the turbulence rumbling under their feet as the turret stowed itself.

"Missiles destroyed," Nancy said, so calmly and self-assuredly that Dannon looked at her to see if she wasn't hypoxic or semi-conscious. "Good work, Huck." She widened the range on their supercockpit displays to check for any additional launches. None were detected, so she sat back in her seat. "Man, I love this job."

ON THE GROUND NORTHWEST OF HAMADAN, IRAN

That Same Time

It was the most exhilarating twenty minutes of his life, Hal Briggs thought as he continued his run through his assigned circuit. Just one more Shahab-2 launch site, about three miles ahead, and he could head to the exfiltration point. He had destroyed about sixteen launchers and scores of other vehicles with the incredible Cybernetic Infantry Device's weapon backpacks, and a few simply by the sheer strength and speed of the CID unit itself—and he was sure he had killed several Revolutionary Guards troops he had encountered at the launch sites or along the way by merely frightening them to death.

"Condor One, Odin," Colonel Kai Raydon aboard Armstrong Space Station called via the secure satellite link.

"Go ahead, Odin," Hal replied.

"You look like you're having more fun than a human should be allowed to have, son."

"I shoulda got me one of these things years ago!" Hal exclaimed happily.

"Well, I got a present for you, One, so don't waste all your ammo or power—I think we found the laser."

"Great! Load me up and I'm on it." Seconds later Hal studied the route to the new target. It was at a military airfield about twenty miles east of the Strongbox, twenty miles northeast of Hamadan, just west of the town of Kabudar Ahang. It was a very large complex, with two three-mile-long parallel runways and one two-mile-long runway roughly perpendicular to the first. Satellite images showed a "Christmas tree" alert parking area on the north side with hangars for eight fighters; a large weapon storage area on the northeast side; and the main part of the base on the east side, with barracks and housing for several thousand personnel and ramp space for about a hundred aircraft.

"Check out the big revetment on the southwest side, One," Raydon said. On the southwest side of the base midway along the southernmost parallel runway was a large aircraft parking area surrounded by twenty-foot-high earth and sand walls. "They made a mistake and operated the radar just as one of our recon satellites crossed overhead and got a direct bearing on it—the radar is sitting in the parking lot near that building southwest of the revetments. We got some excellent pics of the vehicles in the revetment, and I think it's the laser. Looks like they made the sucker road-mobile. Genesis, are you looking at these pics?"

"Affirmative," Patrick McLanahan responded from the White House Situation Room. "I'm downloading the pics to a higher-res monitor so I can zoom in and study it closer. But you could be on to something, Odin. If they made the Kavaznya laser mobile, they could set it up anywhere on earth and threaten any aircraft and any satellite with it, and it'd be impossible to locate. But I'm also concerned about them 'mistakenly' turning on the radar—that could be a trick to lure us into a trap."

"We'll be in position in about ninety minutes to get a moderate oblique ISAR shot of it," Raydon said. "In three hours I can get a perfect overhead shot.

The NIRTSats are good, but we need better resolution to be sure."

"We're not going to wait three hours, guys—I can be there in forty minutes or less," Hal said. "Condor Two, if you're up for it, I want you to finish up my circuit. Just one target left."

"Roger, One," Brakeman acknowledged. "I'm switching my circuit to Condor One's . . . got it, I'm on the way."

"One, this is Three, wait up," Charlie Turlock radioed. "I'll cover you. I've got one more launch site to go and then I'll rendezvous with you. Two and Four can finish their circuits, get picked up at Foxtrot, and then meet us at point Mike for exfil."

"Three, I'll be heading toward the airfield, but I'm not going to wait up," Briggs said. "I've got one partial and one full backpack and battery pack. Looks like the whole south side of the airfield is wide open space. I'm going in."

"It smells like a trap to me, guys," Patrick McLanahan said. "I see all kinds of buildings, gullies, and revetments south of the perimeter fence—they can hide an entire armored battalion in there. Remember the Russians have been helping the Iranians the whole time—we might as well be fighting the Holocaust all over again in Iran."

"Condor One, this is Stud One-Three," Hunter Noble radioed. "I'm beginning deorbit procedures and I'll be on the ground in fifteen minutes. I'll be rearmed and airborne again in less than an hour, and thirty minutes after that I'll place a spread of SPAWs on that spot. You don't need to risk it—I'll take it out for you."

"Negative, One-One," Hal said. "I can be there and out by the time you launch. I've been kicking Iranian ass all morning—I'll take out this laser site for breakfast and join you back at the Lake for a steak dinner celebration tonight."

"Condor One, don't be a hero," Boomer radioed. "I can take it. Assemble your troops and get the hell out of there."

"Hey, stud, mind your manners," Hal said. As soon as he saw Brakeman on his electronic tactical display heading for the last Shahab launch site, he started running toward the Hamadan military airfield. "I'm taking out that laser emplacement. If I miss or didn't get it all, you can clean it up for me—but I'm not gonna miss. Worry about that last Shahab-5 site you missed instead. Deal? Condor One out."

It took less than thirty minutes for Hal Briggs to reach Hamadan Air Base. The entire south side of the base was alfalfa fields and olive and date orchards, with a few rocky hills scattered about—Hal could see the base's perimeter fence from five miles away. The scanners aboard the Cybernetic Infantry Device robot detected all of the outbuildings, irrigation pipes and pumphouses, guard shacks, the perimeter fence, the mobile radar vehicle, and the large building next to the revetment where the mobile laser was placed. Hal was able to compare the latest NIRTSat imagery with his telescopic view of the actual area and was able to correlate everything. "I've got a good eyeball on the objective area," Hal radioed. "I can't see the laser yet, but I see the radar and the few troops they have guarding the place. Piece of cake, guys. Are you guys getting all this?"

"We're getting it, One," Patrick responded. The sensor data from Hal Briggs's CID unit was being uplinked to the Air Battle Force's network and to Silver Tower, so it could be shared by virtually the entire American military. "I can see a few patrols nearby, and those buildings look like they can hold several platoons and armored vehicles. The other Condor units have completed their circuits and are awaiting pickup at Foxtrot. Hold off for twenty minutes and they can join you to assault the area together."

"In twenty minutes I can polish off these turkeys and be at point Mike by the time you guys arrive," Hal said. "I'm going in. Meet me at Mike. Condor One, moving out." He took one last scan of the area, made sure his grenade launchers were chambered and ready to fire, and dashed off.

Hal hit thirty miles an hour across the fields and orchards, and within a minute he was within sight of the perimeter fence. His sensors picked up movement to his right—a Russian-made BMD light infantry support vehicle, firing its puny 7.62-millimeter coaxial machine guns at him. Hal fired one high-explosive round and silenced it quickly and cleanly . . .

. . . and he immediately detected and struck two more BMD vehicles to his left, with one 70-millimeter tank round missing him by several yards and an AT-3 anti-tank missile whizzing just a few yards away from his head. He picked up speed, reaching almost fifty miles an hour now. The BMDs and their weapons seemed as if they were standing still. He hit another BMD even before the aged Soviet-era light tank could get a shot off at him.

"That was three Russian armored vehicles on you, One!" Patrick radioed. "I think it's a trap! Back on out of there and wait for the others."

"Helicopters!" Raydon shouted over the command channel. "Two . . . three . . . four helicopters lifting off from the base, heading your way, One!"

"Bug out, Hal!" Patrick shouted over the satellite link. "It's a trap! Get out of there!" Hal could start to pick up the masses of armored vehicles and aircraft converging on him, but he was determined not to let the laser site stay intact. Just two more miles, less than three minutes at his current speed, and he could wipe out every standing building, vehicle, or human within range of him . . .

A hail of high-velocity, heavy-mass shells hit him from the right side, unexpectedly toppling him over. It was the first time in his short stint as pilot of a CID that he had ever been down on the ground. He wasn't hurt, and his systems seemed fully functional, but he was down—that was something he was not accustomed to. He immediately got to his feet, spotted the weapon system that had hit him—an ancient ZSU-23/4 quad 23-millimeter mobile anti-aircraft gun system, elevated down low to engage him—and he fired two high-explosive rounds into it, blowing it clean off its tracks.

"Hal, get out of there, now!" Patrick shouted. "We can take the site from the air! Get out!"

Hal took one more scan and thought he detected the laser itself inside the revetment. It resembled a Shahab-3 mobile missile launcher but was at least twice as large, with four service vehicles nearby with umbilical cables attached to it. "I've got the laser in sight, Genesis!" Hal called out. "Range less than one mile! I'm going in!"

"Hal, I said pull out!" Patrick shouted. "Your ammo is low! Withdraw now and switch backpacks! Do it, now!"

Hal fired two fragmentation and then two high-explosive grenades at the laser unit . . . which depleted the grenade stores on the backpack. He commanded the spent backpack to drop away. As he ran at almost top speed, he swung his last remaining grenade-launcher backpack off his arm and onto his back . . . but running so quickly, he couldn't make it latch into place. He jumped the base perimeter fence in one effortless leap and landed in a low crouching position, less than three hundred yards from the laser site. He readjusted the backpack, felt it latch into place, and received a good "READY" indication in his electronic visor. He quickly aimed at the laser truck . . .

. . . and at that instant he was hit by an SA-19 "Grison" missile from a Russian 2S6M Tunguska self-propelled air defense vehicle. The SA-19 was a radar-guided anti-aircraft missile with a secondary anti-tank role. It had a two-stage solid-motor missile with a maximum velocity of a half-mile per second and a ten-pound high-explosive/fragmentary warhead with a contact and laser-triggered proximity fuze. Hal was blown clear off his feet and twenty feet in the air by the tremendous force of the hit.

"Hal!" Patrick shouted. "Do you read me? Hal!"

"I'm . . . I'm okay," Hal said. He saw and heard several warning messages and tones, but his dazed mind couldn't sort them all out. He climbed unsteadily to his feet. He could feel cannon shells peppering his body, but they weren't doing a fraction of the damage as the . . .

. . . and at that instant he was hit by a second SA-19 missile, fired from less than a half-mile away. He was blown head over heels in a cloud of fire and smoke. He was still alive, but his electronic visor was dark, and he could barely hear, let alone decipher, all the warning tones beeping and buzzing in his helmet. He struggled to his hands and knees, trying to command the CID system to clear the faults and let him see again. More cannon fire raked his back, and he felt the concussion as the grenade launcher backpack blew apart.

"Hal, hang on!" Patrick shouted. "PAVE DASHER is on the way, ETE five minutes. Hang on!"

"No . . . no, don't come near here," Hal breathed. He couldn't make any of his limbs move. For the first time since training and employing the Cybernetic Infantry Device, he felt like he actually was all along—a human being riding inside a hydraulically operated machine, instead of a running, killing, destroying, avenging superman. "I got hit by some big-ass gun and missile thing, a Tunguska I think. It'll chew up the PAVE DASHER into little bits for sure. Don't let it come near here, Muck."

"No! We're bringing in the Vampires! They'll take out all the air defenses with the Wolverines and the PAVE DASHER will be able to cruise in and pick you up. Hang in there, Hal. They're just a few minutes out."

"Hey, Muck," Hal said weakly. "We've had one hell of a ride, haven't we?" He could hear Patrick yelling something over the satellite link, but that too was fading, getting darker and weaker by the moment. "We kicked some ass together, didn't we, boss? I remember . . . I remember when we first met, Muck. You were the clueless captain, no idea what was happening or what you got volunteered for. I took pity on you, man."

"Hal! Can you hear me?" he could barely hear Patrick yelling. "The Wolverines are sixty seconds out, and the Dasher is three minutes out! Hang in there, buddy! We're coming to get you!"

"Now look at you, you sorry mick genius. You're the boss, Muck, the fucking guru, feared and hated even more than old man Elliott himself." Hal noticed that his electronic visor was working again, and he also found he could raise himself up by his arms. He looked toward the revetment . . . and saw that the object they thought was the laser that had destroyed Nano

Benneton and the XR-A9 Black Stallion was actually just a trailer loaded with steel pipe and tubes. They had moved the laser long ago, probably right after they had commenced their attacks on the Strongbox's deployed Shahab missiles, and put this clever decoy in its place.

Hal's arms lost all their strength, and he rolled over on his back in the hard sandy soil. The 2S6M Tunguska anti-aircraft vehicle was about fifty yards away, its twin 30-millimeter cannons and two loaded SA-19 missile launchers aimed right at him. Hal used the remaining few watts of power left in the CID robot to raise one hand and flash the Tunguska his right middle finger . . . seconds before the cannons opened fire and forever turned out his lights.

The Wolverine cruise missile made short work of the Tunguska and all other Iranian defenders within five miles of the spot seconds later, and minutes afterward the MV-32 PAVE DASHER tilt-jet aircraft swooped in. Charlie Turlock herself ran out of the jet's rear cargo ramp, quickly found the shredded remains, and carried him aboard. With two Wolverine cruise missiles providing cover from anymore defenders from the base, the MV-32 lifted off and headed west toward the Iraqi border.

CHAPTER 9

THE WHITE HOUSE OVAL OFFICE, WASHINGTON, D.C.

"The situation in Iran is far more complex and dangerous than the media is portraying, Mr. President," Director of Central Intelligence Gerald Vista said. He was briefing the President and his national security team on recent events in Iran following McLanahan's operation the day before. "All the media seems to be showing are happy Iranians celebrating the destruction of the Revolutionary Guards. But it's not quite that simple.

"The army is patrolling the streets of the major cities, and there is a dusk-to-dawn curfew, with violators being shot on sight. The curfew was set up because of reports of Revolutionary Guards soldiers in plain clothes, and displaced al-Quds and komiteh irregulars—the religious and government enforcers among the people—roaming the streets gunning down celebrating civilians and ambushing army patrols and checkpoints. There are already reports of terrorists, jihadists, and Islamic soldiers of fortune on their way to Iran from all over the world to help restore the theocracy.

"General Buzhazi has instituted martial law in Iran, but it's doubtful if he has control of more than a handful of neighborhoods in Tehran, let alone control of the entire country," Vista went on. "There are reports of squabbling between Buzhazi, military chief of staff Yassini, and members of the various former monarchies of Iran."

"So we have an insurgency and possibly a three-way civil war brewing in Iran," the President summarized, "with no consensus on who should govern. Meanwhile the theocrats, Islamists, and old government are in hiding and could pop up any time. It's Iraq all over again." No one had any comments after that last remark—it was too terrible to contemplate. "Any idea where Mohtaj and the Revolutionary Guards high command might be hiding?"

"Tehran was the base of support for all branches of the government, of course, with Qom the choice of the clerics," Vista explained. "We'll check all the major cities, but I'd put my money on Mashhad, in the east near the Turkmeni border. Mashhad is the second largest city; it's an important religious city because of the Emam Reza Shrine; and it has an extensive military infrastructure because it was the city farthest away from the fighting during the Iran-Iraq War. The population sextuples during the annual pilgrimage to the shrine, and that would be an easy way to get recruits and smuggle in supplies."

"I don't think we should be hunting down the old government in any case, Mr. President," Vice President Hershel said. "Let the United Nations and the Iranian people deal with it."

There was a nod of agreement around the Oval Office. "That's fine by me," the President said, obviously relieved. "We'll pledge our full support for a peaceful resolution to the conflict and full restoration of democratic institutions and the rule of law, yada yada yada." He rubbed his eyes. "I just want this Iranian thing to be over with, and I certainly don't want to get bogged down in another 'peacekeeping' mission in the Middle East. Patrick? Got all your guys pulled out of there yet?"

"As we speak, sir," Patrick responded. "The last patrol plane should be refueling over the Persian Gulf on its way back to Diego Garcia. But we still haven't recovered the body of Captain Lefferts or our missing equipment . . ."

"As soon as we make contact with Buzhazi or whoever's in charge out there, we'll make sure we expect them to locate Lefferts and our equipment and turn them over to us immediately—it's the least they can do for all the blood and treasure we spent helping them," the President said. Patrick nodded but said nothing. "Sorry if that's not the answer you're looking for, Patrick, but I think we need to back off so hopefully things will simmer down out there." The President turned to the Secretary of Defense. "Joe, I think the Air Force and Navy can keep an eye on things out there—from a distance, a great distance. I want to send McLanahan's boys back to their sandbox."

"We certainly can, Mr. President," Secretary of Defense Gardner said. "I'll brief you and General Sparks on my plan later on this morning."

"Thank you." The President turned to Patrick once again. "Sorry about your loss, Patrick. Briggs was with you almost from the beginning, wasn't he?"

"Yes, sir, he was. He was a good friend and a real asset to everyone at Dreamland and Battle Mountain."

"I'm sorry about the loss of the second spaceplane, too," the President said. "But your losses take nothing away from the job your people did over Iran. I want you to pass along my congratulations and sincerest thanks to everyone out there in Nevada. They took on a hard job and did brilliantly."

"I'll do that, Mr. President, thank you," Patrick said. "But I still want to address the future long-range strike mission. I still believe space is the answer, and I'd like to . . ."

"Hold on, Patrick, hold on," the President said. "I need a little time to recover from the fight, and I want to get the thoughts and reports from everyone before I put the topic of the long-range strike fleet back on the front burner. Your spaceplanes did well, Patrick, but we still lost two-thirds of the fleet in battle. We have to be ready to explain why before Congress will authorize us to build more of them."

"Frankly, General, I'd say your modified B-1 and B-52 bombers and those CID robots did exceptionally well out there," Joint Chiefs of Staff chairman General William Glenbrook commented. "Maybe you should be looking at building up a force of those things instead."

"The small satellite fleet and that resurrected space station did well too," National Security Adviser Jonas Sparks added. "I liked sitting in my office and listening in and watching the battle take place on my computer screen. Your spaceplanes are good, General, but they're too high-tech for my taste."

"Maybe when us old farts are out of the way you can sell them, Patrick," the President said, "but as long as our generation is in charge, I think we'll have to find something else to fly. But I want everyone's reports first and then we'll reopen this discussion. Anything else?" He didn't wait for a response, but got to his feet, prompting everyone else to rise. "Thank you all very much."

As usual, the Vice President and Chief of Staff hung back as everyone else lined up to leave. The President shook hands with everyone as they departed; Patrick, being the youngest and lowest-ranking staffer, went last. After he shook hands with him, the President said, "I'm sending you back to Dreamland, Patrick. I spoke with the staff, and the bottom line is that you made too many folks look bad and stepped on too many toes, to put it mildly, for there to be a suitable work environment here, even with you in the basement. I don't expect you to stay out of trouble out there, but until January twentieth, try to keep me informed of things before you proceed to set the world on fire, okay?"

"Of course, Mr. President. Thank you."

"I hope your son and the ticker are doing okay. Take care of them both."

"I will, sir." The President turned to Carl Minden, indicating he was done with Patrick; he purposely also did not turn to the Vice President, leaving her free to depart as well, which she did.

The Vice President and Patrick walked together without speaking until they reached her office and closed the door. She walked over to her chair in the meeting area in the center of the office, but Patrick did not follow her there. "Patrick, I'm sorry about Hal," she said. "I liked him. He was a good guy. I want to be there for his service."

"Of course. Thank you. It'll be held at HAWC."

"With Elliott and all the other heroes from that place. Good. That's appropriate." There was an uncomfortable silence. "So you'll be heading back to Dreamland. When will you be back?"

"I won't be back, Maureen."

She looked unhappy and a little embarrassed, but not surprised. She lowered her head. "How did you find out?"

"About you and Joe Gardner? Hal discovered it," Patrick said. "He investigated all the possible leaks from the White House and Pentagon to Senator Barbeau's office. I thought it was Minden, but Hal knew it was you. I think he told me, but I didn't—couldn't—believe him." He turned toward the door. "Good-bye, Miss Vice President. Have a nice day."

"You're not going to even ask me why, are you?" Maureen Hershel exploded. "You're going to leave and go back to the Nevada desert without even looking back, despite all the years we've been together. That pretty much sums up the bottom line of our relationship."

"I think I know why, Maureen," Patrick said, still without looking back at her. "I think I knew it ever since you realized I didn't want to give up my career because of my heart condition. You wanted me to be with you. You didn't care if leaving military or government service would make me unhappy."

"You're wrong, McLanahan," Maureen shot back. "It was way before your heart thing, way before you rigged up your own self-monitoring thing that everyone bought off on. It was the flying in the spaceplane, hanging out at Dreamland, being with your boys and girls out there instead of wanting to be with me. I wanted something more than a part-time relationship."

"So you picked Gardner? Gardner is your full-time partner . . . when he's not screwing Barbeau or his wife or the dozens of other women he's got on the side."

"But he was there for me," Hershel said, almost pleading. "That's something you never could do—even when you were with me, you were always somewhere else. At least Joe paid attention to me and treated me like I needed to be treated . . ."

"And we both know what that is, now, don't we?"

"Hey, buster, don't give me advice on how to live a good and proper life!" Hershel spat. "We both know how close you've come to being in prison for the rest of your life! Not even the President of the United States can keep you under control—but that's not the President's problem, it's yours. Even your son can't keep you from unnecessarily risking your life or breaking the rules for your own selfish, nihilistic reasons." That remark seemed to hit Patrick like a physical blow, and he opened the office door.

"I'm not finished with you, mister!" Hershel snapped behind him. "You're pathetic! You're a disgrace! The only one besides yourself who could possibly be proud of what you do was Brad Elliott, and look where he is now!" He could still hear her yelling something as he walked out of her office suite and headed for the exit.

"Dad!" he heard moments later. He hadn't even noticed his ten-year-old son Bradley sitting in the reception area. He came running over to him and gave him a tight embrace, then attempted to pick him up as he always did when they hugged—not too much longer, Patrick knew, he would be able to do it too. "Miss Parks said you were in a meeting with the President and the Vice President. Can we see them? I want to say hi."

"Not now, Brad. They're all busy." He looked a little dejected, but nodded. They started walking downstairs for the exit. "It's pretty late for you to be up, big guy. Did you have dinner yet?"

"Yes. But I didn't have dessert. Can we go to Andrews for dessert? They have the best ice cream there."

"I think it's too late for ice cream, Brad. But we'll go out to Andrews tomorrow morning for breakfast. How about that?"

"Good. Are we going flying?"

"Yes."

"Where?"

"Back to Las Vegas." He looked for any hint of excitement or disappointment, but didn't really see either.

"What about school?"

"You get some time off until I sign you up for school in Las Vegas."

Again, little reaction. Maybe he was getting accustomed to being displaced, having little time to say goodbye to friends and having to face the challenge of finding new friends, just like millions of other kids of military parents had to deal with for most of their youth.

They exited the West Wing and headed toward the parking garage without saying anything else except "good night" to the uniformed Secret Service officers.

Patrick had no reason to fear walking the streets of the District of Columbia late at night: since the American Holocaust, there was plenty of federal and District police, and even some National Guard still on the streets, day and night. Patrick felt Brad lagging behind a bit. "Carry me, Dad?" a sleepy voice asked.

He hadn't asked that in years, or if he did Patrick had to say "no." Bradley was not heavy but he was tall, past Patrick's chin and almost to his mouth when standing together. At the very least, carrying him would have been unwieldy. But he stooped down, scooped him up, and cradled him in his arms. "Thanks, Dad," Bradley said, and fell asleep immediately.

For the first time, perhaps in a long time, Patrick found it easy to keep his mind focused on this important task, rather than the dozens of equally important ones awaiting him.

Epilogue

ARMSTRONG SPACE STATION, OVER EAST-CENTRAL TURKEY

Three Hours Later

"Crossing the Iranian horizon . . . now," Colonel Kai Raydon said. Almost the entire crew of Armstrong Space Station was floating near the radar technicians and displays as the station's powerful sensors began sweeping Iran with its ultra-precise, high-powered, high-resolution beams.

Tehran had mostly been spared destruction by the Iranian Revolutionary Guards. Only two Shahab-2 rockets had hit, both on Doshan Tappeh Air Base, resulting in relatively few casualties. The Air Battle Force had destroyed or intercepted a total of eighteen

Shahab-2s, plus another twenty-four Shahab-2s and twenty Shahab-3 rockets aimed at targets to the west.

But there was one more missile to be destroyed. They had received indications by their constellations of NIRTSats that the third remaining Shahab-5 missile based near Kermān in southern Iran was preparing for launch. It was too dangerous for the Air Battle Force to send in its bombers to try to destroy the silo, and there were no ships available in the area with conventional cruise missiles. There was only one weapon system available to deal with the big Iranian missile.

"Starting to receive imagery of the Zarand launch site, crew," Raydon reported. "Genesis, are you receiving?"

"Affirmative, Odin," Dave Luger responded from the command center at Dreamland. " 'Avenger' has already approved execution—weapons free."

"Copy, Genesis," Raydon responded. "Thirty seconds." As the station got closer to the target area and the radar's line of sight became less angled, they could make out more detail. "Looks like the silo door is open, gang," Raydon reported. "Crew, we have authorization. Weapons free, batteries released. Ann, fire 'em up."

"Roger that, Colonel," Ann Page replied from the Skybolt control module. "Crew, attention in the station, MHD magnetic fields coming alive." The lights dimmed briefly, and then they heard a rhythmic vibration traveling throughout the station.

At that moment Raydon saw a large column of heat burst upward from the Iranian missile silo, completely obscuring their view. The sensor operator zoomed out . . . just in time to watch a Shahab-5 missile shoot out from inside the silo! "Missile launch, missile launch!" the tech shouted. "Confirmed Shahab-5 missile launch . . . veering south now, altitude twenty-five thousand, fifteen miles downrange . . . sensors confirm the target as the north-central Indian Ocean."

"Bastards—they actually launched a missile against Diego Garcia," Raydon said angrily. He floated over to the Skybolt control console to be sure that the radar and targeting lasers were locked onto the Shahab-5 missile rising through the atmosphere. "Ann, do me a big favor and destroy that sucker for me?"

"You got it, Kai," Ann said. "Crew, stand by for weapon release." She hit a button on her console that commanded the Skybolt system to life:

In the Skybolt laser module, two small nuclear reactors began sending a chunk of molten metal through a non-conducting pipe that had a strong electromagnetic field in the middle. When the metal reached the reactor heads it vaporized into a gas, which shot it back the other way through the pipe. When it moved away from the head it turned back into a solid just as it passed the magnetic field, creating a massive slug of electricity that was stored in a capacitor. As the slug traveled through the pipe and reached the other reactor head, it turned back into a gas and was propelled in the opposite direction to start the process over again. The generator could operate for centuries like this with absolutely no moving parts.

The MHD generator quickly picked up speed, sending tremendous pulses of electricity through the capacitors until it filled, then released the electron energy all at once into the laser chamber. This sequence occurred several thousand times a second, creating massive pulses of electron laser energy that were reflected up and down the magnetic laser amplifier, increasing its power even more until the laser light reached its maximum power, then shot out of the amplifier, into a collimation chamber to focus the beam, then out of the module through the directional adaptive mirror and into space.

The higher the Shahab-5 rose through the atmosphere, the more vulnerable it was to the electron laser beam. The intense heat, focused precisely on the rear one-third of the missile where its first-stage liquid fuel was stored, burned through the rocket's skin within three seconds, then detonated the rocket fuel. The plume of fire traveled through the sky for several seconds, blossoming outward as it climbed until the fuel was completely burned up.

"Target destroyed," the radar sensor operator reported. "Confirmed kill."

"Good job, Ann," Raydon said. "I'm very impressed. You sure know how to cook."

"Damn right I do, Kai," Ann said. "Damn right I do."

MASHHAD, IRAN

That Same Time

"Missile destroyed—less than one minute after launch," Russian General Kuzma Furzyenko, chief of staff of the Air Forces of the Russian Federation, commented, shaking his head at the report coming in via secure text messaging from a Russian spy ship in the Arabian Sea. "Amazing. Quite amazing."

"I'm glad you're impressed, General!" retorted Ayatollah Hassan Mohtaj, acting president and Supreme Leader of Iran. "That was a half-billion-dollar ballistic missile that was just destroyed . . . and on your request! I hope you realize your government is going to compensate us fully for the cost!"

"You will be fairly compensated, Mohtaj . . . you just won't be paid anything," Furzyenko said.

"Oh? How, then?"

"By helping keep your asses alive," the general said.

"First we turn over the body of their commando, the robot machine, and the equipment from their spaceplane over to you for free, and then we waste our most sophisticated missile on a test flight for you, and we will not be paid? That is simply not fair, General."

"We can simply take our troops back to Russia and leave you to your fate," Furzyenko said. "Is that fair enough for you?" Mohtaj opened his mouth but said nothing. "Who will destroy you first if we left, priest? Buzhazi? The Qagev princess and her followers? The Americans? The Israelis? Your fellow Iranians? So many enemies, so little protection. Think about it before you speak to me again with that tone of voice, priest." Mohtaj gulped indignantly but said nothing. The Russian glared at him, then picked up his secure telephone and waited for the encrypted connection. "General Furzyenko here, sir."

"How did it go, General?" Russian president Leonid Zevitin asked.

"The Americans took the bait as you predicted, sir," Furzyenko said. "We simply waited until we knew Armstrong Space Station would be in a good position to attack, then had Mohtaj command the

Pasdaran to launch the Shahab-5 missile over the Indian Ocean."

"You didn't actually target it for Diego Garcia, did you, General?"

"It would have impacted in the Indian Ocean but far short of the island, shortly after second-stage ignition—it would have looked like an unsuccessful launch."

"Any chance the missile was shot down by one of their airborne lasers?"

"Their one known AL-52 aircraft has terminated its patrol north of Tehran and is being refueled somewhere over the Persian Gulf," Furzyenko said. "We know they have one or two flyable 747 AL-1 airborne laser aircraft, but we believe if they are operational they were kept back guarding the homeland and were not part of McLanahan's Iran operation. Our picket ships have detected no other aircraft in the area, although their stealth bombers could have sneaked past us. We will get telescopic infrared photographs of the space station that should confirm that the Skybolt laser fired, but I am confident that it was Skybolt that destroyed the Shahab-5."

"So Martindale has resurrected the space laser again," Zevitin said. "This is a major violation of the Outer Space Treaty and a clear and serious escalation of hostilities all around the world. The United States has militarized space, again."

“Agreed, sir. This calls for a quick response.”

“And there will be one, General,” Zevitin said. “I guarantee it. What of our fanar unit?”

“Fanar was moved away from the Strongbox right after we destroyed the spaceplane,” Furzyenko said. “We left its surveillance radar in place and put a decoy trailer at the site, both of which the Americans destroyed. But the laser is on its way here to Mashhad under heavy guard. We’ll fly it back to Russia right away.”

“Very good, General, very good,” Zevitin said. “Gather your analyses and post-strike reports and report to me as soon as possible, and we’ll plan Russia’s next move against the newly aggressive President Martindale and his pet bulldog, General Patrick Shane McLanahan.”

“Nakanyets!” Furzyenko said happily. “At last!”

Acknowledgments

Thanks to Janet and Bryan Raydon and Linda and Richard Offerdahl for their generosity.

Thanks to astronaut Mike Mullane, author of *Riding Rockets: The Outrageous Tales of a Space Shuttle Astronaut* (New York: Scribner, 2006), and Thomas D. Jones, astronaut and author of *The Complete Idiot's Guide to NASA* (New York: Alpha, 2002) and *Sky Walking: An Astronaut's Memoir* (New York: HarperCollins, 2006), for their help on understanding the wonders and dangers of space flight and for their thoughts and opinions on the military use of space.

Thanks to the organizers, sponsors, exhibitors, and presenters that I met at the 2006 International Symposium for Personal Spaceflight, held in Las Cruces, New Mexico, part of the X-Prize Cup weekend demonstrating and rewarding the newest advancements in private spaceflight technology. I especially wish to thank Patricia C. Hynes, Lowell Catlett, and Thomas Burton for their hospitality and help.

I would also like to thank Andy Turnage, executive director of the Association of Space Explorers, for his support, along with ASE members (all of whom had to make at least one orbit around the Earth) Jay C. Buckey Jr., Thomas Jones, and Dr. John-David F. Bartoe, with whom I was lucky enough to hang out with at the symposium and gain some "behind-the-scenes" insight on living and working in space.

Your comments are welcome! Visit www.AirBattleForce.com or e-mail me at readermail@airbattleforce.com. I may not have time to reply, but I read every e-mail.

9/24 Wrapped PG15 AS